Darkness into Light

Natasha Peters

FAWCETT COLUMBINE • NEW YORK

A Fawcett Columbine Book
Published by Ballantine Books
Copyright © 1984 by Natasha Peters

LIBRARY OF CONGRESS CATALOG CARD NUMBER: 83-91177
ISBN 0-449-90104-1

Manufactured in the United States of America
First Ballantine Books Edition: June 1984
10 9 8 7 6 5 4 3 2

PART ONE
THE
GIRL

1

On the day they buried my father and the other miners, the gravediggers used dynamite to open pits in the frozen ground.

I heard the first muffled explosions at dawn. I sat motionless, one bare knee pulled up to my chin, while I stared at the long black lisle stocking that trailed limply across the foot of my cot like an elongated teardrop stained with coal dust.

"Ah, here it is!" My mother's voice echoed from the depths of the trunk she had dragged into the middle of the floor of our sleeping loft. Sitting back on her heels, she held up a large square of sheer black fabric. "Look, Dory, widow's weeds. My Great-aunt Sarah's. Sometimes I'm amazed at the things that turn up in this old trunk. I can't imagine why I never threw this away." She spread the sheer veiling between her uplifted hands and gazed at it for a long time, as if she could see the whole pattern of her life woven into the fabric. Then her hands fell into her lap. "Oh, Frank," she sighed.

I had heard that same note in her voice time and again when my father was alive: desperation tinged with reproach. Whenever Papa indulged in one of his periodic rages at the world, shouting about grievances real or imagined, pounding his fists on the table, grinding them into his eyes, Mother would stand by helplessly and murmur, "Oh, Frank."

Another distant explosion, the third. Still nine to go: twelve graves for the twelve coal miners who had suffocated when the tunnel in which they had been working collapsed. Rescuers had worked for two days to shore up the roof and make an opening. The whole town camped at the mouth of the main shaft during the search. The miners' families kept to themselves, bound together by shared anxiety and the forlorn hope that somehow a stream of fresh air had found its way into the barricaded shaft, enough air to keep twelve men alive for just a few more hours. Then the rescue party broke through and brought out the first body, that of Sam O'Hara, who lived just down the road from us. Mrs. O'Hara broke into a terrifying keening wail. Even so, the rest of us continued to hope. Surely some of the men would survive, the younger ones, the stronger ones. But none did.

As I drew on my stocking, my big toe popped out of the end. The stocking had been darned so many times that even the darns were waffled with darns, and now the worn cotton had simply rotted away. I had no time to mend it this morning, so I pulled out the tip and folded it under my toes, then shoved my feet into my high-topped shoes. They pinched horribly. I was growing too fast, Mother said. Getting too big for my clothes, my shoes, but not too big for the sad ache that seemed to fill up my insides. I would never outgrow that, I decided.

"Oh, dear, whatever shall I wear?" Mother fussed. "I don't really have proper mourning clothes. I suppose this wretched gray coat will have to do, and my old navy blue dress. I'll drape this veiling over my hat, like so." She studied the effect in the cracked mirror over the washbasin. "Yes, yes, that's very nice. I can't see my face at all. Look, Dory, can you see my face?"

"No, Mother." I pulled down my woolen knickers and dragged on my gingham pinafore. It didn't cover my knees anymore.

"We can't have these people saying that Fiona Randall's sister doesn't know how to dress appropriately." Mother struck a familiar pose for the mirror, one hand at the base of her throat, her head thrown back. Like Bernhardt. "And Fiona. What would Fiona say?"

Lowering my head, I worked the buttons on my pinafore. For the past year, ever since she saw a notice in an old New York newspaper that Fiona Randall was appearing in a musical play on Broadway, my mother had talked about her sister. Broadway! From that time on, Fiona was the touchstone, the unseen arbiter of style and behavior. Mother judged everything in terms of Fiona: Would Fiona approve of this or that? How would Fiona act in similar circumstances?

My father had quickly become impatient with Mother's chatter. "Fiona! Fiona!" he roared. "I'm sick to death of hearing about Fiona. If she's such a dear sister, why doesn't she write to you? You've written to her a dozen times, wasted God knows how much money on postage. And you've never heard from her. Not once."

"Oh, Frank, she's so busy, with this wonderful part—"

"She doesn't write to you because she doesn't want to have anything to do with you, can't you understand that, woman? Why should she? You turned your back on your family a long time ago." Then, as he often did, he twisted his rage around and pointed it at himself. "You married a nobody, a failure."

"No, Frank, no, you're not a failure."

But finally Mother refrained from mentioning Fiona's name in Papa's presence. Her delight in her sister's success became a secret that she and I shared. She was a good conspirator, whispering and laughing as she wove fanciful tales about Fiona in the play, Fiona greeting her admirers at the stage door, Fiona riding in a carriage through Central Park. Mother knew all about these things, for she and Fiona had visited New York as young girls. On Broadway they had seen one of Sarah Bernhardt's farewell performances as Camille, a thrill that neither of them had ever forgotten.

Now I sensed that my father's death had freed Mother from the constraints of silence. Even as she readied herself for his funeral, she could talk only of Fiona.

We heard a knock at the cabin door. Mother was still wearing only her sleeveless chemise and her underdrawers, despite the fact that the sleeping loft was so cold that the water in the wash basin was frozen.

"I'll go." I slithered down the ladder and opened the door. A small knot of black figures was silhouetted against the snowy landscape.

"Mornin', Theodora. We've come for your pa," the undertaker said. "He's the last." They stumped into the room, shaking the snow from their boots, doffing their hats as a gesture of respect to the dead.

Up in the loft, out of their sight, my mother laughed, a delighted, girlish titter. The men exchanged eloquent glances as they lifted the lid and covered the simple pine coffin in which my father had lain through the night, his work-ragged hands pressed into a prayerful attitude that he would never have assumed in life. I gnawed my lower lip. Try as I might, I hadn't been able to wash away the traces of coal dust from the deep lines around Papa's eyes and mouth.

The undertaker sank each nail with a single sure blow of his hammer, then the men lifted the coffin from the two rush-seated chairs that had supported it and shifted the load onto their shoulders. I held the door for them. A bitter wind whipped my skirt around my legs and stiffened the tears on my cheeks. The funeral would be brief. The air was too cold for people to stand around eulogizing and reminiscing, and besides, the other miners had to go back to work.

When the wagon on which the pallbearers had loaded the coffin had rolled away down the hill, I called up to Mother. "We'd better leave soon. They've taken Papa."

"I'll be right down. You don't think this old silk rose would be a wrong touch, do you? I know, I'll throw it into the grave. After all, you can't get any real flowers at this time of year. And the red will look so striking against the black of my mourning and the white of the snow. Yes, I think I'll take it. Fiona certainly wouldn't go to a funeral empty-handed."

"Please, Mother." I shrugged into my old coat and swathed

my head and face with a long muffler. "The men said that Papa was the last one. We don't want to be late."

"I'm ready, dear. Just a moment more. Oh, if only I had some gloves without holes in them. I know, if I carry the rose in my right hand, I can keep my fingers curled around the stem, like this."

We trudged along the road that became the rutted main street of Monkey Gulch. The snow was dingy, blackened by the fine silt that fell from the chimneys of the town's new refinery.

I hated the refinery. Our part of Colorado boasted two major mining operations, the coal mines in which my father had died and a quarry that contained a rich vein of iron ore. Instead of shipping the ore by rail to the smelters in nearby Trinidad, along with the coal to fire the blast furnaces that would incinerate the waste materials and melt the iron into ingots, the company decided to construct a refinery right in the town, and extend the railroad line from Trinidad. The association of rich men back east who owned the mines had never been to Monkey Gulch. They never saw what the refinery had done to the town. They never saw how the waste water from the plant had poisoned the wild iris that used to grow along the edge of the Purgatory River, which flowed past the town. As a small child, I had loved to play among the flowers on the riverbank, when the spring sun warmed the earth and the water flowed clear and icy out of the mountains. Now I had to hike more than a mile to find such unspoiled beauty, far upstream from the refinery.

Mother and I joined a ragged band of other women and children, all on their way to the cemetery. Some of the women stared rudely at my mother's getup. Feeling the icy sting of their disapproval, Mother drew herself up and pressed the old silk rose to her breast with both hands. I imagined the gesture was one she remembered or thought she remembered from Bernhardt in *Camille*. I sighed inwardly. Why did my mother have to dramatize every situation? The people in Monkey Gulch had always said that she was odd. Now they would say that she didn't care about her husband, that she didn't mourn him. I knew that wasn't true. My mother simply had her own ways of dealing with suffering and sorrow. She wasn't like the other women in the town. She was a dreamer, a girl who still loved to spin stories and weave daisy chains and race laughing over the fragrant hillsides, her hair flowing loose behind her. The harsh realities of life as a miner's wife had never destroyed her spirit. In fact, the worse things got, the more buoyant and lighthearted my mother became.

"Lift your head, child," Mother said. "We must be noble in our grief." She quickened her step. I scurried to catch up.

We passed the section of town where the Mexican and Indian families lived. I saw my friend Pilar emerge from the smallest of the adobe houses. She pulled her red shawl up over her head and ran toward us. We didn't speak, but Pilar grasped my hand and gave me an encouraging smile. I was grateful. I had an ally now. The women of the town might disapprove of my friendship with a Mexican girl, but I didn't care. Only Pilar could understand the silent depths of my grief. When I was ready to weep, or to talk about my father, Pilar would be there, ready to listen.

The town's Methodist preacher read the service only once for all twelve miners. His weary drone was accompanied by an obligato of keening from Mrs. O'Hara, whose husband's body had been closest to the mine entrance. At the front of the crowd, conspicuous in his black felt hat, shiny black boots, and camel-colored overcoat, stood Mr. Sidney Jenkins, the company's representative in Monkey Gulch and the supervisor of all the mining operations in the region. He was heavyset, bushy-browed, with black moustaches that curved over his thick lips like twin apostrophes. The folks in town said that Mr. Jenkins had no friends except his bright yellow Hudson sedan, one of the half-dozen automobiles in Monkey Gulch.

The pallbearers lowered the twelve coffins into the blasted-out pits one by one and covered them with a mixture of rock, frozen clay, and snow.

"Wait, please." As the men bent their backs into their shovels, my mother stepped up to the edge of her husband's grave. She stood there for a long time without moving, then she lifted the veil from her face and turned it back over the crown of her old felt hat. Her large blue eyes were bright with sorrow, swimming with tears that had not yet fallen. Her full lips trembled dangerously. I felt secretly proud. Even her enemies, the women she called the jealous dragons, would have to admit that for all her foolish ways, Mary Randall Lowery was a beautiful woman.

Mother pressed the silk rose to her lips, then she stretched out her hand over the grave and let the rose fall onto the lid of the crude pine coffin. After lowering her veil again, she stepped away from the grave. Suddenly she swayed, as gracefully as a reed in the wind. The little crowd gasped. She was going to tumble into the pit! I leaped to help her, but Jenkins, the supervisor, elbowed me neatly out of the way and caught Mother around the shoulders.

"I'm so sorry," she whispered. She lifted her head and the veil brushed against his cheek. "Forgive me. I'm all right now."

After a moment's hesitation, the man released her. The town dragons in their battered cloche hats and frayed overcoats swelled and glared, emitting angry puffs of steamy breath in the frosty air.

With the funeral over, the thoughts of the crowd turned to more pressing matters: the paralyzing cold, their gnawing hunger, their responsibilities to the living. It was eight o'clock; the men were already late for the morning shifts at the mill and the mines. Miss Massey hurried down the hill to ring the school bell. Other folks shivered and began to move purposefully away from the fresh graves, down the slope toward the town. Two of Mrs. O'Hara's more stalwart neighbors assisted her. Her wails rose in a steady crescendo, so that her voice seemed to grow louder as she herself became more distant:

"Gone, gone! He's gone! I'm alone now, all alone! He left me with nothing, only debts and more debts. The company owns the house. I don't even have a roof over my head now. What am I going to do? Oh, Lord, what am I going to do now?"

I shivered. The company owned our house, too—owned most of the town, in fact. Mrs. O'Hara's strident question echoed inside my own head: Oh, Lord, what are we going to do now?

"Can I give you a lift, Miz Lowery?" Jenkins approached us where we stood at the edge of my father's grave. His voice seemed to reach Mother over a long distance. After several moments, she moved her head around slowly.

"What's that? Oh, no, thank you. I don't want to trouble you."

"No trouble. I have my car." He glanced at Pilar, dismissing her, then turned his gaze on me. "This your daughter?"

"Yes. Yes, this is Theodora. And you are Mr.—?"

"Jenkins, ma'am. I'm the supervisor of the mines."

"Oh, yes. I have heard my husband mention you."

I cringed. Papa had uttered Jenkins' name often, always prefacing it with "that son of a bitch," or "that bastard." We moved down the hill toward the single dazzling yellow automobile that was parked on the road. Mother admired the car, while Jenkins, smirking in a way that didn't conceal his pride, airily dismissed the Hudson as an old heap of junk.

"These roads aren't exactly kind to machines," he grimaced. "Back east, a car like this might last a good ten, fifteen years. But in this part of the country I can't hope to get more than three or four out of her."

"Oh, are you from the East, Mr. Jenkins?" Mother asked eagerly. She was always on the lookout for Easterners, whom she considered to be more civilized and cultured than those unfortunate persons who hailed from the West or Midwest.

Yes, Mr. Jenkins was from St. Louis. Well, Kansas, really, but he'd spent a lot of time in St. Louis.

"Plenty of room for the three of us in this here baby." Jenkins pointedly ignored Pilar. She and I had stopped about ten feet away from the car.

I gave my friend an anxious look. Pilar said, "I must go to school now. I will be late, I think."

"No," I hissed. "It's not fair." I said aloud, "I think I'll go to school today, Mother. I mean, I have nothing to do at home and—"

"Go to school, on the day of your father's funeral? Dear me, child, what are you thinking? Your place is at home today, with me. People will be coming to call throughout the day, to express their condolences, and I need you to help me receive them. Come along. Pilar doesn't mind, do you, Pilar?"

Casting an embarrassed backward look at my friend, I climbed into the back seat of the banana-colored sedan. As Jenkins pulled away, I turned around and waved at Pilar, standing at the foot of the snow-covered cemetery, called Boot Hill by some of the less imaginative of the town wags. Swathed in red from her head to her knees, she looked fearsome and otherworldly, like a messenger from Heaven or Hell.

I had ridden in a motor car only once before in my life, when I was six years old. I had nearly died of influenza during the winter of 1918, long before the company built the railroad spur between Monkey Gulch and Trinidad. The doctor in Monkey Gulch gave up on me and told my parents to expect the worst. The nearest hospital was in Trinidad, eighty miles away, inaccessible to most of the residents of Monkey Gulch. My father carried me to the house of the leading lumber merchant and richest man in town, Mr. Watson, and asked him to take me into the city. As Papa told the story, Mr. Watson growled something about not wanting to be an ambulance service for every sick kid in Monkey Gulch. But then he looked down at me, lying wan and limp and feverish in my father's arms, and he said, "All right, damn you. But just this once, do you hear me? Just this once." I remembered very little of that journey.

Now I sat on the edge of the seat and stared at the back of Mr. Jenkins' head. His black felt hat looked new enough, but he needed a haircut, and little clumps of hair bristled from his ears. I didn't dare look out the windows; I didn't want to encounter scathing looks from the frozen and footsore mourners we were passing.

"—Boston for seven generations," my mother was saying. "The Chicago Randalls are an offshoot. A small family, virtually extinct by now, since my father died, but we are very distinguished. Perhaps you've heard of my sister, Fiona Randall? She's a famous actress in New York. I used to wheel her pram around Lake Michigan, can you imagine? And now she's a star on Broadway!"

"No kidding?" the man Jenkins said. "I saw a show in New York once a few years ago. Can't even remember the name of it now."

"How exciting!" Mother exclaimed. "Most of the people in this town have never seen a real stage play, much less a Broadway show. Talking to them is rather difficult, as you may imagine. They look at me as though I'd just stepped off the boat from a foreign country."

I slumped down in my seat and folded my arms against my chest. How I wished my mother wouldn't chatter on like this, especially on the day of her husband's funeral, especially in front of a stranger like Mr. Jenkins. For one thing, my father wouldn't have approved. Riding home from his funeral in the bastard's car! No, he wouldn't have cared for that at all.

Mother directed Jenkins to our cabin, a shack located at the western edge of town. We were in an isolated spot, a mile away from the company store and the church. My father had liked his privacy. He hated his work and loathed the townspeople, and he didn't bother to hide his feelings. As a result, I had no friends among the children of the other miners. My father was hostile and my mother was odd, and everybody reasonably supposed that little Theodora Lowery had inherited her parents' peculiarities. My only friends were Pilar and her family, in the Mexican settlement, who were also ostracized from Monkey Gulch society, but for different reasons.

I hoped that Pilar wouldn't be angry with me. How horrible it would be never to see her again, or her little twin sisters, or her handsome older brother, Joaquin. I squirmed as I thought about him. I had never said ten words to Joaquin Garcia, but whenever I visited Pilar's home I was acutely aware of his dark presence, his slender aquiline grace, his unchildlike intensity. He was fifteen, an age which seemed awesomely mature to me, at twelve, and he worked as an apprentice to the company blacksmith. The company had a policy which forbade any boy under sixteen to go down into the deep-shaft mines, but Pilar had told me that Joaquin would try to get a higher-paying job with the company as soon as he was old enough. My first thought when I had heard about the cave-in at the mine was, "Thank God Joaquin isn't down there." And then I had realized that my own father might be trapped a half-mile under ground.

As soon as the car came to a halt, I hopped out and ran into the cabin. I didn't thank Jenkins for the ride; I knew that my mother's thanks would be profuse and elaborate. I felt only loathing for the man who had shoved me aside at my father's grave and who had snubbed my only friend. I crouched down in front of the pot-bellied stove and whipped off my mittens. A few red embers still glowed in the bed of ashes. I added a handful of straw and kindling, then spread my hands out in front of the crackling blaze.

The door opened. "But you must stay for tea," Mother said. "I would never forgive myself for sending you out in this cold without something warm to drink. Theodora, is that kettle hot yet?"

Jenkins followed my mother into the house. I gazed sullenly into the flames. "The fire was almost out. The water won't be hot for hours and hours."

"Oh, I'm sure Mr. Jenkins won't mind waiting for a few minutes."

Jenkins kept his coat on but removed his hat. He looked different without it, balding and less impressive, like a potentate without a crown. He scowled at the bleak interior of the shack in a manner indicating that he couldn't wait to escape. But when Mother divested herself of her mourning, he stared at her as though he'd just discovered a diamond in a manure pile. Her navy blue dress was shapeless and faded, many years out of date, and although her collar and cuffs were scrubbed and white, they were also limp and frayed. She wore no makeup, not even lipstick, but her cheeks were pink and, as always, her eyes were luminous, full of excitement and hope. Silken strands of blond hair escaped from the bun at the back of her head and swirled around her oval face. My mother was only thirty years old, and her beauty had the breathtaking splendor of a full-blown rose.

"How 'bout a little brandy?" Jenkins produced a flat silver flask from an inner coat pocket.

"Why, yes, thank you." Bustling, Mother took a couple of cracked tea cups off the shelf near the sink. "A little brandy on a cold day is so welcome, I think. Of course, my sister Fiona always drinks champagne. I love champagne, don't you?"

"It's okay." Jenkins emptied his cup in a single swallow and poured himself another drink. He looked around at the bare board walls, the uncarpeted floor, the rickety furnishings: a table with one short leg shored up by a coffee can, the two rush chairs and a three-legged stool, a sink without running water. To wash dishes or clothing or make tea, we had to haul water from the river and heat it in the kettle. In winter we melted chunks of ice. "Guess you won't be sorry to leave this place."

I felt myself grow cold inside, and at the same time I broke into a sweat.

"Leave? Well, we hadn't really thought about it," Mother said in her offhanded way. "I had supposed we would just stay here until something presented itself."

"This is a company house," Jenkins reminded her. "Put here for the benefit of their workers."

Mother said, "I'm sure the company won't object if we stay here for a while longer. After all, poor Frank was killed in an accident in one of their mines. I've heard some of the other men saying that the beams they were using to support the roof were rotten, but that the foreman insisted that they use them anyway. They said that the cave-in shouldn't have happened. The company owes us something."

Jenkins shrugged. "They don't always see things that way. They might let you have a week to find another place."

They, I thought; *you.*

"A week! But that's ridiculous, Mr. Jenkins. We have nowhere else to go, and we don't have any money. None." Mother came over to the stove and took an old Prince Albert tobacco tin off the warming shelf. She flipped open the lid, pulled out a single dollar bill and rattled the change in the bottom of the tin. "You see? Only one dollar and fifty—no, sixty-eight cents. We won't be able to move very far on one dollar and sixty-eight cents, will we? The company will just have to be patient. It's their own fault, after all. If they paid their men in real money instead of that silly scrip, we might have something to fall back on."

Scrip. For most of my twelve years, I had thought that all commerce was carried on using the paper issued by the company in place of checks or cash. Only scrip was accepted at the company store, so that the miners and their families were unable to make purchases elsewhere, even if they got better value. A week's salary in scrip bought a small parcel of coffee, tea that my mother swore was half dried weeds, weevil-infested flour, soured butter, some war-surplus dried eggs, and from time to time a length of cloth, a blanket, or a pair of cheaply made boots. Once in a while my father had performed odd jobs for Mr. Watson, who paid him in cash, which Papa spent on liquor. The little bit that remained went into the old tobacco tin.

Jenkins thrust his hands into his pockets. I suspected that his fingers were stiff with cold, even inside their soft leather gloves. "Maybe you could get a job," he suggested.

Mother looked amazed. "A job? My dear Mr. Jenkins, with so many unemployed men in this town, can you possibly think that anyone would hire a woman with no talent and no experience? I can read and write, of course, but Monkey Gulch has no secretarial jobs. Monkey Gulch has no jobs at all, except those the company provides. You don't expect me to go down into the mines, do you?"

"You'll have to do something." Jenkins stood up, hat in hand. "You can't stay here rent-free. The company won't allow it. But I," he cleared his throat, "I'll see what I can do. Get you a month to clear out. But no more."

Mother didn't escort him to the door. After he had let himself out, I moved over to the table and looked down at her as she sat sipping brandy from her teacup. My own understanding of our perilous situation was clear and keen. I waited, hoping that my mother would find a solution.

Mother looked up, a vague smile on her lips. "He's a nice man, isn't he, Dory? How lovely of him to drive us home."

"But where are we going to go?" I said. "We don't have any money. What are we going to do?"

"Is that what's worrying you?" She set down her cup and held out her hands to me. I went to her, and she held me close and smoothed the fine wisps of hair away from my forehead. "I'll write to Fiona," she said. "Right this minute. I'll tell her about Frank, and I'll ask her for a loan. Just until I find some kind of job, and then I can repay her. I'm only asking for your sake, Dory. After all, she's your aunt, your only living relative. She won't refuse to help her own sister's child."

A dark cloud of despair enveloped me, like the rising heat in the vicinity of the stove. Fiona again. I didn't share my mother's faith in Fiona. Fiona hadn't answered any of my mother's letters before this. Why should she respond to this urgent call for help?

2

February brought frigid temperatures and swirling snow. Mother and I scoured the woods above the cabin for twigs and branches to appease the insatiable appetite of the stove. In return we got plenty of smoke and heaps of ashes, but barely enough heat to warm us after those numbing excursions. I lined my shoes with cardboard, and layered newspapers between the blankets on the big bed in the loft, which we now shared. Some mornings, when even the water in the kettle on the stove was frozen, I washed my face and hands with snow before setting off for school.

Every day, Mother grew more worried looking as the full realization of the seriousness of our plight began to sink in. She began to search desperately for work, trudging up and down the main street of the town, asking anyone she saw if they knew of a job or task she could perform for a few cents. Mr. Watson might have given her something in the office of his lumber company, but his wife, who like the other women in the town had long resented Mary Lowery's high-falootin' ways and ladylike airs, forbade her husband to have anything to do with us. Wasn't the company letting us live in our cabin rent-free for a whole month? Well, that was enough.

If it hadn't been for the Garcia family, we would have starved. At school, Pilar shared the contents of her lunch pail with me. I always tucked some morsel of cornbread or biscuit into my pocket to take home for Mother. Pilar's older brother, Joaquin, made the most dramatic contributions to our survival. He had fashioned snowshoes for himself so that he could do some trapping and hunting in the winter, and twice a week he delivered fresh meat to our door: some venison chops, a rabbit already skinned and dressed, a pheasant hen. Each time he would stay only long enough to receive Mother's heartfelt thanks, and to give me a long and enigmatic look that made my blood rush in heated waves to every part of my body. Then he would depart, swiftly and silently, without ever saying a word.

The days passed with no word from Fiona. "Why doesn't she write?" Mother fretted. "I know she's busy, but a little note wouldn't take much of her time. We don't need a gold mine, just enough to tide us over. If we had even a little money, we could leave this contemptible backwater. I'm sure I could find work in Trinidad. As a secretary, or a clerk in a shop. Why doesn't she answer?"

Where would we go when the company threw us out? I asked myself the question twenty times a day. Most of the other families in Monkey Gulch were as poor as we were. As many as eight people lived packed into single-room cabins, where they choked on coal and kerosene fumes and ate barely enough to survive. Even if Mother had succeeded in forming strong friendships over the years, none of those people could help us now. Their own families came first.

About two weeks after Papa's funeral, Mother and I both caught bad colds. I recovered quickly, but Mother became seriously ill. She lay thrashing in bed, feverish and fretful. I stayed home from school to care for her.

"Fiona," Mother moaned. "She didn't get my letter. She couldn't have. If she knew how bad things were, she wouldn't hesitate for a minute to help us. We must send her word at once. Theodora, you'll have to sell my ring." She fingered the wedding band on her left hand. It slipped off much too easily. "Find out how much it will cost to send a telegram to New York. That's how much you must get for the ring. At least that much. And then go to the station and send the wire. Say, 'Husband killed. Situation desperate. In name of family loyalty, beg you send money at once. Child starving—' "

"Oh, Mother," I groaned.

"Do as I say." Mother's voice was sharp. " 'Child starving. Nowhere else to turn.' And sign it, 'Love, Mary.' Can you remember all that?"

I knotted the ring in the corner of my handkerchief and started out. I felt so overwhelmed by shame and guilt that I could barely drag my feet through the snow. Begging money from a relative I'd never seen. Selling my mother's wedding ring, the only piece of jewelry she possessed. Oh, it was horrible, and humiliating, and futile.

The stationmaster told me that the telegram would cost two dollars and sixteen cents. It seemed like a fearsomely high amount. I despaired of ever earning that much from the sale of the ring.

None of the women in the town, I thought, would buy Mary Lowery's wedding ring. And most of the men were down in the mines. But I remembered hearing that one of the older boys in the refinery office was courting a farm girl. I started walking toward the belching chimneys by the river.

Just as I passed the lumber office, I saw Mr. Watson's car pull up. Steeling myself, I decided to approach him first.

"Excuse me, Mr. Watson."

He stood on the running board of his car and frowned down at me from an impossible height.

"Do I know you?"

"I—I'm Theodora Lowery," I stammered, blushing. "Frank Lowery's daughter. Remember, you took me to the hospital in Trinidad when I was sick, a long time ago."

His frown relaxed somewhat. "Oh. Lowery's kid. Sure, I know you. You lookin' for a handout?"

My flush deepened. I wished that the heat of my shame would melt the snow under my feet, enabling me to sink smoothly and rapidly out of sight. "No. Nothing like that. My mother gave me her wedding ring to sell, and I—I just wondered if you'd like to buy it. It's a good ring, fourteen karat. It says so, right inside." With fumbling fingers, I unknotted the handkerchief. "It's real pretty, don't you think?"

Watson squinted at the ring. "Nice enough," he grunted. "But I don't need any wedding rings. I bought one for Mrs. Watson twenty-three years ago. I don't want another." He handed it back to me and stumped off toward the lumber office.

Fear and desperation made me bold. I ran after him. "I only want three dollars for it!" I called. "It's worth much more, I know it is. But I'd be willing to sell it for three dollars."

He turned and gave me a hard stare. "Frank Lowery's kid," he said. "I remember the night I drove you and your folks into Trinidad. I wouldn't have done it, except I saw something in your father's eyes. I knew if I didn't do what he asked, he'd kill me."

I was shocked. "No, you're wrong! He never would have done anything—"

Watson shook his head. "I know what desperation can do to a man. He was desperate. If he was here now, he'd have that same look. I remember your ma, too. She looked so delicate and pretty, like a desert flower. Too bad you don't take after her."

I knew what he meant. Everyone said I was the spittin' image of my father: tall, angularly built, with his reddish brown hair and the freckles to go with it, and an impossibly wide mouth that could form itself into the widest grin you ever saw, or the stubbornest line. Mr. Watson was right. I wasn't pretty, like my ma.

"I'll give you five for it." He reached for his wallet. "Don't tell a soul about this, understand? And don't come sniffin' around askin' me for any more favors. I've done enough for you and your family as it is. More than enough. You Lowerys stay away from me from now on, understand?"

I nodded eagerly. Anything, anything, I would promise him anything. Five whole dollars! I would have enough left over from the telegram to buy some food, and some medicine for Mother.

After I sent the wire, I felt better. No one could refuse such an urgent plea, and a telegram besides. Fiona would have to respond now. She must help us. She must.

Fiona's answer came a week later, a short note enclosed in a heavy buff envelope embossed with the crest of the Hotel Burbage on Fifth Avenue, New York City. Mother opened it with trembling hands. When she had finished reading it, she turned her face to the wall. The note slipped out of her fingers.

I picked it up. Words sprawled over the page, written in large, jagged letters that indicated haste and extreme pique: "For God's sake, will you stop this idiotic pestering! Don't you know I'd sooner give money to a nameless tramp in the street than to you? Find some other relatives to beg from." The note was signed with a boxy, printed F that cut right through the paper at the bottom of the vertical stroke.

I looked on bewildered as Mother wept. I didn't understand this Fiona person. Even if she didn't want to send us any money, she could at least have been kind about it. She could have expressed sympathy, and regret. But no. Her needless cruelty had inflicted immeasurable pain. In destroying her sister's dreams and illusions, Fiona had also destroyed Mother's hope.

I tore up the note and fed it to the flames in the wretched stove. "I hate you, Fiona Randall," I said softly. "I'll hate you forever and ever."

A week passed. Mother's fever abated. Then one morning a man from the company came to tell us that we had until sunset to vacate the premises.

"But we have no place to go," Mother protested. Her eyes were still dull from her sickness; her skin had taken on a bluish tinge. I could see the breath from my mother's words even as she spoke them, little clouds of vapor.

The man shrugged and walked out. It was no business of his.

The time had come for us to leave. Mother moved listlessly around the cabin, packing our few possessions into her old wooden trunk. I carried my few beloved storybooks down from the loft. I kept silent, afraid to speak to my mother of my fears. What could she say that would banish the cold terror that held me in its grip, like a monster made of ice? Words were useless.

By the middle of the afternoon, we were finished. Mother wrapped her old iron skillet in newspaper and tucked it into a corner of the trunk. "I bring bad luck to the people I love. I always have." She sat down on the stool near the table. She was breathless. "Poor Frank. He was so eager, so ambitious when we met. He had so many wonderful plans. He could have been a great man. But he married me. He used to say that a married man isn't free anymore. And now you, Dory. Someone in this town might take you in, if it wasn't for me. It's me they hate, not you. Even Fiona—"

"No!" Alarmed, I cast my storybooks aside. "We don't need her. We don't need anyone. Please, Mother." Kneeling in front of her, I threw my arms around her waist and pressed my face against her bosom. "You're not bad luck. People are just jealous of you, that's all. Because you're so beautiful and fine."

Mother paid no attention. "She's the only family you have left, besides me. If something happened to me, she'd have to take you in. She wouldn't have a choice."

"Nothing's going to happen," I said fiercely. "I won't let anything happen to you. I'll take care of you, Mother. Don't worry. Please don't worry. No matter what happens, I'll take care of you."

Mother looked into my face and sighed. "You always look so serious, Dory. That's my fault, too. You haven't had much of a childhood, have you? So much work, so much worry. You've never had much time for play, and for dreams. Only twelve years old, and you're a grown woman already. You're even more grownup than I am. You've got much more sense. And you've got more courage, too. But it's a pity. You've missed so much."

"No, I haven't," I insisted. "I haven't missed anything. Playing is silly and stupid. And dreaming is a waste of time."

"Oh, no, dear, you're wrong about that. You have to dream in order to survive. That was something your father didn't understand. When he found himself in this town, mining coal, he just gave up. He decided that he couldn't do any better for himself, and he didn't try anymore. Remember how he used to make fun of my schemes? Foolish talk, he called them. Nonsense. But they weren't. If you stop believing that the world has something better to offer you than what you have, you'll stop trying. You won't even bother to live. What's the point?"

A knock on the door startled us. Mother's hands flew to her hair. "Oh, dear, is it time to go? But I'm not ready. Couldn't they give us a few more hours?"

Without waiting for anyone to respond to his knock, Sidney Jenkins opened the door and strolled into the cabin. He glanced around, taking in the naked bedsteads, the cold stove, the brimming trunk in the center of the floor.

"Movin' out, eh? Where are you goin'?"

Mother folded her hands primly in front of her waist. "I don't know. We—we haven't decided."

"Haven't decided," he snorted. "That means you don't have a place yet. You don't have any money, either, do you?" Mother didn't reply. In spite of her attempt to present a dignified front, she looked weary and defeated. "Guess you couldn't find a job that suited your talents," Jenkins sneered.

"No," Mother replied. "I couldn't."

"Too bad." Jenkins hooked the toe of his boot around the leg of a chair and dragged it toward him. Sitting there, with his arms crossed over his chest, he looked like a corrupt judge or senator: sleek, contented, in command. Mother and I, left standing, were transformed into supplicants. "You're a fine-lookin' woman, Miz Lowery," he drawled. "Seems a shame that a pretty lady like you can't find herself somethin' to do, somethin' that might earn her a little cash money." He grinned. "Well, I've been thinkin', how'd you like to work for me?"

"For you?" Mother's eyebrows rose.

"Housekeeper, cook. I need somebody. I've got a big place, you know where it is. Plenty of room for you and the girl. Since my wife left me and went back to St. Louis last year, it's been pretty lonely. I've had a couple of Mexican women comin' in, but I don't like 'em. They don't know how to serve a white man properly. Their cookin's terrible, and they smell bad besides. Well, what do you say?"

I looked at my mother in alarm. I wanted to shout, "No, don't, I don't want to live in his house. No!"

"I'm not much of a cook," Mother said.

"That's okay. I'm not fussy. Plain old meat and gravy, that's what I like. I'll pay you a fair wage, three dollars a week with your room and board thrown in. It's settled, then." He stood up. "Get your coats. I'll send a couple of the boys down for this thing." He jerked his head toward the trunk.

I tried to meet my mother's eyes, to send her a silent plea not to let this man take control of our lives. But Mother was moving resignedly around the cabin, collecting a few last items to put into the trunk.

We walked away from the cabin, I trailing sullenly behind my mother and Mr. Jenkins. As we reached Jenkins' Hudson, Mother suddenly halted. "Wait a minute, I forgot something." She went back into the cabin, and emerged a moment later carrying the old tobacco tin. "I didn't think I was going to need this," she told Jenkins, who was holding the car door open for her. "It's been empty so long." She faced the man squarely. "I just want you to know that I'm only doing this because I have no other choice. I have to support myself and my daughter, and you're our only chance. But you know that, or you wouldn't have come here. Don't worry. I'll work hard, and do my job. You'll get your money's worth."

After seating her, Jenkins grinned and stepped around to the other side of the car. "I never doubted that for a moment, Miz Lowery. There is not the slightest doubt in my mind that I'm going to get my money's worth. I guess you know what I mean."

"Yes," Mother said. "I know." Sitting between them, I gave her a puzzled look but her face remained impassive.

As we drove away, I craned my neck around for a farewell look at the tumbledown shack that had been my home since I was five years old. My father had drifted from job to job before coming here to work in the coal mines, but I had only dim mem-

2019

ories of the various shacks and shanties and roominghouses that had sheltered our family before we arrived in Monkey Gulch.

Jenkins' house was certainly larger and finer than our cabin. Stiff upholstered furniture graced the parlor. The walls were plastered and papered, if somewhat stained, and threadbare carpets lay on the floors. Jenkins boasted of his wife's taste in decoration and blamed his succession of Mexican housekeepers for the deterioration in the house's appearance since his wife had departed.

The second floor had two bedrooms, separated by a bathroom with a porcelain-lined tub and a toilet that flushed.

"You two will sleep in here." Jenkins showed us the drafty back bedroom. "It's not the Ritz, but I guess it's better than what you had before."

"It's very nice," Mother said politely. "Thank you." She gave me a glance that was supposed to remind me of my manners, but I ignored it.

"I like my dinner at six sharp," Jenkins told her. "I got plenty of stuff in the kitchen. You ought to find somethin' to fix. I got to go out now." He gave Mother a crooked grin, winked at me, and stumped down the stairs.

I stood at the window and moved my finger in a widening circle, melting a patch on the layer of frost that covered the pane. Down in the back yard, I could see a twisted pear tree, a board fence drifted with snow. Behind me the bed creaked as Mother sat down.

"I don't like him," I said in a hard voice. "I think he's horrible. Why did we have to come here?"

"It won't be so bad, you'll see." Mother's heartiness sounded forced. "Besides, we didn't have a choice. We'll stay just long enough to save up the money to go to Trinidad, and then we'll leave. Why, with three dollars a week, we can save thirty dollars by the end of April! We can easily get to Trinidad on thirty dollars and we'll have enough left over to rent a nice apartment and to live on while I find work. And you'll go to a good school, a really fine school, Dory, and meet the right kind of people. It's so important, to know the right kind of people. We just need to tell ourselves over and over that whatever happens here, it's only for a little while, and then we'll go away. Come here, darling."

She opened her arms to me. I pouted and didn't move from the window, but in the end I couldn't resist my mother's warm smile. I flung myself into her arms.

"My sweet baby," she murmured. "My little girl. Everything is going to be just fine, you'll see. When spring comes, we'll make a new start, far away from this awful place. New friends, new sights. Mr. Jenkins is right about one thing: Monkey Gulch, Colorado, just can't appreciate a woman of my caliber. Wretched little towns like Monkey Gulch expect women to stay home and nurse their babies and get skinny and worn-out and old. But in a big city like Denver or Chicago or New York I could find a job in a minute. Oh, Dory, wouldn't it be fun to go to New York? We will. We'll do it!" She bounced excitedly. The bedsprings sang. "The theater, the opera—we'll see a different show every night. And I'll go see Fiona. Yes, I will. I'll snap my fingers under her nose like this, and I'll tell her that we managed very well without her money. I'll bet she's sorry." Mother nodded wisely. "I'll bet she's thought it over, and she's sorry she answered our telegram as she did."

"Oh, Mother."

"No, really. You have to remember that actresses are very temperamental, Dory. Temperamental and moody and passionate. Especially the great actresses, like Fiona. How else could she create all those characters, and become a different person night after night? She searches the wellsprings of her spirit, and the things she finds there are not always beautiful and noble. Sometimes the human spirit can be dark, as dark as a dungeon, and sometimes it is as bright as the sun. Artists are sensitive, delicate people. Their only resource is themselves, and yet the world expects miracles, constant miracles of art and loveliness.

Don't blame Fiona, dear. A gift like hers isn't always easy to live with. Sometimes a great talent can be more of a curse than a blessing. And now," she stood up and brushed out her skirt, "I'd better explore the kitchen. If Mr. Jenkins wants his plain meat and gravy at six sharp, then he shall have it at six sharp. Cheer up, baby." She planted a light kiss on my forehead. "Remember, it's only temporary."

That night, I was awakened by whispering. I groped my hand along the mattress. My mother was gone.

"No, please, not tonight. I don't want to wake the child. I beg you—"

"—money's worth. *Now.*"

I sat up in bed. I saw them standing in the doorway, two ghostly forms illuminated by a pale winter moon. "Mother?"

Mother came back into the room and leaned over the bed. The single braid of her hair hung over her shoulder like a flaxen rope. In her white muslin nightgown, she looked luminous, shapeless, like the angels I had seen pictured in the books at Sunday School.

"It's all right, darling," she murmured. "Go back to sleep. Just go to sleep." She kissed me quickly, and whispered in my ear, "We'll go to New York real soon, I promise."

I knew, and I didn't know, what was going on in the room down the hall. My mother and Mr. Jenkins were whispering and embracing in the darkness, engaging in a kind of secret adult ritual that was usually restricted to married people. Thus, in a sense, my mother and Mr. Jenkins were married. I experienced a surge of outrage. My father had only been dead a month, and now a man he despised had taken his place next to my mother in the darkness.

I snuggled down under the blankets. I had never felt so bereft and lonely. When a man and a woman slept together, they achieved a greater intimacy and closeness than I had ever shared with anyone. My mother belonged to Mr. Jenkins now, even more than she belonged to her own daughter.

Somehow, thinking about New York was supposed to make all this bearable. New York? New York, with its vague images of theaters and parks and carriage rides, seemed just as remote and inaccessible as Heaven or Hell. I didn't care if I never saw New York. If people like Fiona Randall lived there, it couldn't be a very nice place.

After an hour, the door opened and Mother slipped into bed beside me. The bed shook slightly. She was crying. I lay stiff, frozen by resentment and anger, but the sound of my mother's weeping made me forget my own anguish. Inching closer to her, I put my arms around her. We clung to each other.

"It's all right," Mother sniffed. "Only for two months, and then we'll leave. You'll see, Dory, everything will be all right."

I didn't speak. I suspected that All Right was as baseless a dream as Fiona or New York or Someday. So long as we lived with Mr. Jenkins, nothing would be All Right.

3

In April, melting snow in the mountains flooded the Purgatory River, swelling it over its banks and sending brown slime swirling into the cabins that lay closest to the water's edge. When the waters receded, the flat prairie along the river was coated with mud for a mile on both sides. Littered with rocks and roots and treelimbs, the landscape looked desolate and permanently spoiled. And then, after only a week, delicate green shoots began to poke up through the caked and crazed mud. Soon the valley was bright with wildflowers.

Pilar and I were wandering along the northern bank of the river, just out of sight of the refinery and the town. We darted here and there, picking the largest and brightest blooms to make nosegays.

"Listen." Pilar lifted her head. "I can hear them on the wind. They are very sad today."

"I don't hear anything." I plucked a blue lupine and stuck it into my bouquet. "You're making it up, Pilar."

"No, no, I am not. My grandmother says that if you come here at night, you can see them, the Conquistadores, along with their leaders Francisco Bonilla and Juan Hermana. They wear suits of armor and helmets with visors, and they carry the flag of Spain."

Pilar's description of the ghosts exactly matched an illustration in one of our Colorado history books, but for a moment I actually believed that the ghosts of murdered men roamed the valley of the Purgatory.

"And Bonilla is carrying his own head!" Pilar added with relish, obviously enjoying my look of horror.

"Oh, you!" I tossed my bouquet aside and chased after her.

Early Spanish conquerers had named the river *El Rio de las Animas Perdidas en Purgatorio,* The River of the Souls Lost in Purgatory, after a band of men who had been slaughtered by Comanche Indians on its banks. A priest who had been traveling with the expedition had turned back after one of the two leaders killed the other in a quarrel. Nothing more was heard about the party until subsequent explorers found their bones. Since the soldiers had died without receiving the last sacraments of the Roman Catholic Church, their souls were presumed still to be in Purgatory, suffering neither the pains of Hell nor the joys of Heaven.

We raced along the riverbank, Pilar's long, dark braids swinging out behind her like the reins of a runaway pony. Making a mighty lunge, I grabbed one. Pilar howled and whirled around, tackling me around the waist. We fell laughing to the ground and engaged in some furious tickling until we both cried out for a truce. Panting, we lay on a blanket of wildflowers and turned our faces up to the great blue arc of the sky.

"I'm glad you're still my friend," I said when I was able to breathe again.

"I will always be your friend." Pilar's voice was very solemn.

"The other kids were so horrible to me today." Lately my schoolmates, instead of ignoring me as usual, had started whispering about me, giggling and pointing behind hands that concealed none of their malice.

I rolled onto my belly in the flowers and sheltered my face in the cave of my arms. But I failed to shut out the memory of the morning.

At recess one of the bigger boys had swaggered up to me in the schoolyard. "I got me a whole dollar," Mike Mullins announced while a little crowd of onlookers snickered. "I bet I could have your ma five whole times for that dollar."

I didn't understand his meaning, but from his tone I knew that my mother was being insulted. "You shut up," I said. "You just shut up about my mother."

"I ain't sayin' nothin' that everybody don't already know," the boy drawled. "Your ma is Sid Jenkins' who-ore. Hey, I bet you're givin' old Sid some of that yourself."

"She is not." I felt my face turn pale, then crimson. "And neither am I!"

"Aw, sure y'are," the boy sneered. "Lowery's a who-ore!" he chanted. "Lowery's a who-ore!" The others took up the song, all except Pilar, who insisted loudly that it wasn't true. "Aw, shut up, you whoring Mex," the ringleader snarled. "Lowery's a who-ore!" he sang. "Pilar's a who-ore, too."

I wanted to kill him. I hated him and Sid Jenkins and all the bullies who worked for the company. I hated the men who had killed my father by refusing to supply decent braces for the mine roof. I hated my mother for exposing me to this abuse, and I hated myself for listening to it.

Without thinking, I hurled myself at the boy's leering face.

The attack caught him by surprise, and before he could throw me off, I had scratched him deeply around the eyes and scored his poxy cheeks with my fingernails.

He began to wail, "Ow, I can't see! I can't see!" Blood oozed out of a half-dozen long red welts. While he pawed at his face with his grubby hands, I aimed a couple of kicks at his shins and some hard punches at his soft belly. Snuffling like an enraged pig, he lurched toward me. His cronies, emboldened by the climate of violence that had suddenly taken over the schoolyard, grabbed me by the arms.

"Get her, Mike," they urged. "Come on, get her!"

"You leave me alone!" I shrieked. "Leave me alone!" Struggling to free myself, I twisted and squirmed and lashed out at them with my feet.

"Lowery's a who-ore!" a few of the girls shrilled from a safe distance. "Lowery's a who-ore!"

Finally the thin but formidable presence of Miss Massey intruded itself into the fray. "What on earth is going on here!" The boys released me, and the crowd in the schoolyard fell silent. "I have never heard such a din, never in my life. All of you, back into the building at once, do you hear me? Theodora, please wait a moment. You, too, Michael. Now, who started this?"

I glared at the boy. "If you ever say anything about my mother again," I puffed, "I'll tell Jenkins and he'll fire your pa from the mine."

"That's enough, Theodora," Miss Massey snapped. "Your behavior is an utter disgrace. You are suspended from school for the rest of the day, and if I hear of any repetition of this incident, you will be expelled, is that clear? Michael, that goes for you, too, but since barring you from school for one day would be no penance, you will stay. Go inside and wash your face. I'll put some iodine on those scratches."

Glaring at me over his shoulder, the boy shuffled off. Miss Massey herded her flock through the door of Monkey Gulch's one-room schoolhouse. She glanced back to where I stood with Pilar in the center of the schoolyard. Pilar's attitude stated firmly that she thought that I had been treated unjustly, and that she intended to join me in my banishment. Miss Massey closed the door with a bang.

"Come." Pilar tugged on my arm. "Forget them, ignorant peoples. Come."

So Pilar took me to the river. But the high clouds, the warm sunshine, the fragrant and colorful wildflowers failed to pierce my misery. I sat on a fallen tree overlooking the water and resisted Pilar's urgings to wade in the still-frigid waters of the Purgatory with her.

"It's not true," I said after a long silence. "Whatever they said about my mother. It isn't true."

Pilar shrugged. "Is none of their business. Pay no attention to them, those stupid peoples." She waded out into the shallows and looked down. "Oh, look," she said excitedly, pointing toward her feet. "Dory, come and look at this."

Unable to resist her repeated urgings, I dragged myself toward the water's edge. Smiling slyly, Pilar bade me come closer. Suddenly she swung her cupped hands upward and showered me with water. I sputtered with outrage and fury. How could my friend do such a thing when she knew how I was suffering? I began to shout and rant. Pilar was a traitor. She was as nasty as the other children at the school, as cruel as Mike Mullins and his odious friends. Finally, I burst into tears and threw myself weeping on the ground. Pilar gave a small sigh of satisfaction and made her way toward the shore.

"My mother always says that when your heart is full of sorrow and anger, your words become twisted and ugly," she said. "Only tears can wash that ugliness away."

After a while, I mopped my eyes on the hem of my dress. "You're right; they're stupid and they don't know what they're talking about. I'm not going to think about them anymore."

The rest of the afternoon was like a holiday. I removed my

shoes and stockings and wiggled my liberated toes in the soft grass. The breeze was soft and warm, full of the promise of summer. Except for the moments when a recollection of the morning's humiliations overtook me, I felt content, almost happy.

We gathered our last bouquets and started home. As the sooty outlines of the town began to take on shape and definition, we saw a figure coming toward us. Pilar cried, "Is Joaquin!" She waved energetically, and started to run toward her brother. I hung back. I had already experienced too many violent swings of emotion that day, everything from black rage and utter desolation to sweet and tranquil joy. Seeing Joaquin now might wrench me into yet another dimension of strong feeling. I wasn't sure I could bear it.

Joaquin and Pilar came toward me. Pilar chattered to her brother in Spanish, speaking more animatedly than she ever did in English. I had lived among Mexicans all my life, and I understood most of what Pilar was saying: "The bad boy called her mother a horrible name, and then he insulted Theodora and then myself. You should have seen Theodora, Joaquin. She fought that boy, bloodied his face for him. I have never seen her so angry. She was like a wildcat."

Joaquin turned his solemn gaze upon me. Then he spoke in soft, strongly accented English. "I am sorry this has happened to you. Pilar is right. They are ignorant. Forget them."

My heart swelled, not from the memory of the incident, but because of his kindness, and Pilar's. Why were they so good to me, these people whom the rest of the town treated as outcasts? My eyes filled with tears. I turned away and covered my face with my hands. I didn't want to cry anymore, but I couldn't help myself. Joaquin made a sympathetic noise, then he put his arm around my shoulders and Pilar took my hand.

Very slowly, we walked back toward the coal-blackened town that was our home.

Sitting cross-legged in the middle of the bed, I watched my mother braiding her long hair. Mother had started spending entire nights in Jenkins' room, changing into her nightgown in the room the two of us shared, then leaving me alone. She no longer even waited for a summons. "Why do you have to go every night?" I asked. "Couldn't you stay with me, at least some of the time?"

Mother shook her head. "It's easier this way. I don't want to make him angry. You don't understand, Dory. He has a power over us. We're dependent upon him for everything, for food and shelter, for our very lives. If he gets tired of having us around, then we'll be out on the street again, with no place to go. No friends, no prospects. No, this is better. So long as he's happy—"

"But it's wrong," I said.

She turned away from the mirror and regarded me with an expression of sadness in her lovely eyes. "Yes, I suppose it is. I know what the people in this town are saying about me, and they're right."

I dug my fingernails into the palms of my hands and lowered my head to hide my tears. I hadn't told her about the incident at school. It would only have upset her.

Mother sighed. "So you've heard the rumors, too, I see. I'm so sorry, Dory." She shrugged. "I never did have any sense where men were concerned. When I was a girl, I chased after every boy I met. I flirted shamelessly. The aunts were always scolding me. I suppose the reason I chased after your father so hard was because he didn't want to have anything to do with me at first. He was right about that. Like I told you before, I'm bad luck."

"I don't like Mr. Jenkins." I pulled my mouth into a stubborn line. "I hate him."

Mother turned back to the mirror. "I keep telling myself that just as soon as we get enough money, we'll pack up and go to Trinidad, and I'll get a real job there."

"How much do we have?" I gave an eager bounce. "It's almost the end of April, and you said we'd have enough by now. How much, Mother?"

She opened the tin. "Well, we've had expenses. You really did need those new shoes, and that fabric I bought will make us both some pretty new dresses for Trinidad. We've got to have something nice to wear when we get there. Nobody's going to hire a woman who doesn't have anything better to wear than a faded old housedress."

"How much?" I persisted.

Mother counted. "Fourteen dollars. Nearly fifteen." I felt glum. Only fifteen dollars, and we needed at least thirty. "We could walk to Trinidad," I suggested without much hope. "The weather's getting real nice, and maybe someone would come along and give us a ride. And if not, we could sleep out under the stars."

Mother laughed. "Walk eighty miles? Are you out of your mind, child?"

A masculine bellow sounded in the hall. "Mary, where in hell are you?"

"I'd better go." Mother leaned down and kissed me gently. "Sweet dreams, darling. I love you."

She turned down the wick in the kerosene lamp near the bed and slipped out into the hall. I heard their voices, Jenkins' low growl and my mother's breathless soprano. Then another door closed, and the house was silent.

I climbed out of bed and went to the window. In the moonlight, the white blossoms that covered the old pear tree looked like a billowing bridal veil. This was my fault, I knew. If my mother hadn't had a child to worry about, she never would have become ... what the people in Monkey Gulch said she was. I didn't blame her. No, I blamed Mr. Jenkins.

I always took the utmost care to avoid Sidney Jenkins. Whenever he entered a room, I tried to slip out of sight. If I saw him approaching on the street or in the hallways, I darted around corners and hid until he passed. When in the evening I heard

2019

the gasping rattle of his car, I made some excuse to my mother about homework and dashed up to my room. I had to endure evening meals with him—he grandly permitted my mother and me to dine at the same table, as though we were a real family. Fortunately, he left for work quite early in the morning, before I was even awake, and we rarely encountered each other during the day. After supper, I washed up the dishes in a hurry and then went up to my room while he and my mother sat in the parlor. She usually had some mending or sewing to do, and he spent the time looking over papers that pertained to his job.

One afternoon, I came home from school to find his car parked out front. Most of the time, he didn't return until nearly suppertime. I entered the house by the back door—no one ever used the front—and looked around the kitchen.

"Mother," I called. Laundry flapped on the line in the back yard. A large open kettle simmered on the stove.

Jenkins came into the room. He had shed his suit jacket and stiff collar and unbuttoned his vest. His shirtsleeves were rolled up above his elbows. "I sent her down to the store. I had a hankerin' for hominy tonight. The company store stocked some pretty good hominy this month, I hear. Better than the slop they usually sell—don't tell anybody I said that."

In what I thought was surreptitious fashion, I edged my way toward the door.

"Where you goin'?" he asked with a grin. "I won't bite. Come on in. Sit down." He gestured toward a kitchen chair. I didn't obey, but hung back, gazing at him expressionlessly, thinking how much I hated him.

He said, "You know, you're not a bad kid, as kids go. Least you're quiet. If you were a yappin' kind of kid, you and your ma wouldn't be here. I can't abide a yappin' kid." He chuckled. "You don't like me, do you? What's the matter? Are you sore that I took your pa's place so soon after he died? You ought to be thankful. If it wasn't for me, you and your ma'd both be out in the streets, eatin' garbage."

I didn't know how to respond. I was a poor liar, and I knew if
I expressed my unfelt gratitude to him for all his favors, he'd
laugh in my face. Or maybe he'd be angry. But I couldn't tell
him the truth, either. I couldn't tell him that I loathed the sight
of him and that I couldn't wait until my mother and I were able
to leave his house.

He sauntered toward me. I wanted to run away, but I didn't.
Maybe I didn't want to behave like a fool in front of him. Instead I hugged my little pile of schoolbooks to my chest and
watched him with wide, wary eyes.

He took the books away from me and looked at the titles.
"Let's see what you kids are studying these days. 'Rithmetic, eh?
You good at math, Dory?"

"No." My voice sounded hoarse, scared. I swallowed. I didn't
like anyone to call me Dory except my mother and Pilar. Everyone else could just cope with Theodora, cumbersome and un-
wieldly though it might be.

"I was pretty sharp at numbers myself. Have to be, if you
want to make a buck these days. Let's see, *Tales from Shakespeare*.
Doesn't interest me. Bet you like it, though. Juliet and Romeo.
Love stuff. You like that story, Dory?"

"Yes, I guess so."

He tossed the books onto the kitchen table. "You're pretty
good in school, aren't you, Dory? You get good grades. You're a
smart girl. That's good. I like smart girls. Smart girls who know
when to talk and when to keep their mouths shut."

He sidled closer to me. I inched away, backing into the door,
which I had foolishly closed as I came in. Suddenly he was
touching me, stroking my face, petting my shoulders. I tried to
wriggle away, but he laughed softly and put his arms around
me. I was trapped like a bird in a cage made of flesh and muscle.
My head darted this way and that as I searched frantically and
futilely for a way to escape him. Except for my father, I had never come up against the solid bulk of a man before. Even that bully Mike Mullins had been soft and childish, inspiring more

scorn than terror. But now, locked in the prison of this man's arms, feeling the pressure of his thighs and belly on mine, I knew I could not escape.

As he rubbed his cheek against mine, I could smell his hair oil. Whiskey and tobacco mingled on his breath. I wanted to scream, but I couldn't. I couldn't even breathe. When he slid his hand under my skirt, into my drawers, between my legs, I made a little whimpering sound. I was terror-stricken, paralyzed, unable to move. I closed my eyes and wished myself far away, out of my body, into Death or some other sweet oblivion.

Jenkins stroked me gently but insistently. His breathing deepened and became slower, as if he were sleeping. "Soft," he murmured. "Nice."

As if through a thick fog, I heard my mother's voice. "Dory, are you home yet?" And then it was over. Jenkins released me and stepped back. Blinking, I looked at him. I hardly recognized him. His face was flushed and his eyelids hung like heavy curtains over his glazed pupils. Through the side window, I could see my mother walking past. Instead of coming straight into the kitchen, she went down to the clothesline at the bottom of the yard and checked the laundry to see if it was dry.

Jenkins thrust my schoolbooks at me. "Get upstairs. Remember: smart girls don't talk. To anybody. You don't want anything to happen to your ma, do you? You say anything and you'll both be out in the street. Or worse."

Up in my room, I flung myself face down on my bed. I was too shocked to cry, too dazed to think about what had happened. It was wrong, I knew, although I wasn't sure why. Jenkins had been revolting and horrible, but he hadn't really hurt me. Yet his furtiveness, and his parting threats, had shown that he recognized that he was committing an improper act. My father had embraced me often, of course, but never like that. And he had never tried to touch me, not down there. I had a clearer idea of what Mother and Jenkins did together in the darkness, and it sickened me. I pulled my pillow over my head, but I could still hear Jenkins' breathing, heavy and throaty, almost a moan.

2019

I ate little dinner that night. Mother asked worriedly if I felt
sick. "No, I'm just not hungry, that's all."

"Dory hasn't acquired a taste for hominy, have you, Dory?"
Jenkins said. His heartiness was so false, and yet my mother
failed to hear it. But I recognized it for what it was: a veil of de-
ceit that he had thrown over both of us, to hide our secret from
my mother and to bind us closer together. As I jumped up and
ran away from the table, I heard him say, "Kids. Always up to
something. That's okay, I'll eat her share."

I lived in terror that the incident would be repeated. I invented a dozen ruses for delaying my return home after school: Miss
Massey had asked me to help her with some special project; I
had been visiting Pilar's grandmother; I wanted to look for wild
strawberries. When I finally did arrive at the house, I could really feel Jenkins watching me. His eyes were like small twin
branding irons burning painful holes into my middle.

The man was a clever fiend, and he chose his opportunities
with care. A week after our encounter in the kitchen, he and I
met on the stairs. I tried to sneak past him, but he pressed me
against the wall and pawed at my chest, where my breasts were
just beginning to bud. He released me when I started to whim-
per. Another week passed without a reoccurrence. I told myself
that it was finished, that he would leave me alone now. But on
Sunday afternoon, while Mother was busy in the kitchen, he
cornered me in the parlor. Grasping my hand, he placed it on
his swollen crotch. I squeezed my eyes shut and turned my face
away. With a laugh, he let me go.

The very next day, Monday, he met me outside school just as
class was being dismissed. He told me he was passing by and
thought he'd give me a lift. Reluctant to disobey him and there-
by risk a scene in front of the other children, I climbed into the
front seat of the grotesque yellow Hudson. Jenkins stopped the
car in front of his house, but before I could jump out, he
grabbed my hand and yanked me back.

"You don't need to run away from me, Dory," he murmured.
"I won't hurt you." Breathing hard, he stroked my thigh. I

gazed longingly at the house I had come to loathe. Why didn't my mother come out and save me? Why didn't someone help me?

Jenkins' first nocturnal assault was like a bad dream. The next morning I wondered if it had really happened at all. Then I felt the soreness between my legs, and detected a rash on my neck where his whisker stubble had irritated the thin skin. I wanted to denounce him to my mother and to the people of the town, but I didn't dare. No one would believe that I wasn't a willing party to his actions, that I hadn't invited his attentions. I finally understood the meaning of the awful word Mike Mullins had used. I was truly Jenkins' whore. My bed, which had been a haven, a place of soft comfort and reassuring warmth, became a prison, a torture chamber.

Mother noticed a change in my behavior, but she decided that girls my age go through stages. And because she slept soundly at night, exhausted by Jenkins' sexual demands on herself, she was unaware that he had started slipping away from her and into my room.

Every night after that, Jenkins crawled under the covers beside me. He fondled and stroked me until he reached a fever of excitement that he could only satisfy by crushing me beneath him. When I cried out, he clapped his hand over my mouth and ordered me to be silent. As he departed, he invariably left me with a whispered warning:

"You tell anybody about this and you'll be out of here so fast you won't know what hit you; you and your pretty ma. Only she won't be so pretty by then."

One night, when Jenkins was bucking and heaving on top of me and I was praying for death or rescue, the door burst open and the golden glow of a kerosene lamp sent the darkness scurrying in retreat.

Mother shrieked, "Leave her alone! Leave her alone!" She attacked him with her fists.

Jenkins leaped up from the bed. He flung Mother away from him, dashing her against the wall. "You say anything about this," he panted, "anything, and I'll beat this kid until she can't walk. You understand? You'll be out of here, you and your crippled kid. You keep your mouth shut, woman. Both of you." He glared at me, lying huddled in a heap in the middle of the bed. Then he stamped out, the tails of his nightshirt flapping around his knees.

Shivering and sobbing, Mother stumbled to the bed and gathered me into her arms. "Oh Dory, Dory, did he hurt you? Oh, my poor baby, my dearest darling. This isn't—is this the first time he's touched you? Tell me." I shook my head. "Oh, my God," she moaned. "Oh, my God, what have I done? I didn't know—I never dreamed. Oh, my God. You should have told me, baby. Why didn't you tell me?"

"He said—he said he'd hurt you." I started to quake, but not from cold. "I—I was afraid."

Mother smoothed the tumble of hair away from my face. "It's all right now. He won't touch you again, I promise. You don't have to be afraid anymore. It's over, darling. It's all over. From now on, everything will be different."

I was too tired to argue, and too exhausted to wonder about my mother's plans. She jammed a chair under the doorknob, then she extinguished the lamplight and climbed into the bed, where she huddled close to me. Eventually we both grew calmer, and I fell asleep in the quiet warmth.

The following evening was unusually fine for June, cool but not chilly. The facades of the buildings along Monkey Gulch's main street caught the orange glow of the setting sun, the reflection of a distant conflagration. Smoke from the refinery and the town's cookstoves created a gentle mist that softened the outlines of the horizon, so that Monkey Gulch appeared to float saucerlike in the universe, a planet unto itself. Mothers called to their offspring, who dragged themselves home to their suppers. Dogs barked, telegraphing excitement or boredom. A factory whistle shrilled.

I dawdled as long as possible after school that afternoon and finally dragged myself home at about six o'clock. I had had a bad day. The memory of the previous night's dark horror and crackling violence enveloped me like a leaden cloak that I couldn't shrug off. Twice during the history lesson Miss Massey reprimanded me for not paying attention. The final humiliation came when she asked me to remain after school. When we were alone in the room, she asked me if anything was bothering me. I shook my head.

"You can talk to me, you know," Miss Massey said a trifle gruffly. After school, she always had difficulty throwing off the brisk and businesslike tone that she assumed during the day. "I don't spread gossip like some people in this town. Anything you say stays within these four walls. Well?"

"I'm just tired, I guess," I mumbled. "I'm sorry. I'll try to pay better attention tomorrow."

Miss Massey sighed. "I certainly hope so. Your work has fallen off badly these past few weeks, Theodora. It isn't like you. Well, if you won't talk to me, you won't. But if you change your mind, I'm always willing to listen. It isn't good to keep things bottled up."

Jenkins' Hudson was parked in the rutted street at the foot of the front steps. I walked around to the back of the house. At this time of day, my mother was always hard at work in the kitchen, preparing the meal that Jenkins wanted served at six sharp.

But the kitchen was empty. The stove was clear of pots and pans, stone cold. This in itself was odd. Since we had moved into Jenkins' house, Mother had never allowed the fire in the stove to go out. Crockery was heaped in the dishpan. I recognized my oatmeal bowl from breakfast.

"Mother!" I called. "Mother, where are you?"

The house was silent. I ran to the front room, the parlor. Everything there was as it should be, tidy and stiff, ready for the guests who never came. The stairs creaked under my slight weight. Odd, how I had never noticed before how much noise they made.

"Mother?" The word came out in a rasping croak. "Mr.—Mr. Jenkins?" Fear constricted my throat. What had happened? Had they fallen asleep, perhaps? Had they lost themselves in their dark pleasures and forgotten the time?

I saw the blood then, a mud-colored smear on the wall between Jenkins' room and the bathroom. Reddish-brown drops dotted the straw matting in the hallway. In the bathroom sink, its blade and handle rusted with dried blood, lay my mother's favorite carving knife. The bathtub was half-filled with water the color of crushed strawberries.

I rushed to Jenkins' room and threw open the door. He lay sprawled on the bed, alone, on sheets drenched with darkening crimson. He was naked, and every inch of his body was reddened with blood that had flowed freely out of a hundred cuts. He seemed to twitch as I stared at him. Then I became aware of a faint hum. Jenkins' body was covered with buzzing flies.

Backing out of the room, I touched the doorjamb and felt something sticky. My hand came away crimson, bloodied. Uttering a startled cry, I wiped my palm on the front of my white middy blouse. But it was too late. I had touched the horror, and it was part of me.

I stumbled down the hall to the back bedroom. Mother was there, hanging like a limp and useless garment from a high hook on the wall. She had put on her new dress, the one she had recently made out of a delicate, green-sprigged cotton. In the corner lay the shabby housedress and apron she had worn at breakfast that morning. They were stiff with dried blood.

The din inside my head nearly deafened me. Cascades of shattering wails seemed to bubble up inside of me as quickly as I vented them. Then I realized that although my mouth was wide open, I was making no sound at all.

4

2019

"The neighbors didn't see no lights in the house that night, and they kinda wondered about it. So the next mornin', when Jenkins didn't show up at the mine office for the second day in a row, Big Jim Beale came lookin'. Well, he come out a' that house lookin' paler'n a ghost. He had himself three drinks of whiskey and he was still shakin'. They didn't find the kid until another night went by. She must a' went crazy when she saw her ma strung up like that, and Jenkins all cut to pieces. She ran up into the hills behind the refinery and hid up thar' until the Garcia boy tracked her down and brought her out. People was askin' her all kinds of questions about what happened, but do you know, she didn't say a word, not one. She hasn't opened her mouth since it happened except to eat a little, and even then we have to kind of force it down."

Mrs. O'Hara paused to catch her breath. Her listeners gaped at me. I paid no attention, but gazed out the window of the train and watched the prairie roll past, as if the tale of horror that held the rest of them in thrall had nothing to do with me at all.

"Maybe she's deaf, too," one of the men suggested.

"Oh, no, she ain't deaf," Mrs. O'Hara assured them. She leaned close to my ear and shouted, "Theodora!" I turned my head and blinked at her in amazement. We were sitting only a few inches apart. Why was Mrs. O'Hara shouting at me? "See?" Mrs. O'Hara looked smug. "She can hear all right, but she can't talk. A doctor in Trinidad looked at her and said her throat and her voice box was okay. He said it was the shock of seeing Sid Jenkins and her ma and all that blood. I saw it myself." Tremors shook the heavy mounds of flesh on her arms. "Oh, Lord, I still have bad dreams about it!"

"Why did she do it?" A young man with deep smallpox scars on his cheeks draped himself over the back of the seat in front of us. "The girl's ma, I mean?"

DEC,
2019

"Just went crazy, I guess," Mrs. O'Hara shrugged. "Of course, Mary Lowery was always a little soft in the head. Like the day of the funeral. Her husband was dead, same as mine and a lot of others, but you might have thought she was the only widder there. You should have seen the way she carried on." A description of the mine disaster and the funeral followed, highlighted by Mrs. O'Hara's graceless imitation of my mother dropping the silk rose onto her husband's coffin and then swooning into Sid Jenkins' arms. "If you ask me," she said, although no one had had the opportunity to pose a question, "that's when Sid Jenkins made up his mind that he was going to have her, one way or the other. Housekeeper!" she snorted. "She was no more his housekeeper than I was. Everybody knew what was goin' on. But she didn't care. Not her. She still sashayed around town like she was better than the rest of us."

"Lordy, she must have hated him." A moon-faced woman fanned herself with her small-brimmed straw hat. The ring of artificial flowers on the crown flapped listlessly. "It must have been abuildin' and abuildin' inside her, and all of a sudden she couldn't take it no more."

"Weren't nothin' sudden about it," Mrs. O'Hara said knowingly. "It was planned. Why, after she did it, she washed the blood off herself and changed her clothes and went into town, just as calm as you please. She went right up to the stationmaster and asked how much it would cost to buy a ticket to New York, one way. He figured it up, and she gave him the money right there on the spot, and all the while that poor man was lying dead in his bed, butchered and bloody."

Her audience shuddered. "Horrible," the moon-faced woman murmured. "Just horrible."

"Oh, it was horrible, all right," Mrs. O'Hara said, " 'specially the cold-hearted way she worked it all out. She left the ticket in an old tin box on her dresser, with a little note. I have it right here. Maybe you'd like to see it?"

The little crowd that had gathered around our seat pressed closer. With tantalizing slowness and all the finesse of a strip-

2011

teaser, Mrs. O'Hara opened her purse and removed a small
scrap of paper. Mary Lowery's suicide note, by now crumpled
and stained, was passed from hand to hand. Everyone in the
front half of the Atchison, Topeka, and Santa Fe coach in which
we were riding saw the words my mother had written before
she died:

"My daughter's only living relative is Miss Fiona Randall of
New York City. Her address is the Hotel Burbage on Fifth Avenue."

Mrs. O'Hara jabbed a plump finger at the paper. "Not one
word about how sorry she was for what she done, or how much
she would miss her kid. She didn't even ask anybody to make
sure and look after the girl. All I can say is, Dory's lucky to have
me along to take care of her. Goin' all this way, clear to New
York City, just to take this poor child to her only living relative." She sighed. "Ain't it strange, the way things work out?
I'm from New Jersey originally, but once O'Hara and I moved
to Colorado, I never figured I'd be going back that way. But after I was widdered—"

Actually, Miss Massey had arranged for Mrs. O'Hara to travel
with me. "The child can't possibly go by herself. She isn't fit.
We will take up a collection, or perhaps we can persuade the
company to pay for someone to go with her. If no one else can
be found, I will take her myself, while school is out."

I wouldn't have minded traveling with Miss Massey, who
probably would have given me history and geography lessons all
the way from Monkey Gulch to New York. But Mrs. O'Hara
had seized the opportunity to return to the land of her birth.

"I'm not surprised," Miss Massey had said sourly. "Everybody in this town is sick of hearing about this tragic business.
What that woman is really looking for is a fresh audience."

And a fresh audience is what Mrs. O'Hara got, every time an
unsuspecting passenger sat himself down within ten feet of us.
Mrs. O'Hara would start by asking the new arrival the reasons
for his or her journey. Once that little formality was out of the
way, she would announce, "This poor child's ma stabbed her

man to death and then hung herself. I'm takin' Theodora to see her only living relative, a famous actress in New York City." Rare was the listener who didn't press for details.

It's funny, I thought. When you don't speak, people think you can't hear. They forget that you even exist.

My muteness was not a manifestation of the stubbornness I had inherited from my father, nor, as some of the women in Monkey Gulch had suggested, was it a bid for attention. I had been as surprised as everyone else when I discovered that I couldn't talk. Well, no, surprised was too strong a word. Along with my ability to speak, I seemed to have lost my power to experience emotion, to react. Nothing touched me anymore, neither heat nor cold, not sorrow nor joy nor anger. I went where people told me to go, ate what they told me to eat, wore what they set out for me to wear. If left to myself, I would have sat toadlike in the middle of the prairie somewhere, losing my human shape, gradually taking on the color and form of the homely objects that surrounded me, so that any but a really keen-eyed passerby would have mistaken me for a stone.

Occasionally I felt a stirring of mild interest or a twinge of regret when I saw how my behavior pained the people who loved me. I had made a genuine effort to speak only once, when Pilar, with tears coursing down her cheeks, had begged me to say a word, just one word. I pressed my lips together and tried to push out a P sound for Pilar's name, but the mechanisms that controlled breath and muscle simply didn't work. I quickly lost interest in the effort. Expelling the air from my lungs in a long sigh, I turned my face away from my friend.

Not even Joaquin could reach me. After he found me cowering in a sort of earthy cave formed by an uprooted spruce tree, he carried me down the mountainside in his arms, all the while keeping up a soothing monologue in Spanish, that beautiful language that always used to remind me of water swirling over rocks, smoothing out the rough places, bubbling and eddying and laughing. At any other time I would have been amazed by this outpouring of speech from one who was normally so taciturn, but that day, and all the days that followed, I hardly noticed.

After that dramatic rescue, Joaquin kept careful watch over me, once even expelling Mrs. O'Hara from the room because he could see that her chatter was making me uneasy. He sat with me by the hour, often holding my hand between both of his. But I couldn't repay his kindness with so much as a smile. When the train pulled out of the Monkey Gulch station and I saw Joaquin running alongside, waving to me, I lowered my head and closed my eyes.

Mrs. O'Hara's sensational gossip didn't bother me. Her flat voice was so much background noise, like the rhythmic clack of the wheels and the labored chuff of the engine. The scenes of America that passed before my eyes, framed by the window of the carriage, might have been pictures in an old storybook, each one flat and colorless and no more interesting than the one that preceded it. Not even the prospect of meeting my mother's sister Fiona could rouse me from my stupor. Fiona had been a central figure in my life, although we'd never met. But I had no feelings left, not even about her. My hatred, like my love, had immolated itself in a raging conflagration that had consumed even its own cinders.

We presented ourselves at the Hotel Burbage. In the dark hush created by deep-piled red carpet and lustrous wood paneling, Mrs. O'Hara's voice sounded like the screech of chalk on a blackboard. The austere-looking man behind the front desk asked in an offended murmur if he could help us.

"You can tell me where I can find Miss Fee-ona Randall, the actress," Mrs. O'Hara said. "I've got a surprise for her."

"Miss Randall is out for the evening," he informed her. "Why don't you telephone later, after midnight?"

"Maybe I will," Mrs. O'Hara said, "or maybe I'll just wait right here 'til she gets back."

"I wouldn't advise it." The man drew his upper lip down over his front teeth. He wore glasses without earpieces, from which hung a black ribbon that snaked its way into the breast pocket of his suit. "We don't permit visitors to loiter in the lobby area. I'm sure if you leave your name and telephone number, Miss Randall will get in touch with you."

"Oh, you're sure, are you?" My companion winked at me. "Well, I ain't so sure, but I guess we'll run along, thanks just the same. Come on, kid." With a speed that belied the idea that bulk impairs freedom of movement, Mrs. O'Hara strode toward the entrance. I picked up the carpet bag containing my possessions and trudged after her. A man dressed in the uniform of a military general held the door for us.

As we passed, I heard him mutter, "Scram, you bums. Come back here and I'll call the cops."

When we were out of earshot, Mrs. O'Hara clasped her fingers pincerlike around my upper arm. "They ain't so smart. Did you see that big bouquet of roses sittin' on the desk? 'Miss Randall, Penthouse Suite,' the tag said. That's where we're headed. Through the back door this time. Anyone asks, we tell 'em I'm the new maid. Penthouse Soote! Mary Lowery's sister's livin' pretty fancy, huh?"

We found the tradesman's entrance and the back stairs. My progress was slow, burdened as I was with my bag, and when we reached the first landing, Mrs. O'Hara snatched the thing out of my hand and charged upwards, so eager was she to be rid of me.

I felt grubby and so weary that I just wanted to curl up in any dark corner and go to sleep. My white middy blouse was covered with specks of soot, and my blue pleated skirt boasted a huge dark stain on one side, where the globe of the ice cream cone Mrs. O'Hara had purchased on the platform in Kansas City had landed as the train lurched into motion.

At the top of the stairs, we were confronted with two doors. "Kitchen," Mrs. O'Hara sniffed, dismissing the first door. We charged through the second, and found ourselves in a small corridor. The double doors of an elevator faced another door that had a knob in the center, at waist height. Mrs. O'Hara dumped my carpetbag on the floor and leaned on the little button to the right of the knob.

An elderly woman wearing a black dress and crisp black apron opened on the second ring. Mrs. O'Hara stared at her gray hair and soft, weathered face.

"You ain't Fee-ona!"

The woman closed the door a couple of inches. "Miss Fiona is resting," she said. "If you'd care to leave your card, I'll tell her—"

Using the advantage of her great size and pioneer-woman's strength, Mrs. O'Hara grabbed my hand and we surged forward. The other woman had the choice of either moving or of being knocked flat by the swing of the door. She moved, protesting that we had no business—

"You just go tell Miss Fee-ona that a relative of hers is here, come all the way from Colorado," Mrs. O'Hara said. "Tell her that. And hurry it up, or I'll go find her myself. Go on, do as I say. Move!"

The woman had sampled Mrs. O'Hara's strength once. Casting us a backward fearful glance, she disappeared through a tall door off to the right of the little foyer. As soon as she had gone, Mrs. O'Hara tested the sturdiness of a small gilded chair.

"Hey, this is pretty fine," she declared, swiveling her head around to gaze at the marble walls, the patterned rug, the tiny table whose surface barely accommodated the pair of gloves and the vase of roses that sat there. "Jesus, my feet are killing me. I sure will be glad to see a bed tonight. My folks are gonna get the surprise of their lives when I turn up. That's why I didn't write or send a telegram that I was comin'. Wanted to surprise 'em."

The tall door opened. Trailed by the elderly maid, who was still looking frightened and murmuring apologies and explanations, a young woman swept into the foyer. I recognized her, of course. She was so much like my mother that for a moment my heart contracted inside my chest, as though it were being squeezed by a large fist. Perhaps it was all a nightmare, and

2019

Mother was still alive, and her incredible dreams for us had come true.

My Aunt Fiona had my mother's wide blue eyes and pert nose, her broad forehead and pointed chin. Her hair was a different color, reddish-gold rather than straw blond, and although her skin was as smooth and as soft as Mother's, Fiona's glowed with shades of rich color that looked like they had come out of a paintbox. My mother had never owned anything so fine as the garment Fiona wore, a black sleeveless tunic, fringed on the bottom, that sparkled with a million tiny sequined lights. Mother had spoken with a breathless, winsome quality. Fiona's voice was firm, forthright, and, at the moment, edged with irritation.

"Thank you, Johanna." She dismissed the maid, who ducked behind a small door that she neglected to close completely. "Now what is all this? I'll give you one minute to explain, and then I call the police."

"Well, I guess you must be Fee-ona!" Mrs. O'Hara tried to launch herself out of her seat, but the slender chair arms hugged her bottom for a moment before the chair fell back to the marble floor with a crash. Mrs. O'Hara was unperturbed. "I didn't really believe until this minute that Mary had a real sister who was an actress, but I guess she wasn't lyin' after all. Mary's dead. Maybe you didn't know that. This is her girl, Theodora."

Placing a meaty hand between my shoulder blades, she gave me a slight shove. I stumbled forward. Fiona's eyes met mine. For a moment I felt a flicker of my old feeling for her, but it was more like the memory of hatred than hatred itself. Then my lethargy reasserted itself, and I yawned and stared at my shoes.

"Dory can't say hello. She hasn't said a word since her ma died." Encouraged by Fiona's silence and rendered eloquent by long practice, Mrs. O'Hara related the gruesome details of my mother's death: "—cut him up in itty bitty pieces, and then cleaned herself up and changed her clothes and went right into town and bought a one-way ticket to New York for Dory here. And then she went home and hung herself on a hook in the bedroom. Can you beat that? Left a little note. I have it right here."

Mrs. O'Hara produced the note and waved it under Fiona's nose. Fiona retreated slightly from the woman's bulk and the stink of her body, but she took the note. "Never a thought for the poor child. Who did she think would find them? Well, it drove poor Dory here right out of her mind. I'm sorry for her, I really am, but to tell you the truth, she wasn't all there before it happened." Mrs. O'Hara tapped her forehead. "A dreamer, like her ma."

"Get out." Fiona closed her fist around the note. "Both of you."

"What?" Mrs. O'Hara gaped at her.

"This girl is no relation of mine. I don't want anything to do with her. Or you. Now get out."

"But she's your kin!" Mrs. O'Hara gasped. "She don't have no one else in the world, not another living soul, just like it says in that note. I'm come a long way, just to bring her here. You hafta take her. You don't expect me to look after her, do you?"

"I'm sure I don't care what you do with her," Fiona said through clenched teeth. "If you're not out of here in two minutes, I shall call the police."

The workings of Mrs. O'Hara's mind were visible on her face. I knew that she was remembering the heat, the cinders, the hard board seats, the bad food, the thousand and one discomforts of travel she had endured, just so she could perform this mission of mercy for a stranger. To put up with all that, only to be turned away at her destination? Oh, no. Mamie O'Hara wasn't going to let this snippet of a female treat her like she was some kind of housemaid.

She darted after Fiona, grasped her arm, and pulled the younger woman around to face her. "Not so fast, you yellow-haired hussy. You can't just walk out on me. This kid is yours now. I done my part."

"How dare you," Fiona snapped. "Take your hands off me!"

"You know damn well this kid is your kin, or you wouldn't be turning her away so quick," Mrs. O'Hara said. " 'Sides, you're the spittin' image of her ma." She dropped her hand. "All right, I'll go, but I ain't takin' Dory with me. She ain't my flesh and blood. I done enough for her. I'm leavin' her here."

"She isn't my child, either," Fiona hissed. "I don't want her, can't you understand that? Take her out in the street, take her to an orphanage, do what you like with her. But she's not staying here."

"Oh, yes, she is. Dory, bring in your suitcase. Come on, step it up."

I ducked out into the corridor and dragged the battered carpetbag inside. It had nothing in it that I wanted: the items that Mrs. O'Hara referred to as "necessaries"—underclothes, nightgown, stockings. It also contained my mother's Bible and my parents' oval-framed wedding portrait, taken a year after that event by a photographer in Denver. Pilar and Miss Massey had assembled the things that they thought I cared about. How wrong they were.

"Get that thing out of here," Fiona barked.

"Leave it there," Mrs. O'Hara commanded.

"I forbid—"

"Don't listen to her—"

Their voices rose shrilly. Suddenly the tall door swung open and a man stepped into the foyer. Like the maid, he wore black and white, a velvety-looking black suit with a wing-collared white shirt and a black tie. But he was no servant. With his hands shoved negligently into his jacket pockets, his fair hair straying down over his forehead, and an air of regarding the world with amused tolerance from under slightly elevated brows, he looked like a god who had forsaken the delights of Olympus in order to observe at firsthand us beings called mortals.

"What in the name of Heaven is going on here?" His voice was soft and slow, almost a drawl. "Can't a man even read his evening newspaper in peace?"

The two women subsided at once. Fiona looked sullen, pink

with rage. Mrs. O'Hara drew herself up and straightened her hat. She seemed to sense that she was in the presence of a real gentleman, like a doctor or a preacher.

"And who might you be?" She demanded.

The man said, "I am Evan Bradford, Miss Randall's husband. Fiona," he turned to his wife, "perhaps you'd be good enough to explain?"

"It's the most absurd mix-up, darling," Fiona began. "This woman claims that this child is related to me. Can you imagine that? This wretched little urchin? But I can't seem to persuade her that the whole idea is just ludicrous, impossible. Darling, you've got to do something!"

"I see. Madame?" Assuming the role of Solomon, the man turned to Mrs. O'Hara, who presented her side of the story with unusual succinctness. When she mentioned the note Mother had left, Evan asked to see it. Fiona handed it over. He unfurled it, and drew his dark brows into a frown. "Mary Lowery," he said, reading Mother's signature. "That's the woman who's been writing to you, isn't it? The one whose letters upset you so much?"

The color rose to Fiona's cheeks. "She has no right to expect me to look after her brat," she said angrily. "I refuse. I absolutely refuse! Look at her." She whirled on me. "She's not even sane. She's an imbecile, a—a moron! It's just like Mary to try and stick me with her wretched bastard. You've got to do something, Evan. It's so—it's so unfair!" she cried.

"Then she *is* your niece," Evan Bradford said. "She has nowhere else to go. I don't see that we have much of a choice."

Fiona's lower lip quivered. She moved close to her husband and put her hands on the front of his dinner jacket. "You can't make me do this," she pleaded in a throbbing whisper. "You can't! I don't want her, Evan!"

"We don't have a choice," Evan repeated. "We have to take her in until we can make some other arrangements for her. You're the only relative she has." He lowered his voice so that Mrs. O'Hara couldn't hear him, but I was standing close enough to them so that I caught every word. "Think of yourself, your career. Can you imagine what something like this could do to you a few years from now, once your career is established? The wrong sort of people could uncover this story, get it from this woman, perhaps. The press would have a field day: 'Famous star spurned orphaned niece.' No, Fiona. We must do something for her. You can see that, can't you? We don't have a choice."

"Well, I do have a choice." Fiona pushed him away from her. "If you want to look after the brat, that's your business. But I don't want anything to do with her, do you understand? I don't even want to look at her: a murderess's daughter! You can put her in a home or in a school, anyplace, just so long as I don't have to lay eyes on her. Do what you want. I don't care. It's your money." In a swirl of tassels and a blinding flash of sequins and diamonds, she swept through the big door and gave it a mighty slam.

Even Mrs. O'Hara was momentarily silenced by the dramatic vigor of the scene she had just witnessed.

"Well, Mrs.—ah," Evan coughed. "We are very grateful to you for taking all this trouble with—ahem—Miss Lowery."

"Yeah, I seen how grateful Miss Fee-ona is," Mrs. O'Hara remarked.

Evan pulled out his wallet. "I hope you'll accept a token of our gratitude. You may be assured, the child will receive the best of care. You need have no further worry on her account."

Mrs. O'Hara took the two fifty-dollar bills he offered and tucked them into her bodice. "Oh, I ain't worried. I guess I done my duty, and I'm not sorry it's over." She glanced around. "This sure is a swell place you got here. But I don't know as Dory wouldn't 'a been just as happy back in Monkey Gulch, Colorado. Lot a' nice folks in Monkey Gulch. Sure ain't nobody like that Miss Fee-ee-ona!"

"No," Evan agreed stiffly. "I suspect you're right about that."

"Well, so long, Dory." Mrs. O'Hara patted my bony shoulder. "Best of luck to you. Don't forget your old friends back home."

Mrs. O'Hara gave Evan a wink and a parting leer as she let

herself out. Evan Bradford stood silently for some moments. Then he turned and gave me a look of thoughtful astonishment. He seemed rather stunned by the enormity of what he had just done: acquired a half-grown child, the daughter of a murderess, and a mute at that.

"Well." He cleared his throat and began again. "You must forgive Fiona for becoming excited. She's had an exhausting day rehearsing for her new play, and her nerves are rather on edge. We open in New Haven in less than a month and the show is still a shambles."

I concealed a yawn behind my fist. This provoked an expression of relief on Evan Bradford's face, as though I had given him a clue on what to do next.

"How thoughtless. Of course you're tired, and hungry, too, I should imagine." He reached over to the wall and pressed a button. The gray-haired woman appeared before the faint echo of a chime had completely faded. "Ah, Johanna, this is Miss Theodora Lowery, who will be living with us until we—for a while. Would you mind seeing to her supper and a bath?"

Johanna's nostrils twitched mutinously. Her trepidation had disappeared. "Yes, sir. Shall I put her in the small room next to mine? The little maid's room?" Clearly she had overheard Fiona's irate rejection of me.

Evan Bradford's eyebrows inched up. "Certainly not. Miss Theodora is a guest. Put her in the spare bedroom for tonight." He bade me a polite but distant good night and strolled off, satisfied that he had shifted the burden onto more capable shoulders for the time being.

Johanna picked up my carpetbag. "I don't care what he says, the bath comes first. Come on, kid. Don't drag your feet."

During my bath and the little supper that followed in my room, Johanna confirmed what I had already begun to suspect, that most people are uncomfortable with silence. Since I made no response to her queries and observations, she was forced to carry on a monologue, in which she revealed quite a bit about her employers. As she herself said, she would have crawled over

broken glass for Mister Evan. But she felt no corresponding loyalty to Fiona.

"I think she must have put a spell on him," Johanna confided.
"He saw her in a musical show, *Girls in a Whirl*—got rotten no-
tices, but he's fond of telling everyone that she was the best one
in it. If you ask me, she just had the sharpest eyes. Saw the bulge
of his wallet and knew she had found herself a live one. Oh,
she's been living better than a cat in a creamery ever since. Singing lessons, speech lessons, fur coats, enough jewels to sink the
Titanic. Not that you'd know it to hear her complain: 'Why does
the show have to open in September? Why do we have to live in
this stupid penthouse? You said the house on Gramercy Park
would be ready in June, and here it is August.' Mr. Evan is just
so sweet to her. He's crazy about her, poor man. His father
would be in a state if he knew that his son had married a common actress. He always hoped that Mr. Evan would amount to
something—be more than just a playboy, if you know what I
mean."

She looked to me for some reaction. Swallowing a yawn along
with a bite of ham sandwich, I managed a feeble nod, although I
had not the slightest idea of what she meant.

"Oh, he's tried his hand at everything. Tennis, racing
cars—twisted himself up real bad in a wreck in France a couple
of years ago. He wrote a book of poetry. Didn't sell ten copies.
Composed a bunch of songs no one ever sang. He hit it lucky
when he met Mr. Max, though. That's Max Feinblatt, the theatrical producer. They're partners now. Mr. Max has the brains
and Mr. Evan has the money. They've already produced one hit,
and this new play is going to be another. Too bad *she* has the
lead. Mr. Evan hired a writer to do the play especially for her.
Still, she's not a bad actress, I have to admit that. I've seen all
kinds of scenes here at home; if she can pull that stuff off on the
stage—I know the theater—my late husband and I did a knife-
throwing act on the vaudeville circuit. That's where I got this
scar." Johanna pulled down her collar to reveal a thin purple
mark on the side of her neck. "The old man got drunk one

night. Pinned me right to the board. I didn't blink an eye. Just kept smiling until the curtain went down. But you should have heard me then."

Seeing me dozing over the remains of my cocoa and sandwich, Johanna declared that it was time for bed. She turned down the covers, plumped my pillows, and tucked me in. As she switched off the light, I heard her sigh, "Poor kid. And I thought my family was nuts."

5

I sat stiffly in the passenger seat of Evan's dark green Hispano-Suiza custom-made convertible roadster. Evan climbed in beside me and pressed the starter.

"Hang onto your hat," he said.

Obediently, I clapped my hand down on the crown of my new straw boater. With a squeal of tires and a deafening blast of its horn, the car whirled into the midst of the traffic on Fifth Avenue.

"The fall term doesn't start until September, of course," Evan said as he guided the car in and out of traffic, "but Miss Frasier says they often have girls living at school between terms, children who can't stay at home because their parents are traveling, or ill."

Or dead.

I was unable to react to Evan's civilized overtures with so much as a grunt or a nod. A leaden stillness possessed me; I felt that I was a stationary object, a structure made of concrete and brick, and that the city, whipping past me in a mad blur, was the living being, a throbbing, vibrating octopus with tentacles composed of people and pushcarts and automobiles. Evan was alive. The Hispano-Suiza was alive. Everything was alive except me. I was stone.

After a while, the suffocating density of the city eased. When we reached the open countryside, Evan accelerated sharply. I remembered Johanna's graphic account of his accident, which had occurred during a rally on the back roads of France, but I felt no apprehension at his sudden burst of speed. Slumped down in my seat, I picked at a loose thread on my new white skirt. When Evan shifted on the next turn, his movements were sharp, irritated.

In my own remote and half-conscious way, I sympathized with Evan Bradford. He hadn't asked for this unexpected intrusion into his life, but he was too well mannered to indulge in any full-blown displays of resentment or regret—only a few signs of annoyance now and then, which he failed to suppress.

In the week that had passed since my arrival in New York, I hadn't set eyes on Fiona again. Johanna and Evan conspired to keep me well out of her sight. I didn't mind. Seeing her was painful and unsettling, because she reminded me of so many things that I wanted to forget.

On the morning following my first night at the Hotel Burbage, after Fiona had left for rehearsal for the day, Evan's mother came over to have a look at me.

"She's frightfully thin, poor dear," she clucked. "Tall for her age, too, don't you think?"

Evan said, "I'm sure I don't know, Mother. It's been a long time since I had any need to concern myself with children. Not since I was one."

"This must have come as quite a shock to dear Fiona." I heard a slightly feline purr of satisfaction in Mrs. Bradford's tone. "Well, now, what shall we do with her? Clothes first. Bring me the telephone."

She rang her favorite department store, explained her problem to the manager, and asked him to send someone over to the Hotel Burbage at once to measure me. The store supplied a skeleton wardrobe immediately, and promised to have the rest of my things ready in a few days. Johanna took special delight in discarding every item of clothing that I had brought with me from Colorado.

"Not even fit for rags," she said, tossing aside my new green-sprigged cotton dress, identical to the one my mother had worn when she died. I remembered my mother's feet, suspended just a few inches off the floor, and the green-sprigged dress, looking starched and beautiful, like a garment hung up for display in a store.

Fiona and the rest of the company would be leaving for New Haven in a week, for the play's first out-of-town tryout. Evan disliked the idea of leaving me alone in the apartment with only Johanna for company, but neither could he take me along; Fiona wouldn't stand for it. Evan's mother offered to look after me at the family's country home on Long Island, but Evan said he didn't want to bother her, and besides, he needed a longer-term solution to the problem. He couldn't keep me at home forever. Once again his mother came up with the answer: Emily Frasier's school. Just the thing. And just in time.

The car rolled between two stone pillars and proceeded up a long driveway lined with evergreens, mostly yews and hollies. The Frasier estate, now The Frasier School, stood on a hill overlooking the Hudson River. According to Evan's mother, Miss Frasier's father had won and lost a succession of fortunes in a series of sensational business maneuvers. He died before he could recover from his last financial reversal. Rather than give up the home that had meant so much to her, Emily Frasier had established a girls' school on the premises. Her friends cooperated by sending their teenage daughters to the new school, which, unlike many similar institutions, offered a challenging curriculum, excellent teaching, a vigorous sports program, and instruction in the domestic sciences. Miss Frasier wanted to prepare her girls for whatever difficulties life might bring them.

Evan stopped the car under the portico of a gray Georgian

2019

mansion. Miss Frasier herself came out to greet us. In the early days of her career as a headmistress, so Evan's mother had told me, Miss Frasier had had to force herself to assume the imposing bearing and authoritative tone that her position required. Now, some thirty years later, she and her role were one. Her manner was capable and solid, her voice firm, her command over her little domain absolute. She was accompanied by a small woman of uncertain age whose eyes blinked behind huge black-framed glasses. The small woman was smoking a cigarette.

"Evan, how delightful to see you again. How is dear Edith? And Ruthie and Margaret?" Evan's two sisters had both matriculated under Miss Frasier's watchful eye. They were married now and currently producing daughters of their own, grist for Emily's mill, as Mrs. Bradford put it.

Unfolding himself from the driver's seat, Evan came around to greet Miss Frasier. He limped slightly, as he always did after a prolonged period of driving or sitting still.

"The girls and their numerous offspring are thriving. Mother sends her love. Her arthritis bothers her now and then, but she doesn't let it slow her down."

Miss Frasier nodded approvingly. "Edith won't let herself become an invalid. She's got too much spunk. Like you, Evan. You seem to have recovered nicely from that awful accident."

Evan grimaced. "You should see me on rainy days. My back is a fiendishly accurate barometer." He opened the door on the passenger side. "Come along, Theodora. We have arrived. I'd like you to meet Miss Frasier and her assistant, Miss Wiggs."

"How do you do, my dear?" Miss Frasier thrust her large hand toward me. I had never shaken hands with anyone before, but after a moment's hesitation, I gave her my own. Flicking her cigarette into the shrubbery, Miss Wiggs extended her hand, too.

"I hope you'll like it here," Miss Frasier said. "We do. Wiggsy, ask for some tea, will you? I'm sure that Mr. Bradford and Theodora are quite parched after that long ride." Miss Wiggs vanished without speaking. A handyman appeared and removed my trunk from the back of the car. Miss Frasier said to Evan, "I am accustomed to dealing with mutes. Wiggsy never says an unnecessary word. Quite a refreshing change from most women, who never say a necessary one."

The three of us strolled down the broad slope of the lawn to a high bluff that commanded a stirring view of the Hudson. The river broadened and curved around the wooded bulge of a mountain on the opposite shore. A few sailboats pierced the water like white arrowheads without shafts.

"Evan tells me you are from Colorado, Theodora," Miss Frasier said. "I have never been there. Is it anything like this?"

I looked out over the Hudson, wide and deep and peaceful looking. The only river I knew, the Purgatory, dried up to a trickle in the summer months and swelled to a killing torrent in the spring, when the snows thawed in the mountains. From Monkey Gulch, the Rocky Mountains looked remote and awe-inspiring, not comfortably accessible like the little knoll across the river. In my part of Colorado, the air was putrid with coke fumes. The screaming of steam whistles, the roar of the blast furnaces, and the incessant rumble and squeal of freight trains assured that the people of Monkey Gulch would never know the serenity and peace that Miss Frasier and her students enjoyed here. I glanced back at the Frasier mansion. The biggest and fanciest house in town, Mr. Watson's, looked like a shack compared to this place, with its broad verandas, marble statuary, and wide solid chimneys. No, Colorado was nothing like this.

Evan nudged me gently, prompting me to reply. After what must have seemed an age, I managed to jerk my head from side to side.

"I thought not," Miss Frasier said. "I would enjoy hearing about it. Perhaps you could describe it to me on paper. Would you be willing to do that, Theodora? To write a little about yourself and your fam—" She caught herself and quickly amended the word to, "home?"

I gave my unenthusiastic assent. I was aware of meaningful glances being passed between Evan and our hostess.

"Thank you. I shall look forward to reading it."

Our tea party on the lawn was a lopsided affair, with Evan and Miss Frasier carrying on a lively conversation in which they tried to include the silently puffing Miss Wiggs and myself. Miss Frasier wanted to hear all about the play Evan was producing.

"I was looking for something really special for my wife," Evan explained. "She's so talented, so brilliant, but none of the properties I saw was right for her."

And so he had commissioned a work from a well-known novelist, who had never written for the theater. At first the writer had refused. Then Evan introduced him to Fiona. Enchanted by her, the novelist had agreed to try his hand at writing plays.

"I hope you'll come and see the show when it opens in New York. I'll send tickets for you and Miss Wiggs," Evan promised. "I'd like you to see Fiona. She has an extraordinary gift, a truly remarkable ability to communicate with an audience. My partner, Max Feinblatt, says that she climbs right over the footlights and embraces every man and woman in the house. She's . . ." He searched for the right word. "She's magical."

As he spoke about Fiona, Evan's expression assumed a new softness. What Johanna had said was true: he adored her. I felt a flicker of interest. This was nothing like what Sid Jenkins had felt for my mother—or for me.

Evan prepared to depart. Rising with him, Miss Frasier said, "Girls with handicaps often fit into things quite well here. The other students get used to them very quickly, and our teachers are competent and caring. I promise you, they will make the necessary adjustments to Theodora's problem. If she keeps up with her work and shows just a little progress, she will be welcome to remain. We will do everything we can to make Theodora feel at home, Evan."

"Thank you, Miss Frasier. My wife and I are most grateful."

"This can't have been easy for you," Miss Frasier said to him as our quartet strolled toward his car. I trailed behind with Miss Wiggs, who sent up little puffs of cigarette smoke as she moved, like a sort of goggle-eyed engine. "Most people get some warning before the arrival of a child."

Evan thanked Miss Frasier again, climbed into his car, and drove away. I thought I detected a joyful note in the roar of the motor when he turned out of the gates. And why not? He had cause for lightheartedness. The crisis was over. He and Fiona could go on as before, as if I had never existed.

"Money certainly has its uses, Wiggsy," Miss Frasier said as we ascended the steps to the front door. "It can rescue a child from poverty, provide an education at a moment's notice, and assure proper care without the nuisance of personal involvement. It can purchase fame, a career, even a play by a first-rate writer. Curious that he doesn't look happier."

Miss Frasier's limousine glided to a stop in front of one of the elegant mansions that faced Gramercy Park. The leaves on the trees in the grassy square were just beginning to turn, introducing frivolous touches of gold and crimson into this otherwise staid and subdued enclave.

Miss Frasier asked Miss Wiggs if she wanted to come inside with us. Pressing herself into the corner of the car, Miss Wiggs sent up furious plumes of smoke. "Suit yourself," Miss Frasier sniffed. "But you'd better open a window."

The front door of the house was wide open. From the center of the high-ceilinged marbled entrance hall, a butler directed workmen on ladders as they hung garlands of live flowers from ornate plaster cornices. Miss Frasier marched up to the butler, introduced herself, and demanded to see Mr. Evan Bradford at once. Recognizing the voice of one who is accustomed to instant obedience, the man rapped smartly at a door to the right of the entrance, announced Miss Emily Frasier, and stepped aside.

We found ourselves in a vast, chestnut-paneled library, a dark but comfortable room furnished with crimson rugs, heavy drapes, and soft leather chairs. Evan was seated behind a mammoth desk. His fair hair glinted like gold under the light of a glass-shaded lamp. With a green velvet smoking jacket draping his slender body and a burnished briar pipe smoldering in his hand, he looked like an illustration in one of the magazines that the style-conscious students of the school passed around: "The Cultured Gentleman in His Study."

Coming around to the front of his desk to greet us, Evan looked understandably apprehensive. Miss Frasier had been unable to warn him of our visit, and her grim expression dimmed any hope he might have had that this was simply a social call.

Miss Frasier gave Evan's hand a single energetic pump, then seated herself on the only straight-backed chair in the room. "The management of the Hotel Burbage directed us here. We seem to have arrived at an inconvenient moment." She pulled off her gloves. "I hope you will forgive me, Evan. I did try to telephone."

"We only finished moving in yesterday." Evan resumed his seat behind the desk. "The phone still isn't working properly. I'm giving a party here to celebrate the opening of Fiona's play tonight."

"Good Heavens, is it tonight? Forgive me, Evan, I would not have intruded at this busy time if I had known."

"The opening is just a formality," Evan reassured her. "Most of the New York critics saw the play in New Haven or Philadelphia. The first month is already sold out."

"I congratulate you," Miss Frasier said. "And I thank you for the tickets you sent. Wiggsy and I are looking forward to seeing Miss, ah, Mrs. Bradford's performance."

"The workmen barely finished the house in time." Evan rapped his pipe gently on the edge of an oversized marble ashtray. He seemed wary, eager to postpone the inevitable unpleasant moment for as long as possible. "I've had the old place completely refurbished. My sisters and I grew up in here, you know. This is my retreat. Hanes, remarkable fellow, has already shelved most of the books, all but the rarest and most fragile ones. I prefer to attend to those myself. Would you like to see them?"

He opened a small leather chest lined with silk, from which he withdrew a slim book. "A copy of Virgil's *Georgics,* printed in the sixteenth century. Not terribly old, but its charm lies in the fact that it once belonged to John Milton. I have Milton, too. A manuscript of 'Lycidas,' which ought to be in the British Museum. And my real treasure, a first edition of *Paradise Lost.* Would you care to examine it?"

Holding the slender book in her lap, Miss Frasier stroked the binding lovingly. At any other time, she would have read aloud from it in her strong, authoritative voice, but not now. Clearly, she could derive no pleasure from any aspect of this visit. She set the book down on the edge of the small table at her elbow and came straight to the point.

"I am returning Theodora to you, Evan," she said. "I cannot tell you how distressed I am over this. Wiggsy is sitting out in the car right now, crying her eyes out. She took a strong interest in Theodora, and gave her long hours of special tutoring. I suppose Theodora's situation has touched her. What am I saying? It has touched me, too. But it is quite impossible for us to keep her on, I'm afraid."

"I don't understand." Evan looked over to where I sat slumped in an armchair closest to the window that overlooked Gramercy Park. I met his glance and then turned my head away. A nurse in a white uniform and blue cape was wheeling a baby carriage along the sidewalk in front of the house. I could see the baby's tiny fist waving a rattle in the air. "You mean Theodora isn't able to do the work? Then she really is intellectually impaired. I was afraid of that."

"No, I do not mean that at all. Theodora is as bright as any girl at the school. The fact that she cannot do her schoolwork is due to factors other than laziness or stubbornness. She is in shock, incapacitated by the events that have occurred to her. Oh, dear, however am I going to explain all this?" Miss Frasier took a deep breath, and forged ahead. "I wrote to the schoolmistress in Monkey Gulch, Colorado. A Miss Bernice Massey."

I glanced around curiously. I hadn't known that Miss Massey's Christian name was Bernice. It seemed an oddly frivolous name for such an austere personage.

"Sensible woman," Miss Frasier went on. "She replied at once to my letter, and at length. She also enclosed some samples of Theodora's work. I shall leave those with you, but let me summarize her letter briefly. Apparently, before the tragedy happened, Theodora was a bright child, good at her schoolwork, as you shall see. Not socially adept, but I understand that for this her mother was more to blame than she. In the weeks that preceded the, ah, mishap, her work fell off dramatically. She ceased to pay attention in class. Miss Massey realized that the child was deeply troubled about something, but Theodora wouldn't confide in her. It's a pity. If she had, perhaps Miss Massey could have interceded, taken her away from that awful man." Miss Massey opened her purse, extracted a handkerchief as big as a towel, and blew her nose with a blast that sounded like the last trumpet. "It makes me so angry," she said. "The way some men behave. Like animals. To interfere with a grown woman is bad enough, but a child. A child!"

"You don't mean—"

"Yes, I do mean," Miss Frasier thundered. "Theodora is pregnant."

"Dear God." Evan clutched at the arms of his chair. "But—but she's only thirteen years old!"

"Thirteen and a half," Miss Frasier corrected him. "Chronologically a child, but biologically, most definitely a woman."

I returned to my observation of the activity in the street outside the window. The baby carriage had moved on. A delivery truck roared up to the front door and two men unloaded another crate brimming with red roses. I had never seen flowers in a box before. New York was full of bizarre sights.

"You're sure," Evan croaked.

"Can't you tell, you silly man? Theodora, stand up, please. Take off your coat."

I obeyed, revealing my bony frame in its shapeless school tunic. Evan stared at the small mound of my belly. After a moment, he looked away, scowling furiously. I sat again.

"She is at least five months along," Miss Frasier told him. "Wiggsy began to suspect—more to that woman than meets the eye, thank God—and she told me at once. I immediately summoned my personal physician." At this, Miss Frasier closed her eyes briefly, as if trying to shut out a distasteful memory. I understood her reaction. The recollection of that medical examination made me shiver, too.

The nurse at The Frasier School had prepared me for the doctor's visit, vesting me in an odd white robe that tied in the back, seating me on the edge of a tall padded table. I sat staring at the little bottles and jars on the shelves of the infirmary until a strange man came into the room. Taking off his coat, he rolled up his shirtsleeves and washed his hands and forearms in the sink.

"Well, now," he grinned at me over the towel the nurse had handed him. "What's your name, young lady?" The nurse answered for me, speaking in a respectful simper. "Theodora, eh? Fine old-fashioned name, Theodora. Your friends call you Dora, I imagine? Well, Dora, I'm just going to look you over. Don't be afraid. This won't hurt a bit."

I braced myself while he listened to my heart and lungs with a stethoscope. Then he asked me to lie down on my back. Reaching under the edge of my robe, he slid his hand right up my thigh and placed it on my belly.

Immediately I began to thrash wildly. I gave the doctor a hard kick in the jaw, sending him reeling into the little screen that the nurse had erected around the table. It fell away with a crash. Jumping off the table, I looked around frantically for some means of escape. The two of them stood between me and the door.

The nurse made soothing noises, while the doctor tried to reassure me in a falsely hearty voice. Moving together, they began to approach me cautiously, like a couple of starving men trying to corner a rabbit in a thicket. As I tried to dart between them, the nurse caught my arm and swung me around, into a stack of open shelves. Glass jars and bottles fell to the hard, tiled floor with a crash. The nurse began to squeal. Furious, the doctor threw himself at me. I sidestepped him easily, but walked right into the minefield of broken glass. Missing his target, the doctor charged into a small cabinet, shattering the glass doors and spilling containers of cotton swabs, bandages, and tongue depressers. By the time Miss Frasier appeared on the scene, the infirmary was a shambles: the nurse was hysterical, the doctor was breathing hard and clutching his chest, and I was standing on bleeding feet in the center of the room, keeping my enemies at bay with a wooden stool.

A few days later, Miss Frasier telephoned a friend of hers, a woman physician, who completed the examination without incident.

"You can see that it's out of the question for us to keep her," Miss Frasier said. "The other girls have already gotten wind of the details of her mother's death, I'm sure I don't know how. Girls are by nature often cruel people. They shunned Theodora, whispered about her, made fun of her. The school uniform hides a multitude of sins, but I simply had to remove her before one of them guessed about the baby. The reputation of my school is at stake, and I confess that that concerns me. But even more important, I know that it would be no kindness to Theodora to let her stay a moment longer at The Frasier. She needs—so many things we cannot provide."

"But what do you suggest?" Evan's eyes were glazed, and he spoke in a toneless murmur. Clearly, Miss Frasier's news had surpassed his worst fears. "Can you recommend a—a home, perhaps, where they treat girls in her, ahem, condition?"

"I suppose such places exist," Miss Frasier said with icy hauteur. "I am sure you can find another institution that will take her off your hands. Any number of sanitoriums and hospitals and asylums are available to wealthy families for incarcerating individuals who have brought them embarrassment and shame."

"Miss Frasier," Evan's voice was filled with desperation, "I can't take care of the child myself, surely you can see that."

Miss Frasier stood. Evan did likewise. "One does what one must," she said. "I believe with all my heart that what Theodora needs is a good home and a loving friend to look after her. I should warn you, Evan, that if you put this girl into a home or an asylum, she will never recover. She will retreat deeper and deeper into herself, and in a few years' time she will be a complete and total idiot. Well, that's all I have to say on the matter. You must do what you think best, of course."

Evan paced frantically, thinking aloud. "The families of my acquaintance. Perhaps one of them would be willing to take in another child? My sisters. No, they both have children of their own. Besides, they'd never be willing to expose their precious darlings to a girl like this. Good home, good home. I'll look for a foster home. Damn it all, I can't keep her here!" He appealed to Miss Frasier, who ignored him.

"Theodora, come here, please." I approached her. Cupping her hand under my chin, the tall woman looked into my eyes. "I want you to listen to what I am about to tell you. Listen carefully, and remember my words. You must never, never blame yourself for what has happened to you. You were not at fault. Some men find it amusing to take advantage of those smaller and weaker than they. Unfortunately, most women fall into that category. And young girls do, most definitely. Do you understand, my dear?"

I didn't, but I nodded anyway.

"Good." Miss Frasier extracted a large envelope from her purse. "The documents I told you about," she said to Evan. "The letter, and Theodora's writings. Also a report from two doctors on her condition. It is not good. She will need the very

best of care if she is to survive the ordeal that is ahead of her."
With a last sorrowful glance at me, she went out.

Evan glared at me. With heaving chest and quivering chin, he
tried manfully to suppress his rage. "Well! Have you nothing to
say for yourself, Theodora? Don't you want to apologize to me
for all the trouble you've caused? Don't you want to tell me how
much you regret being the source of so much anxiety and inconvenience?" He looked down at the envelope Miss Frasier had
thrust into his unwilling hands and pitched it onto his desk. "I
will include this with the rest of your things, as soon as I've arranged a place for you to go. New York City is full of rich wom-
en who delight in rescuing the downtrodden. Let one of them
worry about you. I've done my best."

"Evan, darling!" The door burst open. Looking like a school-
pageant angel in a flowing white dressing gown, Fiona floated
in, her arms full of small white orchids. "How lovely, how heavenly! You're always so thoughtful—" She saw me then, and her
radiant smile vanished. "Oh my God. Where did she come from?
I thought you'd gotten rid of her."

"So did I." Evan rubbed his forehead as if he had suddenly developed a headache. "Miss Frasier brought her back. We have a
slight problem. Theodora is going to have a baby."

How ludicrous it sounded, and how impossible, even to my
ears. A baby? Me? I had hardly been aware of the changes that
were taking place within my body. The nausea, the strange sen-
sations, the weariness all seemed like symptoms of the heaviness
that had weighed on me since my mother's death.

Fiona dropped the orchids into a chair, with no more concern
than if they had been old rags. "A baby! I might have known."
She advanced on me, her fists drawn up to her chest. I retreated
a pace. "I might have known that you'd turn out to be a slut just
like your mother. Trash. Whoring trash!"

"It wasn't that way at all," Evan said quickly. "According to
Miss Frasier—"

But Fiona wasn't listening. "Mary couldn't wait, and neither

2019

could you," she said through clenched teeth. "My God, she had a lot of nerve. She knew all about this, don't tell me she didn't."

With my back pressed against a solid armchair, I could retreat no further. Suddenly I was back in the schoolyard, listening to the taunting chant, "Lowery's a who-ore! Lowery's a who-ore!" The woman in front of me wasn't Fiona at all. She was Michael Mullins, and I wanted to kill her.

Quicker than a cat's paw, my hand flew at Fiona's eyes. Fiona's reflexes were better than Michael Mullins', and she turned her head aside. Even so, my fingernails inflicted shallow scratches along one side of her face, from her temple to just below her jawbone.

Fiona put her fingers to her cheek. "You!" she said in a shocked whisper. "Look what you've done! Evan! Oh, my God, Evan!" She threw herself at Evan, who put his arms around her in a protective gesture. "That horrid child," she sobbed. "That horrid, horrid child."

"There, there, it's all right, darling." Evan patted her shoulder. "No harm done. She didn't draw blood. You know, you really shouldn't have screamed at her like that," he said reasonably. "You can't blame her for being frightened, and for striking out at you."

Fiona drew back. "What are you saying? Surely you're not—you're not defending her!"

"You can't judge Theodora by the same standards you would use to judge an adult," Evan told her. "She's still only a child. If she's somewhat confused—"

"I know what she is," Fiona snarled. "She's a little savage, a brute, and a whore, just like her mother." She ran to the mirror and dabbed at the scratches on her cheek with the sleeve of her dressing gown. "Look at what she's done to my face! Oh, my God, everyone will see. I can't possibly go on tonight. You'll just have to cancel the opening, that's all." She threw herself onto the big leather chesterfield and glared at me over her crossed arms. "I will not perform while that child is in this house."

"I'm sorry to hear that," Evan said after a long pause. "Tonight's performance is sold out. A great many people will be disappointed."

Fiona tossed her red-gold hair. "That's just too bad. But you'll have to get rid of that little monster if you ever want me to act again."

With a deep sigh, Evan sank into the chair behind his desk. He didn't say anything for a long time, then he opened the envelope Miss Frasier had given him.

" '. . . extremely malnourished, traces of ricketsiae,' " he read aloud. " 'Old contusions on thighs and legs. Clearly terrified at the prospect of being touched by a strange man.' " He put the letter aside. "I'm having some difficulty deciding just who, exactly, is the monster in this case."

Fiona leaped to her feet. "You mean me! Well, that does it. You'll just have to get yourself another star tonight, mister." She started toward the door.

Without looking up from his desk, Evan said, "Your understudy will take your place. She's very eager, and rather talented, from what I've seen."

Whirling, Fiona cried, "She's lousy and you know it. If she goes on tonight, that stupid play will close tomorrow, mark my words. The only good thing about that script is the way I say the lines. 'Talented'! You wouldn't know talent if it reached up and hit you in the face."

"I saw your talent before anyone else did," Evan reminded her in a softer voice. "I knew then that you were special, and I wanted to make sure you had every chance to succeed. What a pity. Tonight would have been a brilliant achievement. This is going to put a serious crimp in your career."

"You think you own me, don't you?" Fists clenched, Fiona advanced slowly on the desk. "Just because you pulled me out of that chorus line and bought me a few new clothes and changed my hair and then did me the enormous favor of marrying me, you think that gives you the right to tell me what to do, to dictate terms. It's so easy, because you're rich. All you have to do is pick up the telephone in order to buy out the theater or pay the stage crew not to show up. You can cut off the lights or make sure nobody else ever takes a chance on me in this town. You can get me blacklisted."

"I wouldn't do that, Fiona."

"Wouldn't you? Why not, if that's what it takes to get your own way? I'm in your debt and you know it. If you hadn't seen me in that stinking review, I'd still be struggling to find work, fighting to be noticed. Sweating in summer theaters, scrambling to prepare for auditions, smiling, always smiling, playing the game by the rules but breaking my heart to achieve something special, something the big boys would remember, that would set me apart from the rest. I would have made it without you, but it would have taken a long time. You know damned well that I'd cut off my legs before I'd give up this show. After tonight, I'm going to be a star, and when that happens, you won't be able to touch me. No one will. But right now, I have to do as you say. All right, keep the kid. I'll go on, and I'll be brilliant. But I won't forget this, Evan."

Evan looked dismayed. "Hurt you? Dictate terms? My God, Fiona, you're wrong, so wrong. I love you," he said. Both of them had forgotten I was there, seated in my armchair again with Evan's old copy of *Paradise Lost* open in my lap. "You act as though I were trying to wield some sort of power over you. How could I? I only want you to succeed. You're brilliant and talented, and you deserve success more than anyone else I've ever known. I never meant to sound as though I were blackmailing you. Never."

"I'll do my bit tonight," Fiona sniffed. "But you can just forget your party. Tell your fancy friends that I'm tired, that I'm sick."

Standing behind her, Evan rested his hands lightly on her shoulders. "You know the sort of thing people said when we were married: that I wanted a bangle for my watch chain; that you were just using me to get ahead. They were wrong. I fell in love with you the minute I saw you. You were so soft and vulnerable, with a little crooked smile that seemed to mock all the fierce and determined things you were telling me. Remember? You wanted to play everything, serious drama and high comedy, Shakespeare and Shaw. You wanted to be as famous as Bernhardt. Remember?"

Bernhardt. I flinched at the name. Of course, Mother and Fiona had seen her together, when they were children.

"I remember." Fiona caressed his hand. "You didn't laugh at me. You believed in me."

"And you believed in me. You put yourself in my hands. You never became upset when I criticized your walk or your accent or made suggestions about how you could improve yourself. You wanted to learn everything you could. I think you care about me, too, Fiona. You didn't have to marry me, after all. The play and the production would have been yours even without marriage. That's what I promised you. I don't go back on my promises. I have a special reason for wanting you to come to the party tonight. I want the rest of the world to fall in love with you twice, as I did. Once when they see you onstage, and the second time when they see you here, as yourself, in your new home, with a husband who thinks that the sun and moon and all the stars revolve around you."

Fiona turned slowly and faced him. They gazed at each other for a long moment, then she slid her arms around his neck and kissed him. Evan's eyes flickered open and he saw me watching them. Flushing, he slipped out of Fiona's embrace.

"And what about her?" Fiona jerked her head in my direction.

"I have to do my duty. You are my wife and she is your sister's child. I can't turn her out. Miss Frasier was right: what Theodora needs is a home, a family. I'm going to keep her here with me. I'll make her my ward." As soon as he had said the words, Evan looked stunned, as though he couldn't quite believe what he had just heard.

Fiona couldn't believe it either.

"You're joking!" she yipped. "What are people going to think when they find out you're harboring a little piece of gutter trash who's been knocked up? They'll think that it's your kid, that's what."

Evan shook his head. "I will not advertise the tawdrier aspects of this affair, and neither will you. I'll make sure the servants are discreet. And when the, ahem, the time comes, I will take the girl away, to a hospital in another city. No one need know anything about this, if we're careful."

"Well, I don't want anything to do with her. Just keep her out of my way." Fiona set her lips in a stubborn line. "That's what I said the night she came, and I still mean it."

"You don't need to see her at all, Fiona." Evan sounded relieved that they had reached a compromise. "Theodora is my responsibility now. I'll see to everything. Miss Frasier thinks she's intelligent. With just a little work and the right kind of attention, I can bring the child around. I'm sure I can."

"I knew it. I knew it!" Fiona crowed. "The bored little rich boy has found himself another hobby. Only instead of racing cars and poetry and theater, this time it's educating the savage. Evan Bradford, Modern Educator! You're going to try your hand at bringing up the kid, aren't you? What a joke."

Evan stiffened. "I am perfectly capable of teaching the child the rudiments—"

"She's a moron," Fiona said. "A dummy. Do you honestly believe that she's going to snap out of this and start quoting Shakespeare one day? You're such a dreamer, Evan. You cook up these stupid schemes, and when you fall on your face, you wonder what went wrong, why you keep on failing."

"I didn't fail with you."

"You couldn't. I knew what I wanted and I was willing to work. But you've never finished anything on your own, have you? If it wasn't for Max, you wouldn't be Broadway's fair-haired boy now. Theater is just another plaything as far as you're concerned, but it's Max's living. Without you, he'd be starving, and he knows it." Fiona narrowed her eyes shrewdly. "You know what your problem is, Evan? You don't have any idea what it's like to be desperate, on the edge of starvation. You've never had to put your heart and soul into anything. If you fail, so what? You won't go hungry, you won't be out walking the streets, without a nickel to your name. You keep on trying to be somebody, but you'll never make it. You'll just go on spending money that somebody else earned, coming up with half-baked ideas that never pan out. The best thing that could happen to you would be to lose every cent you had."

"You'd leave me."

"Would I?" Fiona thought for a moment. "I don't know. You might be surprised. You might find out that we weren't so different after all, that we really had some things to talk about. But we're not equals. We can't be. You'll always be the good-hearted philanthropist and I'll always be the little girl you dragged up out of the chorus line. We're a thousand miles apart." Fiona passed her hand over her eyes. "God, I'm tired. If I don't get some rest now, I'll fall asleep during my big speech in the third act. The critics will have a field day, won't they? 'Would-be Actress Lulls Self to Sleep at Debut.' "

"I hope you'll get over your feelings of resentment toward the child," Evan said. "In time, you and Theodora will get to know each other. You might even become friends."

"Don't bet on it." Ignoring the bouquet of orchids she had dumped in the armchair, Fiona made a sweeping exit.

Evan let out his breath in a long sigh. Lowering himself wearily into the chair behind his desk, he rested his head in his hands. After a long time, he looked up and saw me flipping through his priceless copy of *Paradise Lost.*

"What do you think you're doing?" He shot out of his chair. "Put down that book at once!"

Hastily, I slammed the book shut and handed it to him. He examined it to make sure that I hadn't damaged it.

"Have you been reading this?" he demanded. I lifted one shoulder in a weak attempt at a shrug. "Did you understand it?" I shrugged again. "Tell me. I mean, write it for me." He fetched a scrap of paper and a pencil from his desk and handed them to me. "Now just tell me what you think this poem is about. A short sentence will do."

He went to his desk and packed some tobacco into an old pipe. I suppose he wanted to give me some room to think. Miss Frasier could have told him that it didn't make any difference whether or not someone looked over my shoulder while I wrote. I still couldn't do it.

Still, I wanted to make an effort to please him. I was Evan Bradford's ward now—whatever that meant. Picking up the pencil, I made a vertical stroke on the paper, the beginning of the word Evil. I had seen Satan's name mentioned in the poem, and as an infrequent visitor to the Monkey Gulch Methodist Sunday School, I knew that Satan was Evil, Evil Incarnate. Struggling, I made a short horizontal stroke at the top of the E. The shape reminded me of something: an old game Pilar and I used to play.

In the space just under the horizontal bar I drew a stick figure. A hanged man. With a quick mark I joined the legs together at the knees. A hanged woman. The pencil slipped out of my fingers.

"Well, let's see how you've done." After some minutes had passed, Evan approached my chair and picked up the paper. "Dear God." He stared down at me. The paper rattled in his hand. He beat a retreat to his desk, dropping the paper into a wastebasket as he passed. After a while he picked up the volume of Milton again, as if he preferred the company of Evil Incarnate to my own humbler version. The minutes passed, marked off by the mellow pock, pock, pock of the grandfather clock in the corner.

" 'A mind not to be chang'd by place or time,' " he read in a low voice. " 'The mind is its own place, and in itself can make a heaven of hell, a hell of heaven.' "

Looking up, he stared at me for a long time. "Poor child," he murmured. "What in the name of Heaven am I going to do with you?"

6

this book has 459 pages

One night in December, just two months after I came to live in the Bradford house on Gramercy Park, I was awakened by twisting pains in my belly. I lay in bed thinking, "I am dying. I am dying." The prospect didn't frighten me. In fact, I was glad. Despite the care I received in Evan's household, I had grown progressively more frail as the weeks passed. Johanna had pleaded with me to eat, but much of the time I was too sick to keep anything down. Now I felt eager for The End.

When the pains subsided a little, I rang for Fanny, the new maid Evan had hired to care for me. Fanny, in her nightgown and robe, took one look and rushed out to summon Evan.

Through a fog of pain, I saw him leaning over my bed. He had just come in from a party, for he still wore a dinner jacket and black tie.

"The doctor warned that this might happen at any time," I heard him say, "even though she isn't due to deliver the baby for another two months."

"Shall I telephone an ambulance, sir?"

"No, I'll take her myself. It will save time. Call for the car, and then phone the hospital." He touched my shoulder. "It's all right, Theodora. Don't be frightened. Everything will be all right."

Another spasm of pain wracked me. Being unable to scream, I sucked in my breath and grabbed his hand. He stiffened, trying to pull away, then he gave my hand a reassuring squeeze.

"Don't worry," he said into my ear. "You'll be fine, Theodora, just fine."

Wrapping me in a blanket, Evan carried me down the stairs and out to the waiting Rolls. I didn't fight him. I thought that I was a little girl again, and that he was my father, taking me to Mr. Watson's house to demand a ride to Trinidad. His arms felt

79

safe and strong. I trusted him, and didn't fear his touch. Then, over Evan's shoulder, I saw Fiona standing outside the door of her bedroom, watching us. Her face looked pinched and furious.

Evan held me close by his side during the short ride to a private hospital on East Twenty-sixth Street. Every time he heard me gasp, he murmured soothing words. As the car drew up in front of the doors, orderlies rushed out pushing a stretcher. As they wheeled me inside, I saw that Evan's white shirtfront was smeared with blood. So much blood. Sidney Jenkins' blood. My mother's blood. And now my blood.

I was aware of people running, rows of white glaring suns rushing down long corridors, spasms tearing at my insides. A white room. People shrouded in white. Lights so intense I could almost feel them like screams inside my head.

In a panic, I tried to sit up. I wanted to run, to run away from my fear and my agony. Strong hands pushed me down and held me while I struggled. A black cone descended over my face like a corner of night, shutting out light and noise and pain.

To my surprise, I didn't die. I awoke from the anaesthesia in a small, white room. The noise was gone; the pain had subsided. For a week I had no visitors. I was dimly aware of the white figures who fed me, turned me over, bathed me. Then one day I opened my eyes and saw Evan sitting on a chair by the side of my bed. He seemed even more stiff and ill-at-ease than I remembered. I knew that he would have preferred not to come, but duty demanded it, and he obeyed.

He offered hollow reassurances, telling me that I would soon be well and strong and ready to participate in the games and amusements so dear to the hearts of young girls. Then he told me that my doctor had prescribed fresh air and a less hectic environment for my convalescence. In his typical unstinting fashion, Evan had promptly bought a farm in Connecticut, only an hour's drive from New York. "That way, Fiona will be able to relax in the country but she'll still be close to the theater. I've

always rather enjoyed the country myself, and of course you
grew up there."

Monkey Gulch, the country, with its fuming smokestacks and
heaps of slag?

"Besides, it's time we expanded your area of study," Evan
went on. "The city is a fine laboratory for the arts, but we need
to pay some attention to the sciences. We can study botany, and
biology. You know, Theodora,"—he flicked a particle of soot off
his fawn-colored fedora—"you're lucky you fell into the hands
of a dilettante, no matter what Fiona may say. I have limited ex-
pertise in any number of areas." He stood up. "But I mustn't
stay any longer. You look tired. I'll be in to see you tomorrow."

I closed my eyes. I heard the door open, but it didn't close
right away. Evan spoke to me again, in a firm voice that carried
an underlying note of command.

"I want you to promise me one thing, Theodora. You're going
to put all this behind you. We will never refer to it again. Your
child was stillborn. It could not have survived. And I cannot say
I'm sorry. It's for the best. You have a chance to start over.
Please believe that I will do everything I can to help you. Good-
bye, then."

He went out. A pretty nurse came in and popped a thermom-
eter into my mouth. "He's your guardian, isn't he? He's very
nice. And so good-looking. You're a very lucky little girl."

Even now, people spoke to me as if I were stupid, as if I didn't
understand what had happened. But I knew very well that the
baby that had been growing inside me was gone. I had had experience with dead babies. My mother had borne two more children after me. One was stillborn, but the other had lived for a
few weeks. Now my own child was dead. Dead. Like my father
and mother, like Sid Jenkins. But I was supposed to forget them
all. I was supposed to be happy.

Turning my head on my pillow, I looked out the window.
Snow was falling, covering the naked branches of the tree outside with soft puffs that reminded me of the blooms on the pear
tree in Sid Jenkins' yard in Monkey Gulch.

Yes, I was lucky. My mother's absurd and farfetched dreams for me were actually coming true.

That very first evening after Miss Frasier delivered me to Gramercy Park, Evan had taken me to the theater to see the opening of Fiona's new play. The occasion had been more splendid and elegant than anything Mother had ever described to me. The women in the audience wore fur coats and ropes of pearls. Diamond tiaras sparkled in their hair. The men all smelled of soap and spice. Their hands were as soft and clean as the hands of the women. They spoke in soft, beautifully modulated voices, like Evan's, with never a curse or a spit for punctuation.

I hadn't been able to keep my mind on the intricacies of the plot, which seemed to concern a woman who couldn't make up her mind which of two men suited her best. I didn't understand the jokes; the place names meant nothing to me; the subtle exchanges might as well have been spoken in Greek for all the meaning I extracted from them. Instead I thought about my mother, and how thrilled she would have been to see me in such dazzling company; sitting in a box overlooking the stage of a Broadway theater; riding home in a long black limousine; munching crab salad in a glittering, flower-bedecked dining room that was bigger than Sid Jenkins' whole house.

My room at Gramercy Park looked like the frothy bedchamber of one of those little princesses who used to play such a large part in my reading and daydreams. My bed was soft, one vast pillow, with sheets that smelled of flowers even in the wintertime. I had a desk all to myself, and a bookcase that held more volumes than the whole Monkey Gulch school. The room was so comfortably warm that one could forget that it was nearly winter, and when I wanted hot water, all I had to do was to go into my bathroom—my own *private* bathroom—and turn on the spigot.

When Johanna had put me to bed that first night after my expulsion from the Frasier School, she had kissed me on the fore-

head and told me that it was good to see me again. Even Johanna
had caught the kindness disease.

My education had begun the very next day. Evan took me to
the Metropolitan Museum of Art to show me suits of medieval
armor. I had never known that the knights and ladies I had read
about in storybooks had really existed. I felt vaguely sorry.
When we got home, Evan gave me a novel called *When Knight-
hood Was in Flower.* A year earlier such a romantic story would
have captured my imagination and held me in thrall, oblivious
to everything else, for hours. But no longer. I understood a little
of the first few pages of the book. They conjured up a world of
sentiments and emotions that seemed utterly frivolous and shallow. I set the volume aside, never to pick it up again.

I could no longer use fantasy as an escape; nor hazy daydreams; nor birthday wishes; nor beautiful lies. Nor bright
hopes for the future. The plays and the musical shows and the
movies Evan took me to see left me unmoved. I despised the storybooks he gave me, books whose fantastic plots and absurd adventures seemed to have been invented for smaller, happier
minds; the minds of children. Nothing stood between me and
the harsh truth about reality that I had learned in the past few
months.

Life, I had discovered, was like an immense and powerful engine that pulls you along, heedless of where you really want to
go. Some people are crushed to death in its gears, some are man-
gled, a few manage to survive unscathed. The machine was
mindless and undiscriminating, an unthinking, unpredictable
monster. Why had it taken my father, a good man? Why had it
destroyed my mother? Why had it spared me?

From the very first, Evan had devoted a great deal of time and
effort to broadening my cultural and intellectual horizons. I
made some attempts to please him, but since I was unable to
concentrate for more than a few minutes at a time, I made little
progress with my lessons. I listened attentively when Evan explained something, but when he asked me a question later, I
couldn't answer it. "Where is your mind, Theodora?" he de-

manded once, trying hard to control his anger. I wondered about that myself.

My mind wasn't in Monkey Gulch, with my mother and Sid Jenkins. My mind wasn't with Pilar and Joaquin, or even with the little baby growing inside my abdomen. I felt as though someone had stuffed a big sponge into my brain, which was soaking up all the things I was supposed to be learning and hiding them away in little dark holes where I could never retrieve them again.

Evan had bought me more clothes. Theodora Lowery, who had never owned more than three patched and ragged dresses at one time, now possessed a closetful of beautiful things. My dresser drawers were crammed full of undergarments that were thin and delicate, and warm besides. I had five or six pairs of new shoes that didn't pinch, not even the first time I wore them. Whenever a stocking developed a hole, it disappeared from my wardrobe. Johanna or Fanny just whisked it away, and put a perfect one in its place.

The nurse took my pulse and made a note on a chart. "You've lost a lot of blood, you poor child. You're lucky to be alive." She went out.

Yes, lucky. I knew I was lucky. Everyone told me so. Johanna. Fanny, the new maid at Gramercy Park. The nurse. I was lucky to have Evan for a guardian. Lucky to live in a fine mansion in New York City. Lucky to be the niece of the famous Fiona Randall.

I didn't hate Fiona anymore. How could I? Fiona was the only person in the world who knew what kind of person I really was. Everyone else, Miss Frasier and Miss Wiggs and Evan, called me a poor child and showered me with kindness. But Fiona knew, as I knew, that I didn't deserve their kindness. How could I? If it hadn't been for me, my mother would still be alive. I was evil, wicked. Just what Fiona had called me: whoring trash. I must be wicked, or Sid Jenkins wouldn't have used me as he did. I must be vile, or I would have run away the first time it had happened, or told my mother or Miss Massey what was happening. But I didn't. I didn't speak and I didn't run. At the time I told myself that I was frightened by what he might do to my mother if I betrayed him. But what if, deep down inside, I had really liked his clumsy, loveless caresses? What if I hadn't wanted them to end?

When I went into labor, and the pains wracked and twisted my body, I felt a sense of gratitude and relief. At last I was getting what I truly deserved.

One month after I was released from the hospital, Evan and I drove up to Connecticut. He knew I wasn't strong yet, and he promised that we would stay just long enough to look over his purchase and to form some ideas about what we wanted to do with the place. We both knew that he was only pretending to include me in his planning. I wasn't capable of contributing a single creative or helpful thought.

Evan called Elf Hill a farm, but it was unlike any of the farms I had seen on the Colorado prairie outside of Monkey Gulch. Those ranches were barren, dusty, and dry. In Colorado, just getting sufficient water for livestock and crops was a problem. But in addition to a grand swimming pool, Elf Hill also boasted a long, shady natural pond, which Evan said was stocked with trout. We looked inside the huge stone barn, the stables, and the greenhouse. We discovered a vegetable garden, and a formal rose garden, with acres of rolling pasture and woodland beyond. The house was a large, rambling place with endless bedrooms and bathrooms, two kitchens, a vast dining room, and several sitting rooms.

"Just tell me if you feel tired," Evan said as we wandered through the first floor. The sale had just been completed, and the house was still bare of furniture. "We'll take a quick look around, and then have lunch at a nice little place I know near here." I trailed him into an airy sitting room. One whole wall was lined with glass doors. They opened onto a terrace overlooking the swimming pool and the south lawn. "This isn't too bad. At least furnishing the place won't be a problem. My mother has attics full of stuff she's been aching to get rid of." He turned to me. "What do you think? Do you like it?"

I shrugged and nodded slowly. Yes, I liked it more than any place I had ever seen. The house had none of the Gramercy Park mansion's stiffness and formality. Elf Hill was the kind of place that should hum with the noises of a half-dozen children and their toys and pets. Instead, it would have to endure the silence of one teenage mute.

The fact that Evan had bought Elf Hill on my account saddened me. He had wasted his money. I didn't care where I lived. I would have been happier in a dank, miserable, airless room, like a prison cell.

"I needed something like this," Evan declared. "A real home. Not a museum like Gramercy Park. A place to get away from it all."

The next time I saw the house, a month later in February, it had been transformed. The sitting rooms were bright with figured chintz and hothouse flowers. Plump armchairs invited me to take off my shoes and curl up in front of a blazing fire. Books lined the log shelves of Evan's rustic study. Upstairs, a decorator had turned one of the bedrooms into a parody of a bridal chamber, a dream of Virgin White and Country Blue: my room. The bed was covered with white eyelet cotton over a blue satin spread. Blue ribbons restrained the curtains at the broad bay windows, which overlooked the east lawn and the rose gardens. On the other side of the valley, apple and peach trees stood in perfect rows like soldiers waiting for springtime and the order to bloom and bear fruit.

One day, as I washed my face and hands, I happened to glance at my image in the mirror over the sink. I was amazed at how old I looked. In the past year, a spurt of growth combined with a lack of appetite and a difficult pregnancy had pulled my skin taut over my bones. Blue veins throbbed on my temples and bulged on the backs of my hands. My eyes looked huge and sad, ringed with shadows, like my mother's.

I dried my hands hastily and walked down to the library, where Evan awaited me. It was time for my morning lesson.

Evan took his duties as a teacher seriously. In giving me lessons in Latin, French, and history, he tried never to be dull. So many of his instructors in prep school and college had been boring, he said. He was constantly jumping up to raid his shelves for a picture or a poem or a quotation that would illustrate what he was saying. But no matter how hard he worked, how entertaining he made his lectures, they made no impression upon me at all. I listened, nodding occasionally, trying not to doze off, but when he asked me a question, I didn't even try to respond. I either shrugged or looked down at my hands.

Evan controlled his irritation, but when at the end of three hours I was still unable to conjugate a Latin verb properly, he lost his temper. He threw down his book and stalked out of the room. I waited. In a few minutes he returned.

"That's enough for one day," he said. "I shouldn't have expected so much from you. God knows, I was slow enough at Latin myself. Let's take a walk, shall we? I have another surprise for you."

Bundled up in coats and mufflers, we trudged through the snow to the stables. Evan called to Boyd, the groom, and asked him to bring out Muffin. She was a sleek and drowsy bay mare who seemed annoyed at being dragged away from her feed trough.

"She's yours." Evan patted the horse's nose. "Have you done any riding? No? Well, she's the perfect animal to teach you. Yes, I know she's big, but she's quite gentle. If you fall off, she'll probably reach down, pick you up and dust you off, and toss you right up on her back again. I thought about starting you off on a pony, but your legs are so absurdly long. Do you want to get up on her?"

I shrank from the animal. Evan looked annoyed.

"Well, another day then, when the weather's nicer. I'll have Boyd saddle her up, along with Custer, my old gelding. I haven't done much riding since the crash, but Custer has a nice even gait, not too jarring."

The horse and I exchanged skeptical appraising glances. I had never had a pet, not even a kitten or a mongrel puppy, and now Evan had given me a horse.

My shoulders drooped. Every thoughtful thing he did for me only added to the awful burden I carried. If only he would leave me alone. If only the world would leave me alone.

"This really is a lovely place, Evan. Does Fiona like it?"

"She seems to. I'm teaching her how to play tennis. She's become quite excited about it, especially since someone told her that it was good for the figure. She stays in town most of the time, of course. More convenient to the theater. But I send the car for her on Saturday night, and we spend all day Sunday and most of Monday here together. On those days Theodora keeps herself busy."

The voices of Evan and his mother drifted up to my bedroom. I was supposed to be using the hour before lunch to copy a list of Latin verbs. My cushioned window seat seemed like a fine place to study, but once there, I had dropped my notebook and given myself up to an unscientific contemplation of the clouds. In the rose garden below, gardeners were busy among the neglected canes. They pruned and snipped, ruthlessly eliminated weeds, and cut away the sod that had crept over onto the brown earth. Spring had come to the country, and with it a burst of activity.

"And how is Theodora's education progressing?" Mrs. Bradford asked.

"Not very well." Evan's tone was glum. "If only she'd show some enthusiasm, Mother. Just a spark. I'm doing the best I can, God knows. I've got her copying a few words at a time now. I'm straining my brain trying to think up new ways to reach her. But she just sits and gazes at me with those large, limpid eyes. I suspect she doesn't even see me. Most of the time she doesn't hear me, either."

"Oh, I wouldn't worry about it," his mother said. "It seems to me that I did a lot of woolgathering when I was that age. Particularly this time of year. It's so difficult to concentrate on verbs and participles when the birds are singing and the sun is warm."

"I doubt that Theodora takes any notice of the weather," Evan said. "I hold class outdoors when the weather is fine. Very Socratic. I read Thoreau and Rousseau—makes no impression on her at all. I might as well be reading from the works of some wretched female poet, extolling the glory of the robin and the rose. And last week, the Kingstons came up from New York with Fiona. This country's most brilliant acting couple, really delightful people. We spent an entire evening reading Shakespeare, everyone taking a part. Except Theodora, of course. You should have heard them, Mother. They were extraordinary. And of course Fiona was delicious."

"Of course."

"You know, Mother, I'd really like to mount a *Twelfth Night* for her. She could do Juliet, too. She'd be incredible, heartbreaking. Anyway, do you know what that wretched child did, while three of this country's greatest actors were performing for her? She fell asleep."

"How inconsiderate!" Mrs. Bradford clucked. "Clearly she doesn't know that she's supposed to show eternal gratitude for all that you're doing for her. I'd better speak to her."

Their footsteps halted on the gravel path just under my window. "That's not fair, Mother. I do not expect fawning displays of appreciation. I don't even want her thanks. God knows, when I embarked on this project, I didn't expect instant results, or any kind of renown. But the least the child could do is make an effort." Evan's tone grew plaintive. "Just a small one, so I wouldn't feel that I was wasting my time."

"You know, Evan, children are difficult enough to teach even when they are healthy and normal. Poor Theodora has been through a lot."

"Poor Theodora has had plenty of time to recover," Evan grumbled. "She's got to get on with life, after all."

"Yes, I suppose witnessing a murder-suicide is a little like falling off a horse," Mrs. Bradford mused. "Bounce right back on again, and you'll soon forget all about the hurt. If you ask me, any child who didn't react strongly to something like that wouldn't be normal."

"Miss Frasier and the woman back in Colorado seemed to think she was bright enough," Evan said. "I don't see why she just doesn't snap out of it."

"She may never," his mother cautioned him. "Although children are remarkably resilient. She may just wake up one day and begin noticing things again. But when she's ready, Evan; not when you tell her to."

"She's impossible." Evan sighed. "But I'm not going to quit."

How could he? Fiona would never let him hear the end of it. Whenever she saw me, she asked how his "star pupil" was getting along. Evan always made some vague and utterly false reply about my rapid progress.

"Good for you, dear," Mrs. Bradford said. "I love seeing you engaged in something useful and unselfish for a change. Children are really very nice people, you know. I rather enjoyed watching you and your sisters growing up. Like flowers. They do the same thing, year after year, but for some reason, they never get boring. A child is always new, always fresh."

"Theodora Lowery isn't like most children," Evan grunted. "She's as boring as milk."

I felt like thanking him for that. I would have compared myself to tepid water, or yesterday's oatmeal.

7

"We'll take a slow canter down to the woods this morning." Evan tightened the girth under Custer's belly. I was already seated astride Muffin, who danced and tossed her head as if eager to be under way. It was a fraudulent show. As soon as she left the stableyard, she would try to turn around and go back. I was barely able to discourage her.

Evan hoisted himself into the saddle and thanked Boyd, the groom who had held his stirrup. "We're going to study some rudimentary botany today. The wildflowers are up. Did you ever see purple trillium in Colorado?"

Muffin followed Custer at a sedate trot. The morning air was cool, and although the sun was shining now, the dark clouds building in the northeast promised rain.

I liked riding. I enjoyed it as much as I was able to take pleasure in anything. For one thing, Evan and I were usually too far apart for him to talk to me. Although he tried to be amusing and instructive, the close attention and intense concentration he expected of me were tiring. But trailing behind him and Custer, Muffin and I were alone, a single, welded unit of surging energy without thought or feeling.

Evan led me to the edge of a sprawling woods, where we dismounted and tethered our horses to a couple of saplings. The forest felt cool after our vigorous exercise in the morning sun, but it was by no means a quiet temple of greenery. A low breeze rustled last autumn's crisp leaves. Birds chattered, irritated by our invasion of their domain. A rabbit scurried for cover.

The ground was steep and rocky, dropping down to a small stream that emptied into the pond at the far edge of the woods. Evan pointed out various ferns and wildflowers as we walked. He limped slightly, either in anticipation of a change in the weather or from a jolt Custer had given him. He never com-

91

plained about his pain, but sometimes I could see a tightness around his mouth and a strained look in his eyes, and I knew that he was suffering. I was dimly aware that the further aggravation I caused must have added to his discomfort.

"You might find this interesting, Theodora. *Sanguinaria canadensis.* Bloodroot."

We crouched over starlike white flowers that gleamed above still-furled hands of gray-green foliage.

"The roots have a substance, an alkaloid called sanguinarin, that's sometimes used in medicine." Evan pushed back a layer of leaves. His long fingers probed into the loamy earth. "I'm sure this plant won't mind sacrificing a bit of itself in the interests of science." He pulled up a piece of fleshy root, about half an inch in diameter. "This is rather unusual. The root actually bleeds when it's cut. Hence the name. See?" He snapped the root. Beads of red-orange sap appeared at the broken ends.

I stared over his head, at a space between two old hemlock trees.

"You're not paying attention again," Evan said sharply. His backache made him short-tempered. "Can't you even make a show of being interested? I shall repeat what I said. This plant is known as bloodroot because its roots secrete a bloodlike substance when they are wounded. Like this." He took my hand and smeared a little of the juice on my palm. "Red. Blood. Bloodroot. Now do you see?"

I saw the slash of crimson on my hand and stood up quickly. The redness was spreading over my fingers, climbing up my arm, engulfing me. It felt hot, like boiling water or acid. It was burning into my flesh. Frantically, I wiped my hand on the front of my blouse. But I couldn't cleanse myself, couldn't stop the flowing and the burning.

"Theodora, what's the matter with you?"

My mouth worked silently, opening and closing. Then I started to moan. "No, no, no!" My voice was harsh and rasping, rusty from long disuse. I couldn't catch my breath. "No, no, no, no, no!" I started to tear at my own flesh with my fingernails.

"Theodora!" Evan grasped my wrists. "Stop that. Stop it at once, before you hurt yourself."

My head rolled. He shook me roughly, and after a moment, my eyes focused on his. I felt that I was seeing him for the first time.

"*Let—go,*" I screamed. "*I—hate—you!* LET—ME—GO!" I tried to pull away from him.

Evan tried to calm me. "Theodora, it's all right. Look at me, please. You have nothing to be afraid of. I'm not going to hurt you. It's Evan, Theodora, Evan. Don't you know me?"

"*Don't—touch!* LET—GO!" My voice rising in a scream, I broke free of him and ran. Evan followed, calling after me, begging me to stop. Then his toe caught in a branch, and he fell. I heard the crash of branches and an agonized cry of pain.

Low scrub snatched at my eyes and my hair as I plunged headlong through a thicket. Briars snagged my long-sleeved blouse and jodhpurs. Thorns lashed my face and neck. Run, run, run away from the past, the hideous blood-soaked past. Get away from Sid Jenkins, naked and bloody and twitching with flies. Outrun the shadow of your mother with her dark face and swollen tongue and her feet that never touch the floor. Escape Fiona's knowing glances that see right into the black core of ugliness that is your soul. Once and for all, get away from Evan Bradford's killing kindness.

I reached the edge of the pond. Beavers had been busy in summers past, felling maple and birch saplings that grew along the edge of the water. Two of the young trees had fallen across each other and caught at an angle to the ground. Honeysuckle and bittersweet vines had covered them with the first new leaves of spring, making a sort of tent. Pawing an opening, I scrambled inside, and sat in a tight crouch, my head bent over my updrawn knees.

A chill rain started to fall, penetrating even my leafy shelter. Through the interstices of the leaves, I could see droplets pocking the smooth surface of the pond. The water looked dark and calm and quiet, like sleep.

I knew what I would have to do. At long last, the fog had lift-ed. My brain was working furiously, spinning out thoughts and ideas with dazzling speed. I saw everything so clearly now: my own unworthiness, the impossibility of my leading any kind of normal life. The ghosts of my past would haunt me forever, and wherever I went, people would say, "That's Theodora Lowery. Her mother cut up a man into a thousand pieces, and then hung herself." If my mother was crazy, and a whore, and a murderess, what did that make me?

Amo, amas, amat. The things Evan had been drumming into my poor befuddled brain rushed to the surface now, squeezed out of the sponge. Gaul was divided into three parts. Rome wasn't built in a day. Too bad he would never know that at the end, his teachings had finally taken hold. I could conjugate verbs like a Latin native, discuss Gibbon and Caesar and Jesus Christ.

I looked down at my crimson-smeared hands. The bloodroot had jolted me into consciousness, prompted me to recognize the simple fact that my life was unbearable. Up to now, I had been too dazed and stupified to do anything about it. But at last my mission was clear. I had to rectify the Machine's mistake, hurl myself under its wheels, end my suffering and everyone else's.

I don't know how long I sat in my leafy cell before I heard the sounds of a search party. A horse whinnied, an automobile en-gine roared, a dog barked. I frowned. I hadn't expected to have to hurry the business, but now I saw that I had no time to waste. I started to pull off my riding boots. They were sturdy and heavy, and I wanted to be able to move freely in the water, so that I could reach the deepest part. It occurred to me then that the balloon hips of my jodhpurs might fill with air and keep me floating on the surface, so I stripped those off, too. That left me clad only in my blouse, chemise, and knee-length drawers.

I heard voices then, coming from the thicket at the edge of the woods. Boyd, the groom's: "—that last ditch, hurt your back, sir. Better go back home and call the doc—whiskey and a hot-water bottle."

And Evan's: "—got to keep searching. You don't know how distraught she was—never saw anything like—no telling what she might do."

I would have to wait until they went away. The pond was fairly exposed, visible from various points on the farm. I didn't want any would-be rescuers to see me wading into the frigid water.

Evening closed in. I listened to the sounds of rain falling on the fresh green leaves of the trees, rustling the tender grasses at the edge of the pond. From far away came the voices of the searchers calling to each other. By this time I was thoroughly chilled, so stiff and numb that I could hardly move.

I stared down at my long braids, flopped over my chest. They reminded me of Pilar, and of our long afternoon on the banks of the Purgatory. The memory of that day's happiness pained me even more than the gruesome specters of the dead. I unwove my plaits quickly. My hair fell around my shoulders, warming me a little.

"Dory!"

I peered through the curtain of honeysuckle vines. Evan was limping along the edge of the pond, coming straight toward me. He stumbled a couple of times on the slick track, but he pulled himself up and kept coming, moving swiftly and purposefully. He knew where I was hiding. Of course: he had read Miss Massey's letter. He remembered that once I had found shelter in a sort of cave on the mountainside, and he had been looking for just such a natural hiding place.

"Dory," he called. "It's me, Evan. Don't be frightened. I want to help you. I know you're in there. It's all right, I won't hurt you, I promise. It's late, Dory. Time to go home."

I scrambled out from the thicket and clambered over the felled trees. Sitting on the grassy edge of the pond, I slid into the water. Evan, twenty feet away from me, called out my name. I waded out from the shore until I could no longer touch bottom, and then I threw myself forward into the icy blackness.

The mucky bottom of the pond pulled at my feet. Under the

water the world was as black as death. I couldn't begin to see through the mud, the algae, the slime. Something caressed my legs: the water plants that were beginning to push their way out of the ooze on the bottom.

Suddenly I saw light again. The air in my lungs had buoyed me up to the surface. I heard a wheezing shout, and sounds of splashing. Evan was treading water just a few feet away. He lunged toward me. I dove, paddling hard. My head snapped back as a strong hand closed around my hair. I felt myself being dragged up, up through the thick black water. Evan locked his arm across my chest and started to pull me toward shore.

He hauled me up on the grassy bank, flopped me over onto my belly, positioned my face to the side, and straddled me. He pressed down on my waterlogged lungs, eased back, pressed down again, shouting, "Come on, Dory. Breathe. Breathe, damn it. Dory!"

I heard his voice coming from a long way away. Then a shuddering spasm knotted my body. I vomited, and gasped, and vomited again. Evan continued to pump, squeezing every drop of pond bilge out of my lungs. Finally, when I began to groan and cough, he ceased, and gathered me into the warm shelter of his arms.

"Leave me—alone," I muttered, giving his sodden sweater a feeble push. "Go away. Die. Want to die."

"No you don't. You don't want to die." He sounded angry. "Dying is easy, a coward's choice. That's why your mother killed herself, because she wasn't strong enough to deal with what was going on."

"No—no—my fault—."

"It wasn't your fault, you stupid child. Who do you think you are, taking the blame for that whole miserable business upon yourself? Life isn't easy for anyone, Dory. You've had a rough time, worse than most, but lots of things are worse than bad memories. You have a whole future ahead of you, filled with love and pain and sorrow and joy and all the other things the poets talk about. The only future at the bottom of that pond is mud and darkness."

"Hate—you," I gurgled.

"Come on. We're both chilled through. If we don't get warm soon, we'll catch pneumonia."

Grunting, he lifted me. I may have been skinny, but I was nearly five feet seven inches of flesh and bone and wet hair.

"Hell," Evan said. "I've left my shoes on the other side. Forget it. I'll send one of the boys back in the morning."

As we approached the farm, golden orbs of lantern light bobbed toward us. Men shouted and cheered. Evan set me down. Someone threw a heavy coat around my shoulders and forced some whiskey down my throat.

"Leave me alone," I sputtered, pushing their hands away. They laughed. Not only was the mute alive, but she could speak!

Boyd picked me up easily and carried me toward the house. Two of the other lads threw Evan's arms around their necks and half-dragged him along. As we neared the front porch, I heard a peculiar rattling noise and cast a sleepy look over Boyd's shoulder. Evan's teeth were clicking like castanets.

Evan came into my bedroom. He had bathed and washed the pond muck out of his hair and changed into a fluffy sweater and tweedy slacks. He held a cane in his left hand, the walking stick he used from time to time when his back was bothering him. In his right hand, he cradled a snifter of brandy.

"I know you're tired, but I think we should talk now, Theodora."

I glowered at him from the middle of my bed. My skin felt raw and sore, thanks to Fanny's vigorous scrubbing. My hair hung damply around my shoulders. In order to ward off a chill, Fanny had made me put on a long-sleeved flannel nightgown.

"Go away," I growled. My voice sounded rough and absurdly deep for a child's, rusty from disuse. "Leave me alone."

"Ah." Evan lowered himself into a chair near the bed and set his glass down on the nightstand. "You're still angry with me for saving you."

"I hate you." I couldn't bear to look at him, my guardian, my savior. I felt no gratitude toward him.

"If you're thinking of trying again, I warn you, it won't be easy. I'll watch you like a hawk. I'm responsible for you, after all."

"You're a liar," I shouted, rising up on my knees. "You don't like me. You don't care anything about me. You only tried to teach me because you were afraid Fiona would make fun of you." Throwing myself over on my side, I buried my face in my pillow.

Evan sighed. "I plead guilty as charged. You're right, I didn't care about you, not at the beginning. But I had committed myself, and my pride wouldn't let me admit defeat. I was trying out a new hobby, just as Fiona said. I should have been more sympathetic to your problems, more patient. But I ignored your suffering. I told myself that you would soon come to your senses and forget the past. I refused to admit that you were in constant pain. I treated you like an object, rather than like a human being. And for that I am most truly sorry, Theodora."

I wriggled, embarrassment momentarily supplanting my fury. It didn't seem right for a grown man to be apologizing to me, a child.

"I never made any effort to understand what had happened to you, Theodora. I expected too much of you. You needed time, a cheap enough commodity, but I denied you time. I treated your affliction lightly, trying to force you to learn Latin and French and botany, when all the while your mind was trapped in a single terror-stricken moment. I've been an awful ass, calling myself an educator, imagining that single-handedly I could erase your past and mold you into a cultured, civilized human being. My mother was wiser than I. I should have listened to her."

"My fault," I said into my pillow. Tears started to spill out of my eyes. "She did it for me. To give me a good life. I should have run away. I should—I should have told someone. Then he couldn't have hurt her. She wouldn't have done what she did. She wouldn't be dead."

I began to sob, making wrenching, choking noises that sounded so sad and pathetic and ugly that they made me cry all the harder. Evan coughed and shifted in his chair, but he made no move to leave. I was surprised. I had observed that people like the Bradfords of Gramercy Park hated scenes of any kind. They didn't engage in shouting matches. They never made a public show of grief or joy or anger. But then Evan was accustomed to dealing with Fiona's displays of emotion. He handled her theatrical rages with the cool aplomb of a natural diplomat, which made Fiona all the angrier.

"Look here, Theodora, you can't really believe that," he said. "What your mother did, for whatever reason, was the sad product of her own mind and her own will. She could have done any number of things to spare you, to stop that man from forcing his attentions on you. My God, how ludicrous and quaint that sounds. As if he'd been pestering you with invitations to dance. Forgive me. It must have been hell for you. For both you and your mother."

My weeping intensified. I wanted to stop, because I could tell from the strained note in Evan's voice that my tears distressed him. But I could no longer hold them back. My horror at what had happened had dissipated, but an infinite sadness remained.

My mother had truly believed, in her poor, half-crazed fashion, that by killing Jenkins, stealing his money in order to purchase a train ticket for me, and then killing herself, she could buy a brilliant new life for her daughter. It was so sad, so useless. As sad as it was terrible.

"You really can't keep this up, you know," Evan said in a concerned voice. "You'll make yourself ill. Please, Theodora."

Knees updrawn, arms laced tightly around my middle, I twisted my body into a hard knot of grief. Evan's words only increased my despair, because they showed me that I was truly alone with my sorrow. His words of comfort were as empty as air, as meaningless as passionate words of love that are unaccompanied by simple gestures of caring. My grieving heart had no ears for his words.

The bed sagged slightly as Evan sat beside me. Placing his hands on my shoulders, he exerted gentle pressure and drew me upwards, gathering me close to him. I pressed my face against his chest and gripped his sweater fiercely, and I wept for my father, for my mother, for my child, for myself.

Gradually, my sobbing abated. Evan's warmth calmed me as his words never could. So long as I had a friend who could hold me and comfort me, I wasn't alone. Somehow, Evan had sensed that need. He patted me awkwardly.

Johanna tapped on the door and looked into the room. She seemed surprised to see Evan there. "Oh, excuse me, sir. I was wondering if the young lady wanted anything before she went to sleep. She didn't touch her supper."

Evan looked at her over my head. "You might bring us some hot chocolate and some sandwiches. And I'll take another brandy, please. Make it a double."

Johanna went out. I made a snuffling noise and wiped my eyes with my hands.

"Feel better?" Evan handed me a handkerchief. I nodded. "Good. You've been waiting a long time to do that, haven't you?" Another nod. Evan looked solemn. "I hope we won't have any repeats of what happened today. I'm too old and weak to go chasing after long-legged little girls who can run faster than I can."

I managed to smile bleakly over the snowy billow of his handkerchief. He smiled, too, a genuine relaxed smile which I had seen only rarely.

"Seriously, Theodora, if you're ever troubled or worried about anything, I want you to come to me and tell about it. Will you do that? You've been silent too long. It's not a natural state of affairs, to hold things back. Whatever happens from here on, I want you to know that I'm your friend. I truly mean that."

I retreated into the depths of the handkerchief and blew my nose. "Thank you, Mr. Bradford."

"You're quite welcome, I'm sure. You might as well call me Evan. We've shared too many adventures to be on such formal terms. Now, go and wash your face. Johanna will be here soon with our midnight snack."

When I came out of the bathroom, I saw Evan standing in front of my desk. He was reading the family history inscribed on the front page of my mother's old Bible, which usually stood at the end of the row of books on my shelf. I knew that chart well, having spent hours poring over it as a child.

"The Randall Family Bible" was written at the top in faded sepia ink. Ardis and Malcolm Randall of Chicago had had two daughters, Mary and Fiona. Mary had married Frank Lowery on the fifteenth of September, 1911. Their daughter Theodora was born on the seventh of March of the following year. Theodora's name was followed by two other names, with the dates of their deaths following soon upon their birthdates. Frank Lowery had died in February, 1925. No one had filled in the date of Mary Lowery's death.

Evan looked around. "Your mother had a neat hand. Her writing is very beautiful."

I stood beside him. "She was beautiful," I said in a halting rasp. I was still unaccustomed to talking. In fact, I had difficulty remembering that I could speak at all. "Would you—would you like to see her picture?"

"Yes, I would. I'd like that very much."

I opened the bottom drawer of my desk and took out a small framed photograph.

The photographer had posed my parents in front of a cheap painted backdrop. My mother was seated, one gloved hand in her lap, the other resting atop the handle of an old umbrella. Her wrist was cocked in a charmingly theatrical manner. She wore a fitted suit with a straight skirt pulled up just enough to reveal a pair of trim ankles. Her head was tilted back so that her face could be seen plainly under her dreadful hat with its broad, flat crown and piles of cloth fruits and flowers. Mother was smiling right into the camera lens, taking it into her confidence.

Evan grunted. I knew that he was trying to imagine this sweet-faced woman slitting the throat of a sleeping man and then hacking at his dead flesh again and again.

Frank Lowery stood behind his wife, his hand resting on her shoulder in a way that suggested either possession or restraint. He looked uncomfortable, stiff, unsmiling. Father's clean-shaven face was rigidly handsome, but with none of Mother's light and warmth. He probably didn't realize until after he saw the developed photograph that his wife had been flirting with the camera.

"It's incredible," Evan said softly, "how much she resembles Fiona. I would even say—and you must swear never to breathe a word of this to Fiona—that she was the more beautiful of the two." He glanced at me. "Amazing."

I knew what amazed him: that I resembled my mother hardly at all. Instead, I had inherited my father's strong features and long, lanky build. To Papa I owed my straight nose, straight hair, firm chin, and the no-nonsense expression in my eyes.

Evan handed the photograph back to me. Instead of returning it to the drawer, I propped it up on my nightstand. Johanna came in with a tray and set it down on the desk. Inviting me to sit, Evan pulled up another chair for himself. I devoted my full attention to my sandwich, and a moment later was astonished to find it gone.

"Take mine," Evan said. "I had quite an ample supper. What I really need now is more medicine."

Just as he reached for his brandy, he sneezed and jostled the glass so that half the contents sloshed out onto the tray and splashed his sweater.

"Damn," he said, dabbing at the spots with a napkin.

I giggled.

"Laugh all you like, Missy," he scowled. "I'll probably spend next week in bed with chills and fever, not to mention lumbago, thanks to you."

We finished our little meal. "It's odd, but I don't know very much about Fiona's family," Evan said. "She never talks about them. I didn't even know she had a sister until your mother's letters started to arrive. I suppose their parents died when they were still children?"

I swallowed the last crust of my second sandwich. "Their mother died after Aunt—after Fiona was born. My Grandfather Randall worked for the railroad. He died in a train wreck. Mother and Aunt—she and Fiona were raised by two old aunts. I think they're dead, too."

"Too bad. So Fiona really is the only family you have in the world. What was the family like, do you know? I don't mean to pry, but Fiona doesn't seem to like to discuss them, and I am a bit curious. She is my wife, after all. Were they well off?"

I sipped cocoa. "They came to New York once. They saw Sarah Bernhardt in *Camille,* and rode in beautiful carriages, and ate in fine restaurants. Just the way you do now."

"Er, yes," Evan said. "Interesting, about Bernhardt. Fiona mentioned her, too. The first evening we met. That must have been quite an experience for a couple of little girls from the Midwest." Evan drained his brandy glass and stood up. "We still have a lot to talk about, but nothing that can't wait until tomorrow. I will understand if you'd rather attend a formal school, like Miss Frasier's. I'm sure she would be delighted to take you back. But if you want to give the Bradford School another chance, I'd be willing to try again, too. You don't have to give me your answer now. You've had a long and exhausting day. We both have. But think about what I've said. Remember, Theodora, I'm your friend. I want you to do what makes you happy. After all, that's what your mother wanted, for you to be happy. Into bed with you now."

I climbed into bed and pulled the blankets over my lap. "Evan?"

"Yes, Theodora? What can I bring you?" I didn't reply at once. He came over and sat on the edge of the bed. "You look so serious, child. Tell me."

I threw my arms around his neck. "I'm sorry," I said. "You hurt yourself because of me. I'm sorry for that."

"No, no, that's all right." When he recovered from his surprise at this spontaneous demonstration of trust and affection, Evan returned my embrace. "This back of mine acts up from time to time whether I'm pursuing little girls or not. Don't think anything of it." He planted a gentle kiss on my forehead and stood up. "Good night, Theodora. Get some sleep now."

I lay back. "I will. Good night, Evan."

After Evan had left the room, I got out of bed and took down the Bible from the shelf over my desk. I opened it to the front page, picked up a pen, and filled in the date of my mother's death: June 17, 1925. Then I closed the book and put it away. The last thing I saw before I turned out the light was my mother's face, full of excitement and hope.

8

"Fiona, honey, I want to take your picture under that arch of flowers over there. The light's perfect, couldn't be better. Sit on that bench like a good girl, and pretend to smell the flowers or something."

Max Feinblatt propelled his leading actress toward the rose arbor. Fiona applied her nose to a late season blossom on the Paul's Scarlet climber.

"Good, good, wonderful. Now just hold still a minute while I get things adjusted."

"Hurry up, Max, for God's sake. I'm dying for a drink and a cigarette. Theodora," Fiona called out, "bring me my cigarettes, will you? They're in the house someplace." She made a face and said to Max in a voice meant for me to hear, "Might as well make her useful. Looks like she's here to stay."

Max shrugged. "She's a nice kid. Okay, why don't you try looking up at the flowers over your head? My God, the line of your throat is so beautiful."

Seething inwardly, I ran to the house. I wanted to tell Fiona to get her own stupid cigarettes, that I wasn't her slave or her errand girl, but I held my tongue for Evan's sake. "Please try and get along," he pleaded from time to time. "I know she's difficult. But try and understand." Yes, try. Fiona loathed me and I loathed her. I didn't understand why I had to hide my feelings while she was allowed to give full vent to hers. But any friction between us seemed to hurt Evan, and more than anything, I wanted to spare him distress.

I returned to the arbor. Fiona didn't bother to express her thanks. She snatched the flat silver case from my hand, extracted a cigarette, and snapped the flint on the matching silver lighter.

Ducking out of the frame of the picture, I stood beside Max. "What kind of camera is that, Mr. Feinblatt?"

"A Soho Reflex, sweetie, one of the best cameras made today. It's like magic, Teddy, all done with mirrors. If you look down through this hood you can see the image as it is reflected on the mirror at the back of the lens. Would you like to see?"

He handed me the camera. Peering down into the viewfinder, I saw Fiona, her white summer dress vivid against the backdrop of dark leaves and roses. She had smoked half a cigarette while waiting for Max to take the picture.

"Can we get on with this so that I can get back to my guests?" Fiona said.

"Of course, of course, darling," Max said in a distracted murmur. To me, he said, "If you want to move in closer or to step back a little, you adjust your focus by moving this little lever here. Do you know how cameras work, Teddy?"

I hated it when Mr. Feinblatt called me Teddy, but he was so sweet that I couldn't bring myself to make my objections known to him. "Um, light comes through the lens and makes an impression on the film?"

"Something like that," Max said. "Instead of roll film like the Kodaks, the Soho uses little plates that have some kind of special coating on them. You put the plate in back here, take your picture, take the plate out, and put in a fresh one from the case here. Now, the size of the opening and the speed of the shutter when it opens to admit the light are very important. Too much light will give you a washed-out, white-looking picture. Too little will do the opposite, give you harsher contrasts, less gray area. Do you understand?"

"Yes, I think so."

Max had launched into an explanation of f-stops and focusing, when a waspish voice from the bench under the arbor demanded, "Can we shoot the picture, please?"

"Sure, sure, Fiona," Max said, "I'm just showing Teddy here—"

"School is out for Theodora for this week," Fiona said. "She can learn about the mysteries of photography some other time, when I'm not here."

"Of course, darling." Giving me an apologetic wink, he announced, "I will now take the picture." He instructed Fiona to please put out her cigarette and to arrange herself on the bench. "Now look emotional, my darling."

"What kind of emotional?" Fiona asked. "Theda Bara?" She gave him a sultry and seductive look. "Or Mary Pickford?" Widening her eyes, she pushed her lips into a moue of girlish innocence.

"What an actress." Max gave an ecstatic sigh. "Listen, why don't you put yourself into your character? If these pictures turn out okay I can use them in our London publicity. 'The actress at her estate in Connecticut.' They'll love it."

"Mr. Feinblatt," I whispered.

"Anything you say, darling," Fiona said. "How about that nice scene at the end of the second act? 'What a fool I've been!' You know."

"Mr. Feinblatt."

"Yes, yes, that's beautiful. Now don't move, darling. What is it, Teddy?"

"You've put the cap back over the lens."

"Oh, so I did. Thank you for telling me."

"My God," Fiona moaned, "how much longer is this going to go on?"

Evan called down from the terrace above the swimming pool, "Max, telephone. Your secretary's had a wire from London."

"It's about the theater." Max shoved his camera at me. "You play with this, Teddy. Go on, take some pictures. Fiona, if you move I will shoot you, not with the camera but with a gun. This sun won't last forever. I'll be back in five minutes, no longer. I swear."

"I hope you got me a nice place to work," Fiona called as Max trotted toward the house.

"The best for you, darling. Only the best."

The other guests were all sitting around the pool, drinking and laughing. No one was swimming. Evan admitted that Connecticut wasn't the best place in the country for an outdoor pool. The water had finally warmed up at the end of July, and even now, the cool August evenings sucked the heat right out of it. According to Max, California was the only sensible place to have a pool. He hinted that Fiona might find herself in Hollywood one of these days. Her face was made for the movies, he declared: expressive, beautiful. But Fiona sneered at film actors. Any monkey could get up in front of a camera and emote on cue, she said. It took a real talking actress to sustain a characterization for more than a few minutes.

Fiona yawned and lit another cigarette. I aimed Max's Soho at her and clicked the shutter.

"What in hell do you think you're doing?"

"I just took your picture," I told her. "It's all right," I added. "Mr. Feinblatt said I could."

"You'd better put that thing away. You might break it."

"No, I won't. I'll be careful. May I take another of you?"

Fiona shrugged. "Suit yourself. It's not my toy. It would serve Max right if you ruined it."

I removed the exposed plate, inserted a fresh one, and looked into the viewfinder again. Fiona reduced to the miniscule size of one inch by one inch wasn't nearly so daunting as the Fiona I confronted in person. The woman in the tiny blue-colored mirror could say what she liked. The camera made her seem like a tiny nuisance, a mosquito. The camera cut her down to size.

"You know, I don't think Mr. Feinblatt had these openings adjusted right," I said half aloud. "The sun was bright where he was standing, but you're still in the shade."

"Where in the hell is Max?" Fiona fussed. "He has two minutes to get back here. Two minutes. And then I go swimming. My hair will be a mess, but I don't care. He can take his pictures some other time."

I ran around to the back of the bench, into the shade. I moved the lever on the f-stop to make the opening larger, and adjusted the focus.

"Look over here, Fiona."

Fiona swiveled around, bracing herself on one stiff arm. She held her cigarette in her other hand, just under her chin. The smoke swirled lazily upwards, disappearing in an aura of golden hair and sunlight. The expression on her face was one of intense irritation. I took the photograph.

"What do you think you're doing, you little monster?" Fiona hissed. "I don't want you spying on me, understand? We'll make a deal. You stay out of my hair, and I won't spoil your Cinderella story." She narrowed her eyes at me. "You've got a pretty nice thing going here, don't you? Poor little Dory," she simpered mockingly. "Well, poor little Dory's show of childlike innocence doesn't fool me for a minute. You know exactly what you're doing, don't you? You've got Evan eating out of your hand; nothing's too good for his star pupil. But not me, baby. Not Fiona. I know where you came from, remember?"

Turning away, Fiona took a long drag on her cigarette. I moved around to the front of the arbor again. Fiona's face fascinated me, especially the shifting play of light and shadow on its graceful contours as her expression altered.

"Your mother should see you now," Fiona said with a soft, bitter laugh. "I'll bet even she never imagined you'd end up like this—and she could come up with some pretty fantastic dreams. Little Dory, a rich-man's darling. Well, why not? Makes a good story."

During her speech, I had changed plates. Now I clicked the shutter again. I was concentrating so hard on the world I saw through the viewfinder that I hardly heard Fiona's words.

"Jesus." Fiona looked disgusted. "I've had enough of this." Click. "Leave me alone, will you?" Click. Click. "Just stay out of my sight!" She bounced off the bench and ran toward the pool. Max Feinblatt came toward her from the house, his arms open wide.

"We got Her Majesty's," Max shouted jubilantly. "The most beautiful theater in London. Now you will be a star for the whole world, Fiona."

Fiona called for champagne to celebrate. In his excitement, Max forgot all about his Soho Reflex until I approached him just before supper and confessed that I had used up all his plates.

Max laughed, and said to Evan, "Your girl has been bitten by the shutterbug, Evan. You'd better get her a camera of her own."

"I have an old one somewhere," Evan said. "Bought it a few years ago, used it for a month, and then forgot all about it. You can have it if you like, Theodora."

I gave an excited bounce. "Oh, yes, I'd love it! Thank you, Evan. Thank you, Mr. Feinblatt. I'm sorry about the plates."

"That's okay, honey. We'll wait and see what develops, huh?"

"These pictures are damned good. One of them is so good I'm going to use it for a press handout in London. But look at these, Evan. We can't use them, of course, but they're Fiona, all right. Down to her toenails."

The partners gazed down at the enlargements spread out on Max's desk. In one of them, Fiona looked like a sullen Broadway golden girl surrounded by wreaths of flowers. But in the others, she had dropped her mask of saucy civility. She glowered at the camera, her teeth clenched, her eyes blazing.

Max said, "I never could have gotten shots like these. How did you do it, Teddy?"

"Just lucky, I guess, Mr. Feinblatt."

Evan and I exchanged glances. We both knew it wasn't luck. Fiona plainly loathed the person holding the camera.

"I want to give you a little something for the good one, Teddy," Max said. "I like to encourage young talent."

Evan smiled. "Theodora doesn't need encouraging. The camera I gave her last week has hardly been out of her hands. I think she sleeps with it."

"I've been reading a book that says the real art of photography takes place in the darkroom." I gave Evan a hopeful look.

"If that's supposed to be a hint, I'll ignore it." Evan turned to Max. "Dory's been begging me to buy her some darkroom equipment so that she can do her own developing. So far I've resisted. I'm afraid she'll blow us all up."

"Better pack plenty of film for the trip," Max advised me. "Nice hobby for a kid. Keeps you out of trouble."

He wrote out a check and handed it to me. I gasped. "Fifty dollars! Oh, Mr. Feinblatt, that's too much. I didn't do anything. I just . . . took the picture, that's all. And so much! Evan, tell him I can't take it. I didn't do anything," I protested again.

"You managed to secure some very intriguing glimpses of a very intriguing woman," Evan said. "That's hard to do, even for professionals like Stieglitz. Maybe it was just beginner's luck, but I don't think so. I think you have a good eye. Max thinks so too. No, Dory, you keep the money. You've earned it. I can't imagine that Fiona was terribly cooperative in posing for you."

"I didn't know you could get paid for taking pictures." Folding the check, I tucked it into my pocket. I knew exactly what I would buy with it: a yellow filter that I could use in bright sunlight to reduce glare.

"You can always get paid for doing something well," Evan told me. "Talent of any kind is in short supply. And if you can make a living doing something you love, then you're luckier than most people."

The door burst open and Fiona breezed in, bringing a sunny sparkle to an otherwise bleak afternoon in Max's dingy Broadway office. She parked her dripping umbrella in a corner and tossed her raincoat over a chair.

"It's foul outside, darlings, simply foul. Good practice for London, I suppose." She perched on the corner of Max's desk. "Quick, who has a cigarette?"

We were sailing on the twentieth of September, 1926, just two weeks away. All Evan's plans had gone smoothly, except for Fiona's shrill insistence that the London cast include one of her male co-stars from the New York production.

While Evan lit Fiona's cigarette, Max covered the photographs on his desk with some other papers.

"I've been meaning to talk to you about London, Fiona," Max said. "I just heard that Nigel Norwood, who was such a hit over there in *Hamlet* last season, will be available during our run. He's a star in the silents, too, real popular in England, like Doug Fairbanks is here. Norwood would really help our box office if we could get him to appear with you."

Fiona shook her head. "Gregory *is* the character," she declared. "After a year of doing the play with him, I couldn't possibly act with anyone else. The British critics will love him, I know they will. Please, darlings. I haven't made a nuisance of myself before this, playing the temperamental star, but I must insist on this. All my instincts tell me it's the best thing for the play."

And the best thing for Fiona, I thought. Young Gregory had been a good deal in evidence lately, accompanying Fiona whenever she came up to Elf Hill, escorting her to the noisy parties and dinners that Evan preferred to forgo, sending her flowers, candy. Fiona seemed determined to transport her co-star across the ocean. Both Evan and Max knew that she was capable of refusing to go on without him. And without Fiona, the play would fold.

"Would you really refuse me this eensy little favor, Max?" she asked in a pouty coo. "That part's not much, just a juvenile role without much depth and a decent speech or two in the third act. Your great English actor would be bored to tears. Like putting a Barrymore in *Abie's Irish Rose*. Please, Max? I wouldn't ask, except it's for the good of the show. Evan, darling?" Smiling irresistibly, she appealed to her husband.

The two men looked at each other and shrugged. Evan said, "If that's what you really want, Fiona. We'll take Gregory to London with us. But if the critics don't like him, he can swim home."

"I adore you both!" Fiona beamed. "And now I must run and tell Greg the good news. Don't forget, Evan, you promised to come to the performance tonight to see my new gown for the third act. It's smashing."

"When you see the hole that thing put in last week's take, you won't think it's so pretty," Max growled.

Evan said, "The ladies in the audience seem to like the idea, new gowns every month. Some of them have been back to see the play two and three times, I hear, just so they can look at Fiona's dresses."

"Bah, dresses." Max threw up his hands. "In my day, theatrical costumes were made of glitter and gauze. Up close they were nothing—old muslin painted to look like brocade and velvet, a few sequins pasted on net to make a nice sparkle. Now everybody wants the real thing. If they want real life, why don't they go to Macy's?"

"Because you don't find Fiona Randall at Macy's," Fiona said gaily. As she slid off the edge of the desk, her skirt caught on some of the papers and pulled them aside, revealing the photographs. "What's this, some new publicity stills? Let me see them."

Max tried to stop her. "No, my darling, they are not good enough—"

When Fiona saw the unflattering shots, she blanched. She knew who had taken those photographs. "You little bitch," she hissed, glaring at me. "I told you to stay out of my way. You think this is very funny, don't you?"

"Really, Fiona," Evan said, "Dory meant no harm."

"Dory is a goddamned little nuisance. Well, I'm not letting anyone else see these. They're fit for the trash." Scooping up the glossy black-and-white enlargements, she prepared to rip them into shreds.

Evan grasped a corner of the bundle. "You don't need to carry on this way. We weren't going to use them."

"Let go, damn you!" They wrestled with the photographs for a few seconds. "I said, let go!" Fiona slapped Evan's face. Shocked, he released the photographs immediately.

Fiona made short work of them. In a moment fragments of black and white and gray covered the floor around Max's desk. "You're always defending her, no matter what she does," Fiona snapped. "I'm sick of it, do you hear me, sick of it!"

Scooping up her coat and umbrella, Fiona whirled out of the office, slamming the door behind her with a force that made the pane of glass on the top half rattle like stage thunder.

No one moved for at least half a minute. Evan's cheek blazed pink where she had struck him, but I knew he wasn't thinking about his physical pain. The scene had been grotesque, a parody of a childhood quarrel over a toy. I felt the sting of Evan's humiliation as if it were my own. He had incurred Fiona's wrath by defending me.

Turning his back on Max and me, Evan gazed out the streaked office window and down at the cars streaming past on Broadway, their headlights creating a tangle of golden threads on the rain-washed streets.

Max gave me a worried look. For the past three years, he and Evan had enjoyed an amiable and profitable partnership. Max had savvy, Evan had cash, and together they shared an understanding of popular taste and a strong love for the theater. An odd couple: the son of immigrant Russian Jews and the crown prince of New York's Four Hundred. But the theater was responsible for a lot of bizarre matches. Like Evan and Fiona. If they separated and Evan lost interest in the theater, Max would have to find another banker.

The jangle of the phone broke the sickly silence. After a brief conversation, Max hung up. "My broker," he said jubilantly. "Telephone's just hit two-forty and a quarter. I told him to buy me a hundred more shares. You play the market, Evan?"

After an uncomfortable moment, Evan let out his breath and shook his head. "You know how it is with old money, Max. We're conservative. I have a few thousand shares of blue-chips, but I can't bring myself to buy more. Certainly not at these prices."

I felt relieved. He sounded like himself. I knew that he wouldn't refer to this incident again, and neither would I, but I suspected that the memory of his shame would burn in us both for weeks, perhaps months, to come.

"You're making a mistake," Max said, cheered that their relationship had returned to normal. "I've cleared three hundred percent profit on my initial investment in just two years. Three hundred percent! You're missing out on a good thing, my friend."

"No, Max. It scares me. Like Dory and her darkroom. I have a feeling that if I bought now, the whole thing would blow up in my face." He gave me a sad smile. "Come on, Dory, we'd better go. So long, Max."

When Evan and I got back to Gramercy Park that evening, we found the loathsome Gregory seated at the piano in the drawing room. Fiona stood behind him, her arms draped casually around his shoulders. She greeted Evan with a bright smile, as though nothing out of the ordinary had occurred.

"Buy me an operetta, darling," she demanded. "Something whipped cream and Viennese, sweet and frothy. My voice is plenty good enough for that sort of thing, and Gregory thinks

I'd be marvelous, don't you, Greg? Sing something for Evan, darling. I want him to hear your voice, too. Such a marvelous baritone."

"Another time, if you don't mind," Evan said stiffly. "I have a bit of a headache."

Fiona put on a concerned face. Gregory smirked. As I followed Evan out of the room, I could hear the two of them giggling.

I spent the next hour poring over some new books on photography in my room. They helped me forget the embarrassment of the afternoon, and my intense hatred of Fiona. I had never felt so interested and excited about anything before, and I wanted to learn everything I could. I had already become a familiar figure at the camera store over on Third Avenue. Every servant at Gramercy Park and Elf Hill had posed for a portrait at least five times, in five differently lighted locations.

After a while, I ran downstairs to remind Johanna that Evan and Fiona were planning to dine out together after the evening performance, and to ask if I could have my supper on a tray in my room. At the foot of the staircase, I met Hanes carrying a brandy snifter on a silver salver.

"Is this for Mr. Evan, Hanes?"

"Yes, Miss. He's in the library."

"I'll take it to him."

Evan was seated at his desk, his chin resting on his folded hands. I set the salver down in front of him. He looked up. "It's just a silly flirtation," he said in a faraway voice. "It doesn't mean anything. She's always loved to play the coquette. She flirts with everyone, but she married me. Not any of the Gregorys or the Peters or the Arnolds she was always going around with. Me."

I didn't remind him that the Gregorys and the Peters and the Arnolds were all paupers compared to Evan Bradford.

Just then Fiona came in, Gregory trailing behind her on an invisible leash. "Time for us to run along," she said. "An hour and a half until curtain, and it always takes me at least an hour to get my face on right. Will you come now, or later, darling?" she asked Evan.

"I think I'll postpone my visit, if you don't mind," Evan said. "I'll see the gown another time."

Fiona clucked. "Head still hurting? That's all right, darling, I'll ask Greg to bring me home. Why don't you run along up to the country and breathe in some of that nice, clean air?"

She slipped her arms around his neck and kissed him warmly. "I love you, darling," she said in a husky theatrical whisper. "Sorry about this afternoon. You know the kid makes me see red." Evan patted her hand, grateful for the apology, grateful for that crumb of attention. I turned away.

When Fiona and Gregory had gone, I dragged a little hassock closer to Evan's chair. "I've been thinking, Evan. Maybe I should go away, to Miss Frasier's school."

Evan looked down at my upturned face. "Go away? What an idea, Dory. Go away! What's the matter? Aren't you happy here?"

"Oh, yes, I'm very happy. But Fiona's angry at you because of me. You spend so much time with me, even more than you do with her. I'd much rather stay with you, but if you think it would be better if I left—"

"No, no. What happened today wasn't your fault, Dory. I've been touchier than usual, but it has nothing to do with you, I promise. Go away," he repeated softly, shaking his head. "Strange, I can hardly imagine life without you. Things have been so different since you came. I'm not sure why. I'm still interested in the same things, only now I have someone to share them with. Poetry, painting, music, ballet—they were beginning to bore me. But I've caught some of your excitement. I feel like I'm seeing everything through fresh eyes, the eyes of a little girl who has forgotten poverty and hunger and want, and who now thinks that the whole world is a beautiful miracle."

"It's true," I said. "It is a miracle."

"And I'm the architect of that miracle. Without me—why,

God knows what would have happened to you. You really need me. I'm a necessary part of your life. It's important for a man to feel needed."

I put my hands on the arm of his chair. "Tell me what to do to make you happy, Evan. Tell me and I'll do it, anything, anything you say."

"Don't go away yet." He placed his hand over mine. "That would only make things worse. I'd be all alone, without any distraction, without any good work to do. A man can't live like that." He was silent, then he shook himself and smiled. "Forgive me. I shouldn't burden you with my problems. Go tell Johanna that we'll take our supper in here tonight. We'll read a little Dickens, and get to bed at a reasonable hour. We need to get an early start tomorrow so that we can meet the man who's going to set up a darkroom in the old root cellar at Elf Hill."

"Oh, Evan, really?"

"Yes, really. But don't come crying to me when you blow yourself up. It will be too late then to pick up the pieces."

"That's silly." Leaping up, I flung my arms around his neck. "You can burn yourself with those chemicals if you're not careful, but you can't blow yourself up." I hugged him tightly.

He didn't go stiff, as he had the first time I embraced him, the night he had pulled me out of the pond at Elf Hill. I had battered down his reserves through sheer persistence. I wasn't articulate; I could never find the right words when I wanted them. Often I could express my feelings through touch alone. Evan had become used to my unrestrained displays of affection and high spirits.

He returned the hug, then demanded laughingly that I unhand him. I obeyed, and ran off to find Johanna. I felt like singing. I had won. Angry with Fiona, Evan had turned to me for comfort. He needed me as much as I needed him. I made him feel important. And tomorrow, the two of us would go home to Elf Hill.

Away from New York and Fiona, he would be happy again.

December

9

Hugging my camera to my chest, I leaned over the rail and watched the ocean slide past in a rush of foam. Behind me the S.S. *Franconia* hummed like a little city. Nearly as large and populous as the whole town of Monkey Gulch, the ship offered many more amenities and comforts. I marveled that people could live so splendidly while traveling—enjoying films and games and books, fine meals, music and dancing. But of course, the *Franconia*'s passengers weren't like Colorado coal miners; the poorest among them was richer than Mr. Watson, who had bought my mother's wedding ring. In the eight days of our crossing, I took hundreds of photographs of the ship and its sleek inhabitants.

"If only Pilar could see them," I said into the wind. Something within me contracted painfully. I hadn't thought about my old friend for a long time.

After my recovery from the long nightmare that had begun with my father's death and ended, at last, in the muck at the bottom of the pond at Elf Hill, I had written to Pilar. I told her a little about Evan and Fiona and Elf Hill, and described some of the things I was doing. In my heart I still felt as close to her as I had long ago, when we raced laughing through the wildflowers that grew along the banks of the Purgatory River.

Pilar answered my letter promptly. Nothing much had changed in Monkey Gulch. When he turned sixteen, Joaquin had gone down to the mines. Soon after he started working, they had another accident. The cave-in wasn't a bad one, like the one that had killed my father, but it had cost Joaquin his right leg. And it had destroyed his serene silence. The once quiet and thoughtful boy now raged constantly at the absent owners of the mines, the need for stricter safety measures, the obligation of the miners to unionize.

Pilar wrote somewhat wistfully, "Now we wish Joaquin would be quiet once in a while!"

I understood. Joaquin had become an unsettling influence, what the miners called a troublemaker. My father had been like that, always telling the others that if they wanted better working conditions, they had to band together. The company had ways of discouraging such incendiary talk. Frank Lowery's overseers at the mines had given him the most dangerous work to do. They hadn't increased his pay, but they had made it clear that if he refused to do what they wanted, he would lose his job. Instead, he lost his life.

The chilling memories that Pilar's letter evoked contrasted strongly with my new life—the beautiful miracle, as Evan had called it. I never felt hungry now, never cold, never isolated. Under Evan's tutelage I was learning French and Latin, music and art, history and biology. In my mind, Monkey Gulch was forever linked with misery and terror. Try as I might, I couldn't separate Pilar from her bleak surroundings.

I never wrote back to Pilar. How could I describe the wonderful things I was seeing and doing, knowing what deprivations and hardships Pilar and her family had to endure? It would be cruel, I reasoned; it would seem like gloating. Eventually my memories of my old life faded, pushed out of my mind by the onrush of new experiences, new adventures, new delights. Except for moments like this, when I longed for a friend my own age, someone to confide in, to share with.

"Hi, Dory. Gonna dance with me tonight?"

Gregory joined me at the rail. Deeply tanned and tousled, he wore his white flannels and red muffler with a nautical dash. His college-boy good looks and stagy charm didn't appeal to me. He wasn't a real gentleman like Evan, only a cheap copy. I gave him a hostile glance and sidled away from him.

"What's the matter with you, Dory? Don't you like me?" Gregory's tone was plaintive. "I only want to be friends."

No, I didn't dislike him. Gregory was nice enough, I supposed. But he was Fiona's friend, and I, like Evan, had no interest in Fiona's friends. Like most of them, Gregory's favorite topic of conversation was himself. But more than that, I had a special reason for not wishing to share his company that afternoon. For the past few nights at dinner, Gregory had been teasing me to dance with him. It had become a joke, which Fiona encouraged by laughing at my persistent embarrassed refusals.

I said, "I don't like people to call me Dory."

"Oh? Sorry. I didn't know. Evan calls you Dory all the time. I've heard him."

"It's all right for Evan. It isn't all right for anybody else." I shoved my fists into my coat pockets and moved away from the rail.

"Wait a minute." Gregory bounded after me. "You haven't answered my first question. Are you going to dance with me tonight?"

"No."

"Why not? I'm a good dancer. I won't step on your toes, I promise."

"Because." I found myself blushing. I hated to admit the truth, but lying always made me uncomfortable. "Because I don't know how to dance," I confessed in a rush.

Gregory seemed relieved. "Oh, is that all? Well, I'll teach you then. It's really easy. We don't have to do any of the lively stuff, if you don't want to. Charleston and Black Bottom. But you ought to know how to waltz and fox-trot at least. Everyone knows how to do that. It's not so hard, you'll see. Come on." He saw my reluctance and said, "Look, nobody has to know. We'll surprise 'em, right? And if it doesn't work out, we can just forget the whole thing."

"Don't you have to rehearse with Fiona or something?" I asked.

"Nah, I know my part backwards and forwards. Fiona and I did a little work on a scene this morning,"—he reddened slightly—"but she has a headache and she doesn't want to see anyone until tonight." He sounded wistful, like a small boy who had lost his playmate. "Come on, what do you say? Let's just give it a try. A few minutes."

Finally, I consented. We found a deserted corridor and commenced the dancing lessons.

I was stiff and awkward at first, but Gregory put me at my ease by telling me that I was the same age as his little sister, whom he had also taught to dance. He was barely twenty, as close to me in age as he was to Fiona. But Fiona was demanding, difficult, temperamental. Perhaps Gregory found it a refreshing change to be spending some time with a kid like me.

"One, two, three. Follow my lead. Don't look at your feet. Hey, not bad, not bad. See, it's not so hard."

No, it wasn't hard. I was well coordinated and light on my feet, and as soon as I managed to forget the slight pressure of Gregory's hand on my waist, I was able to relax, to smile, and, finally, to laugh at my own clumsiness.

"I think you're ready for your debut," Gregory said after an hour's practice. "We'll do it tonight. I'll ask you to dance, but instead of saying no, like you always do, you say yes. Everyone will be surprised. It'll be fun."

I wore my prettiest dress to dinner that night, a pale blue silk frock with a dropped waist and long sleeves. A matching blue ribbon held back my long hair. As she helped me get ready, Fanny declared that I looked quite grown up. Gregory gave me a broad wink as I took my place at Evan's table. I had to bite my tongue to keep from laughing out loud.

As we were finishing dessert, the orchestra struck up a Strauss waltz. As he had every evening since we left New York, Gregory asked me if I would care to dance. As always, Fiona smirked, Max grinned, and Evan glowered, wishing he could do something to spare me—and himself—the annoyance of Master Gregory.

But this particular evening, I said, "Yes, I would, thank you." Gregory helped me out of my chair, and the two of us walked arm in arm to the dance floor.

"Well," I heard Fiona say. "What's all this?"

Gregory and I began to whirl sedately. Evan's scowl deepened. Fiona riveted her eyes on us.

"Looks like our little girl has inherited her mother's fatal charm," she drawled as we passed their table. "I'd better warn Gregory not to step on her toes. He doesn't want to end up like a jigsaw puzzle, scissored into a thousand pieces."

I felt almost sorry when the music ended and Gregory escorted me back to the table. I was flushed and breathless, smiling triumphantly.

Max and his wife laughed and applauded. Fiona said, "Well, Gregory, you're full of surprises, aren't you?"

I glanced at Evan, and was startled to see him glaring at me furiously. When I spoke his name, he stood up and stalked out of the dining room. I stared after him, bewildered and ashamed. I had angered him. How, I didn't know. But I did know that I was the target of his wrath—not Fiona, not Gregory, but I, who would have cut off my arm rather than hurt him.

I ran after him, and caught up with him on the windy stretch of deck outside his stateroom.

"Evan, wait for me. Evan, please!" I grasped his arm. "Why are you so angry with me?"

He shook off my hand. "How could you betray me like this? Plotting secretly with Fiona's lover, a man I regard as little better than a male whore. You couldn't have found a better way to humiliate me."

"But I didn't plot anything, it was just a game—a surprise. Please, Evan."

"Just a game, was it? You made me look like a fool. Fiona and her fancy boy cooked up a scheme and you fell right into it. You enjoyed it, didn't you? You're no better than Fiona, or your mother. You've got no sense of what's right or appropriate or— or *decent*. I don't know why I bother with you. I should have kept my mouth shut when Fiona told that woman to take you away. If I had, I wouldn't be plagued with you now."

His words pierced my flesh like so many fire-tipped arrows. Fiona always used words as weapons, but her barbs didn't hurt because no love existed between us. But Evan—Evan was my friend, my brother, my teacher.

Evan lurched along the deck and disappeared through a white steel door.

Shivering in my thin dress, I gazed out at the dark ocean. Its endless heaving blackness mirrored my own desolation. I tried to understand what had made Evan lash out at me, but I couldn't. A simple waltz, perfectly harmless, as innocent as a game of quoits or shuffleboard: what was wrong with that? I winced again as I remembered his parting shot; he wished me dead, out of his life.

I staggered drunkenly as I made my way back to my cabin. My legs felt like someone had chopped at them with a sledge-hammer.

Later that night, after I had gone to bed, Evan tapped at my door.

"Theodora, I know you're awake. Open the door, please."

I turned my face to the wall. I couldn't answer him. As always when I was troubled, I lost my power of speech. Instead I retreated into myself and pulled my old silence over my head like a carapace.

For the next few days, until the ship docked, I avoided Evan and met his attempts at reconciliation with mute expressionless stares. During the drive between Southampton and London, he pointed out landmarks and chatted about the history of the British Isles. I remained silent.

"Just like an honest-to-goodness lovers' quarrel," Fiona observed brightly. "Why don't you send the poor kid some flowers and candy, Ev? You know the way to a woman's heart as well as I do."

We checked into rooms at the Claridge, where we planned to stay until Evan found a townhouse to rent. Evan came into my room as Fanny was unpacking. I was sitting on my bed, listlessly thumbing through a guidebook to London. Evan sat down beside me. Fanny, catching his look, left us alone.

"I know it's not enough to apologize," Evan said. "I just want you to know that I am most heartily ashamed of my behavior, Dory. I don't know what made me act as I did that night. I'd been drinking too much, for one thing, and seeing you and that fellow together—. I wouldn't expect you to understand, but I'm not particularly fond of young Gregory."

"You think he's sleeping with Fiona." I tossed the book aside and dug the toe of my shoe into the deep pile of the carpet.

Evan jumped. My occasional flashes of insight into the adult world seemed to startle him. He had forgotten that my own introduction to sex had come early, and violently.

"Yes," he said. "But whether it's true or not, I've been behaving like a jealous husband—brooding, drinking, snapping at people. I shouldn't have taken out my anger on you. It was unforgivable. I said the most vile things to you that night—I didn't mean any of them. I hope you know that. You are very dear to me, Theodora. I hope you know that, too. I jeopardized our friendship by my crude behavior. I don't blame you a bit for being angry with me. If you choose not to forgive me, I would understand."

I turned my head to the side. "That's silly. Of course I forgive you, Evan."

He gave me a grateful smile, and squeezed my hand. "Thank you. I don't deserve it. I'll try to make it up to you."

"You don't have to do that."

Evan stood up and moved to the window. He was silent for a long time, then he said in a low voice, as if he were speaking to himself, "I don't know what's the matter with me. I've never behaved this way before. It's Fiona, of course. She has the most maddening way of getting under my skin. I've never known a woman like her. She knows I'm a fool. She knows she can carry on as she likes, and I won't say anything. I can't help it. If that's the price of loving her, I'll put up with it."

He looked around, a frown distorting his handsome face. "I'd better run along. We have a lot to do. We'll be auditioning the rest of the cast this week. You won't mind entertaining yourself

for a couple of days, will you, Dory? After the show opens, we'll
do something special to celebrate, just the two of us."

He went out. I felt more anguished and unhappy than I had
before he came in; I wasn't sure why. It had something to do
with Fiona and how beautiful she was and how much he loved
her.

"I love you, too," I said softly. "More than she does. You don't
need anyone but me, Evan. Why can't you understand that?"

Armed with map, guidebook, and camera, I explored London
on my own. When foul weather discouraged walking, I spent
my time in Madame Tussaud's or the British Museum. Every
evening Evan made a point of spending a few minutes with me
before rushing off with Fiona and their London friends. He
asked me how I had spent the day, what I had seen, where I had
gone. I sensed that he wasn't really interested. He was tense
and preoccupied these days, immersed in preparations for the
play. Rehearsals had begun and they weren't going well.
London was to see an entirely new production of the play, with
Fiona and Gregory the only members of the original New York
cast. Fiona and Dexter, the director, quarreled constantly.
Dexter walked out twice, and only Evan's diplomatic cajolery
and promises of a percentage of the profits had persuaded him
to return.

The sad mood that had possessed Evan on shipboard clung to
him like a sickness, a cold he couldn't shake in London's chill
dampness. I knew that Fiona was seeing less of Gregory these
days, but that didn't help. Fiona had found new friends, members of London's fast set. She stayed out late with them, dancing
and drinking. She began to arrive late for rehearsals. Evan spoke
sharply to her about it one morning, and a noisy argument en-
sued. Fiona began screaming and throwing things. White-faced
and furious, Evan stalked out of our suite at the Claridge. He
didn't come back until the following afternoon.

On my way to Regent Street one morning, just a few days before the play was scheduled to open, I passed through Hyde Park. A crowd had gathered at the corner near the Marble Arch. The young man who addressed them was tense and gaunt, dressed in rough clothes and heavy boots. I stood at the back of the crowd and listened.

"We working men have no voice. Oh, we speak out individually, one man to another, but who listens to us? We elect a spokesman, but who listens to him? I tell you, the ears of the lords and the barons of business are closed to any sound but the jingle of gold coins and the rustle of pound notes being passed from hand to hand. What will it take to make them listen? Can we go to them and tell them, 'We have no food to feed our families. We have no place to live. We have no warm clothes.' Ladies and gentlemen, you know that their ears will be deaf to such pleas."

The speaker was as good an actor as any I had ever seen. His words cast a spell over his listeners, who were largely silent except for an occasional angry mutter of agreement or a lustier, "Hear, hear!"

"No, my friends," the young man went on, "in order to make them listen, we must speak their language. The language of money. We must deny them the profits that keep them sleek and fat. We must turn off their machines, close down their mills, refuse to go down into their mines. We cannot fault our overseers for not meeting our demands if we don't make our demands known. And how shall we tell them? In the only words they can understand: Strike! Sabotage! Strength!" He beat his right fist on the palm of his left hand. "We'll speak not with words, but with actions. Strike! Sabotage! Strength!"

The crowd caught fire, repeating the three words in a chant. I turned to the woman beside me. "Who is that man? The one who's speaking?"

" 'Im? Oh, everybody knows Donal McAllister. 'E's a rich man's son from the North who went to work in his father's mines and got all the other miners to form a union. A Member of Parliament now, 'e is, but still a laborer, just like us. Some say 'e's a Commie, but I don't believe 'em."

"What's a Commie?"

The woman gave me an exasperated look. "Communist, dearie. Reds, like the Ruskies. That whole country belongs to the workers now. Somethin' like that ought to 'appen 'ere, that's what I say. Strike! Sabotage! Strength!"

I wriggled my way to the front of the crowd and pointed my camera at Donal McAllister. At that moment he looked down from his little soapbox and saw me. He grinned and lifted his arm, clenching his fist.

"Send me a copy if it's a good one," he shouted.

Embarrassed that he had noticed me, I moved away. My brain was buzzing with what I had heard. What would have happened if the miners in Monkey Gulch had refused to work? Their families, always so close to starvation, would surely have died. The company would only bring in new workers, and things would go on as before.

I wondered about the company, those rich men from the East I had heard so much about. What would happen if the son of one of those rich men went to work for the company, as Donal McAllister had? Men like my father and Joaquin would rally around him. The other workers would see that they were right. Theirs was the only way. Speak with actions. Strike, sabotage, strength.

So many things were hard to understand. Why were some people rich and others poor? Why didn't the company pay their men more generously? Rich men like Evan didn't really need two or three homes. Why, Evan could give one of his houses to someone else, a poor family with lots of children.

Elf Hill. I pictured grubby-faced children riding Muffin and Custer, throwing rocks at the frogs in the pond, rampaging through the stables, smashing down the gorgeous flowers in the gardens. They would spread their possessions all over the sunny downstairs sitting room, where Evan and I spent so many comfortable and gentle afternoons in the winter. No, it wasn't fair. I hated them, those faceless children who wanted to usurp my place. They didn't belong there. They couldn't possibly appreciate the special beauties of Elf Hill.

2019

As evening fell, the haze that had shrouded London during that strange, windless day grew thicker. Tramping over the more remote stretches of Hampstead Heath, I heard none of the warnings that were being broadcast over the radio, nor did I take any notice of the insidious yellow fog that had begun to settle over the city below. According to my guidebook, the poet John Keats had lived in a small house just south of this wooded oasis. There he had met Fanny Brawne, with whom he had fallen in love. Earlier, as I had visited that shrine, a small white cottage faced by a haphazard and autumn-blighted English garden, I imagined that John Keats must have been a lot like Evan: vulnerable behind a facade of civility and good manners, devoted to his family, loyal to his friends. I wondered how Fanny Brawne had charmed him and persuaded him to love her.

At five o'clock, rumbles from my stomach reminded me that it was after teatime. I started home, knowing that I would have no difficulty finding a bus or cab. After spending two weeks on my own in London, I had become quite expert in getting around town.

The fog was so thick at the north end of the Heath that I couldn't read the street signs unless I stood directly beneath them. Traffic was unusually light for that hour of the day. I waited for twenty minutes for a taxi to pass, then searched vainly for a bus stop. I decided to walk toward Camden Road, which would take me down to Regent's Park. From there, I could easily find my way back to the Claridge.

After walking for about ten minutes, I found myself in a congested industrial neighborhood. The streets were so narrow that only one car could pass at a time. The air reeked of sulfur and smoke and rotting garbage. I found breathing difficult as well as unpleasant, and I kept my handkerchief pressed tightly over the lower half of my face. Suddenly a cat darted across my path, followed by a leggy little girl of eight or nine years.

"Excuse me," I called out, "I'd like to get to Camden Road. Can you tell me how to get there?"

Having retrieved her cat, the child walked back to where I stood. She was thin-faced and solemn, so grubby that I could hardly make out the color of her hair and skin. Even her blue eyes seemed dull, like dirty porcelain.

I repeated my request. The girl hugged the cat, who kept up a continuous low yowling. I shivered. The child's shabby dress, thin arms and wretched shoes looked so strange, and yet so horribly familiar.

When the cat had had enough of being held, he lashed out at the girl, who promptly released him. His body made a furry arc in the air, and then he disappeared, like an animal in a magic act.

"Ow, the bloody beast," the girl wailed. "I'm gonna kill 'im, I am."

"I'm sorry if he hurt you," I said. "Are you bleeding?"

" 'Course I am." The girl displayed two long red scratches on her dirty forearm. She gave me a suspicious look. "You talk funny. Where you from?"

"America. New York." We studied each other warily. I was conscious of my own prim and tidy dress, my warm jacket and fluffy beret, my polished boots.

"What's that?" The little girl pointed to the camera that hung from a strap around my neck. I explained in detail, removing the case, pointing out the lens aperture, the view-finder, the little door that opened so that I could remove exposed film and insert a fresh roll. Other children appeared from the shadows and crowded around us. They had a rank and sour smell, as though their bodies and their clothing hadn't been scrubbed for ages. Their noses were red and runny. Several of them had cold sores on their lips. Fresh bruises darkened the complexion of one scrawny little girl.

" 'Ere, take me picture," the first girl demanded, giving my arm a proprietary tug.

The others clamored to have their pictures taken as well. I balked, telling them that I really had to go home, but they surged around me, stretching out their grubby fingers toward my precious camera. In order to keep them at a safe distance, I agreed to photograph them. I grouped them in front of the arched brick entrance to an alleyway, the least hideous background I could find.

Looking at them through the viewfinder, I forgot who they were and how they disturbed me. As always, I lost myself completely in the challenge of taking a good picture: looking for strong contrasts, making a balanced arrangement of figures, finding an interesting camera angle, adjusting the lens openings and the focus. I took three shots of the group before my film ran out.

"Sorry." I snapped the case shut. "I don't have any more film."

"We want to see the pictures," a large boy said. "Come on, open that thing and show us the pictures."

"You don't understand." I explained that the film had to be developed before the pictures could be seen. The boy insisted that the pictures must be inside the camera. He tugged at the strap. "No, don't touch that!" I pulled away. "Please, leave me alone."

"Aw, whatsa matter?" the boy sneered. "You 'fraid of us? T'ain't nuthin' to be 'fraid of 'ere. We're all nice and friendly like."

Another boy snatched my beret off my head. My guidebook slipped out of my jacket pocket and was trampled in the mud and slime underfoot. The children converged on me, shoving, laughing, poking fun at my clothes, jerking at my long braids. I clutched my camera to my chest. I didn't care what these little ruffians did to me, but I wasn't going to let them damage my camera.

Their laughter took on a sinister sound; the pushing and shoving got rougher. These children hated me as much as I hated them. They wanted to hurt me. Fear immobilized me, like

blocks of ice that had formed around my feet. I couldn't run,
couldn't even move. In a moment they would push me down
into the mud, take away my camera, tear my clothes, kick me
and beat me. As I opened my mouth to scream, the scenario of
my worst nightmares became real. I couldn't make a noise, not
even a squeak. The muscles of my jaw moved, but no sound
came out.

" 'Ere, what's all this? What's goin' on 'ere?"

A burly man entered the crowd, his arms whirling like the
blades of a windmill. Children scattered in all directions. The
little girl with the bruised face arched her arms over her head
and ran squealing to her ma. The big boys who had taunted me
most severely backed off and stood glowering at me.

" 'Oo're you?" the man demanded of me. When he saw my
good wool jacket and my expensive camera, he screwed up his
mouth and spat at my feet. "You're in the wrong place, Missy.
Better get out of 'ere."

Run, run. Run from Sid Jenkins, run from the leering boys in
the schoolyard, run from the hunger and the horror. I pelted
down the narrow street. Behind me I could hear the faint jeers
of the children, but the fog soon swallowed the sounds. I was
running through cotton. I couldn't see, couldn't breathe. My
legs moved mechanically, like twin pistons. I didn't know where
I was going, and I didn't care. I just had to run, to escape.

A woman shrieked. Brakes screamed and horns blared. A
huge red double-decker bus screeched to a halt as strong arms
pulled me clear. When I opened my eyes, I saw a policeman's
large-pored nose and graying moustache, and the strap of a helmet just under his lower lip. He asked me, not unkindly, what
was wrong, where I wanted to go.

I struggled to answer him. "Taxi—Claridge," I gasped finally.
"Taxi—Claridge Hotel." A taxi was found. I leaned back gratefully on the cushioned seat as traffic crept along through the
fog. The cabbie chatted easily. Apparently, this fog was going to
be severe. The autumn ones were always the worst, he said.

By the time we reached the hotel, I felt calmer. I found a

pound note in my pocket, money Evan had given me that morning for food that I had neglected to buy. I gave it to the driver, who said, "Change, Miss. Wait a bit." I shook my head and ran past the doorman into the lobby. At that moment I loved the Claridge Hotel more than any place on earth.

Up in the Bradford suite, I retreated to my own room and closed the door. When Fanny poked her head in to ask if I would be dining out with Mr. Evan and Miss Fiona and their guests, I said that I wasn't hungry. I was tired, and I just wanted to bathe and go to bed. That's all. Fanny turned on the taps in the bathtub and left me alone.

I soaked and scrubbed myself vigorously. I felt defiled, filthy. The squalor and the misery on that street had shocked me, not because they were new and strange, but because they were so appallingly familiar. I recognized myself in those scrawny little girls. I knew those rough boys, and the rough man who had come to my rescue. I could have described the insides of their homes: the small spaces stinking with coal and kerosene and the emanations of too many bodies, the cold, the dirt, the darkness.

After my bath, I put on a clean nightgown and warm robe and sat patiently while Fanny combed the tangles out of my hair. She had already turned down my bed. A flattish bulge at the foot revealed the presence of a hot-water bottle. The room smelled of rose sachet and lavender-scented steam from the bathroom. Heavy curtains at the window shut out the darkness and the choking fog. A fresh bouquet brightened the dresser. This was Evan Bradford's world, where everything was warm, soft, and unbearably beautiful.

When Fanny left, I opened my camera and removed the roll of used film. I unfurled it, exposing it to the light. I didn't want to see those children again. I didn't want to see Donal McAllister, the wealthy boy who had given up his comfortable home in order to go down into the black hell of his father's mines.

I was thinking about the mine that had claimed my father's life and maimed Joaquin Garcia when I heard a tap at the door and Evan came in. He was wearing evening clothes, black tie

and dinner jacket. He limped slightly, in anticipation of a change in the weather most likely, and although he looked tired, his smile was warm. I thought he must be the handsomest man in the world, and the kindest.

"Ready for bed so soon, Theodora?"

"Oh, Evan!" I hurled myself at him and flung my arms around his neck. "I don't want to go back. I don't ever want to go back!"

"What are you talking about? Go back where? To Elf Hill?"

"No, no," I gasped. "To Monkey Gulch. To being poor again. Oh, Evan, it was awful!"

We sat together on a small love seat in front of the gas fire and I told him what had happened to me that day. Evan listened solemnly. He didn't try to laugh away my fears. As always, he treated me as if I were an adult.

When I had finished my recital, he nodded and stood up.

"I'll tell Fiona and the others to go ahead without me. I've been neglecting you, you poor child. While I'm gone, you get dressed. We'll dine together, just the two of us. I know a nice little Italian restaurant just around the corner."

"But I'm not hungry," I protested.

"Not hungry, after an adventure like that? You're starving and you know it. Now hurry and get dressed, like a good girl."

Over dinner, I told him about Donal McAllister. Did the fact that Donal had forsaken the comforts of a wealthy home for the rigors of life in the mines mean that he was a good person, I wondered? Surely he was better than the rich men who owned the company. Those men lived thousands of miles from their mines and left their operations to overseers who cheated and abused the workers.

I found that I couldn't look at Evan while I posed these questions. Evan didn't reply at once. He drained his wine glass and signaled to the waiter to refill it. When the man had gone, he smiled at me.

"I think I understand," he said. "In a way you're worried about my immortal soul, aren't you, Theodora? You see me enjoying my money, not giving ostentatiously to poor people like the children you saw today. If life were fair, you think, then all the world's wealth would be distributed equally and everyone would have a share of the comforts that you and I now enjoy. I agree with you; it's a pleasant thought. But life isn't fair, Theodora. Some men are rich, some are not. Some are handsome, some are ugly. Some are intelligent, some are morons. Fate hasn't distributed any of these gifts on an equal basis, and it isn't in the nature of man to help fate along. Unfortunately, men are self-centered. Or perhaps it isn't so unfortunate. That selfishness contributes to our instinct for self-preservation, which includes the protection we extend to the ones we love. No mother having only a cup of milk to give her hungry child, would give half that milk to a stranger's baby. However cruel and unjust that may seem, it is a fact of life. We protect what we have, we give only when it doesn't inconvenience us, and if we need to, we rationalize our reasons for acting as we do. Am I making any sense?"

"Yes, a little."

"Good. You know, Theodora, every man has to make a decision about how he wants to live in this world. Can he ignore the inequities in life? Or does he want to change them? Your Mr. McAllister realized that he couldn't tolerate the gap between himself and his workers, and so he eliminated it completely, by joining them. He found a solution that made sense to him. But that doesn't mean his answer is right for every other rich man's son. Another man in his position might decide he could do more good for these people by building hospitals and schools for them, providing education so that those workers' children who are eager and intelligent won't be compelled to follow their own fathers' footsteps down to the mines."

A waiter removed our plates. I asked for ice cream, and Evan ordered coffee. I said, "What about you, Evan? How did you decide how you wanted to live?"

Evan lit a cigarette. "I agree that conditions in some mines and mills are shocking, and should be changed. I would hope that the companies on whose boards I sit treat their workers fairly, and with respect. However, it is not in my character, as it is in Mr. McAllister's, to organize men, to exhort and inspire and compel them to act. No, Donal McAllister has found a role that he is peculiarly able to fill. I admire him, but I could never do what he's doing. The Bradfords have always given generously to charity, and I like to think that I have continued that tradition. As for myself, I happen to believe that bringing light and beauty into the world is as important a mission as encouraging workers to strike, to sabotage, and to join unions."

I was silent for a few minutes, ingesting ice cream while I digested Evan's words.

Evan said, "I don't have any special talents, Dory. Oh, I can do a few things adequately—play the piano, ride a horse, produce a decent sketch or a coherent paragraph. Above everything else in this world, I admire the people who have been gifted with the ability to create something out of nothing: the artists, the poets, the players, the painters. I suppose I fell in love with Fiona's talent even before I fell in love with the woman herself. Not that you can separate the two."

I sighed inwardly and set down my spoon. As always, it depressed me to hear Evan extolling Fiona's virtues.

"You see, Theodora," Evan went on, "I feel a certain responsibility toward artistic genius. I can recognize talent—which is, I suppose, a talent in itself. I use my money to develop talent, to bring it out, to nurture it. At certain times in every artist's life, he may be tempted to give up. The myth of the starving artist is, alas, no myth. And Fiona is not the only one I've helped. I gave Dexter, Fiona's director, his start, and I've given encouragement and financial support to other theater people and to some writers, even a composer. I'm not boasting. I just want you to know that these people are as important to me as Donal McAllister's miners are to him. The changes he will bring about are important. But more important, I think, are the works of art that I will sponsor in my lifetime. Those works of art will last. They'll be with us long after McAllister's mines are filled with mud and his workers are gone. Well"—he sat back and gave me a gentle smile,—"are you still ashamed of me?"

My eyes widened. "Of course not, Evan. I was never ashamed of you. Never!"

"But you were a tiny bit afraid that I wasn't quite so noble as Donal McAllister. Weren't you?" he teased. "Come on, admit it."

I squirmed and looked down at my lap.

"It's all right," Evan said. "I'm glad you wonder about these matters. It shows that you're sensitive to the things you see and hear, that you're curious about the world. You know, Theodora, of all my projects, you're the one I'm proudest of." I looked up quickly. "Oh, yes. After we got over our initial hurdles, you responded so eagerly to everything I taught you. You've learned an amazing amount in the past few months. I'd like to think that even in a first-rate school like the Frasier, you wouldn't have made such rapid progress. I don't want to take all the credit; you deserve a good bit yourself. But it's worked out pretty well after all, hasn't it?" His eyes shone warmly. "Don't you think you're at least as important as one of Donal's miners?"

"I don't know."

"Well, I do know. You are important. I have the feeling, Dory, that someday I'm going to be very proud of you."

I glowed. Evan had never spoken to me like this before. He thought me worthwhile, important.

We stepped out into the street. During the short walk back to the Claridge, Evan put his arm around my shoulders, as if to shield me from the odorous, oppressive fog and the horrors it concealed.

"Let's hear no more about going back to Monkey Gulch. Look ahead, Dory. Never feel guilty because you're not stuck in the grinding, demeaning poverty you knew as a child. All that is behind you now. Look ahead," Evan said again. "And speaking of looking ahead, we'll be leaving London right after the opening. I'll only be in the way, and frankly, Fiona's new friends bore me to distraction. We'll run over to Paris for a few weeks, and then we'll roam around Italy until we feel like going home, to Elf Hill."

"Keats died in Rome," I said. "Near the Spanish Steps."

"We'll go there," Evan promised. "A little pilgrimage. You see? Poor Keats could have done with a patron like me."

After we got up to our rooms, I sat at Evan's feet while he read Keats' "Ode to Beauty." We talked about the poem until I fell asleep, my head resting on Evan's knee.

10

Snuggling into the corner of the sofa, Fiona sucked the olive from her martini. "I know Hollywood's ready for me, Max, but I am not yet ready for Hollywood."

From the depths of his chair in the drawing room of the Gramercy Park townhouse, Max Feinblatt appealed to Evan. "You tell her, Evan. Tell her about the money she can make in movies. Tell her about the millions of people who could see her act, not just the few who have enjoyed her performances on the stage. Tell her." In the more than two years since Fiona's Broadway triumph and comparable London success, Max and Evan had produced two more Broadway hits starring her.

"I wouldn't try to persuade anyone to go to California, for whatever reason." Evan didn't look up from the table in the corner where he and I were examining an expensive new book of art prints. "Nice enough place if you like deserts, I suppose."

"Bah, deserts." Max flapped a chubby hand. "Tell her about the wonderful sunshine, the fruits, the flowers."

Evan grunted, clearly unable to work up any enthusiasm for California's wonders.

Max attacked Fiona again. "Think, Fiona, think what it

means to make a film. When you play on Broadway, even your most brilliant performances are lost forever as soon as that curtain goes down. But a film lasts. Twenty years from now, people will look at you and say, 'That's why Fiona Randall is a great star!' Look at what has happened to the great actors of the past. Who knows anything about David Garrick and Mrs. Siddons these days? But if they had made a few pictures, they would be stars even now."

"And Dr. Johnson would have been the first film critic." Evan turned the page from Botticelli to Michelangelo. "I'd like to hear his opinions of the current cinema. Dory, pour me another drink, will you? Snowy afternoons always make me feel so lazy."

Fiona also wanted a refill. I collected their glasses and went to the sideboard. Evan had already consumed several bourbons in the course of the afternoon. He claimed he needed alcohol to calm his nerves. I had noticed that he always drank more in the city than he did at Elf Hill, except when Fiona made one of her periodic journeys to the country.

"Max, I'm not saying that I never want to make a movie. I just don't want to leave the theater right now."

"You won't be leaving." Hoping to press his suit physically as well as verbally, Max joined Fiona on the sofa. "Think of it as a leave of absence, a sabbatical. This is a wonderful opportunity, darling. And believe me when I tell you that the studio has a really worthwhile project lined up for you." He leaned forward, his tiny eyes gleaming behind his gold-rimmed glasses. "A musical!"

Fiona laughed, a bright, rich sound. Her head fell back, unfurling the long, slender line of her throat. "Naturally it's a musical, my dear. They're all musicals these days. Tell the boys in Hollywood to forget it. I'll wait until they come up with something that calls for a real actress rather than a chorus girl."

"This isn't just another *Jazz Singer*," Max assured her. "This picture has class. This is 1929!"

Evan rolled his eyes as I handed him his bourbon. I bit my tongue to suppress a giggle. In the year and a half since Hollywood's first hit talking picture had opened, theatrical and artistic circles had been buzzing about *The Jazz Singer*. They weighed its artistic faults and merits, pondered how its popularity would affect business in the legitimate theater and vaudeville, postulated what the future of the talkies would be. Evan hadn't particularly cared for the movie. He said he preferred to see musical comedies on the stage, where the flash and dazzle came over in full color and glorious sound. I agreed with him that *The Jazz Singer*'s music could have been squeezed out of a gramophone horn.

Fiona and Max argued back and forth. Max was busy forging links to Hollywood these days. Since the advent of talkies, the movie industry was desperate for voices, and Max, whose ear was pressed to the heart of the legitimate theater in New York, knew thousands of voices. The movie men wanted new talent, and he, Max Feinblatt, could provide it. Now if he could only persuade Fiona Randall to turn her eyes westward.

I leaned over the back of Evan's chair. "I need to run over to the camera shop. The new filter I ordered should be in by now."

Evan looked around. "Why don't you call first, and have them send it over?"

"Because I want to make sure it's the right one. I won't be long."

"We have tickets for *Il Trovatore* tonight," he reminded me. "Remember, we need time to go over the score before dinner."

Whenever urgent business forced Evan to forsake the bucolic joys of Elf Hill for the bustle and din of the city, he rewarded himself—and me—with massive doses of art and culture. In the past two weeks, we had attended two theatrical openings, including Fiona's new play, three symphony concerts, one operetta, four operas, and a lecture on the headhunters of Borneo. The last had been my favorite, since it had been illustrated with slide pictures.

"The store's only ten blocks away. I'll run."

"Why don't you ask Hanes to ring for the car?"

Evan was always trying to persuade me to take one of the limousines whenever I went someplace, and I always refused. "You can't take pictures from the window of a car." I laughed. "Don't worry, I'll be back soon."

"Well, be careful. The sidewalks are slippery."

"Listen to the mother hen," Fiona said. "Cluck, cluck, cluck."

Evan flushed at her jibe. On my way out of the room, I flashed her a furious look, which she ignored.

Out in the hall, I threw on my new coat and the floppy beret Evan's mother had given me for Christmas, then I burst out the front door, as happy as a puppy to be liberated from the house for the afternoon. The snow was still falling in the park, draping the statue of the actor Edwin Booth in an ermine mantle, coating the trees so that they looked like pale skeletons silhouetted against a dark background, or like reverse images on a photographic negative. I smiled to myself. I couldn't help seeing everything in photographic terms. Since Evan had given me my first camera three years ago, my enthusiasm hadn't abated. Instead, it had matured into a full-blown passion.

My errands took longer than I expected. I made my way home through the muffled cottony twilight, knowing that I was late and that Evan would be worried. As I approached the house, I saw that the drawing room curtains were still open. Evan stood at the window, his arms crossed in front of his chest. I could tell from the set of his shoulders that he was annoyed. I waved energetically and nearly tumbled down in the snow. He shook his head slowly as if to say, "I did warn you about that."

Once inside, I didn't wait to shed my outer garments before dashing into the drawing room. Fiona and Max were still ensconced on the sofa. Evan, seated at the piano, pounded out the heroic tenor aria "Di Quella Pira" with one admonishing finger.

"I'm sorry I took so long," I said breathlessly. "Mr. Warren didn't have the right filter after all, but he looked around the back room and found one that I could use until mine comes in.

I'm going to need it if I want to shoot pictures in the snow. All that glare—"

"Let's get on with this, shall we, Theodora?" Evan said. "We've barely an hour before dinner."

"Look at the child's shoes," Fiona exclaimed. "My God, Theodora, don't you even bother to wipe your feet before coming into a house?"

I looked down at my sturdy English brogues, shedding muddy pools of water onto the pale blue Aubusson carpet. "Oh, sorry. I forgot."

"It doesn't matter," Evan said. "If we could get on with this."

"Yes, it does matter," Fiona barked. "You teach the kid French and botany and Shakespeare, but you haven't taught her anything about manners. I think she ought to pay for the cleaning. That would make her think twice. She wouldn't have so much lovely spending money to waste on gobs of film and new lenses."

I stooped down and blotted at the puddles with my handkerchief. "I really am sorry, Evan."

"I don't want to hear any more about it." Evan snatched the opera score off the music rack and stood up. "Come into the library, Theodora. We'll go over the story in there, without the piano."

I didn't obey at once, but stood smiling and twisting my hands in the ends of my scarf.

"Well, come on." He paused in front of the door. "What are you waiting for?"

"I was walking up Third Avenue," I said, "and I looked up and just happened to see a sign for a coiffeur in one of the windows. Monsieur Henri from Paris. I went up, and Monsieur Henri himself was there. I spoke French to him, but he didn't seem to understand me. I guess my accent still isn't very good."

"He's probably Henry Friedman from the Lower East Side." Fiona crushed out her cigarette. "I'll bet you a nickel the only Paris he's seen in his life is the plaster kind."

"Anyway, I did it." I whipped off my beret.

The long braids that used to hang to my waist were gone. Monsieur Henri had cropped my hair as short as a boy's, parted it deeply on the left side, and brushed it away from my face. An errant strand fell over my eye, and I pushed it aside.

"It feels so strange and light, like great weights have been lifted from my head," I said with a giddy wave of my hand. "It's going to be wonderfully easy to take care of. Fanny used to spend hours doing it every morning, and now I can use that time for other things, like reading or studying or photography."

Evan stared. "What in the name of Heaven have you done to yourself?"

"Don't you like it?" I gave him a bright smile that concealed my nervousness. "Monsieur Henri thinks it looks wonderful."

"Monsieur Henri is a fool," Evan snapped. "You look like a common flapper. All you need now is a little black paint for your eyelids and some crimson stuff for your mouth. I'm surprised you didn't let him sell you on those items while you were at it."

"I don't think it looks so bad," Max ventured. "Actually, Teddy looks very pretty."

"Gamine as hell," Fiona agreed. "You're going to have to keep the boys at bay with a shotgun, Ev. Your little Dory's almost a woman now. What is she, nearly seventeen? That's a dangerous age for any girl. It makes my blood run cold to think about all the trouble she could get into."

Turning his back on me, Evan refilled his glass from the decanter on the sideboard. "I think it looks horrible—grotesque. I don't even want to look at you."

"It will grow back," I said, hating myself for capitulating to his anger.

"And what do you intend to do in the interim?" he demanded. "Join a convent and take the veil?"

"All this fuss just because the kid bobbed her hair," Fiona said. "You wouldn't be any more upset if she came home and announced she'd had an abortion."

Glaring at her, Evan slammed down his glass and stalked out

2019

of the room. I felt sick with anger, so shaken that I could hardly stand. I sank down on the piano bench.

Fiona stretched languidly. "Get me a glass of seltzer water, will you, Max? I've got to be romping around on that stage in a couple of hours and I might as well start sobering up. God knows it isn't easy when Evan's around. I learned a long time ago that the things he said were a lot more interesting when I had a few drinks under my belt. He certainly is in a fine mood tonight."

"He is concerned about Teddy." Max gave me an encouraging smile as he squirted seltzer into a glass. "I remember when my own kids were that age."

"He's so touchy lately," Fiona said. "Always fussing about this, that, and the other thing. Do you know what he said the other day? He accused me of overdramatizing. He said that I always acted out my side of an argument as if I were in front of an audience. But what can he expect? Honestly, if he didn't want a wife who knew how to bare her soul in public and in private, he shouldn't have married an actress."

"Maybe it's not your soul he's worried about," Max suggested.

"Evan?" Fiona laughed. "Oh, he doesn't mind my little friendships."

"You might be surprised."

"Come on, Max. Evan doesn't act like any jealous husband I ever saw. Jealous husbands hire detectives. They follow you around and listen in on your phone calls and read your diary. They fly into rages and swing their fists and utter the most awful threats. Evan jealous? He couldn't be less interested in what I do."

"Evan is a gentleman." Max spoke warily. "He would not want to behave like a common bully."

"Evan is overbred, overcivilized, and overwrought." Fiona sniffed. "If he didn't have the Bradford millions to play with, he wouldn't have a friend in the world. How long would you stay with him if he went broke? You don't have to answer that." She stood up. "I'd better get going. I need to make a stop before I go to the theater. An appointment with my hairdresser," she added with a wink in my direction.

"Wait, darling," Max hauled his bulk out of an armchair. "What can I tell the boys in Hollywood?"

Fiona paused, her hand on the doorknob. "Tell them to get themselves a piggy bank the size of this room. By the time I'm ready to go to the West Coast, they're going to need plenty of dough."

"But sweetheart, they've already offered twenty-five thousand," Max said.

"Because that's all I'm worth now. But in a few years I'll have a couple more stage hits under my belt, plenty of magazine and radio exposure, lots of good publicity. My name will be one of those proverbial household words, and those boys of yours will be panting to sign me up. I just want to make sure they pay plenty for the privilege. Why not?" She lifted one shoulder. "Whores and actresses make their livings on their looks, and looks don't last forever."

"You are a marvel, Fiona." Max waggled his head admiringly. "You are one of the few actresses I've met who has any idea of what the world is really like beyond the footlights. Most of them can't see past tomorrow."

"That's because they can't remember past yesterday." Fiona opened the door to the hall. "Not me. I've never had vision problems in any direction."

Max bade me a friendly farewell and followed her out. I banged the cover down over the piano keys so hard that the strings inside reverberated for a full minute, then I went up to my room. I hated them all: Max, and Fiona, and especially Evan.

What was the matter with him? He had been so edgy lately, always nagging me about my studies or my clothes or how much time I was spending in the darkroom. He lectured me on my appearance, on my behavior at the theater, at the dining table, on the street—as if he had any right to chastise anyone for

NATASHA PETERS

breaches of conduct, after the disgusting way he'd behaved downstairs. It had been a long time since he had humiliated me in front of Fiona. Normally we managed to present a united front to her, but tonight he had lost all reason.

Almost seventeen. Almost a woman, Fiona had said. But I didn't want to be a woman. In my mind, I was still a girl, a child, the only child Evan Bradford was ever likely to have. Fiona had declared long ago that she didn't want to distort her figure or hamper her career by having babies. Evan had agreed. Why not? He never cared for children; he hadn't been acquainted with any until I came along. He told me once that he hadn't recognized the void in his life until I arrived to fill it.

I looked at the framed photograph on my nightstand. Along with my parents' old wedding picture, I carried this one with me wherever I went. It showed Evan and me seated on a fat chunk of marble in the Coliseum in Rome. Our arms were wrapped around each other's waists and we were laughing. Originally I had posed Evan alone; "a ruin among ruins," he'd called himself. His back had been bothering him that day, and he was carrying his cane. Just as I was about to shoot the picture, I saw an Italian urchin of the type that follows tourists the way seagulls follow steamships. I called him over and explained what I wanted. The picture was in focus and the camera was ready; all he had to do was press a small lever when I gave him the word. I ran over and flung myself down beside Evan, who called out in Italian, "Now! Take the picture now!" I was furious with him, but that picture had turned out better than all the rest of my Roman snapshots.

As we were leaving the Coliseum, the boy shouted after us, "*La sua figlia è una bellissima ragazza, Signor.*"

"*Sì,*" Evan shouted back, "*bellissima.*" A very beautiful young lady.

"*Figlia* means daughter," I said as we climbed into our rented car. "But I'm not your daughter. Why didn't you tell him that?"

"I don't have to explain my relationships to every little ragamuffin I meet," Evan had said as he threw the car into gear. "Besides, you're as dear to me as any daughter. That's all that matters."

After washing my face and changing into the dress Fanny had set out for me to wear to the opera, I went down to the library. I felt curiously calm, as though the amputation of my braids had removed some of my childish insecurities and doubts. Evan didn't like my new hairdo? That was too bad. I liked it fine, and I was going to keep it.

I sat in my accustomed chair across from Evan's desk and I waited. The assertive tilt of my chin could speak for me. I would not apologize for what I had done. Why should I? It was my hair, not Evan Bradford's.

After a while Evan glanced up from the book he was reading. He seemed surprised to see me, although I had been sitting there, breathing and making small rustling noises, for a full ten minutes. "Oh. Theodora. I've been thinking that there's no point in going to this opera tonight unless you just want to listen to the music. You'll never be able to figure out what's going on."

"Yes, I will. We saw a production of *Il Trovatore* in Vienna last year," I said. "Don't you remember?"

"What's that? Vienna? Oh, that's right. Well, then you'll be able to explain things to me if I become confused. Refresh my memory, Theodora. What is this opera about?"

I launched into a description of the Byzantine intricacies of the plot of Verdi's masterwork. "The gypsy Azucena sees her mother burned at the stake as a witch—"

Neither of us referred to my shorn hair. We dined at home, as we always did on the evenings before we went to the theater. Nowhere else was Evan able to drink the wines he liked with his meal. Prohibition, he used to say, had made civilized dining in public an impossibility. We rode in silence to the Metropolitan Opera House.

As we entered the Bradford box, we saw that Mrs. Bradford and Emily Frasier were occupying two of the red velvet chairs.

Evan shook Miss Frasier's hand and kissed his mother's cheek. "Why didn't you let me know you were in town? You and Miss Frasier could have dined with us."

"My dear, we've had the most exhausting day," Mrs. Bradford said. "We've been attending a college reunion, our thirty-fifth. Can you imagine? You wouldn't believe how terribly some of those women have aged. But after a while, Emily and I decided that we were really rather tired of those boring stories about children and grandchildren. After all, we didn't care about those women when they were girls. With good reason, I see now. I remembered the opera tonight—why, Theodora, how delightful you look! You've cut your hair. It's about time. Evan, don't you think Theodora looks delightful?"

Evan was spared from answering by the applause that greeted the conductor's entrance into the orchestra pit. The houselights dimmed and the musicians began to saw away at the overture.

During the first intermission, two visitors came to our box to greet Evan and his mother. Edward Fairbank was a prominent man on Wall Street and the Stock Exchange. He and Evan served on some of the same corporate boards together. Mr. Fairbank presented his son Tom, a gangly, painfully polite young man of twenty, who shook my hand gravely and asked me if I were enjoying the opera. "Not really," I said. "I don't particularly care for the story."

Tom tried to cover his discomfiture with a bright society smile. "But don't you think the singing is wonderful?"

"No," I said. "I don't."

That stumped him. "Oh. I'm sorry to hear that."

I took pity on him. "Actually, Caruso and Tetrazzini sounded better in last week's *Otello.*"

"Oh?" Tom looked lost. "Well, the costumes are certainly colorful," he observed with another strained smile. I couldn't argue with that, and didn't bother to comment. We were both relieved when the time came for the two gentlemen to return to their seats for the second act.

"They say Tom Fairbank is some kind of scientific genius,"

Miss Frasier told Evan's mother. "He's lucky. His father has enough money to equip a dozen laboratories, if that's what the boy wants."

Mrs. Bradford had a more romantic turn of mind. "I think he liked Theodora, don't you?"

The ripple of pleasure I experienced at her comment was almost buried under a wave of incredulity. What could Tom Fairbank possibly have found to admire in me? I had been brusque, cool, socially awkward in spite of all Evan's instruction. Could Tom have enjoyed our halting conversation? Perhaps he liked my plain, straightforward features and my unremarkable green eyes, or maybe the honest sprinkling of freckles across my nose attracted him. But no, I had the answer: he had been charmed by my bobbed hair.

After the performance, Evan invited the two ladies to come back to Gramercy Park for a light supper, but they declined. We parted company at the corner of Broadway and Thirty-ninth Street. Just as her chauffeur was about to pull away, Miss Frasier opened her window.

"You've done a remarkable job with Theodora, Evan," she called out. "If you want to send her to me for some finishing, please do. Wiggsy will be delighted."

I glanced at Evan to see if this compliment to his teaching had pleased him. He was busy packing tobacco into the bowl of his pipe. I climbed into the Rolls and slumped down on the base of my spine. We rode home in smoky silence.

As soon as Hanes admitted us to the house, I murmured a stiff good night to Evan and started up the stairs.

He said in his firmest tutorial voice, "Would you mind stepping into the library for a few minutes, Theodora?"

I followed him into the room, closed the door, and braced myself. I knew I was in for one of those talks about how ladies do not submit to the irrational whims of fashion without first considering the ultimate wisdom of their actions.

Knocking his pipe against one of the andirons in the fireplace, Evan poked a stray ash into the grate with his toe. "I just wanted to say that I think your new hairstyle is very becoming. It suits you even better than the old one did. You looked charming at the opera tonight. Quite charming."

I couldn't speak. Relief and happiness flooded over me. Evan didn't hate me.

"I hope you'll overlook my absurd behavior this afternoon, Theodora. I don't know what came over me. I don't want you to think that I don't care about you. I do care, more than you'll ever know. I've showered you with many favors in the past few years. I know you're grateful, and that you think yourself undeserving of them. That's not true. You have returned my gifts a thousandfold, with your unquestioning love and trust. I don't — I don't know how I would have survived without you."

I understood. My love had helped shore up Evan's self-respect, which had eroded because of his inability to do anything about Fiona's infidelities. In the past three years, I had poured out love and affection for Evan Bradford in an attempt to restore and replenish the love he was giving to Fiona, who couldn't return it. I fancied that without my love, Evan would have dwindled away, diminished, vanished like a piece of ice on a griddle. My love kept him whole.

He said, "You're hovering on the brink of something that I have never really understood: womanhood. I suppose I don't want you to grow up. I'm selfish, I know. But I'm afraid that when you do become a woman, your feelings for me will change."

Evan didn't want me to join the ranks of women who valued him for his good looks, his clever conversation, his sports cars, and his money, not necessarily in that order.

Crossing the room to him, I slid my arms around his neck and pressed my face close to his. I didn't speak. I knew that at some moments words were superfluous and unnecessary. An embrace was something Evan could never misunderstand, whereas words were subject to all sorts of misinterpretations.

I became conscious of the pressure of Evan's arms, the firm smoothness of his cheek, the warm gust of his breath on my neck. A vision appeared behind my closed eyes. I was lying in a field, on a blanket of wildflowers and fragrant green grass. Evan smiled down at me. Reaching up, I grasped his hands and drew him down beside me. We lay together, holding each other while the sun warmed us like a kiss.

I felt a contraction in my middle, like a cramp except that it wasn't painful. It was more like a fiery ball, a tiny sun, that in spinning gave off waves of heat that flowed to every part of my body. Then the beautiful vision vanished abruptly, and I was back in a dark hallway. Sid Jenkins pressed me against the wall. I couldn't escape.

With a little cry I pulled away from Evan, who dropped his arms and turned back to the fireplace. "It's late, Dory." His voice sounded hoarse. "You'd better go to bed."

"Evan—"

"Go to bed," he repeated. "Good-night."

Up in my room, I undressed and crawled under the coverlet. I didn't quite understand what had happened. I knew only that my mind had betrayed me, and I, in turn, had betrayed my dearest friend. The darkness, the terror, the tangle of sweating limbs and grinding bodies belonged to the past. I thought I had put that nightmare firmly behind me. It was gone, dead, forgotten, until suddenly it had leaped out at me from the darkness like a grotesque jack-in-the-box. Sid Jenkins and his foul, oppressive presence—no, that had nothing to do with Evan. Evan would never hurt me like that.

But these things were all part of being a woman: lying in the darkness with a man, having babies, growing old together in the same bed. My mother and father. My mother and Sid Jenkins. Sid Jenkins and me. I shuddered.

I lifted my hands to my swelling breasts. One of Evan's friends had told me once that the rounded form of the champagne glass had originated as a tribute to the perfection of Queen Marie Antoinette's breasts. Mine were just that size now, round and full. I had hardly noticed the changes in my body.

But I no longer had the slim shape of a boy. Overnight, my hips and breasts seemed to have blossomed. I had become a woman.

I didn't want to grow up yet! I had been forced into woman-hood while I was still a child; I wanted to remain a child for just a little while longer. But all the same, I didn't want to lose the lovely vision of the two of us, Evan and me, melting together in the warmth of the sun.

A car pulled up in front of the house. Fiona was home. She came up the stairs and went straight to her room. Her new role was a demanding one, and most evenings she was too exhausted to party.

After a few minutes, I heard the library door close with a muffled boom. The stairs creaked under their thick wad of car-peting. Evan paused for a moment outside his own room, then he moved on down the hall and tapped at Fiona's door. I heard a murmur of voices.

Fiona's door closed, and the house fell silent.

11 Dec. 2019

After a triumphant but ennervating Broadway season, Fiona demanded a complete change of scene. Edward Fairbank, who had come to our box at the Metropolitan Opera with his son Tom during the performance of *Il Trovatore*, told Evan that the property next door to their house on Cape Cod would be vacant that summer. Fiona expressed such delight at the prospect of a month at the seaside that Evan immediately ar-ranged to rent the place.

So the Bradford entourage, complete with servants, trunks of linen, china, and glass, two limousines, and crates filled with bootleg liquor and champagne, moved up to the sea shore in the middle of July, to a large house located near the town of South

Orleans on Pleasant Bay. Cape Cod was a favorite retreat for writers, artists, and theater people. Scores of friends and visitors began to arrive from Boston and New York. The Fairbank and Bradford households became one on those long summer afternoons. Servants went wherever they were needed, setting up tables on the lawn at either house, carrying trays of food and drink from one kitchen to the other.

Upon discovering a common love of fashion and gossip, Fiona and Lydia Fairbank became as close as sisters. Evan shared no interests whatsoever with Ed Fairbank, an important figure in the world of high finance. Evan never set foot in Wall Street or the Stock Exchange if he could help it, preferring to leave the care and feeding of his trust funds and investments to his bankers.

The Fairbanks had two children, Tom and his sister, Susie, a student at The Frasier School. Susie was entertaining two of her absolutely most bosom friends for the summer. We were all the same age, and although I spent a lot of time with them, I always felt excluded from their intimate group. Still, I learned to play tennis, and I got some new freckles while they tanned and exchanged idle talk about boys I had never met.

Evan told me that he was pleased we had come to Cape Cod. "You need to be with people your own age. I'm too old to be good company for a young girl. Too much of a fuddy-duddy." He couldn't help grimacing as he used one of Fiona's slang phrases. Evan was thirty, but he imagined that to my seventeen-year-old eyes he seemed positively venerable.

In spite of my efforts to hold back the pull of time, I grew up that summer, quite literally. I added another inch to my height, much to Fanny's despair, because my clothes never fit properly anymore. That hardly mattered at the beach, where my usual costume consisted of light dresses, tennis whites, or bathing suits. And besides darkening the freckles on my nose, the sun streaked my otherwise ordinary brown hair with strands of pale gold.

Evan also changed that summer. He drank more, but instead

of calming his nerves, the alcohol seemed to quicken them. He prowled around the house like a nervous, watchful tomcat, ready to arch and bristle at insults, eager to pounce with criticism, sulky and slow to apologize. Fiona, busy impressing her new friends, ignored her husband's morose behavior. But as I was not very interested in Susie Fairbank and her crowd, and since Evan and I were still carrying on a limited program of study, I came in for more than my share of his bad temper.

"You have two great faults, Theodora," Evan said one evening. He had just overheard me telling a Provincetown playwright that I considered most of the modern plays I had seen a waste of time. "Stubbornness and indiscriminate honesty."

I drew myself up so that our eyes were level. Evan still topped me by two inches, but his current slouching posture diminished his stature. We were standing in a corner of the dining room, near the sideboard that served as a bar.

"I only told him what I thought."

"It would have been better to prevaricate or to keep silent. You were rude. Whatever you think of the man's plays, you should keep your thoughts to yourself."

"I didn't say anything bad about his plays in particular, Evan. In fact, he agreed with me."

"You were rude. I insist that you apologize."

I refused, thus providing proof of Evan's first accusation of stubbornness. Furious, Evan declared our lessons at an end until I did as he asked.

"Then I'll just have to study on my own."

"Fine. I can use a rest."

This, our worst rift since the shipboard quarrel, lasted a full week, until I presented the wretched playwright with an enlarged photograph of himself, looking very melancholy and artistic. Although I uttered no word of apology, the man was obviously delighted, and Evan chose to accept this gesture as a fulfillment of his terms.

"I hope you've learned your lesson," Evan said. "Someday you'll thank me for teaching you how to behave."

I felt myself reddening. For the first time in our acquaintance I wanted to strike out at him. Instead I snarled, "I doubt that. I couldn't thank anyone for making me act like a hypocrite."

Bouncing out of the house, I ran toward an isolated beach at the north end of Pleasant Bay. Throwing myself down on the sand, I wept and kicked until I was thoroughly damp and encrusted with sand. Then I stripped off my clothes and plunged into the salty water.

"Someday." The word had bowled me over like the unexpected slap of a wave. I had grown up listening to my mother chatter on at length about her fantasies and daydreams and wishes. In my heart, I had known they were all lies. As I grew older, I found that I couldn't bear to listen to anything that was shallow or false or silly. Everytime I heard anyone say, "Someday," I ground my teeth. "Someday" had been my mother's pot of gold. Because of "someday," she had prostituted herself and her daughter, and when "someday" turned out to be a pit full of poisonous snakes, she couldn't live with the consequences.

Words were treacherous, like a vicious undertow that lurks under the otherwise placid water of a quiet cove. I had learned very early that even the sweetest and most innocent-sounding words could mask scurrilous intentions. Sid Jenkins had spoken kindly to me most of the time, but his actions had been brutal and hurtful. My mother's dreamy talk had never revealed the depths of violence of which she was capable. Fiona called everyone "darling," but she loved no one, and she often savaged her closest friends behind their backs. Even my beloved mentor and tutor, Evan Bradford, was skilled at throwing up verbal smokescreens to conceal his true thoughts and feelings.

Photographs, I decided as I hauled myself out of the water and trudged across the sand to where I had left my clothes, were the most honest reflections of reality. I knew, of course, that in the hands of experts, like the masters in Hollywood, photography could raise falsity and sham to high art. I, too, had learned a variety of darkroom tricks that enabled me to alter, distort, clarify, or even falsify negatives. The person taking the picture might be filled with all kinds of prejudice and emotion, but the camera itself, that all-seeing insensible eye, never lied. The camera penetrated falseness to expose the truth. I wondered how many of Fiona's adoring friends would have been shocked by those first pictures I had taken of her with Max Feinblatt's Soho Reflex, those which revealed a cruelty and cunning that most of them had never seen, the side she usually masked by bright talk and laughter.

One lazy Sunday afternoon late in August, hosts and guests *2019* from both Bradford and Fairbank households assembled on the Bradford veranda to admire the sunset while they sipped fruity drinks made from bootleg gin. After helping Hanes, our butler, serve this dubious punch, I retired to the most remote corner of the porch and aimed my camera at the crowd.

An invisible spotlight seemed to light Fiona from above, transforming her blond hair into a heavenly aureole. Her dress, a sheer summer voile with a white and blue print, brought out the azure in her eyes. As always, she made a lovely picture, but it was one that I declined to take. On principle, I had taken no photographs of her since those first ones under the rose arbor at Elf Hill. Instead I trained my view finder on my favorite subject, Evan, held captive by Miss Jemimah Fairbank, who turned out to be an old flame of his grandfather and an expert on Bradford family history. The old woman rambled on about long-dead Bradfords and long-forgotten scandals. Evan listened politely and shot me an occasional desperate glance.

After a while, I saw Tom Fairbank coming from the other house to join the party. He wandered over in my direction and sat beside me on the porch railing. I could have predicted his first conversational gambit: "Have you seen any operas lately?"

"A few. Have you?"

"No, I've been busy at school." In the six months since I had seen him last, Tom had shed some of his adolescent gawkiness. His voice and his bearing were imbued with a new solidity. He was a nice-looking boy, although I'm sure that the cowlick on the side of his head was the despair of his life and his barber. On his otherwise smooth, dark head, it stood out like a horn bud on a calf. "I'm at Harvard Medical School," he told me, "going into my second year."

"You're going to be a doctor?"

"That's right. I really want to work in a research laboratory. We have a lot to learn yet about how the body functions; there are so many diseases that we can't prevent or cure. Are you interested in science, Miss Lowery?"

I shrugged. "I like plants and flowers, and I've learned the constellations and the planets, but I don't know very much about any of the other sciences. Except chemistry. I need to be able to mix up the right proportions of solutions when I develop my film." *Time out for me!*

Tom, who had just come down from Boston, hadn't known I was a photographer. He told me that he had owned a Brownie since he was thirteen, but that he'd never used any more sophisticated equipment. He seemed quite interested in my new camera, a German Leica that Evan had bought me for my seventeenth birthday. I asked if he wanted a demonstration, and he responded enthusiastically. We walked down through the sand to the edge of the water, so that I could better explain the workings of my light meter and my various lenses and filters.

Tom listened closely as I talked about the advantages of the Leica's modified viewfinder. Our heads touched as I talked. But when I glanced up, I saw that he was gazing not at the Leica, but at my face.

"I hope you pay better attention to your lectures in medical school," I said. "I'd hate to be your first patient."

He gave me a sheepish smile. "Sorry. I'll try to do better. You were saying that the f-stop—"

"You're not a bit interested," I said. "Why on earth do you want me to talk about something you don't care about?"

"Because I like to hear you explain things."

"That's silly." I closed the case around my camera with an impatient snap. "I have better things to do." I started back toward the house.

Tom ran after me. "Theodora, wait!"

I halted. What had happened to the proper formality of Miss Lowery? I felt my cheeks getting red.

"I really am sorry. I don't quite know how to say this. It's just that you're so different from the other girls I've met. You seem so sure of yourself, so grownup. Not at all like my sister and her friends. I want—I wanted to get to know you better, that's all. The camera seemed like a good excuse to get you away from the others so that we could talk. I guess I'm not like Mr. Bradford," he said with a self-conscious smile. "I'm not very good at conversation."

I relented. "That's all right; neither am I."

"Listen, would you like to come down to the yacht club for a few minutes? Dad just bought me a new sailboat, a seventeen-footer. She's a beauty. I named her for you, you know."

"For me?"

"Well, indirectly. We were trying to think of a name, and I remembered meeting you at the opera, and I remembered the gypsy in the opera, so I said I wanted to call her *The Sea Gypsy*. Do you like it?"

Secretly I like it very much, but I said simply that *The Sea Gypsy* sounded like a perfectly good name for a boat.

It was nearly dusk when Tom escorted me back to the house. I didn't see Evan on the veranda or in the downstairs rooms, and I guessed that he had retreated to the little octagonal tower at the top of the house, which we had chosen for a study. Windows on seven of the eight sides offered unobstructed views of the Cape, Pleasant Bay, and the ocean beyond Chatham Lighthouse, and even Monomoy Island. After our first session there, Evan declared that I should be forced to study in a dark closet furnished with only a table, a chair, and a naked lightbulb.

I admit that I found the sea a source of never-ending fascination and delight. I loved to watch the waves crashing over the rocks, the sea birds diving for their food, the great pyramids of clouds building on the horizon whenever a storm approached. The colors of the sea and the sky changed constantly, making my fingers itch for my camera. The Atlantic Ocean had more moods than Fiona Randall.

Evan was seated at the little desk, a bourbon in his hand. "You and young Tom seem to have found plenty to talk about," he remarked.

"He was interested in my Leica." Flopping down in my accustomed chair, I opened our copy of *War and Peace* to the proper page. We had reserved the hour before dinner for reading aloud, and it was a custom I hated to break.

"You certainly must have explained things in detail. I suppose you offered to reveal to him the delights of the darkroom as well?"

The waspish note in Evan's voice warned me that I could expect an argument. I said, "How could I? My darkroom is at Elf Hill. We walked over to the yacht basin to see his new sailboat. It's lovely. He wants to take me out in it tomorrow. Would that be all right?"

"If you want to risk concussion and drowning in the company of that irresponsible young idiot, it's no affair of mine." Evan swallowed bourbon.

I stared at him. He didn't look up. He knew that his behavior was irrational and ridiculous, but he couldn't stop himself.

"What's the matter with you, Evan? Why are you acting like this? I haven't done anything wrong."

"Nothing's the matter. Nothing."

"That's not true," I persisted. "You've been so strange all summer, always staring at me as though you hated me. But whenever I ask you what's troubling you, you say it's nothing. But it can't be nothing, or you wouldn't be doing this. Why won't you tell me?"

"Because what goes on inside a man's head and heart is nobody's business but his own," he retorted.

"But if it affects other people—"

"Then the other people will simply have to put up with it and have the good manners not to remark upon it, won't they? Honestly, I don't know where you got this passion for direct utterance, Theodora."

"Not from you," I said, my temper flaring.

"No, thank God. At least I understand that little things like diplomacy and tact are necessary if the world is to function smoothly and in a civilized manner. The whole idea of civilization is to tame the savage. Why else do we refrain from burping in public, or breaking wind, or sneezing in other people's faces? No reason, except that the ability to control our bodily functions and to temper our appetites is one of the few things that sets us apart from the beast. But you, with all your clamor about honesty, you'd have us all rutting in the streets like dogs, snatching food from each other, slaughtering our neighbors if they had the ill luck to stray into our back yards. And conversation. What would happen to civilized conversation in your totally honest world? We'd have no need for wit, for clever turns of phrase, or for elevated discussions of philosophy or ideas, only boring descriptions of the horse's twisted bowel and Uncle Martin's bladder troubles. Well, what can I expect? I know the kind of background you come from. You never knew ideas existed before you met me."

By this time Evan was beginning to slur his s's, and his eyes had taken on a glazed look. My anger faded. I had seen plenty of drunken men in my childhood, and I knew that he wasn't responsible for what he was saying.

I turned to the window that faced south.

"Oh, look, you can see the boat basin from here," I said. "Tom's boat is—there it is, the fourth one from the left, near that little cabin cruiser. And look, there's Tom, walking along the dock."

"What did you see down in that little cabin?" Evan blurted out.

I looked around at him. Slouched low in his chair, he was star-

ing at a pair of binoculars that sat on the table a short distance
from his hand. The glass he was holding wavered, sloshing
bourbon onto his sleeve.

"You were watching Tom and me, weren't you? Spying on
us. Oh, Evan. That's silly. We weren't doing anything wrong."

"Get out," he rasped. "Go away and leave me alone. I'm tired
of you and your talk. Talk, talk, talk. I'm sick to death of talk.
Damned waste of time."

I picked up my camera. "That's the first truthful thing you've
said tonight. Good night, Evan."

"We'll walk today, shall we?" Evan said at breakfast the next
morning. Normally, we would have gone up to the tower room
for an hour or two of Greek—Evan's project for the summer
was to have me translate Plato's *Lysis* from the original.

I slung my camera around my neck and we set off. We
tramped until we reached the southernmost spit of the Cape.
Monomoy Island was invisible behind a morning haze. The
ocean and the sky merged into a single gray entity broken only
by an occasional glimmer of white foam.

"I want to take your picture."

"You've taken thousands of pictures of me," Evan protested.
"You know what I look like. Don't waste your film."

"No, this one is going to be special," I promised. "Now sit on
that rock and look out at the ocean."

Evan knocked the cold ashes out of his pipe and clambered
wearily over the boulders to the perch I had indicated. "You're
getting very brazen these days, Theodora," he grumbled. "Always ordering people around. Sit here. Do this. Hold that. I've
been meaning to speak to you about it."

"Really, Evan?" I fiddled with an adjustment. "Am I becoming obnoxious?" The wind whipped my skirt around my legs.
As usual, my feet were bare. I hated wearing shoes in the summertime.

"Thoroughly. You are as obnoxious as you are ugly."

I grinned at him over the top of my camera, then I ordered him to hold still. Just as I was about to take the picture, a ship passed behind Evan's head. I told Evan to relax. "We have to wait. Otherwise it will look like the ship is coming out of your ear."

"I knew I had bats in my belfry, but not ships." Evan gnawed his pipe. In the throes of a hangover, he looked rumpled and exhausted. "I want to talk to you about something, Dory. I've been thinking that it might be a good idea for you to spend the next year at The Frasier School. Miss Frasier is willing to have you back. We both agree that a year in a place like hers would be an excellent preparation for college. You'd make friends—something you haven't done since you've been living with me—and it would round out the gaps in your education. I'll be the first to admit that my approach to teaching has been more idiosyncratic than thorough. I've stressed the arts, which appeal to me, and I've neglected the sciences, which do not. You really ought to learn a bit of calculus and trigonometry, you know. These days no man wants to marry a woman who can't understand sines and cosines." He managed a weak smile.

"You—you want me to go away," I said faintly. "But I don't understand, Evan. Why? What have I done? Is it because of yesterday? I didn't mean to make you angry, but I can't seem to help it lately. Everything I do—"

"You haven't done anything except grow up, Dory." He sighed. "You knew it couldn't go on forever, just the two of us, teacher and pupil. It isn't right, it isn't natural. You need to meet people your own age."

I said, "I don't need any more people my own age. I've already met Tom and Susie."

"Well, you like them, don't you?"

"They're all right," I shrugged. "But neither of them are as smart or as interesting as you are."

"*Is,*" he corrected me. " 'Neither of them is.' Thank you for the compliment. I'm sorry if this has taken you by surprise, but I've been thinking about it for a long time. You know, I've spent many hours these past four years thinking about you. I don't regret those years, not a bit, but it's time I gave some thought to other things, don't you agree? It will seem strange at first, for both of us. But we need to get used to doing without each other."

He turned his face seaward. I moved around so that I could see his expression. He looked so lonely sitting on that rock, so vulnerable. I didn't know what to say to help him; I didn't know what to do.

I balanced myself precariously between two rocks on the jetty below him. The sea surged and splashed beneath me, tugging at my feet, soaking my skirt.

"Evan, look at me." The diffused light touched his face with soft shadows that emphasized the sadness and desolation in his eyes. I clicked the shutter. "I had to take that picture." I wiped my cheeks. My face was wet, awash with tears or sea spray, I couldn't tell which. "You looked so—so far away. Isn't that silly?" I started to laugh, and my laughter quickly became choked sobs. "My heart is breaking and what do I do? I take a stupid picture."

Evan stretched out his hand and pulled me up beside him. Weeping, I huddled against him. He held me as a child for the last time.

"We'll still be friends," he promised. "You'll come and see me on weekends and holidays. You'll come often at first, until you've made other friends. You'll see, Dory, it won't be so bad. You and Susie Fairbank will both be seniors, so it isn't as though you'll be totally among strangers. Miss Frasier has all sorts of contacts in the colleges and universities around. She'll steer you in the right direction, I promise you."

"But I don't want to go to college," I mumbled into the coarse knit of his sweater. "I just want to take pictures, and to be with you."

"I don't know any law that says photographers have to be ignorant hermits," he said. "You need to see the world, to find new things to photograph. Surely you're getting tired of this old face? Come on, cheer up. It's time we started back. As I recall, young Tom wanted to take you sailing today."

"I don't want to sail, with Tom or anybody else," I said. "I just want to stay with you. What's wrong with that? I won't be any trouble, Evan, I promise. I'll even learn calculus, if that's what you want." I looked up at him.

Taking my hand, Evan led me over the rocks, down to the beach. "I want you to have a full, rich life, Dory. I want you to meet lots of fine young men, to choose a husband from among them, to marry and raise a family."

I dug my bare toes into the sand. "I won't do it. I won't marry anyone."

"Suit yourself," Evan sighed. "Lots of old maids lead full, rich lives. Look at Miss Frasier. Maybe she'll let you stay on at the school as Mistress of Photography."

I turned away. "I wish you wouldn't tease me, Evan. This isn't funny."

"I know. I'm sorry. But I'm trying to make it easier for myself, too, can't you see that? I'll miss you terribly, Dory. You know what I was thinking about back there? Elf Hill. It will seem so empty and silent without you. I'll have to sell the place, or go away for a while. I don't want to be alone there."

"No, Evan, you can't," I cried. "Please don't sell it. I won't—I won't have any place to come home to."

"All right," he said. "I didn't really want to get rid of it. But I'll have to find something to do with my evenings, while Fiona is at the theater. And the mornings, before she wakes up." He gazed out at the ocean. "I'll get myself a mistress or a dog or a drinking buddy—somebody," he said under his breath. "But I will not be alone."

It sounded like a vow, a promise he was making to himself. Throwing myself at him, I hugged him around the waist. "Oh, Evan, I'll miss you, too. Terribly. Terribly."

Grasping my shoulders, he held me away from him. "No

more of that," he said. "You're a woman now. What is appropriate behavior for a young girl is not appropriate for a young lady
about to embark on a new life and a new career. No more lively
and uninhibited demonstrations of affection, if you please. Save
them for some lucky young man like Tom Fairbank."

I felt hurt and confused, but I complied with this new order.
The physical distance between us widened as we walked back to
the house.

We might have been solitary strollers on the beach, two
strangers coincidentally heading in the same direction, who had
no reason to speak or so much as look at one another.

12   Dec, 2019

Boyd met me at the train station in his old Model A. "The
Rolls is down in New York, pickin' up some more fancy
movie folk from Hollywood." He gave me an apologetic wink as
he piled my suitcases into the trunk. "Hope you don't mind ri-
din' home in this old piece of junk."

Filling my lungs with country air, I looked around at the tiny
rural station, badly in need of paint, the daisies pushing up
through the cinders alongside the tracks, the gnarled pines that
leaned over the road, the wooded hills beyond. "I'm so happy to
be here, I'd ride to Elf Hill in a dog sled or a push cart," I said.
"How are the children, and Mrs. Boyd?"

The members of Boyd's family were all fine. The butler
Hanes and Johanna and the girls were fine, too. "Miss Fiona,
she's been in a real good mood since she made that new movie.
She's gonna be makin' another picture soon, goin' back out to
Hollywood in September. Good place for her," Boyd muttered,
and added hastily, "I mean, you can't make movies here in Connecticut."

I climbed into the front seat. Boyd pushed my door closed before climbing in on the other side. "And Mr. Evan?" I asked. "How is he?"

"Oh, Mr. Evan's okay, I guess." Over the grinding of the starter, Boyd's tone sounded disturbingly vague. "I get the feelin' that he didn't take to Hollywood much. He sure was glad to get back here."

"I can imagine." We rode past small fields bounded by low granite walls and orchards heavy with summer fruit. I had never seen Evan's California house, but I couldn't imagine that any place could be so beautiful and perfect as Elf Hill.

"Mr. Evan says it's not a real world, out there. I reckon I could'a told him that 'fore he left. For one thing, they don't have no Depression in Hollywood. Everybody's a millionaire. They all have swimmin' pools and palm trees. Lots of folks in these parts wouldn't mind being poor if they could do it where it was warm come Febr'ary."

We turned into the drive at Elf Hill. At the bottom of the slope on my left I could see the pond, its surface green with algae and lily pads. The little cave that had been formed by felled saplings and honeysuckle vines, where I had hidden on that memorable day, had long since been cleared away. I could picture the woods where Evan and I had found the bloodroot: deep green, cool and dark and heavy with leaves.

The house appeared on the knoll just ahead of us. Long and white, roofed in gray slate, it presented its simplest and most appealing aspect to the arriving visitor. Over the years the plain colonial rectangle had swelled with successively smaller additions, so that the original structure resembled a mother hen stretching her wings over a brood of chicks that spanned several generations.

Heedless of Boyd's good-humored scolding, I hopped out of the car before it came to a full stop. Hanes, stiff and correct in a white summer jacket, permitted himself a small smile as he opened the front door.

"Everyone is on the terrace near the pool, Miss. May I say, welcome home?"

2019

"Thank you, Hanes." I didn't go up to my room to bathe or change, even though I had spent the entire day sweating on trains pulled by coal-fired locomotives. More than anything, I wanted to see Evan. I ran through the cheerful downstairs sitting rooms and went out through open French doors to the terrace.

A dozen people lounged in chairs around a vast umbrella-shaded table. They were just finishing lunch, flicking their cigarette ashes into the melting remains of strawberry ice in crystal goblets. A few heads turned as I came out of the house. I saw Evan standing at the portable bar, his back to me. I started toward him.

"Well, look who's here," Max Feinblatt shouted. "Come over and say hello, Teddy."

Casting a longing look at Evan, who hadn't yet noticed my arrival, I approached the table. "Fiona's niece," Max announced to the other guests, some of whom I recognized but had never met: film people.

Fiona, sleek and cool in white linen, bobbed her floppy-brimmed straw hat in a jerky movement that the others might have mistaken for a greeting, but which I recognized as a shudder of disgust. I kissed Max and his wife, Vera, who told me that I was looking too thin for good health. Max introduced the rest of the company: a gaunt British character actor who made a career out of playing butlers and villains; Fiona's first cinematic leading man, a handsome near-midget who reputedly played his love scenes standing on specially constructed stilts; a striking dark-haired woman whose lips were puckered in a perpetual simper; a balding script writer, lurking behind glasses so thick and dark that they made him appear blind; and "the man who made Fiona's last picture a hit," her director, Hugo de Graaf.

I nodded politely to all. The leading man said with a touch of bitchiness, "My God, Fiona, who would have thought you were old enough to have a niece her age?"

Fiona shot him a look intended to shave several more inches

Dec.
2019

off his height. "My sister was a sexual prodigy, darling. She was many years older than I, and she married young, didn't she, Dory? Run along now, dear. I'm sure Evan's dying to see you. If he's able to see, that is."

The character actor snickered. Hugo de Graaf jammed an obscenely large cigar between his lips. "Anybody have a match? Christ, it's hot out here."

Evan was watching Jackson, the black barman, polish martini glasses. He turned when I spoke to him, blinked several times and squinted hard. Then his face creased into a slow smile.

"Hello, Dory." He straightened up and took one uncertain step toward me. My heart constricted as I saw the truth of Fiona's barb: Evan was drunk. "Forgot you were coming today. Did you get here all right?"

"Yes, no trouble. Boyd met me at the station."

"Good. Good." Evan rubbed his forehead, as if he were trying to recapture a thought that had flown. "It's already the end of August, isn't it? You've been in school rather a long time."

"Don't you remember, Evan? I wrote to you that I was staying to take a summer course with a professor who's going on sabbatical next year. Elizabethan drama. I didn't have any reason to come home in June. You weren't going to be here."

Evan grunted and turned back to the bar. "Fiona was finishing her film. Couldn't leave until it was finished. Jackson, fix Miss Theodora a drink or something, will you?"

"No, thank you, Jackson." Seeing Evan sway slightly, I moved closer to him. I wanted to put my arms around him, but I didn't dare. Except for crisp and formal handshakes upon meeting and parting, Evan and I had hardly touched each other since that day on the beach at Cape Cod. "Why don't we go inside, Evan? It's awfully hot out here. I have some new pictures I want to show you."

"Good idea," he nodded. "Cooler inside."

Evan's study, at the other end of the house from the pool and terrace, felt more like Connecticut than Hollywood. Thick stone walls insulated us from the heat. Outside the window a lusty mockingbird did his best to drown out the shrill poolside chatter of Fiona and her guests.

Evan sank down into the old leather chair behind his desk. I drew up a hard chair and sat directly opposite him. I wanted to study his face, to measure the effects of time and drink and loneliness.

My bold scrutiny must have made him uncomfortable, for he twisted around, turning his back to the light and throwing his features into shadow.

Hanes came in, carrying a plate of sandwiches and a pitcher of lemonade. "A light lunch, Miss Theodora. Johanna thought you might be hungry after your long train ride."

"Yes, I'm famished. Thank you, Hanes." I glanced at Evan. "I think I'd like some coffee, too, if you don't mind."

"Of course, Miss." Hanes went out.

I removed a linen napkin from a silver ring and spread it over my lap. Comforts that might have seemed extraordinary in other places were part of life here. As I ate, I talked about the last semester of my sophomore year at Radcliffe, the courses I had taken, the new friends I'd made.

"I saw Tom Fairbank last May. It was sad. He's working as an orderly at Massachusetts General, trying to earn enough money to finish medical school. He had to quit for a while, you know, after his father died."

"Um, I remember. Ed Fairbank made quite a splash on Wall Street, all right." Evan gave a grim little laugh. "Sorry, Dory. Poor joke. You see Tom often, then?"

"No, not really. I just happened to meet him by chance one day. Susie's married. Their mother still isn't herself, Tom says. She never got over the shock."

"Don't know why Ed had to kill himself," Evan sighed. "He could have brazened it out. He wasn't the only man in the country who went broke. Trouble with men like Ed Fairbank is pride." Evan sipped from the tumbler he had brought into the house with him. "Too much pride is a terrible thing. Look at Max. When the market went into a tailspin, he was left without a penny to his name. What did he do? He asked me for a loan, then he went out to the West Coast, opened an office, and set himself up as an agent. Before you know it, he's on top again. Good old Max. Didn't let his pride strangle him."

I finished my second sandwich and filled two cups with the coffee Hanes had brought. I set one cup on the desk in front of Evan, who looked up at me and grinned. "Trying to sober me up? It won't work. I haven't been sober in months. Years, really."

Johanna had told me that on the day I left Elf Hill for my year of finishing at The Frasier School, Evan took a bottle of bourbon up to his room and locked the door. He had stayed there for three days, warding off the loneliness before it had a chance to set in.

"Oh, Evan, why?" I asked softly. "Why?"

Evan lifted his shoulders. "I don't know. Boredom, I guess. After you left, I should have tried to do something serious for myself. Like write a book, paint a picture. But I don't have any talent, Dory. Anything I did would be third-rate, and I couldn't stand that. The world has enough bad art and third-rate literature already. I guess I've been critical too long. I know very well that my work wouldn't meet my own high standards."

"I shouldn't have gone away." I knotted my fists. "I shouldn't have listened to you."

"It would have happened anyway." Evan emptied his glass and looked around for more bourbon. The decanter on his desk was empty. He seemed annoyed. "I was already working up to a pretty high level of dissipation before you left. Do you think I like having you see me like this? I'm glad I sent you away, Dory. You're doing so well. Proud of you. Still taking pictures?"

"Yes. I brought some of the best ones to show you. Would you like to see them now?" I started to rise.

"No, no, thank you, Dory. Later. Later."

He couldn't even pretend to be interested. Neither had he shown much joy in seeing me. Alcohol had blocked all feeling, pleasure as well as pain—which is just what he wanted.

I sat back. "The yearbook committee at Radcliffe has hired me to do the portraits of the seniors next year. I'm charging them less than any of the professionals in the area, and I'll still make a small profit. I've arranged with the boys at the *Crimson* to let me use their darkroom. It's fairly well equipped, and I won't have to buy anything except paper and chemicals. I sold some photographs to the *Boston Globe* this spring. Local stuff, students-at-play sort of thing. I had other pictures they didn't want that I thought were better. You know, Evan, I still can't believe that I can make money taking pictures. It's always been more like play than work."

"Lucky." Evan gave me a bleary smile. "I envy anyone who can make a living doing work he loves. You. Fiona. Maybe I just haven't found my metier yet. I can't imagine how it's managed to elude me. God knows, I've tried everything under the sun: poetry, cars, music, golf. I even spent a year at an art school in Paris when I was your age, did you know that? I've written bad poetry, modeled lumpy sculpture, composed wretched sonatas. I suppose the only thing I'm really good at is spending money. Odd, isn't it? I neglected my investments as rigorously as Ed Fairbank pampered his, and in the end, I didn't loose a cent and he lost everything. I was a success as a producer of plays because I was smart enough to let Max Feinblatt do my thinking for me. I've made some good purchases: paintings, books, antiques. I suppose I even bought Fiona. It was the only way I could get her. Really, I wonder sometimes why she continues to put up with me."

"She stays with you because you're good and wise and wonderful," I said fiercely. "She couldn't find another man like you in the whole world and she knows it."

"Bless you, sweet child." Evan fingered his empty bourbon glass. He hadn't touched his coffee. "You're good for my ego,

Dory. You always have been. You never saw the vulnerable, frightened man behind the smooth, polished facade. You really believed in me, didn't you? I am sorry to disillusion you. One of the prices of growing up, I'm afraid. Disillusionment." He stood, holding onto the back of his chair for support. "I think I'll go lie down for a while. I usually take a nap at this time. Got into the habit in California. Siesta, you know. I wanted to be fresh and bright for Fiona when she came home from the studio. But she was usually too tired to notice."

He walked toward the door. He moved slowly, with the heavy deliberateness of the inebriated or the handicapped, for whom each step is a triumph. I followed, and watched as he ascended the stairs.

When he was out of sight, I touched my face. My cheeks were wet with tears.

Our numbers were enlarged that evening by the arrival of some theater people from New York, and the head of Fiona's studio from Hollywood. Evan came downstairs at seven o'clock wearing black tie and white dinner jacket. Except for his pink-rimmed eyes, he looked perfectly sober and subdued. He asked Jackson for a glass of seltzer water, then joined me on the terrace, away from the music and babble in the drawing room. I had changed out of my travel-stained suit into a long, fitted frock made of white dotted swiss.

"Sorry about this afternoon," Evan said. "I wasn't myself. I really had forgotten you were coming, or I would have made an effort to behave. You see"—he raised his glass of seltzer to me—"I'm trying to redeem myself in your eyes."

"You don't have to do that," I said. "No matter what you do, I still think you're better than all the rest of these people lumped together."

"Really, better than Mr. Big and Hugo de Graaf? You flatter me, Dory. I'm sorry you don't like my new Hollywood friends."

"Excuse me." I snapped a white rose off the old climber that grew on a trellis on the south wall of the house. "I didn't know they were your friends."

Evan laughed. "I doubt that most of them even know who I am, even though they're guests in my house. I admit, when I'm out in Hollywood, I'm not worth knowing. I can't join in their studio gossip, I won't go to their parties, and I refuse to take a screen test. Someone actually suggested that I do that, can you believe it? Evan Bradford, idol of the silver screen. You should have heard Fiona laugh."

"I think you'd be wonderful in the movies," I said. Evan made a derisive noise. "No, it's true. You're not patent-leather handsome, like that stupid little actor inside. Men like him always make me uncomfortable, as though they'd rather be watching themselves in the mirror. And you do photograph well, Evan. I ought to know."

The photograph of him I cherished most was the one I had taken that awful day at Cape Cod, when he had told me I must go away. Hunched on the rock, the wind ruffling his fair hair, he looked lost and forlorn, a shipwrecked sailor marooned on a rocky and forbidding coast. I carried a small print of that picture in my wallet. Whenever I looked at it, I felt sad all over again.

"Now you're trying to butter me up, and you're succeeding. For your next birthday, I'll buy you a car. Would you like that? A little red sporty model, like the kind the movie stars drive. You should see them speeding along under the palm trees on Hollywood Boulevard, sounding their little horns, converging with sporty little crashes at intersections. The blond star leaps out of her little red sports car and rushes over to the brunette star, who has leaped out of her little red sports car. The two of them glare at each other for a moment. You wonder, what will these two goddesses do? Will they hurl thunderbolts? Will they exchange sneers and walk regally away from each other? No, my dear. They roll up their sleeves, curl their little hands into fists, stamp their tiny high-heeled feet, and start screaming at each other, using the most vulgar language you have ever heard—which I shall not repeat. Don't laugh, Dory. I actually saw it happen. The studios paid thousands to keep it out of the newspapers."

A few people had gathered around Evan as he told his story. The simpering femme fatale I had met earlier slipped her hand around Evan's arm and drew him away with her to another corner of the terrace.

"He'd better watch out. That woman has the strength of a boa constrictor and the appetite of a whale."

I looked around. Hugo de Graaf stood just behind me. He was massive, not fat, but broad-shouldered and burly, with a squared-off beard and an unruly mop of grizzled reddish hair. In his huge paw the martini glass he cradled looked absurdly small and fragile. Only his eyes didn't quite match his teddy bear softness. They were pale blue, keen and intelligent.

"You're the niece," he said. His voice was deep, a low boom roughened by whiskey and cigars. "Edwina, was it?"

"Theodora."

"Hell of a name." Hugo looked around. "Christ, when's chow? My goddamned stomach's about to cave in."

"I'll get you some canapes."

"Don't bother." Hugo looked gloomy. "They'd only make it worse. Don't want to get any action going down there until I have something substantial to give it. Hope Fiona has a decent cook. Can't take what people here call French cuisine. One cutlet as big as my thumb, swimming in a tablespoon of greasy sauce—Jesus. Couldn't keep a canary alive on that crap."

"I think Delilah's roasting a moose," I said with utmost seriousness. "She stuffed it with a whole pig, which she stuffed with a turkey, which was stuffed with cornbread and sausage."

Hugo gave me a dark look. "Not funny," he said. "You should hear what that's doing to my stomach." Right on cue, his hard, rounded belly rumbled indelicately.

"Sorry."

"Haven't eaten moose in years," Hugo sighed wistfully.

"Damned good meat if you prepare it properly. Not as tender as gazelle, but a better flavor."

I stole a look at Evan and the dark-haired woman, whose gown of tangerine-colored crepe de chine threatened to ignite at any moment. She moved her face close to Evan's cheek, practically touching his ear with the tip of her nose. I gnawed my lower lip.

"Don't worry about her," Hugo said. "She's only doing that because she knows I'm watching."

"Why?"

"Wants to make me jealous. We're getting divorced."

"Oh." I looked around. "She's your wife?"

"Not for long." Hugo's beard tilted slightly. He was grinning. "Stupid bitch. Boring as hell. Should have learned my lesson about actresses. They're all alike. Don't stop acting when the camera's turned off. I thought she had a brain, but she was only pretending. Thinks she's getting a nice fat settlement. Doesn't know that I hired a detective. I got the goods on her, all right. Whoops, look at that."

Fiona swept across the terrace toward Evan and the other woman. Slipping her hand around Evan's elbow, she gave Hugo's wife a dazzling smile and bore Evan off in triumph. Hugo's almost-ex-wife ground her teeth audibly.

"The bitch hates Fiona." Hugo rubbed his hands with glee. "She wanted that part in Fiona's picture; would have killed for it. Almost did. Thought I'd give it to her because I was directing and I was her husband. Ha. I knew she was no damned good. Fiona's the only one who could have done that part. Lousy story, but she made it live. Damned good actress."

"I know," I mumbled. I wished someone else would come up to us so that I could excuse myself and move away. As an article of faith, I made it a point not to like anyone who adored Fiona.

"A bitch," Hugo said, taking a fresh martini off a passing tray, "but a damned good actress. You act?"

"Heavens, no," I laughed. "I've never had any interest in acting."

This book has 459 pages

"Come on, every girl in this country wants to be a movie star. Even the ugly ones. And you're not ugly." He gave my figure a quick, professional appraisal. I could see him making notes in his head: hair needs color and curl; wide mouth and long nose, could be corrected with makeup; good eyes. A big girl, not delicate like Fiona. Some problems with wardrobe. "Bet you photograph pretty well."

"I do not. My hair and eyes and skin are all the same color: mud. No contrasts at all. Besides, I hate having my picture taken." I grimaced. "I'd much rather do the photographing."

Hugo squinted. "I remember now. You're the kid that takes the pictures. Evan told me. He's proud of you. Still working at it?"

"As much as I can, between schoolwork and everything else."

"What kind of camera are you using?"

I told him about my trusty Leica and the new Rolleiflex I had bought in the spring. We spent the next few minutes in a purely technical discussion about the advances the Germans had made in photography in recent years. After some hesitation, I said, "I brought some of my latest prints home with me. Would you—I don't suppose you'd care to see them, would you?"

To my surprise, Hugo said, "Sure. I used to be a pretty good cameraman myself, before I got into directing."

I led him through the house to Evan's study, where I had left the portfolio containing my most recent prints. I spread them out on the desk while Hugo made himself comfortable in Evan's chair.

"I went down to Lowell, Massachusetts, one weekend this summer," I told him. "It's an industrial town. A lot of the factories have closed because of the Depression. The workers don't have any place else to go. Besides, most of them have lived in Lowell all their lives. They have children and families and parents in that town, and it would be impossible for them to pull up stakes and go elsewhere. But their faces—look at their faces, Mr. de Graaf."

Seeing the pictures again brought back the sadness and poi-

2 0 / 9

gnancy of that visit. I had seen men and women whose gaunt features already revealed the urgent tug of starvation; old women who seemed to have retreated into their memories; children who looked lost and frightened, even though they were huddled against their parents' bodies. I had a photograph of two boys sitting outside the walls of an idle shoe factory, their own shoes in tatters. And one of a Catholic priest, frayed and harried, an aged shepherd worn out with worrying about his flock.

"I showed them to the editor at the *Boston Globe*," I said as Hugo turned over the last of the photos. "He said he couldn't use them because they didn't tell people anything they didn't already know."

"Damned idiot." Hugo studied a photograph of an empty warehouse, its windows shattered and dark, vacant like sightless eyes. "Like all the rest, doesn't want to face up to the mess this country's in. These are damned good, Alice. Have you shown them to anybody in New York yet? Look, I know the top man at *Mode*: Gabe Rosati. My name will get you in to see him, and these will do the rest."

"That's very kind of you, Mr. de Graaf, but I still have two years to go before I graduate from college."

"What in hell are you doing at Radcliffe? I didn't know they taught photography there. Least they didn't when I was at Harvard."

"They still don't. College was Evan's idea. I'm rounding out my education."

"Damned waste of time," Hugo grunted. "I dropped it after six months. Is that old fart Harris still teaching Chaucer? He was the best man in the place. The others didn't know their elbows from their—never mind." Hooking his hands behind his head, Hugo leaned back in Evan's chair, which groaned alarmingly. "Is taking pictures just a hobby with you, or are you really serious about it?"

"I love it more than anything else in the world," I said. "I don't want to do anything else. When I don't have my camera with me, I feel naked, like part of my body is missing. I can't look at things properly. I can't see. I feel like a nearsighted person without glasses. Do you know what I mean?" I had to grope for words. I had never spoken of my feelings about photography before, not even to Evan. "So many people go through life without looking at things. And if you don't see things, you can pretend they don't exist, can't you?"

I picked up a print of a girl I had met in Lowell. She had turned to prostitution after losing her job at the mill. At first she had been hostile, refusing to let me photograph her until I gave her a little money. She sat on a worn stoop, my miserable two dollars clutched in her hand. My camera had captured the cold fear behind her sneering smile.

"If you don't see how people are suffering, you can pretend that things like starvation and pain and ugliness don't exist. I like things to be honest, Mr. de Graaf. I'm not crazy about movies or plays or novels, because they're full of lies. But people believe in them as if they were real, and after a while they can't tell the truth and the lies apart. I think that the people who make movies are cruel and dishonest. They never think about what effect they're having on people's—" I noticed that Hugo was grinning, and I closed my mouth with a snap. "I'm sorry. I shouldn't have said that."

"Why not? It's what you think, isn't it? Go on, kid. What's so bad about us Hollywood types? Don't you think we're performing a service? People like to get away from their troubles now and then, Annie. If they don't go to movies or plays, they go to church, or they drink, or they get themselves a little loving. Anything to forget the real world for a while. Is that so bad?"

"It's bad because the situations you depict are false," I said. "You never put hungry children in movies, or old men with no teeth. The world you depict doesn't have anything to do with war or politics or any of the really important things in life. The stories you tell are silly, misleading. People expect their lives to have the same happy endings that they've seen on the screen, but they're always disappointed, aren't they? They expect love to be happy ever after, and marriage to be like a game."

Hugo grunted. "Hell, if I were married to a woman with a face like a horse, I'd be glad to close my eyes and make believe I was with somebody like Fiona. What's wrong with that?"

I started to gather up my photographs. "It's false, that's what's wrong with it. If you knew what Fiona was really like, you'd be happy to be married to a horse-faced woman, especially if she had a kind heart, and if she loved you. Fiona can't love anybody. She pretends to be nice and funny and warm, but it's not real. Remember what you said about actresses, that they don't stop acting when the camera's not watching? Well, that's Fiona. She never stops."

"Is that so?" Fiona stood in the open door, her arms braced on the frame. She looked like a beautiful martyr nailed to an invisible cross. Her gown was blue silk, with billowing sleeves that were slashed between the shoulder and the wrist so that they hung from her arms in airy festoons. The bodice dipped to the waist in the front and the back; only an emerald and diamond brooch between her breasts preserved her modesty.

As she advanced into the room, her hips and shoulders moved with silent strength. Hugo murmured, "Reminds me of tigers I've known, just before they pounce."

"So I can't love anybody," Fiona echoed softly. "It's all pretending. I don't stop acting. Interesting, that you should say that to Hugo. You've never had the guts to say it to my face."

"Now, look, Fiona—"

"Shut up, Hugo. I'm not talking to you. I'm addressing myself to poor little Dory here. I'm extremely interested in what she has to say about me. I never suspected she felt that way."

I faced her. "I never pretended to love you. Why should I? You never pretended to care about me, not from the very first day."

To my surprise, I was unafraid. Strange.

Now that the scene that had been building between us for all these years was finally taking place, I felt strong and confident.

Hugo stood up. "Whoops. Sounds like a good time to make a graceful exit." He lumbered out.

I braced my arms on the desk. "You've just lost your audience, Fiona. Don't bother to throw a tantrum for my benefit. I've seen too many of them to be impressed."

"You know"—Fiona narrowed her eyes at me—"sometimes I think you're a better actress than I am. So sweet and innocent, so damned grateful for the least little thing that Evan does for you. Now you're trying it out on Hugo. What can you possibly want from him, I wonder? You already have Evan wrapped around your little finger. I heard him offering you a car."

"He was joking. I don't want—"

"The hell you don't. You've done pretty well, haven't you? You've had ocean crossings, trips to Paris and Rome and Vienna. Expensive toys, cameras, darkroom equipment. Clothes. Horses. Riding lessons, tennis lessons, golf lessons, languages. Radcliffe. Dates with rich boys, who can't look down their long noses at you because they don't know who you are. Evan Bradford's ward? Fine and dandy. You must be a proper little lady, then. I wonder what they'd do if they found out about your mother?"

I laughed, a single short bark. "What are you trying to do now, Fiona, work a little blackmail? Don't bother. If I liked a boy well enough, I'd tell him the truth about myself."

"I'll just bet you would. Your little eyes would fill with tears, your hands would tremble, your voice would shake—I know just how you'd play that scene, dearie. In a few minutes, those boys would be in tears themselves, putting their big strong arms around you, telling you it didn't matter. Poor little Dory. Then you'd tell them about your mean old Aunt Fiona, wouldn't you? How she didn't want you. How she's never cared for you. My God, how you've suffered! No love, only luxury."

179

2019

"I never asked for any of this," I said.

"Maybe you never asked for it, but you're not about to give it up, are you? What if you could turn the clock back and make a choice? Which would you take, I wonder? Life with Mary and her caveman and all the squalid pleasures that Monkey Gulch, Colorado, had to offer? Or all this?" Fiona waved her hand. "You know as well as I do that you've got it made here, honey. You're not about to head back to Monkey Gulch or to any other slum. You'd hate it. You wouldn't last a week in that filth. You know, the best thing that ever happened to you was when Mary stabbed her lover and then tied that rope around her own neck. As much as you'd hate to admit it, you're glad she did it. Aren't you? You're glad she's dead."

"That's a lie," I cried. "I'd give anything to bring her back, anything."

Fiona took a cigarette from the malachite box on Evan's desk and hovered over the built-in lighter. "You like being Evan's white-haired little rich girl, don't you? I don't blame you. I like the lap of luxury just fine myself. But the big difference between us, kiddo, is that I work for what I have. I work damned hard. I started working the minute I came to New York, and I haven't let up since. But you, you've had it all handed to you. You haven't earned any of this. But that hasn't kept you from taking it, has it?"

Silver spoon

Evan came in and closed the door. "Hugo sent me in to prevent bloodshed."

"No blood." Fiona didn't take her eyes off me. "We Randall women are just having a long overdue discussion about rights and responsibilities. I was about to ask Dory here how much she thinks she's taken from you in the past seven years. How much have you spent on her, I wonder? Add it up, Evan. How much has it cost you to feed, clothe, entertain, and educate this kid? Five thousand? That's what you spend on her in a single year, I bet. Tell me, Dory, when was the last time you looked into your closet and couldn't find anything to wear? When was the last

Dec
2019

time you felt hungry, and didn't have something brought to you by a butler or a maid?"

"Please, Fiona, it's my money and I don't begrudge—"

"I'm not talking about whose money it is," Fiona said, "only about where it's going and what you're getting for it. Do you know what a parasite is, Dory dear?"

"Fiona, don't—"

Fiona ignored Evan's protestations. "Come on, tell me. What's a parasite?"

Tight-jawed, I answered her. "A parasite is a creature that attaches itself to another creature, and lives off it."

"Good girl. All that education hasn't been a total waste, I'm glad to see. Would you define yourself as a parasite?"

"What about you?" I countered. "You married Evan for his money, everybody knows that."

Fiona shook her head. "No, not quite. Let's get our facts straight. This baby gives as well as takes." She tapped at the brooch on her bosom with a long, scarlet-tipped finger. "You don't believe me? Do you know what Evan got when he married me? He got an identity. Instead of being a rich nobody, he became Fiona Randall's husband. He got the satisfaction of telling himself and whoever else would listen that he pulled me out of the chorus of *Girls in a Whirl,* that he was the first one to recognize my talent, that he was the one who groomed me for stardom. Not a bad life's work, when you think about it. And that's not all. He gets sex whenever he wants it, which is surprisingly often. Don't let his puritanical posturing fool you. From the waist down, he's like every other man. Ask him. He'll tell you that I'm not selfish. When he wants to screw, I screw. I am his wife, after all."

"Fiona, for God's sake," Evan moaned. He sank down onto the long tufted leather chesterfield that occupied the wall opposite his desk.

"Don't worry, Evan, Dory doesn't have virgin ears. It's been a long time since she was a virgin, remember? And so you see,

2019

Dory, being a wife is a whole different thing from being a para-site—excuse me, perhaps I should say 'ward.' As far as I'm con-cerned, I don't get something for nothing from Evan Bradford. I'm still earning my keep, making my way."

"You're such a liar," I cried. "You're just using him, every-body knows it—"

"That's enough!" Fiona angrily stubbed out her cigarette. "Let's go to the real point of this discussion. I am sick and tired of having you underfoot, Dory dear. Yes, I know, lately we've been busy in Hollywood and you've been away at school, but it seems that we can't make a trip back to the East Coast without running into you. Mostly, I don't like the way you and Evan gang up on me and my friends when you're together. You de-spise us, and you make that perfectly clear. I find that embar-rassing and annoying, and I want it to stop. I don't like the way you attach yourself to people like Max Feinblatt and Hugo de Graaf. After a few minutes with you, they start looking at me funny, like I had horns and a tail. Now you may think that I'm just jealous of you. After all, you're young and you're smart and you're not exactly ugly. Old Fiona's suffering by comparison, you might say. Well, let me tell you, I am not worried about competition from you, my dear. I can hold my own against any woman on this planet, young or old, when it comes to looks or brains or talent. But honest sinners like me have a hard time de-fending ourselves against imputations from phony saints like you. You've been slandering me, child, whether you know it or not. I can't bring myself to pretend that you and I are bosom pals, and when people see how sweet and tender you are, they start to wonder what's wrong with me. I come out looking like a villain, which is not a role that I enjoy. How many of my friends besides Hugo have you talked to about me the way you did to-night? How many of them have heard you say that I can't feel anything, that I'm always acting, that I'm a fake and a fraud?"

"I have never spoken about you like that before," I said. "I shouldn't have done it tonight, Fiona. It just happened. We were talking about movies and being honest."

Fiona moved her head from side to side. "No good. I don't believe you. And besides, that doesn't undo the harm you've done already. I'm sick of looking at you and Evan with your heads together. Evan was your first success, wasn't he, Dory? He never knew what a really cruel and heartless bitch I was until you came along. I was supposed to clasp you to my bosom, a child I'd never seen, just because you were my sister's kid. But I didn't want anything to do with her while she was alive, and I certainly didn't want anything to do with you after she was dead. And because I didn't try to pretend, I found myself cast as the wicked witch."

"Fiona, that's not true," Evan protested. "We never thought of you—"

"I tried to behave myself." Fiona lit another cigarette. "I kept my mouth shut. You two went your own way, and I went mine. For a while I really believed that something must be wrong with me. Everybody likes kids, right? And who can resist an orphan, for God's sake? I was glad that Evan had something to keep him busy. At least he wasn't always following me around with his tongue hanging out of his mouth. But you're not a kid anymore, Dory. You're all grown up, and that puts a whole different complexion on things. I could share my house and my life and my husband with a child, but I'll be damned if I'll share them with another woman."

"Oh, really, Fiona, Dory's only twenty years old."

"Her mother was fifteen when she got herself pregnant and ran off with Frank Lowery," Fiona said. "Forgive me, Evan, but this dolly's no kid anymore, not by anyone's definition." She went over to the sofa where Evan was sitting, and looked down at her husband. "Are you in love with this girl, Evan? She's been in love with you for years, anyone can see that. But what about you?"

Flushing slightly, Evan said in a stuffy, offended tone that conveyed nothing, "I'm very fond of Theodora. You know that."

"I didn't ask you that. Are you in love with her, or are you in love with me? It's ultimatum time, darling. If you love her, then tell me so, and I'll go. Not quietly, but I'll go. But if you want to keep me, then you'll get rid of her, now, this minute. Tonight. It's up to you."

All of a sudden I saw our lives as loose strands that had become woven into the fabric of the present moment. Although my past had become entangled with Fiona's even before my birth, I would not see her again after tonight. Those skeins were finally falling free of each other. At the same time, the hard knot of love and friendship that Evan and I had tied was also unraveling. Powerless, I waited for the strands to reform, for the future to take shape. In that instant, my life, my happiness, my future hung on a word.

"Evan." I took a step toward him, but he refused to meet my gaze. He sat with his hands clasped firmly between his knees. When he spoke, his voice sounded defeated, weary.

"I love you, Fiona."

In the few seconds that had elapsed before Evan gave his answer, I had hardly moved, hardly even breathed. Now I felt as shaken and disoriented as if I had plunged to earth after tumbling across half a million light-years.

Fiona brushed a lock of hair away from Evan's forehead with her fingertips. He closed his eyes. "Poor Evan," she murmured. "You would pick tonight to get sober, wouldn't you?"

I drew myself up stiffly. "It's all right, Evan," I said. "I'll go."

"See?" Stepping away from Evan, Fiona turned her bright, false smile on me. "No tantrum, no big dramatic scene, just good old honesty. I don't like Dory, and Dory doesn't like me. It's silly for us to keep up the charade any longer." She walked to the door. "I'd better get back to my guests. Dinner's late and Delilah's probably having fits."

"Fiona, couldn't we discuss this?"

"No, darling, we couldn't. I'm all talked out." Fiona paused with her hand on the doorknob. She looked back over her shoulder at me. Before she went out, the corner of her mouth twitched, not in a sneer but in a brief victorious smile.

I watched a thin strand of smoke working its way out of the crumpled butt of Fiona's cigarette. I could taste the ashes.

"I'll ask Fanny to pack your things," Evan said. "You can stay at Mother's tonight. I'll take you up to Boston myself, when you're ready to go back to school. I'm sorry about this, Dory. You don't know how sorry."

I ran out of the study and up the stairs. Below me, I could hear laughter and talk, the ripple of a piano, Fiona's voice saying, "You poor dears must be starving. Come into the dining room," and Hugo de Graaf's rumble: "Jesus, it's about time."

In my room, I flopped down in the window seat that overlooked the rose garden. A light rain had started to fall, driving a few straying nature lovers indoors. Minutes passed, I don't know how many.

The door opened, and Evan came in. "Fanny's busy downstairs. I thought I'd give you a hand." I couldn't reply. Evan glanced out the window over my head. A rising wind tossed the hemlocks that overhung the western edge of the lawn. "Looks like it's going to storm. I've asked them to bring the Rolls around in half an hour. Mother's expecting you. What do you want to take with you tonight?"

"Nothing." I gripped the edge of the cushion on which I was sitting. "I don't want any of the things you've given me. I came with nothing. I'll leave with nothing. So you won't be able to call me a—a parasite."

Evan smiled down at me. "Now you're being silly. What am I supposed to do with all your things? Give them away? Burn them? Decorate a shrine in your honor? Now, that's not a bad idea." The lightness in his tone must have sounded as shallow and unconvincing to his ears as it did to mine, for he abandoned it at once. "Dory, don't pay any attention to what Fiona said just now. 'Parasite' is an ugly word. You have always given me back more than I gave. I want us to part as friends." He put his hand on my shoulder.

I shrugged him off and averted my face.

He sat down beside me. "I know I can't say anything that will make this easier, Dory. I won't even try. I suppose I always knew this would happen. But I couldn't stop it."

I jerked my head around. "You couldn't stop it!" I exclaimed. "You could have done a hundred things to stop it, Evan, but you didn't do any of them. You let her talk to me like a servant. You let her order me out of your house. You listened to her call me all sorts of names, tell all sorts of lies about me, and you didn't say one word in my defense. Not one! I don't understand it, Evan. In the past, you were always the peacemaker, the healer. But not this time. You didn't even try to deny any of the horrible things that she said. That means you believe her. You agree with her!"

"That's not true, Dory. You know how much I value your love and friendship."

"Oh, yes, you value it so much that you didn't speak up when she told me to get out. Why didn't you tell her that this was your house and I was your ward and that you wanted me to stay?"

Evan looked grieved. He hated scenes, and this one promised to be even more painful than the one downstairs. "Because she was right about one thing: it's better that you leave. The two of you can't live under the same roof anymore."

I jumped up. "But you bought this place for me. For us. And now you're tired of me. She always said it would happen, and it has. You're going to drop me the way you've dropped all your other projects. You've finally lost interest. You're bored with me. You'd rather spend your time with a bottle of bourbon and a lot of Hollywood frauds." Striding across the room, I yanked open the top drawer of my bureau and started to toss the contents onto the bed.

"That's not true, Dory. I haven't lost interest in you. But things have changed. You're a grown woman now."

"I'm the same person I always was." Underwear, stockings, sweaters landed in a pile in the middle of the bedspread. "You're the one who's changed. We used to be friends; we could talk. But not anymore. You haven't talked to me in years."

"We've had nothing to talk about. My problems are my own. You couldn't help me. In fact, you rather complicated matters."

" 'Complicated'! Well, forgive me, Evan. I knew I was a bore and a burden, but I didn't realize that I had made your life so unbearable." I crouched down on the floor and dragged my suitcase out from under my bed. For once I didn't have to swallow a lot of dust. Fanny had unpacked for me only that afternoon. "Well, you don't have to worry about that any longer. I'll get out of your life and things will be as simple and straightforward as they were before I came. I certainly don't want to interfere any longer."

"Dory, please listen to me."

I dove into the depths of my closet, where I found an old knapsack. With a single sweep of my arm, I scooped the contents of my dressing table inside: framed photographs, lipsticks, hair brushes, manicure set. I heard a tinkle of glass and smelled the strong stink of perfume.

"Oh, God, how can I explain this to you?" Evan dragged his fingers through his hair.

"Explain what? You don't have to explain anything, Evan. For once you've made yourself perfectly clear: you don't want me around anymore. That's fine. I won't stay where I'm not wanted."

He shook his head. "You really don't understand, do you? You wonderful child. You naive, beautiful, wonderful child."

I blinked at him. "You're not making any sense. I can't stay here because I'm grown up, but you're still calling me a child. You've been drinking too much bootleg liquor, Evan. It's muddled your brain."

I plunged into the closet again, to emerge with an armload of woolen clothes that I would need for the winter. I looked down at my suitcase. It would never hold everything. I'd have to borrow another, and ask Hanes to load the rest of my possessions into a trunk and send them on later.

Evan stood up, wincing slightly. The old pain in his back still bothered him from time to time. "You don't have the faintest idea why you have to leave, do you? You think I'm letting Fiona have her own way because I'm tired of you. You couldn't be more wrong."

I stood in front of the dressing table and started to pull down the photographs that I had tucked around the edges of the mirror. Theodora and Evan, Rome, 1926; Evan in the Jardins de Luxembourg, Paris, 1926; Theodora and Evan with the Houses of Parliament in the background, 1928. Evan and Custer at Elf Hill. Theodora and Muffin. The view from my window, encompassing the rose garden and the apple orchard. I started to shred them all into tiny particles.

"Dory, stop." Evan came up behind me and put his hands on my shoulders.

"Leave me alone, Evan." I tried to shrug off his hands, but he wouldn't let me go. "I can't stand to look at them anymore. It was all a lie, a dream; a beautiful, lying dream. I don't want—"

Evan spun me around to face him and kissed me full on the mouth.

"Now do you understand?" he said softly.

I gaped at him, and rattled my head like a moron.

"You really are simpleminded," he sighed. "What will it take."

He drew me close and kissed me again, slowly and searchingly.

I had never known anything like that kiss, never even imagined it. Like a powerful and delicious drug, it paralyzed my brain, sent spasms through my middle, robbed my legs of strength.

Feeling me start to sag, Evan eased me down on the bed, on top of a heap of clothes and underwear that smelled faintly of lavender and mothballs. We lay there together. It was like that old fantasy of mine, only not like it at all.

A clap of thunder shook the house. The lights went out. I could hear the faint startled exclamations of Fiona's guests, and their relieved laughter as Hanes appeared with boxes of candles and matches. At that time of year, we were accustomed to dealing with interruptions in electric service.

Evan's lips moved along my cheek to a place just below my ear. I had never experienced anything so magical, so sweet and powerful and warm. His hand dropped away from my waist, stroked the line of my hip and thigh, traveled upwards again under the hem of my skirt, gently caressing and exploring, urging me to open to him, to welcome him, to give up my secrets and to banish the last vestiges of strangeness that existed between us.

Slipping my arms around Evan's neck, I pressed closer to him. The small sun whirled inside me, casting off white-hot sparks. So this was what I had waited for. This: not Sid Jenkins' animal gropings or Tom Fairbank's artless good-night kisses or the ludicrous tussles outside my dormitory a few minutes before curfew. I understood now. At long last, I understood everything.

The lights blinked on again. Before I could open my eyes, I felt Evan pulling back, taking himself away from me.

Breathing hard, he stood over me. "I'll find Fanny, somebody else to help you pack. The car's probably waiting." He turned and started toward the door.

"Evan, wait!" I ran after him and gripped his arm with my two hands. "I love you, Evan. I love you! Come with me tonight. We'll go away together, just the two of us. Things will be like they were in the old days, before you sent me away to school. Just you and me. No more Fiona, no more silly actors and movie stars. Only poetry and music, all the things you love, that you've taught me to love. Life will be so wonderful."

"Stop it, Dory." His face had gone as white as his dinner jacket. "Don't you know that if I had had one iota less of self-control and discipline, I would have taken you to my bed long ago? I wanted to, God knows. It was hell sometimes, that summer at Cape Cod. But I kept telling myself that you were still a child. A child!" he repeated bitterly. "I wouldn't have had to force you, not like that other man. You would have done anything I asked, willingly, because you loved me and wanted to please me."

"Yes, I would, because I do love you," I said. "I never knew how much. Please, Evan. Leave her. Come with me."

"No, Dory." He looked away from me and stared resolutely at the wall. "It's impossible."

"It's not! Fiona doesn't love you, but I do. I'll look after you, and take care of you, and love you until I die. I swear it. Say you will, Evan. It's so easy. Just come downstairs with me now and we'll drive away together, to New York or Boston or Paris —wherever you say."

"I can't do that."

"But you're not happy with her. She makes fun of you. She sleeps with other men and doesn't even try to hide it from you. She humiliates you over and over again, and you—you just stand there and wait for more!"

Evan said, "I learned a long time ago that if I wanted to keep her, I would have to accept her the way she is. I don't know why I stay with her. I've known other women who are more beautiful. A few others who are more talented. But Fiona is strange and wild, a woman unlike any I've ever known. I'm willing to overlook her infidelities simply because I know that none of her other lovers will possess her either, any more than I can. She belongs to herself. Not to me. Not to anyone."

"But she doesn't love you." I continued to insist, even though I knew my cause was hopeless. Evan had already made up his mind.

"The French say that in every relationship, there is always one who loves, and one who permits himself to be loved. And at least Fiona permits me to love her. I've never asked for more than that." He detached my hands from his arm. "I'll telephone you tomorrow at Mother's, after we've both had a chance to cool off. Meanwhile, forget that this ever happened. A good-bye kiss, nothing more. I'd better get back downstairs. Fiona will wonder what has become of me."

The door closed. Standing at the window, I saw a jagged dagger of lightening plunge into the earth's breast. I wished one of those daggers would strike me where I stood.

Evan's repudiation of me had slashed through me like the cutting edge of a sword, cleaving me in half from my neck to my bowels. For the first time I experienced love not as a wish or a dream, a poem or a line from a play, but as a physical ache, a gnawing, raging hunger, an all-consuming pain. I understood Evan's torment. He loved someone who couldn't return his love. One who loves, one who permits himself to be loved. Evan was both.

Fiona was right not to trust me, I thought. In a single instant my childlike love for Evan had exploded into a full-blown passion. Only a woman in love could feel as I did now, shaking and empty and aching inside. Only a woman in love would have humiliated herself as I had, pleading for love, offering herself with a desperation that approached madness.

I realized that I had been guilty of the very sin I most despised. My mother's bitter experiences had taught me nothing. I had permitted myself to dream when I had no right to dream; to hope when I had no reason to hope. Yet I had always pictured myself and Evan together, without Fiona. Someday, she would tire of him, and then he would turn to me for comfort. Someday. Blithely ignoring reality, I had constructed a beautiful someday out of tissue paper and glitter. When touched with a single spark of truth, the whole dream had gone up in flames. Evan loved Fiona. Maybe he loved me, too, but he had chosen. Someday would never come.

Fanny came in lugging an empty suitcase. "Look at this mess, Miss Dory! And that window wide open and the rain pourin' in! I declare, you young girls get sillier every day. Now you hurry and change your clothes while I pack these suitcases. You can't go anywhere in that old crumpled dress."

I stripped off my long dotted-swiss gown and put on the same wilted summer suit in which I had arrived. I glanced around the room. Once so familiar and dear, it had already ceased to be home to me. The dream was over.

yes, the nightmare comes but you can do this

Fiona was right: Well brought up men don't fall in love with the daughters of murdering whores. They sleep with them, unless they happen to be superbly well-controlled gentlemen, like Evan. But they don't love them.

I picked up my Leica from the dresser and looked through the viewfinder at my image in the mirror. My body had no head, only a camera, with a single staring eye.

"You won't get much of a picture of yourself that way, Miss Dory." Fanny looked up from the suitcase she was packing. "I'll take it for you, if you want."

"No, thanks, Fanny. I don't need a picture of myself. I know what I look like." Portrait of the Photographer as a Fool.

The Rolls turned out of the lane at Elf Hill. I had slipped away without fuss or farewell, without seeing Evan again. I didn't look back.

After we had gone a few miles, I asked Evan's chauffeur to take me not to Long Island but to Manhattan, to Pennsylvania Station.

"Mr. Bradford didn't tell you, we've had a change in plans. I have to go back to Boston tonight."

The car arrived in New York one hour later. After the chauffeur had unloaded my bags and hailed a porter, I thanked him and told him that he could go. As soon as the car was out of sight, I picked up my two suitcases and trudged toward the subway entrance.

I was on my own now. *yes, you are!*

PART TWO

THE

WOMAN

14

2019

Rounding the corner onto 96th Street from Central Park West, I saw Evan's Hispano-Suiza standing at the curb in front of my boarding house. With a thumping heart, I let myself into the foyer. My landlady was waiting to pounce.

"The gentleman has been here for over three hours, Miss Lowery. I told him you might not be home 'til after eight, but he said he'd wait."

More than a month had passed since I had left Elf Hill. I didn't let Evan know where I was living. He would find me sooner or later, I was sure, but meanwhile I needed time to think over what I wanted to say to him.

I slid open a door and stepped into the parlor, a stale, dark, unwelcoming chamber designed to weed out the faint of heart from among the boarders' male visitors. After three hours of pacing the musty faded carpet in this dungeon, Evan had certainly passed the test. He looked hungry, hot, and thoroughly angry. My throat tightened. I had never loved him more.

"Well, Theodora, here you are at last. I was beginning to think that someone had given me the wrong information. I couldn't really believe that I'd find you in a place like this. I don't suppose it makes any difference that we've been worried sick about you. What can you have been thinking of? Do you know how frantic we've been, trying to find you? Why on earth

2019

did you have to disappear without telling anyone where you were going?"

My feet hurt and my bottom ached. I had spent a tiring, nerve-wracking day in the company of an undistinguished Russian violinist who expected all women, even female photographers, to respond eagerly to his crude attempts at seduction. I dumped my possessions onto a chair and perched carefully on the edge of my landlady's horsehair sofa.

" 'We?' " I echoed. "You mean that Fiona was worried about me too?"

His eyes flashed. "I mean Mother, of course. She was terribly upset when you didn't turn up."

"I am sorry that I distressed your mother so terribly." I folded my hands in my lap and crossed my ankles, the perfect little lady. "I'll send her a note with some flowers in the morning. That should make it all right."

Evan frowned. "What's the matter with you, Dory? I've never known you to behave like this before."

I wanted to say, "I've never suffered like this before," but I didn't. I bit down hard on my lower lip.

Evan must have seen my distress, for he said more gently, "Why didn't you write, or at least send a wire? How are you living? And on what? You haven't drawn any checks on the account into which I pay your allowance. I still wouldn't have known where to find you if Hugo de Graaf hadn't happened to hear from his friend Gabe Rosati at *Mode* that he'd hired you as a photographer. Surely he's only paying you a pittance—not nearly enough to get by."

The other roomers in the house were all women, most of them young. I could hear them giggling and whispering on the other side of the door, which I had inadvertently left open a half-inch.

"And what about your education?" Evan lowered his voice. "You have two more years until graduation. Why don't you forget this absurd job until—"

"I'm not going back to Radcliffe," I said. "I don't need a col-

2019

lege degree to be a photographer, and I don't want you to spend any more money on me. I'll pay you back what I owe. I can only manage three dollars a week at first, but Mr. Rosati has promised me a raise after six months if he likes my work, and so far he seems to."

"That's the most ridiculous thing I've ever heard." Evan strode over to the door and closed it firmly on the giggling eavesdroppers. "I don't want payment. I don't want anything but for you to come to your senses. What are you doing in this awful place? If you must live in the city, at least let me find you—"

"My room here is perfectly all right," I interjected firmly. "It's the best I can afford on my salary. I won't take anything more from you, Evan. This is the way I want it."

"I don't know what's gotten into you, Theodora." Evan tried to adopt a reasonable tone, but he wasn't in a reasonable mood. "You say you're grateful to me for what I've done, but your actions don't show it. I respect your desire to live a life of your own. That's only natural for a person your age. I won't interfere, if that's what you're worried about. I'll be joining Fiona in California in a few days, but I'll be coming to New York from time to time for board meetings, that sort of thing. We'll see each other when I'm in town. I'll take you out to dinner, to the theater. It will be like old times."

"No, Evan. I can't. I—" I took a deep breath. This was the hard part. "I don't want to see you again."

He was silent for a long time, then he sat beside me. "This is my fault. You have every right to be angry. That scene with Fiona at Elf Hill upset you badly, I know. I'm not proud of the way I handled that whole wretched business. And I sincerely regret what occurred between us afterwards." He shifted uncomfortably, moved either by embarrassment or by a lumpy spring, I couldn't tell which. "It should not have happened. It wouldn't have, if I'd been sober."

That was a silly lie. We both knew he had been perfectly sober.

"And it will never happen again?" I spoke softly.

"Never," he promised. "We'll forget all about it and go on as before. Friends." He reached for my hand. "Best friends."

I gazed down at our meshed hands. Evan's long fingers were pink and clean, with buffed, manicured nails. I kept my own nails clipped short; the chemicals I used to develop my photographs had stained my fingertips. These weren't the hands of a lady. But I wasn't a lady. My father had mined coal and my mother had been a murderess.

"Can you imagine what it would be like," I said with a soft laugh, "the two of us sitting over dinner in an elegant restaurant, discussing music and the weather and current events, and all the while pretending that what happened that night at Elf Hill was only the product of your drunkenness and my dreaming? I can't do it, Evan. I can't forget and I won't pretend. I'm not ashamed of the way I acted. How can I be? I haven't stopped loving you. And you—have you really forgotten? Tell me the truth."

I watched him struggle with the answer. He wasn't accustomed to speaking honestly about his feelings. I half expected him to brush the question aside, to laugh at my childish yearning for romance. But he shook his head.

"I'll never forget the way you looked. Or how you felt in my arms. Soft. So incredibly warm and beautiful."

The pressure of his hand increased. I fought to keep my voice steady. "You said then that the only thing that kept you from making love to me in the past was my age, and the fact that I trusted you and depended on you. But that's all changed now, Evan. I'm independent, and I'm old enough to know what I'm doing. You know that I'm in love with you. More than anything else I want to be close to you." I met his gaze squarely. "You'd like to sleep with me because you're lonely and your wife doesn't want you. Sooner or later it would happen, because we both want it: a love affair."

Evan smiled. "I'm glad to see you haven't lost your talent for indiscriminate honesty, Theodora. Obviously, we've come too far. We can't go back. Which means we'll go forward. That's what I want, too. A love affair." He touched my cheek. "But you already knew that, didn't you? You're so wise. And you're right. It's inevitable. We might as well accept it, and rejoice. And I do feel like rejoicing." He put his arm around my shoulders. "You won't be sorry. We'll be good for each other. Friends, as always. But more than friends."

He kissed me tenderly. I felt the old dreams tugging at me like a tidal pull: Someday he'll fall in love with you. Someday.

Jumping up, I moved across the room to the gray slate fireplace. "It sounds like a perfect arrangement, doesn't it?" To stop my hands from trembling, I gripped the edge of the mantelpiece. The stone felt reassuringly hard and cold. "I'll be your mistress, your confidante. I know all about Fiona, and I understand the situation. I won't pester you to marry me, and I won't make unreasonable demands. You'll indulge me and pamper me as you've always done, and I'll show my gratitude in a hundred new ways. I can take you into my arms whenever you come to visit, I can love you, I can make you feel important. You'll teach me about love, as you've taught me everything else. Just the two of us together, in what the newspapers call a love nest, with no Fiona around to sneer at us. Yes, you'd like that, Evan. You'd feel like a man again, with your beautiful wife on one coast and your loving mistress on the other. You could have it both ways."

"You'd have what you wanted, too," he reminded me.

"Oh, yes. The idea of a future without you is so cold and horrible—the way it's been ever since I left Elf Hill. Even now, it's a struggle just to get through the day. I get up, I drag myself to my job, I immerse myself in my work, and I try to forget what happened. I keep hoping the pain will go away, but it never does. Every night before I go to sleep, I think about you and the wonderful times we've shared. I try not to cry, but I can't help it. After all that, you'd think I'd be eager for a chance to be close to you, even for a few weeks out of the year. We could probably keep up appearances: people are used to seeing us together and no one would suspect. Your mother would never have to know that we were sleeping together. Nothing would change."

"Well, what's so terrible about that?" Evan wondered.

"Everything. I'd love you more, but you wouldn't love Fiona less. I suppose if I were really clever, like she is, I could win you away from her. But I can't fool myself. The last time I forced a confrontation, I didn't fare very well, did I? I can't compete with her. And I couldn't live knowing she was my rival. I couldn't bear it." I drew my hands into fists. "I will not spend my whole life waiting for 'someday.'"

"You're not making any sense," Evan said impatiently. "You've admitted that you're unhappy, and we both know how to change that. Don't be foolish, Dory. Come with me now. I'll get you a suite at the Burbage, and send someone back for your things in the morning. We can discuss all this over dinner. I don't know about you, but I'm famished."

"A month ago, I asked you to come away with me. You refused, because you didn't want love on my terms. Now I have to refuse. Your terms aren't good enough."

"What do you mean? I thought we'd decided—"

"No, I've just explained to you why it's impossible. You'd better go, Evan. Don't try to see me again. I'll move away if I have to, I'll quit my job and go to another city and change my name. But I won't be your mistress or your ward or your friend."

Evan intercepted me as I ran toward the door. "I don't understand you, Dory." He held me firmly around the waist. "You want to be with me, and you don't want to see me again. You can't have it both ways."

"No, and that's why I can't love you, Evan." I struggled, trying to wriggle away from him. "I won't tear myself apart anymore. Loving you is like dying. If I can get away from you, I might have a chance for some kind of life."

"You're being silly. Your life is with me."

"No, Evan, no. Please let me go."

"I need you, Dory, and you need me!"

"No!" Sobbing, furious, I jerked myself free. "No, I do not
need you, Evan, any more than you need Fiona. Everybody's
chasing a dream that won't come true, except her. She has too
much sense to break her heart over somebody who can't love
her. You're so afraid to give up your dream. You keep waiting
for her to love you: 'Someday, someday, someday!' But it's never
going to happen. Why can't you admit that you're wrong, that
the dream's gone bad? Because you don't want to. Fiona's right.
No wonder she despises you. You're weak, a coward. You're a
fool."

I saw the sudden surge of anger in his eyes and the quick upward movement of his arm, but I didn't pull away. The flat of
his hand struck my cheek with a sound like ice cracking. Tears
sprang to my eyes and spilled over, but I didn't move. We stared
at each other for a stunned moment, horrified that our friendship, which we had always considered so deep and enduring,
could be sundered by a few cruel words and a single sweep of
the hand. Evan's mouth twitched. He didn't apologize.

I picked up my camera case and slung my raincoat over my
arm. "I know all about people who sacrifice themselves on altars
made of dreams," I said. "I'm not going to end up like my mother, hanging from a chandelier or a doorknob in some fancy
apartment or hotel room."

Up on the third floor, as I fumbled blindly for my key, I heard
the roar of the Hispano-Suiza engine outside. The girl who lived
in the room next to mine thrust her head out into the corridor.
"Ooo, who was that man you were with, Theo? He's absolutely
gorgeous. And that car!"

I fought down the urge to laugh, or to scream. "He's my uncle."

"Wow, lucky you. That means he'll be coming around again,
huh?"

"No, he won't be back."

"Oh. Too bad." She sighed. "He sure was a honey. But I bet
he's married. The good ones always are." She ducked back into
her room without waiting for an answer.

Gabe Rosati walked through the crowded Madison Avenue offices of *Mode*. "Does anybody in this godforsaken place speak Spanish?"

"Sure," came the responses. "Vaya con Dios." "Olé!" "Malaguena." "Los Angeles, San Francisco, San Diego."

Mr. Rosati didn't match my mental image of a friend of Hugo de Graaf. Small, reed-thin, elegant to the tips of his soft suede shoes and manicured cuticles, he had never hunted any game bigger than the roaches who found their way into his expensive New York apartment. The only time he ever drew blood was when he pricked his finger on a thorn from the red rose he always sported in his buttonhole. He and Hugo had been freshmen at Harvard together, a couple of scholarship students from poor families who had taken a liking to each other but whose interests and abilities had drawn them in different artistic directions.

When Mr. Rosati had seen the Lowell photographs in my portfolio, he groaned. "Heaven help us, another social conscience. Why can't the teachers at Harvard and Radcliffe leave politics alone?"

"I didn't go to Lowell on a classroom assignment," I told him. "I went because I wanted to see what was going on in the world outside the ivory tower."

"People who live in ivory towers ought to know when they're well off," he informed me. "Especially these days. You could have stayed at that school for another two years, soaking up Henry James and William James and James the First. Instead, you've thrown yourself into an already-overcrowded job market in the middle of a depression, just because you think you're ready to turn professional. Give me one good reason why I should hire you instead of a man who has a wife and family to support?"

I handed him the print of the Lowell prostitute. "Because I

take better pictures than most of the men who call themselves photographers."

He leaned back in his chair and grinned. "Okay, I'll give you a job. But leave your social conscience on the shelf, Theo," he advised. "The whole idea behind *Mode* is style: changing styles in art, literature, fashion, music—anything that's new and interesting. We focus on people who have style or stylish ideas. That's what our readers want, and that's what we give them. Think you can handle it?"

I did. I needed work, and I did my best to ignore the little voice inside my head that kept hinting that taking pictures of actresses, writers, and politicians wasn't very important in a world where people were starving.

My first week at *Mode* found me taking closeups of chicken feathers, dog noses, seashells, flowers, peach pits, textured fabrics and materials—all sorts of things that people see every day and seldom examine carefully—for a series entitled, 'Visions: Intimate Views of Reality.' Two weeks later I received my first promotion, from photographing inanimate objects to doing candid portraits of minor celebrities.

Many of these people, expecting a hard-eyed professional photographer burdened with equipment, seemed a little confused when I came into the room bearing only my Rolleiflex and a light meter. I could see the question in their eyes: Could this demure young woman possibly capture the hidden facets of their complex personalities? They didn't realize that I had come of age among people who had an exaggerated idea of their own importance. To put them at ease, I always asked my subjects a few questions about themselves. As they expanded on their favorite topic, they relaxed considerably and forgot that I had come to take pictures. I got some very interesting and revealing portraits that pleased even our publisher, a man known for his wealth and his taste, and the frequency with which he changed his wives.

Now Mr. Rosati poked his head into a cluttered work room

2019

• 204

DARKNESS INTO LIGHT

ing. Know any Spanish?"

I looked up from the proof sheet I was marking with a black
grease pencil. "Enough to get a room and a meal in Mexico City,
I guess."

"You're not going to Mexico City. Eddie Powell is on his way
to interview a distinguished visitor from abroad, and since Eddie can barely speak English, I thought I'd line up a little insur-
ance. Take your camera. Diaz has been in this country for six
months and nobody's interviewed him yet except one left-wing
rag. He was an also-ran in the Nobel competition last year, one
of Spain's best-known writers."

Ambling into the room, Eddie attempted to hide a yawn behind his hat. "Anybody who calls himself 'the Poet of the People' has got to be a Communist. Do I really have to ask him all
the standard questions? Everybody's tired to death of that stuff."

"No, use your imagination," Rosati suggested. "Ask him what
he eats for breakfast and if he sleeps in the nude."

"I've never heard of this person," I admitted to Eddie as we
left the office.

"Luis Diaz Albareda"—now that he was out of his boss's
sight, Eddie indulged in a more elaborate yawn—"is a Spanish
poet and playwright, rich boy turned friend of the working
man. His poems haven't been translated into English yet, which
is why no one in this country except the Communists has ever
heard of him. God, I hate interviewing poets. They're so self-
centered."

I smiled to myself. Eddie hated interviewing anybody. He
complained about every assignment Mr. Rosati gave him. But
when I asked him once why he had become a writer, he replied,
"Because I can't do anything else."

"This guy lives in the Village." He looked glum. "Shall we
take the subway, or do you want to spring for a cab?"

"Subway." I hitched my camera case higher on my shoulder
and dug into the pockets of my navy blue cashmere overcoat for
a nickel.

"Tightwad," Eddie grunted. "Somebody told me you were rich."

I said, "I lost everything in the Crash. Now I'm just another poor working girl."

We got off the subway at West Fourth Street and climbed the stairs to the sidewalk. "He lives on Bedford, wherever that is," Eddie puffed. "We'll never find it."

"It's on the way to the Provincetown Playhouse," I said. "I know where it is."

Moaning, Eddie pulled his collar up around his ears. A biting November wind tugged at his hat. "I hate this town," he muttered. "I never should have left Kansas City."

"Why did you?" I clamped my hand down hard on my own blue felt cap.

"The last time anybody had an interesting idea in Kansas City, he was lynched."

The poet lived on the top floor of a four-story walkup. Eddie complained about the stairs, the cold, the stink, the darkness. An old man opened the door to our knock. A fine down of white hair covered his head. His eyes were bleary and blue and infinitely wise.

"Mr. Albareda?" Eddie said. "I'm Edward Powell from *Mode* magazine. I'd like to know your impressions of this country, how you're getting along, that sort of thing. Miss Lowery will take a few pictures, then we'll push off. It'll only take a few minutes. May we come in?"

The old man looked puzzled. I attempted, in my halting Spanish, to rephrase Eddie's request. The bleary eyes narrowed into an uncomprehending squint.

After what seemed like ages, a dark form loomed up behind the old man. "This is Mr. Blumberger from the second floor," a rasping baritone said. "He is slightly deaf and he speaks no Spanish, I fear."

At first glance, this Nobel-class Poet of the People was unimpressive. His collarless white shirt and black waistcoat, both frayed, hung on his bony frame like afterthoughts. Cigarette

ashes sprinkled his black serge trousers. His cheeks were bearded, indicating, I suspected, a disinclination to shave rather than
a desire to appear Bohemian. His straight dark hair, also in need
of washing and barbering, had been pushed back from his forehead with an impatient hand, not with a brush and comb.

"Great," Eddie sounded relieved, "you speak English. That's
just fine. Can we talk for a few minutes? This is Miss Lowery,
our photographer. She'll want a few pictures to go with the article."

Diaz nodded and invited us in. Our eyes, I noticed, were on a
level. The poet was tall for a Spaniard. While he showed Mr.
Blumberger out, Eddie murmured, "This place looks worse
than my office, and that's going some."

The single bed-sitting room was small and sparsely furnished,
with a small iron bedstead under the windows and a couple of
hard-seated chairs. No rug covered the stained floor. The flak-
ing walls were bare of paintings or photographs. Limp burlap
curtains drawn over the windows shut out the shabbiness of
Bedford Street. The oversized table in the center of the room
was clearly the heart and nerve center of this otherwise bleak
and monastic cell. Its surface was laden with papers and books,
all heaped in precarious piles and interlaced with pencils, soiled
coffee cups, brimming ashtrays, envelopes with notes jotted on
the back, scholarly journals bristling with markers, students' essays, copies of *The Daily Worker* and *The New York Times*.

Coming up behind us, Diaz said, "Mr. Blumberger tried to
form a union in the clothing industry here many years ago.
Management thugs beat him so badly that he could not work for
five years. Now he runs a little tailor shop down the street."

His English was British accented. When Eddie remarked
upon it, Diaz explained that his father had permitted him to
travel abroad for further study after he finished college in Madrid.

"A gesture uncharacteristic of Spanish fathers. I am sure he
looks back on it as his greatest mistake." With a wave of his
hand, Diaz invited us to sit in the two chairs while he seated

himself on the narrow bed and extracted a cigarette from a crumpled pack. "If I had stayed under the watchful eyes of the Jesuits, I might have become a priest myself. Instead, I was exposed to the corrupting atheistic influences of the Sorbonne and Cambridge University. I lost my faith in God, in the Spanish King, and in the sincerity of governments who say they want to improve the lot of the people."

"So you became a Communist." Barely stifling another yawn, Eddie pulled out his notebook.

"No, I am not a Communist, Mr. Powell," Diaz said carefully. "I have no politics. In my heart I am more of an anarchist than anything else, I suppose. I dislike any organization that dominates the individuals who comprise it: governments, the Roman Catholic Church, the military. I am in favor of labor unions because I know that no solitary worker can hope to oppose the forces of money and management. But when unions cease serving workers and demand that the workers serve them, then they, too, should be abolished."

I unpacked my camera. "Please don't pay any attention to me, Señor," I told our host. "I just want to take a couple of informal shots. May I open this curtain?"

Diaz nodded briefly and went on speaking to Eddie. "I am a poet in exile, Mr. Powell, a wanderer. My father has disinherited me, and so has my country. Under the new Republican government, I could return, I suppose, but I find that I can observe Spain more clearly from a distance."

"What are you doing in the States, Mr. Albareda?"

"Excuse me," Diaz said, "but in Spain all people are burdened with two surnames: that of their father, which comes first, and their mother's maiden name. I may be referred to as Diaz or Diaz Albareda, but never as Albareda. I just wanted you to know that, Mr. Powell, so that your editor won't take you to task for a glaring inaccuracy."

I suppressed a smile. I hadn't seen many people who could put Eddie in his place.

Grimly, Eddie applied his eraser to the page. "Gotcha," he

said. "We were talking about what you're doing in New York, Mr. Diaz."

Diaz lit another cigarette. He explained that he had received an invitation to teach at Columbia University. Soon after arriving in this country in the summer, he had become ill, too ill to teach. He hoped to extend his visa another six months, if the American Department of State would permit it.

"I would like to see more of this country of yours," he said. "I am accustomed to scenes of want and despair in Spain. They are part of the Spanish landscape, the product of centuries of oppression and stupidity. But I didn't expect to see them here in America." He shook his head. "So much horror in the midst of plenty."

I pressed myself into the corner near the bed and snapped a couple of quick pictures. The light from the window glanced off the planes of Diaz's forehead and jaw and accented the fierce thrust of his nose and bearded chin. He wasn't terribly old, thirty-five or forty at the most, but years of illness and self-denial had pared his flesh down to the minimum needed to cover his bones.

The cigarette that Diaz held between his thumb and middle finger looked like a sixth digit. He used it as a conductor might use a baton: to emphasize a point, to draw out the line of a thought, to curtail a phrase.

Those hands fascinated me. They were long, whiter than alabaster, veined with blue. Their movements reminded me of the ballet: smooth, precise, well-defined. Diaz's tobacco-roughened voice provided the perfect music for their dance. Shaping their movement to his words, his hands dipped and halted, arched and glided.

I wanted to capture those hands against the black background of his vest, beneath the haggard mask of his face. I adjusted my focus, then moved quickly into a crouch in front of him and snapped three pictures in quick succession. Diaz paused in mid-sentence and gazed at me with an expression of mild astonishment.

"Excuse me." Conscious of the unwavering intensity of his gaze, I took two more closeups of his face and one medium-range shot. "I have what I need, Eddie." Retreating to the greasy corner of the apartment that served as a kitchen, I waited for Eddie to finish the interview. I could still feel Diaz watching me.

I had never experienced anything like that before, the sensation of being physically touched by someone's glance. No, that's silly, I thought, and looked up at him. Sure enough, his eyes were waiting for mine. I felt a strange hollowness inside me, as though Diaz had robbed me of something vital.

"What about the Nobel Prize for Literature, Mr. Diaz?" Eddie wanted to know, "How did you feel when you heard you hadn't won?"

Diaz shrugged. "I felt nothing, because I didn't know that I was in competition for the prize. Still, it might have been amusing to use some of Mr. Nobel's profits from dynamite to denounce the system that makes the accumulation of such obscene fortunes possible."

Eddie made a few final scratches in his notebook and stood up. "I think we have enough for now. Thanks a lot, Mr. Diaz. The article should appear in next month's issue."

I had the impression that the interview had wearied Diaz. Nevertheless, he thanked us for coming and escorted us to the door. Eddie didn't bother to hide his relief at having completed yet one more boring assignment. He gave Diaz's hand a perfunctory pump and told me that he'd run ahead to find a taxi. I hung back, feeling that I wanted to thank Spain's most distinguished modern poet more graciously for his cooperation.

"You were very devious." For the first time I saw the hint of a smile lurking in Diaz's eyes. "I almost forgot that you were there, then you jumped out in front of me. I have never been photographed from that angle before. I will be interested to see the results."

"I hope the pictures turn out well," I said.

"They will." He sounded confident. "You are an expert. But

you really ought to practice your Spanish, Miss Lowery. In a short time you could become fluent."

I was surprised that he remembered my name. "It's been a long time since I've spoken any Spanish."

"Your accent is Mexican, is it not?"

"Yes. I grew up in southeastern Colorado. My friends were Mexican. But I've forgotten most of what I knew."

"Not at all," Diaz said. "I would have rescued you from Mr. Blumberger sooner, but I enjoyed listening to you. From your voice I guessed you to be a very charming young lady. Your appearance only confirmed that judgment."

Ducking my head, I pretended to check the closure on my camera case. I decided that Diaz, like many continental men I had met, was trying to uphold the reputation of his fellow Europeans for gallantry. Like many American women, I didn't know how to receive a compliment gracefully. Nevertheless, his words brought a flush of pleasure to my cheeks.

"Theo, cab's waiting!" Eddie bellowed up the stairs.

"I'd better go." After a moment's hesitation, I offered my hand. "Good-bye, Señor Diaz."

His handshake was firm, although his fingertips felt cold. "*Adios, Señorita.*"

I ran down the stairs. I didn't feel safe from Diaz's penetrating scrutiny until I was sitting beside Eddie in a taxi headed uptown.

"That was the bore of the year," Eddie yawned. "I knew you'd be in a hurry for lunch and wouldn't mind sharing a cab. God, the things I do for Gabe Rosati. That guy was a monumental windbag."

I rose to the poet's defense. "I didn't think he was boring."

"You weren't even listening. Oh, why didn't I learn how to take pictures? Take the shot, keep your mouth shut, collect your money. Not a bad life."

"He didn't look well, did he?" I murmured.

Eddie snorted. "Don't let that consumptive pallor fool you. Any man who looks that much like a saint has to have some vices. I'm betting that Diaz's is small boys. He probably dopes, too."

Eddie was right, I thought. Diaz did resemble a saint: weary, disillusioned with men, yet willing to sacrifice his own health and comfort for their sake, because they were blind and weak and he had the vision and the power to help them see.

15

2019

Gabe Rosati didn't run the Diaz interview for two months, until January, but when he did, he introduced the text with a full-page closeup of the poet's long, brooding face. The article ended with a cropped shot of those wonderful hands gesturing to the reader.

"Nice work, Theo," he told me on the day the article appeared. "Better than Eddie's," he added, rolling his eyes.

That afternoon, I studied the prints of the other pictures of Diaz I had taken that day. They were as good as I had hoped they would be. In three successive shots, taken only a few seconds apart, Diaz had assumed three different expressions, each more intense and fascinating than the last. His hands were prominent, as dynamic and stunning as twin sculptures.

Too bad Diaz won't see these, I thought. Why not? prodded a little voice inside me. *Mode* had no further use for them. We often gave extra copies of photographs to the subjects, as a cheap way of generating goodwill. Why not send these to Diaz? Better still, why not take them? Because I can't. I don't want to see him again. Why not? the voice demanded. Because he makes me nervous. He sees too much. He makes me uncomfortable. No, you're comfortable with men like Eddie Powell, the voice sneered. Oh, you are a coward, Theodora Lowery.

Two nights later, I found myself on the subway after work, only this time traveling south toward Greenwich Village in-

stead of north to my boarding house on Ninety-sixth Street.
Even as I mounted the stairs to Diaz's fourth-floor apartment
and tapped on his door, I asked myself what I was doing. I could
just as easily have mailed him the pictures. I adjusted the stylish
black hat on my head, smoothed the feather that curved down
alongside my cheek, and gave the belt of my overcoat a nervous
tug.

The door opened with teasing slowness. Before me stood one
of the most beautiful boys I had ever seen. His head was turned
to the side, displaying a strong classic profile topped by showers
of curling black hair. I wondered why he didn't look at me,
when suddenly he whirled and grinned. I jumped back, smoth-
ering a shriek with my gloved hand.

A wide purple welt pulled the outer corner of his left eye
downwards into his cheek, and drew that corner of his mouth
into a grotesque leer. The eye was milky white, blind. Another
vivid scar traversed his neck, just under his chin.

It took me a moment to regain my composure, then I asked to
see Señor Diaz Albareda. The young man opened the door wider and, with a mocking bow, motioned for me to enter.

The air inside was thick with cigarette smoke, but decidedly
chilly. A fizzing radiator under the window provided more
noise than heat. Someone had pushed the litter of papers on the
table aside in order to clear a space for a couple of bottles of
wine and some pieces of fruit and bread.

Seated in the middle of the narrow bed, the poet was surrounded by a dozen or so young men and women. A few sat beside him on the bed, the rest knelt like adoring disciples at his
feet. All of them had the look of intelligent college students, serious and attentive.

How young they are, I thought. Yet until just a few months
ago, I had been one of them, listening intently to some lean and
romantic Harvard professor talk about Renaissance poetry.
Now I was on my own, a working girl. Everything I did these
days was geared toward survival. I felt oddly distanced from the
days when I had so casually absorbed learning for its own sake.

2019

213 ◆

NATASHA PETERS

Sunday
Dec. 26
2019

Diaz looked up. His eyes flashed a special greeting. "Ah, my young friend," he rasped. "I am glad you have come back."

The others turned and stared at me. I said, "I didn't mean to intrude. I have some leftover prints from the *Mode* article, Señor. I thought you'd like to have them."

"Please, let me see." He extended his hand. I gave him a large envelope, along with a copy of the issue of *Mode* in which the interview had appeared. Diaz flipped through the photographs. "Ah, they are most interesting, Miss Lowery. You are an artist with a camera. Sit down, please. Angel, give Señorita Lowery your chair."

The man with the scarred face, who had been slouching in one of the two chairs in the room, rose reluctantly. I hesitated to usurp his place, but I felt ridiculous standing opposite him with the empty chair between us like disputed territory. I sat, pulling my coat tighter around me.

"Angel is an artist, too." Diaz pronounced the name "Anhell." "Forgive him for not speaking, but he is mute. The Guardia Civil in the town where he lived arrested him for thieving when he was just a boy. They tortured him, and when he continued to protest his innocence, they became impatient and slit his vocal cords. He speaks with his hands now. He is a painter."

An earnest young girl wearing dark-rimmed glasses said, "Did you discover him, Señor Diaz?"

"I saw him making drawings with colored chalk on a sidewalk in Barcelona. I took him with me to Paris, then to London. He has had no formal instruction. It would only spoil him. Like all great artists, he paints with his heart instead of his mind. He likes America. I think the savagery of your country appeals to him."

"Does he live here with you?"

Diaz shook his head. "Angel requires strong light, while I shun the light. When he is working, he fills the room with distractions that I really cannot bear: bad smells, naked women, rags covered with paint. We cannot live together, but we have found that we cannot live far apart. I give him words. He gives

2019

me color." He looked at me. "You might like to photograph Angel in his studio sometime, Miss Lowery. When he is working,
he is a wonderful combination of the Marx Brothers and Michelangelo."

Glancing up at Angel, I forced myself to smile. He stared
crudely at my breasts and licked his lips.

Picking up the threads of the discussion that had begun before
my arrival, one of the students asked Diaz what he hoped to ac-
complish on behalf of the Spanish worker.

"I want for the workers of Spain what I want for workers everywhere," Diaz said. "Dignity, respect, a fair wage for a good
day's work. Any time a company hires a worker, it assumes the
role of a father. It is the responsibility of the owners to guarantee the worker a decent shelter, sufficient food, schools for his
children. After five or ten years, a loyal worker should be rewarded with an additional share of the profits he has helped to
earn. He should become part-owner of whatever mine or factory
or mill he has helped to build. Why not? He has given the owners his blood, his youth, his strength."

"And sometimes his life," I said, thinking of my father.

"Yes, frequently his life. I have seen working men in this fine
country of yours. In some areas they are no better off than they
would be in Spain, where they are treated like animals. Old civilization or new, it seems that rich men require human flesh to
fire the stoves that warm them."

"But surely the new Republican government is trying to
change things in Spain," said a boy whose protruding teeth and
pointed nose lent him an unfortunate resemblance to a mouse.

"No matter whose hands hold the reins of government, some
things in Spain never change," Diaz said. "King Alfonso abdicated in 1923 because he was unable to stop the killings and the
acts of terrorism that were tearing Spain apart. After his departure, the dictator General Primo de Rivera used military might
to suppress rebellion, but the country was still wracked by unrest. The liberal government elected just two years ago has been
equally powerless to restore peace and calm. As you see, the

monarchy, the army, the elected representatives of the people themselves have all failed. Why? Because none of those groups could attack the root causes of discontent."

"You mean the need for land reform, Señor Diaz?" the Mouse said.

"Many reforms are needed in Spain," Diaz told him. "Reform in education. The emancipation of women. A fair distribution of land among the people who cultivate it. But powerful forces discourage change. The influence of the Church is still strong. The wealthy still retain their death grip upon land not rightfully theirs. These two groups are supported by a corrupt military top-heavy with officers who have no wish to jeopardize their pensions. In the smaller towns, the Guardia Civil rules with impunity. This body is autonomous, answerable only to itself and to the government in power. The Guardia was organized expressly to keep order in the more remote parts of the country. Their officers never serve in their home provinces. They are cold-hearted and ruthless, loyal to an ideal Spain rather than to the real Spain, the Spanish people."

" 'Patent leather hats and patent leather souls,' " murmured the girl with glasses. I recognized a line from one of Diaz's poems that I had recently read.

Diaz nodded. "Perhaps no other group is so hated and feared. They symbolize a Spain eternally at war with itself, bullies who terrorize innocent children, like Angel." All heads turned to look at the painter, who stood behind my chair noisily munching an apple. I ground my teeth. I had my doubts about Angel's innocence. Diaz concluded: "Certain regions like Catalonia and the Basque country feel no kinship with the rest of Spain. That sort of regionalism is destructive to a nation, as the lesson of your own Civil War proves. But how do you change the yearnings of men for freedom?"

"Does that mean that Spain will never know peace?" a boy asked.

Diaz sighed. "Does any one of us know peace? As long as we live, we struggle, we grow, we learn. The history of a nation is the history of struggle. I can only hope that the people of my homeland will resolve their differences as we have tonight, through conversation rather than conflict." He looked around the circle of rapt faces. "But it is late, and I have work to do. We will meet again soon," he promised.

The little group prepared to depart. Seeing me rise with them, Diaz asked me to wait. While he escorted his guests to the door, Angel wandered over to the bed where Diaz had left my photographs. He flipped through them, selected two or three, and stuffed them inside his shirt. The cocky grin he gave me further distorted his ravaged face. The sight sickened me, and I looked away.

After closing the door behind the last student, Diaz rejoined us. "No one offered you wine, Miss Lowery. It is crude Spanish wine, the kind our peasants drink."

I had learned about wines from Evan, who had been able to afford the finest champagnes and clarets. The stuff Diaz gave me tasted raw and astringent.

Diaz spoke to Angel in Spanish too rapid for me to follow. The young man lifted his shoulders in a surly shrug and jammed his hands into his pockets. In a gesture of utmost tenderness, Diaz placed the palm of his hand on Angel's scarred cheek. Casting me a searing glance, Angel jerked away from Diaz and slammed out of the apartment.

"You must forgive him," Diaz sighed. "He is badly behaved at times. He never learned the rules of conduct that so constrict and paralyze the rest of us. Angel is a true anarchist. He disregards all rules and systems, because in his world they don't exist. Please, Miss Lowery, sit down." He drew the two chairs closer to the table.

"I shouldn't stay." I resisted the urge to sweep the scattering of crumbs and ashes off my chair seat. "I only wanted to drop off the pictures."

"Ah, yes, the photographs." Diaz fetched them from the bed and looked through them again. "I see that the best ones are

2019.

What is the world

expecty

missing. Angel, of course. Whenever he sees something he likes, he takes it."

"I still have the negatives. I'll send more."

"It is not necessary. The cluttered condition of this apartment belies my words, but I do not wish to become encumbered with possessions. My books, for example. When I leave this country, they will stay behind. I take what I need from them and make it my own. Gypsies—literate gypsies, that is—carry their libraries in their heads." He tapped his graying temple with his forefinger. "Do you smoke?" I declined his offer of a cigarette. "I knew you would come back." He met my gaze over the flare of his match. "We had no opportunity to talk before. Nevertheless we spoke to each other, did we not?"

I smoothed out a nonexistent wrinkle in my coat. Diaz's probing glances unsettled me. He saw too much. "I'd like to apologize for the way Eddie Powell treated you. As though he had no respect for your work."

"Do you?"

I told him that I had bought one of his books and read it with the help of a dictionary. "Your poetry is very moving. Strong, like the people you write about."

"I thank you. Like your photographs, my poems are little abstracts of reality. Windows that shed light on areas so small that they might otherwise go unnoticed. I see you brought a copy of your magazine. Have you taken any other pictures in it, besides the ones of me?"

Flipping through the pages of *Mode*, I pointed out an informal portrait of a showgirl relaxing in her dressing room at the Shubert Theater. The chatty column "Noses and Weathercocks" was headed that month by a lucky picture I had taken of President-Elect Roosevelt conferring with an aide in the back of an enclosed car; I had happened to be standing close to the curb when his limousine passed. The future President looked deeply worried about something: the State of the Nation, perhaps? His digestion? I had made several contributions to the regular photo-feature "Personalities," including a shot of an acquitted murderess strutting out of a courthouse in New Jersey. Her gloating expression made one doubt the verdict.

"Such a waste of a fine talent," Diaz murmured. Seeing me start, he said, "Does this really satisfy you, Miss Lowery? Taking pictures of whores and politicians? If a visitor from a foreign country looked at this magazine, he would never know that here in America men were out of work, children were going hungry." He studied the pictures of himself again. "You are showing off your technique with these, telling your audience that you are a very clever girl, to be able to see the arrangement of hands and face against this dark costume. But these are not honest photographs, are they, Miss Lowery? Where is the soul of the man in them? Where is the soul in any of them?"

He tossed the magazine and the pictures aside, a frown pleating his forehead.

A hundred excuses sprang to my lips: I was still polishing my technique, I needed the experience, I needed a job. But I knew in my heart that Diaz was right. Working with the other professionals at *Mode*, enjoying my new freedom and independence, I had turned my back on the questions and issues that had touched me in the past.

Diaz said gently, "You are very unhappy."

I denied it. "I'm not!" Then I looked into his eyes, and the last vestiges of my reserve crumbled. Tears spilled down my cheeks. "How—how did you know?"

"I could see it in your face, in your eyes. It surprised me, the first time you were here. You are so young. Too young to feel such sadness. You decided that I could be trusted, that I could help you. That is why you came here tonight, isn't it?"

"I don't know why I came. I don't—I don't know what to do." Weeping, I covered my face with my hands.

"What is your Christian name?" Diaz asked. I told him. He repeated it softly, several times, "Theodora, Theodora, Theodora," dropping the th in favor of a soft *t* sound, rolling the *r* the

way Joaquin and Pilar used to do. I heard them calling me,
voices from the past, the past I had so resolutely put behind me.
"Trust me, Theodora." Leaning forward, Diaz gently drew my
hands away from my face and turned the dark force of his eyes
upon me. "Trust me. I am your friend."

Words spilled out like tears. I found myself telling him about
my father's funeral. I hadn't thought about that day in months,
but suddenly long-forgotten details came flooding back: the
traces of black grime on Papa's face, the scarlet rose Mother had
tossed onto his coffin. My life had changed decisively on that
day, even though I didn't know it at the time. I talked about Pilar and Joaquin, about Sid Jenkins and my mother. When I fal-
tered, Diaz encouraged me to go on. Memories tumbled over
each other: Mike Mullins jeering at me, Pilar running through
the wildflowers that grew along the Purgatory, Sid Jenkins
kneading my thigh, bloody water shimmering in a bathtub.

I described my life with Evan and Fiona, telling Diaz everything, even the shameful details of my last quarrel with Evan.
My voice grew angry when I repeated Fiona's charges that I had
become a parasite, a spoiled rich girl who would do anything
rather than go back to my squalid origins.

"You were afraid that she was right, weren't you?"

I recalled that day in London: Speaker's Corner in Hyde Park,
Donal McAllister haranguing the crowd, prodding something
in my conscience; the wretched children; my terror; and finally,
Evan's eloquent apologia, his justification for hanging onto his
wealth.

"You didn't believe him even then, did you?" Diaz said. "In
your heart, you were afraid that he was a coward who wouldn't
have soiled his hands with an urchin like you if circumstances
hadn't forced him to do it. You feared he was like the men who
owned the company, the ones who were responsible for your father's death, and ultimately, for the tragedy of your mother.
You love this Mr. Bradford, yet part of you despises him. Is that
not so, Theodora?"

"How can you know all this?" I shook my head dazedly. "It's as though you're looking right into my heart. How do you do it?"

Diaz mashed out his cigarette. "Because I have been lost in the same dark forest. I was like the old saints Augustine and Francis, those sons of wealth and privilege who ran from their consciences. Like them, I was arrogant, spoiled, self-indulgent. I had traveled the world, I had become the intimate friend of artists and writers and musicians. My writing was clever, conceited, full of obscure allusions and baroque images. I wasn't interested in communicating my thoughts. I had no thoughts. I was only concerned with turning out one bravura performance after another."

I winced, knowing that he had included this last remark to tease me.

"My life changed during a visit to the home of my family in Granada," Diaz said. "I had finished my studies, and my first poems and plays had already been published in Madrid. I had achieved some notoriety. My father, although baffled by my work, still took pride in the accomplishments of his literary son. One evening I went for a walk on the Paseo. Most Spanish towns have a central square where the good citizens take their constitutionals in the evenings. The young men eye the young girls, perhaps make an arrangement to meet again, under the watchful eye of a duenna, of course. A girl caught my fancy, a peasant girl but very beautiful. I was with my little brother. I remember that I felt somewhat foolish because he was much younger than I and I had to hold him by the hand. The girl walked with her cousin. The two of them were strolling arm in arm. A delightful picture." He smiled as he recalled the scene. "One that you would have photographed very well."

Grateful for that sign of his confidence, I returned his smile.

"I spoke to her. And do you know what she did, this charming girl? She spat in my face. Her cousin was horrified, and frightened. The Diaz family is very important in Granada. I was more surprised than angry. She had no reason to do it, having never seen me before. I found out later that she was the daughter of a man who had lost both his legs in my father's saw mill. She hated the Diaz family, and with good reason. The profits from that mill had paid for my education, clothed and fed me, enabled me to live well in Madrid and Paris. I owed everything to that mill, but strangely, I had never seen it. I went there the very next day. I saw how poorly the workers were paid, how wretchedly they lived."

Diaz paused to refill my wineglass and to light another cigarette for himself.

"Like any young man who has been converted, I wanted to change things right away. My father and I quarreled, and I left my home. I did not leave Spain immediately. I went to Madrid, where I started to write essays that I hoped would prod my backward country into wakefulness. I was bold, reckless, fired by a new awareness, a new sense of justice. I attacked everybody, the monarchy as well as the Church and the army and the Guardia Civil. Perhaps if I had been more restrained, I would be in Spain at this very moment, lampooning those figures that I detested like a Molière or a Beaumarchais, arousing laughter and scorn instead of anger and hatred. Shame is a powerful weapon, Theodora. Perhaps I could have shamed them into reforming their corrupt and oppressive ways." Diaz shrugged. "But it was a long time ago. I think I always knew that I could not live in my father's world, or in the world of artistic bohemians that I had recently embraced. So long as I ignored the forces inside me that were pulling me toward my land and my people, I suffered. As soon as I heeded them, I felt that I had been washed clean. I felt that I had found my purpose."

I had tried so hard to forget the past, to run away from it. Instead I had come full circle.

Here, in this bleak room, in the company of a stranger, a foreigner, I had come home again. I had come face to face with myself.

"What should I do now," I asked him. "I can't go back to Monkey Gulch. It would be horrible, like walking into an old nightmare."

"Your happiness, the success of your work does not depend on a physical location," Diaz assured me. "Your past has shaped you, Theodora. In spite of the years you have spent living in luxury, you do not see with the eyes of an Evan Bradford, but with the eyes of a worker's daughter. You must be true to your vision. Use your understanding of your own people. Use it to give the world an honest reflection of itself."

I sat quite still for a long time, thinking. Diaz respected my need for silence. At length I said, "I want to open the windows on those small spaces. I want the world to see how Americans live, the real Americans."

As I said the words, I felt a sense of exhilaration, of joyous liberation. The fragments of my life were coming together at last. There had been two Theodora Lowerys: the child of a grim mining town, and the pampered ward of a wealthy man. Each had despised the other. But no longer. Diaz had shown me how extremes of experience can work together to broaden understanding. I could never romanticize poverty, because I had been poor. Likewise, I would never long for wealth, because I had seen that money was no barrier against loneliness and unhappiness.

"The rich wouldn't exist without the poor." My brain worked faster now, and my excitement rose. "I need to show both sides. I'll photograph the upper classes in their country clubs, their nightclubs, on their yachts and in their racing stables. And I'll photograph the poor, in their slums and dirt farms and tenements. I'll put the two worlds side by side, so that everyone will see what I have seen: two Americas, as foreign to each other as if they were different countries."

"Your photographs might anger some people," Diaz warned. "Like your Mr. Bradford. He will feel that you have betrayed him."

At the mention of Evan's name, I stiffened. "Evan Bradford

has nothing to do with my life anymore," I said. "I have to do what I think is right. If that means exploiting my relationship with him in order to reveal the truth, then so be it. I know his friends. They'll let me photograph them. Why not? They're not ashamed of the way they live."

"You have courage." Diaz gave me an approving smile. "Your project sounds like a good one. Not quite suitable for the pages of *Mode*, however."

"Then I'll have to find someone else to publish my pictures, that's all. *Mode* isn't the only magazine in the country. Besides, this is something I need to do whether it's published or not. For myself." I saw Diaz nodding, and I looked at him curiously. "It's almost as though you knew all these things before I told you. How? How did you know?"

Diaz said, "We have known each other for a long time, Theodora. I felt it at once: a sense of familiarity, of being comfortable with an old friend."

"Yes. I felt it, too." Once again I was aware of a strange hollowness in my core and a strong sense of losing something. What was it? What was this man taking from me?

I glanced at my wristwatch, an expensive gift from Evan. "I didn't know it was so late. I must go."

Diaz rose with me. "You want to run away. You are still frightened of me."

"Oh, no, Señor Diaz."

"My name is Luis." He brushed my cheek lightly with his fingertip. I shivered. "You came here tonight for another reason, didn't you? Will you tell me, or will you force me to tell you?"

"I can't." I didn't want to run; I didn't want to stand still. The space between us seemed too wide, and not wide enough. I was frightened, and I was eager. "Tell me what to do," I whispered. "You know."

He shook his head. "You know it, too. Tell me."

"I want to stay here, with you." I slipped my arms around his neck and placed my cheek alongside his own. He shuddered, and held me. "I want you to make love to me."

He brushed my lips with a breathless kiss that felt like the strokes of a feather. His tenderness evoked memories of Joaquin. If Joaquin had ever kissed me, it would have been like this, sweet and innocent.

At length my coat slipped to the floor. Diaz jerked the pull-chain on the light, plunging the room into soft darkness. The glow from the street lamp outside the window filtered through the burlap curtains. I was at Elf Hill again. Evan was holding me, awakening in me a fierce yearning and a terrible hunger. I wanted to believe that I was in love with the man who was caressing me. Evan, I told myself. This is Evan, and I love him. Diaz moved his long hands over my breasts and hips and thighs. I shivered and pressed myself close to him.

Trust me. Believe in me. Love me.

I will. I will. I will.

This was Evan, igniting the swirling sun, capturing a lifetime of hopes and dreams and holding them in his loving hands. Evan, who loved me. Evan. We stumbled to his bed. In a fever, I pulled off my skirt and jacket and wrenched at the buttons on my blouse. He was no stranger to the intricacies of ladies' undergarments, this man, this Evan. Sliding the straps of my slip down to my waist, he caressed my breasts with his tongue. I moaned, experiencing the sheer powerful joy of being a woman. Flesh melted into flesh.

Labored breathing in the darkness: I tried to push the sound back down into the depths of memory. Hands probed. Lips burned. I felt the weight of another body on mine, heavy and solid and irresistible. I remembered. A man wanted to invade my body, and I couldn't stop him. Panic choked me, preventing me from crying out or even breathing. But I could do nothing. I was small and helpless, and if I made a sound, if I told anyone, he would hurt me, he would hurt my mother. Sid Jenkins wrenched my legs apart. I wanted to die.

And then, finally, it was over. Diaz pushed the damp hair away from my forehead. "You will learn to forget."

No, Luis. I couldn't forget. I was still two people: the woman who craved intimacy, and the child who was terrified by it. I had hoped, perhaps, that you would make me whole again, that you would force these two disparate physical entities to unite, even as you had brought the two thinking Theodoras face to face with each other.

After a long time, I opened my eyes. I lay under a scratchy blanket on Diaz's narrow bed. Diaz sat at his cluttered table a few yards away. He was writing, squinting through the smoke from the cigarette that dangled from the corner of his mouth. The sole light in the room, the naked bulb, cast an ugly yellow glare on the streaked walls, the stained curtains, the clothing lying in a heap on the floor. My clothing.

It was done. I wasn't sorry. Or maybe I was sorry, because Luis Diaz Albareda wasn't Evan, and I didn't love him.

Diaz glanced up at me. "It is still night, Theodora. Go back to sleep." He looked down at the paper, muttered a curse in Spanish, and attacked it savagely with his pen. He paid no more attention to me.

When it was nearly dawn, I threw off the blanket and began to pull on my clothes. Diaz was still working.

Shivering, I made a quick trip down the hall to the bathroom shared by all the tenants who occupied the top floor. Back in the kitchen, I found some ground coffee in a cupboard and boiled some water. As I set a cup down in front of Diaz, he grasped my hand.

"You are not sorry?"

No, Luis. No.

"You weren't pretending. A woman acts a certain way—"

A woman, yes. A child, never.

"Sit with me while you drink your coffee. I like to have you close to me. You and Angel: two mutes who inspire poetry."

An hour passed. I moved around the apartment, straightening the bed, cleaning the sink and the hot plate, refilling Diaz's coffee cup. He scribbled intently. After a while, he put his poems aside. He had started teaching two courses at Columbia after the Christmas holidays. Rummaging in the pile for some books he needed to take to his morning class, he complained that he couldn't find anything, couldn't even locate a pencil when he wanted it. *Cojones,* he grumbled. Balls. I smiled at that, and he stroked my cheek.

"I am meeting with a group of graduate students in the afternoon," he said. "You will be here when I get back?"

I didn't know.

After he had gone, I stared at the mess on the table in front of me. Bills for heat, electric, books, food—some three months in arrears. Letters from publishers begging for permission to translate his works. Books sent for review from American and British and French presses, ignored, their bindings uncreased. And snatches of poetry, hundreds of little scratchings on envelopes, newspaper margins, notebook pages. How could Diaz possibly work in such haphazard surroundings?

Having been paid just the day before, I had some money in my checking account. I sorted through the pile, finding bills, writing checks, getting them ready to mail. I separated the books. Those that had been sent for review I relegated to a distant corner; obviously, Diaz hadn't the time or the interest to bother with them. Those that seemed useful or important I classified according to category: poetry, drama, fiction, history. The newspapers, except those that had lines of poetry jotted in the margins, I put into bundles, ready to be discarded.

Diaz may have been a genius and a Nobel-class poet, but he was hopelessly disorganized, incapable of coping with the demands of the real world.

Taking the key he had left in the lock, I went down to Bedford Street. I located two bookcases in a secondhand furniture shop and arranged for immediate delivery. At nine o'clock I telephoned the *Mode* office and told them I wouldn't be in that day. I mailed Diaz's bills, put in an order at the corner grocery for staples like rice, coffee, sugar, cereal, and milk. By midmorning, I had found a neighborhood seamstress who was willing to spend a few hours cleaning and repairing some heavy velvet curtains that I bought from a peddlar. If Diaz wanted to work in the daytime and pretend it was night, that was fine, but that hideous burlap wouldn't help the illusion. The bookcases arrived and I set them up against a blank wall near Diaz's big table. Finally, I bought a secondhand floor lamp with a reasonably clean shade. No poet should have to write under the glare of a naked bulb.

At four o'clock, I stood back and surveyed my handiwork. The room wasn't the library at Gramercy Park, but at least it was better suited to Diaz's needs: books shelved, windows shrouded, papers sorted and arranged, larder stocked. He would probably be furious with me, but what did it matter?

I locked the door behind me, slipped the key underneath, and went home.

One evening a couple of weeks later, I emerged from the *Mode* offices on Madison Avenue to find Diaz standing on the sidewalk in front of the building. Away from his accustomed environment, he looked strangely vulnerable, almost pathetic. I realized for the first time that he was a stranger in this country, a man with no family, many admirers, few friends. A fierce January wind roared across town from the East River, ruffling his long hair and whipping the tails of his threadbare coat around his legs. He wore no scarf and no gloves.

"Did you think you had to pay me for my advice and counsel, Señorita Theodora?" he asked in lieu of a greeting.

"No, of course not. But I couldn't bear the clutter. And I saw that you hated it, too. I suppose you're angry. One of those men who thrives on chaos."

Other *Mode* employees were leaving the building. They glanced at us curiously, especially Eddie Powell, who recognized Diaz at once.

"I'm on my way home," I told Diaz. "You can walk me to the subway if you wish."

"I would be delighted," Diaz said.

He had difficulty matching my brisk pace. After I had gone about two blocks, I looked around. He was leaning against a lamppost, trying to light a cigarette. I walked back to him.

"I despise chaos," he said, resuming the conversation where we had left it, "but I can't seem to help generating it. What you did for me is quite wonderful, and I thank you. But I warn you, I cannot possibly maintain that beautiful order for longer than one day."

"I'm sure you have plenty of students who would love to help you keep your house in order," I said.

"Oh, Theodora, why are you so afraid of me?"

I couldn't meet his gaze. "Because I don't love you, Luis. I can't."

"Indeed not. I am a member of the race you despise: a poet, a dreamer. I do not blame you for feeling shy of love. You are wounded. You need time to heal."

Snowflakes swirled around us. Diaz hunched his shoulders inside his wretched coat. I felt impatient with him. This apparently grown man, this supposed genius, had no more idea of how to take care of himself than a child.

"I would like to show you a poem." He reached into the pocket of his vest.

"For Heaven's sake, let's get out of this wind," I said. I took him to a nearby cafeteria, where we picked up a couple of meat loaf specials and coffee. We chose a table, and Diaz handed me a piece of paper.

"Do you remember the flower you told me about, the one that has roots that bleed?" Diaz warmed his hands on his coffee cup. "I wrote this poem for you, on the morning we spent together. I was surprised that I was able to work with you there. But you know how to be silent, a rare gift among women."

I saw that the words were Spanish. "I don't have my dictionary."

"No, but you have the poet," Diaz said. "Surely that is even better? I will help you translate:

> " '*Flowers grow on the banks of Purgatory,*
> *where the river flows between Heaven and Hell.*
> *Flowers from a sad mortal place,*
> *a gray world without love.*
> *Their fragrance is sweet, the color of angels,*
> *the color of nothing.*
> *Drawing from Hell the ancient waters of sin,*
> *their roots are the color of pain, the color of life.*
> *Drinking this sorrow, their petals open to the sky.*
> *White.*
> *The color of truth.*
> *The color of hope.*' "

I sat quite still amid the rattle of china and the tinny babble of conversation in the cafeteria. The stained scrap of paper in my hand felt oddly warm and weighty.

"Beautiful words," I said. "I don't understand them all."

"A poem is not a piece of journalism," Diaz told me. "A poem should not give up all its secrets on the first meeting, any more than a woman. Someday you will understand it."

Someday. He had used the word deliberately. For the first time that afternoon, I smiled at him.

We began eating our meatloaf. Diaz devoured his food quickly. I offered him my bread and butter, and I went back and picked up two pieces of apple pie for dessert. I suspected this was his first meal that day.

"What about your project," he asked. "Are you still going to do it?"

"I don't know." I lifted my shoulders. "Thinking about it later, I decided that it sounded naive and silly."

He grunted, swallowing. "You have lost faith in yourself because of what happened between us." He buttered another chunk of bread. "I frightened you. I should have been more patient."

"No, Luis, it wasn't your fault. It's me. I didn't know—I expected it to be different, that's all. I need time."

"I would never ask anything of you that you were not prepared to give, Theodora."

I set down my fork. "What do you want from me, Luis?"

"I am tired of solitude," he said simply.

I shook my head. "I'm nothing special. I'm not a particularly good housekeeper. I don't even know if I can cook. I'd rather take pictures than talk. You probably have twenty students who would love to keep house for you, fifty who are more clever than I am. I'm only twenty-one, practically a child in your eyes. Inexperienced in love. Terrified of it."

Diaz reached across the little cafeteria table. "Give me your hand." I hesitated for a moment, then complied. He said, "Do you know that I envy you? It's true. You are more alive than anyone I have met in this city, in this country. You struggle, you suffer, you cry out, but you know what it is to live. You love justice and you despise falsehood, even when you see it in yourself. You will see it in me, I fear. I have fought it all my life, and I still have not conquered it. I need your truth, Theodora. Need can bring people together more quickly than love. I need your youth, your strength, your honesty."

Evan, too, had spoken of need, but not like this. I gazed at our joined hands for a long time, then I said, "I've got to have a reason to keep going. Something to live for. Someone."

"Then you will come home with me?"

I nodded. Because we needed each other.

"I think you've lost your mind," Gabe Rosati said. "Do you know how many people in this town would like to have your job?" I didn't answer him. "What are you going to do for money, if you don't mind my asking? Ask Fiona Randall's husband for a handout?"

"No." I brought my head up sharply. "I don't want anything from him. Thank you for seeing me, Mr. Rosati. I won't take up any more of your time." I started to rise.

"Don't be in such an all-fired hurry, Miss Lowery. Your masterpiece of photographic exposé has waited this long, it can wait a few minutes longer." Leaning back in his chair, Rosati locked his hands behind his sleek head. "I'm curious about all this. I thought you were happy here."

"I am." I looked down at my hands. "I mean, I was."

"Then what?" He narrowed his eyes. "Eddie said that dago poet bowled you over. That's it, isn't it? You swallowed what Diaz had to say about the rotten establishment and magazines like *Mode* being mouthpieces of a corrupt society. Well, if Diaz wants to fix up a corrupt society, why doesn't he go back to Spain? At least the people in this country haven't taken to burning churches and destroying private property."

Rosati flicked his hand at that morning's *Times*. Page one featured an article about strikes and acts of violence in Barcelona. Apparently the newly elected Republican government was unable to maintain order. Rumors were spreading of a possible military takeover, a coup.

"He couldn't go back there while the monarchists were in power," I said. "They would have arrested him."

"I'm not sure that jail isn't the best place for troublemakers like Diaz," Rosati growled. "How are you going to live if you don't work? Tell me that."

I shrugged. "We'll—I'll get along. I have a little money set aside."

"Sure, and I suppose when it runs out, Diaz will get a job waiting tables." He snorted. "Like hell he will. Well, Miss Lowery, I do not accept your resignation. I told you when I hired you that I was going to take you on for six months, on a probation basis. But probation works two ways. You're supposed to be sizing us up at the same time. Our six months hasn't run its course yet. You haven't given us a fair chance. Stay until March, and then let us know how you feel."

"Mr. Rosati—"

"I don't want to hear any argument," the little man said crisply. "We made a deal. If you're not happy with the assignments I've been giving you, then tell me about it. Maybe we can work something out. Now, just what is this so-called project you're in such a hurry to work on? You want to change the world and I want to sell magazines. If it's interesting, maybe we can work together."

I told him my idea about photographing America's extremes: showing people from the upper classes in their typically luxurious settings, juxtaposing those pictures with shots of the less fortunate in their humbler environments.

"Family groups, for example. The Southampton crowd in their drawing rooms, the South Boston poor in their tenements. Or horses. The races at Saratoga, and a farmer with his team of old work nags. Mothers, rich and poor. Nurses pushing prams in Central Park; a teenage girl in a tenement with her illegitimate baby. Children's games. Swimming holes versus swimming pools. This probably sounds naive to you," I said, "but the pictures would tell the story better than I ever could. I know these people, you see. I've lived in Gramercy Park, and I've lived in the most miserable coal-mining town in Colorado. I want to show how wide the gulf is between the two classes. I don't know if it will change anything—"

"No, but it might sell a few magazines," Gabe Rosati said with a grin. "Well, go on, get out of here. You were in such a hurry to get started."

I gave him a radiant smile.

As I reached the door, Rosati said, "Oh, Theo, I just want to say one more thing. If you start out on something and you find out that it's a mistake, the worst thing you can do is stick with it. It's no disgrace to back down because it isn't right for you. Do you understand me?"

I nodded. "Yes, I do, Mr. Rosati. Don't worry, I'm doing the right thing."

16

A larger apartment on Bedford Street became vacant in mid-February, two rooms with a closet-sized kitchen and a bathroom so small that seating oneself on the toilet, under the edge of the sink, required feats of agility and cunning. Most miraculous of all, the bathroom possessed a miniature tub with hot and cold running water. That alone made the toilet-related contortions worthwhile.

I spent two days cleaning furiously and sealing cracks against roaches. A couple of Diaz's students helped me shift furniture and books. We hung the heavy velvet drapes over the bedroom windows, so that Diaz could sleep undisturbed during the day. A few more pieces of secondhand furniture, an old-fashioned hooked rug for the living room, a Boston fern on the worktable, and one of Angel's wilder canvasses on the wall completed the move to our new home.

When Mr. Blumberger called on us for the first time, he kissed my hand and presented me with a bouquet.

"Mrs. Diaz, may I offer my sincere congratulations and best wishes for a long and happy life together?" The old man thought that Diaz and I were married. I didn't correct him. Our living arrangements were our own business; we owed no explanations to anyone. None of my co-workers at *Mode* knew that I had moved in with Diaz. I didn't even give my old landlady a forwarding address.

I decided that Angel resented the prominent role I had assumed in Diaz's life. Although the frequency of his visits did not lessen, he made no attempt to hide his scorn. Most of the time he ignored me, but once in a while, he sketched me in the little notebook he always carried with him. On those occasions, his hideous face would twist into a knowing grin. I loathed him. That glaring good eye of his saw too much.

Once Diaz asked me to take Angel's picture. I pretended that I had just run out of film. I couldn't explain that everything I photographed became part of my visual memory. Years afterward, I could look at a print and remember the exact circumstances under which I had taken the picture. I had to be selective about the people and places that I absorbed through the eye of my camera. I didn't want Angel's warped face lodged in any part of my mind or memory.

Most of the time, Diaz and I got along fairly well. At its worst, his behavior could be even moodier and more temperamental than Fiona's. When his writing was going badly, when he struggled over each word and phrase, he became touchy and irascible. His thoughtful silences would erupt into towering rages, in which he settled his dissatisfaction with everything—the boorish deans at the University, his thick-skulled students, his bothersome editors, the hazards of living in New York City—squarely on my shoulders.

I didn't mind his outbursts. I was the natural focus for his anger, the one who overcooked the rice, who made the coffee too weak, who mislaid his socks, who thoughtlessly shifted a notebook from one spot to another. What had my mother said so long ago, referring to Fiona? Talent can be a curse as well as a blessing. Whenever I saw Diaz agonizing over a poem, I pitied him. His soul was not his own. He was a servant to his genius. And while his words scratched and abraded, they never cut deeply. I respected and liked Diaz, I even needed him, but I wasn't in love.

Diaz was highly esteemed in Marxist as well as literary circles. Almost every evening, the apartment hummed with conversation, more often about politics than poetry. Professors from New York University and Columbia, union leaders, journalists from left-wing publications gathered around the Spanish poet-in-exile. They were joined by intellectuals enjoying a flirtation with socialism, and from time to time by prominent writers, painters, and actors who wandered in to observe and be observed. I could always distinguish the dabblers from the real

Communist Party members, particularly those who had achieved some power within the organization. They were zealots, as passionate as Diaz himself, but without his careful judgment.

Diaz's friends usually arrived at about seven or eight in the evening. They talked and drank until the early hours of the morning, when Diaz announced that it was time for him to write. Exhausted by my work, I frequently excused myself from these meetings at midnight or even earlier. I rarely slept. Instead, I lay in bed and listened to the buzz of talk and laughter in the next room. Every once in a while a new guest in search of the bathroom would open the door, flood the room with light, mutter an apology, and retreat. I waited, drifting into sleep, starting into wakefulness, until the last guests shuffled out and blessed silence fell. Then Diaz wrote until dawn, when he stumbled into the bedroom and flopped down beside me.

Under my care, Diaz began to regain his health and strength. I made sure he ate substantial, regular meals and dressed warmly before going outdoors. I couldn't deny him the cigarettes he loved, but I did manage to air the apartment frequently. Diaz's lack of concern about physical comforts astonished me. Sometimes I felt that I was living with a pure spirit, a mind that would have been happier liberated from its cage of flesh and bone.

Under his care, I gradually lost my fear of intimacy. We shared the same bed for an entire week before he approached me and asked if I felt ready to try love again. Afterwards I felt better about living with him. I wasn't just his cook and housekeeper; I was his companion, his friend, his lover. I found to my relief that the hideous events of my past hadn't left permanent scars. My sense of freakishness faded, along with my terror. I was a normal, healthy young woman.

As the weeks passed, Diaz taught me how to lose myself in passion. On those infrequent occasions when we found time for lovemaking, I could forget everything else: Evan, and Elf Hill, and my bruised and battered heart.

No, I didn't regret my decision to share Diaz's home. He was a brilliant poet who had achieved greatness by throwing off a way of life that forced him to be dishonest. Diaz defended Justice and he loved Beauty, but he insisted that both of these must serve Truth, and Truth was something he felt he never attained. I remembered words that I had learned long ago in Sunday School: "Blessed are they which do hunger and thirst after righteousness." I felt that in searching for truth, Diaz had already found it.

Although I continued to accept regular assignments from Gabe Rosati, I devoted every spare minute to my own project, which I called "America the Beautiful: Another Look." During the winter and spring of 1933, I took dozens of photographs of America's rich and poor, pictures that would doubly damn the wealthy, once for their own hedonistic self-indulgence, and again for ignoring the crying want of so many.

I traveled up to Boston in May to call upon old friends of the Bradfords, who introduced me to others of their class. All of them graciously granted me permission to photograph them. As Evan Bradford's ward, I was a member of the privileged class, like them. And so I followed the rich to their tennis courts, to their garden parties, to their weddings. They opened their homes to me, and I took full advantage of their hospitality.

For every image of wealth, I found a corresponding image of want. A return trip to Lowell, Massachusetts, revealed worsening conditions in that depressed industrial town. Families were being evicted from their pathetic houses, the ownership of which reverted to the banks that held the mortgages, banks owned and presided over by people like the Bradford's Boston friends. I never criticized the wealthy to their faces, never suggested that they be more compassionate to the unfortunate. My camera would provide all the damning evidence I needed to convict them of cruelty and callousness in the court of public opinion.

The disparity between the classes was an old story, but never had the extremes of want and wealth seemed sharper than at the height—or depth—of the Great Depression. Faces started to emerge in the developing pans in the darkroom at *Mode*. When I placed my prints side by side, the people in the photographs seemed to look at each other with wonder and hostility.

Gabe Rosati saw some of the early pictures. To my amazement, he suggested an exhibition in an uptown gallery.

"I'll give you four pages in *Mode*, two double-page spreads. We'll run them to coincide with the opening," he said. "Plenty of publicity all around. If the magazine gets a good response, we might be able to interest one of the publishing houses in doing a book."

I was delighted. With four pages in *Mode*, a gallery showing, and a book, my pictures would reach a wide audience.

"You will need words," Diaz declared that night when I told him about these plans. I had persuaded him to let me trim his hair, and he sat draped in a sheet, which quickly became sprinkled with cigarette ashes and snippets of hair. "Captions for the photographs."

"But Luis, that would spoil it." I combed the graying strands away from his temples. "The pictures tell their own story. Captions would only be a distraction. They'll dilute the effect."

"They will make the purpose behind your work so much clearer," he argued. "I can write them myself. Not long paragraphs of Marxist dialectic, but snatches of verse, perhaps. A poem to go with each pairing of photographs."

"That's very kind of you, but I don't think it's necessary." His hair had grown so long that it was beginning to curl up in back. I heartlessly butchered a lock.

"What do you know?" he shouted. "You will show faces, but they will be as mute as Angel unless someone gives them a voice. Yes, voices! That's good," he exclaimed. "I will write dialogue, little speeches, as if the people in the pictures were speaking to each other."

That would spoil everything, I told him. Photographs have an instant effect on the viewer. Once people paused to read speeches, the impact of the pictures would dissolve.

He continued to press his point. I stood back, scissors in hand, and looked at him sharply. "Why are you being so adamant, Luis? What difference does it make to you how I handle this? It's almost as though you were jealous of all the attention I'm getting."

He exploded. I was a vile ignoramus, an ingrate, insinuating that he, Diaz, one of the world's foremost poets, would even dream of coupling his name with that of an unknown child whose talent consisted of nothing more than an ability to press levers on a little box. Throwing off his shroud, he staged a rather theatrical walkout, snatching up his notebooks and cigarettes, whirling out into the cold without even a coat, like a child who wanted to spite me by hurting himself.

He must have gone to Angel's studio. When he returned the following evening, he reeked of turpentine and linseed oil.

"Why is it so easy for you?" he demanded. "How do you see things so clearly?"

I took this to mean that I had been right. Luis was apologizing. "If you'll sit down, I'll finish cutting your hair," I said, and the incident was closed.

Diaz accepted an invitation to speak to the Labor and Craft League in Chicago in mid-June. The weeks before he left were busy ones. The spring semester at Columbia was just ending, he was polishing an article for a new socialist weekly, and a London publisher had offered him a good-sized advance on his first book of poems in English, *Songs of the Soil*. He complained that he barely had a minute to himself, yet when a group of Spanish-American scholars asked him to address their monthly meeting in Brooklyn, he could not refuse.

"Everybody wants something from Diaz," he grumbled. "They can't even let me have a peaceful Sunday afternoon with my—where are those notes for my talk? Why are you always moving my things? I can't find anything since you came here."

"You couldn't find anything before I came, either," I said calmly. "Here are the notes. Can you remember how to get there, Luis? Take the BMT. Maybe I should go with you."

"I am quite capable of finding Brooklyn without your assistance. Why must you always treat me like a child? Look at this." He pulled his pockets inside out. "Not a penny to my name. Why is it I never have any money? It's your fault, always spending it on clothing and flowers, as though you were still living with your rich uncle."

I didn't remind him that he spent all his pocket money on cigarettes and books and handouts to impoverished students. The only clothing I had bought since meeting him were necessary additions to his own wardrobe.

"What time was this talk? Three? Bah, I'll never get there on time. Go out and call them. Tell them I cannot come."

"They have a business meeting at three-thirty." I put a few dollars in his wallet and slipped it into his jacket pocket. "You're not scheduled to speak until four. You have plenty of time."

At last he departed, still protesting that he hated these demands on his time. I knew how much he loved meeting a new audience, and he always came home from these events full of new ideas.

I made myself a pot of coffee and spread some proof sheets out on the table. I worked happily on those for an hour or so, crossing out the pictures that were bad or useless, making notes on the others about how I could improve them in the lab. Then I sorted through a couple of dozen of my best enlargements. I wanted to crop them and arrange them in an experimental layout. Four magazine pages wasn't many, and I wanted to make the best possible use of the space Mr. Rosati was giving me.

The door flew open, and Angel strolled in. I cursed myself for not locking myself in, but Diaz despised locks, and we were always losing our keys.

"Luis has gone out," I said in Spanish. "Why don't you come back later?"

Angel helped himself to bootleg wine from the jug under the sink. I bent my head over my work to hide my displeasure. It was always like this when Angel came around: no manners, no self-control. He was like an untrained child, a savage. Luis was

no help. He seemed to think that chastising Angel, or even asking him to obey a few rules, would somehow dampen his creative impulses. I happened to believe that art springs from
discipline, but I had never tried to argue the point with Luis. He
would tolerate no ungracious behavior toward a guest in his
house, even though that guest was intolerably crude and uncivi-
lized. Angel was Diaz's special pet. "He paints like a free man,
like an innocent," Diaz would declare. "He is the only truthful
artist working in this country today."

Personally, I disliked Angel's work, which was wildly colorful and abstract. To call his garish scrawls art seemed an insult
to the painters whose work Evan had taught me to love: Michelangelo, Delacroix, Renoir, even the iconoclastic Whistler. No
matter how chaotic their private lives, at least their art reflected
a love of order.

As a rule, serious scars and blemishes didn't upset me. I had
noticed that many people with severe disfigurements had
learned to ignore them, and in that way they helped others to
forget them too. But Angel seemed to take special delight in
drawing attention to his hideously warped face. He was always
grimacing, touching his scar, thrusting his cheek at unsuspecting strangers. Sensing my revulsion, he never missed an opportunity to flaunt himself in front of me.

Now he pulled a chair up next to mine—his milky eye and
twisted left profile turned to me, of course—and watched me
work. Ignoring him, I marked the sections of a print that I
wanted to crop out, drew a couple of lines with my ruler, and
picked up my scissors.

As I was about to make the cut, Angel reached over and
grasped my wrist lightly.

"What are you doing, Angel? Stop it."

He took the print, redrew the lines, and trimmed it his way.

It was a portrait of an enormously rich old woman, a German-
Jewish grande dame. Her frail body was hung with jewels, ropes
of pearls and diamond eardrops, bracelets and rings on all ten
fingers, even her thumb. A jewel-encrusted cigarette holder

forged a dramatic link between her dark-painted mouth and her flashing fingers. I had intended to frame the picture vertically, in order to display the jewels that carpeted her ancient breasts. But Angel cut the picture in half horizontally and trimmed away most of the background, so that only the face, cigarette holder and one glittering hand were left. The effect was exactly what I wanted: a bold, straightforward depiction of decadence grown old and complacent.

I was irritated that I hadn't seen it myself.

"I don't like that," I said stubbornly. "Kindly leave my pictures alone."

As usual, Angel paid no attention. He sorted through the enlargements and picked up another photograph, this one showing a Lowell mother with her hungry brood. I had made a couple of tentative marks in grease pencil where I thought I wanted to crop the photo. Angel wiped them away with his finger and drew them in differently, shifting the focus of the picture from the weary mother to one of the sad-faced children, whose expression epitomized the suffering of his whole family.

"You're right," I muttered. "I should have seen that."

Our heads were very close together. Suddenly Angel leaned over and brushed his scarred cheek against mine. Horrified, I jumped away from the table.

"How dare you! Get away from me!" I spoke in English. I was never sure how much of that language Angel understood. No matter; the anger in my voice communicated itself quite clearly.

Leering at me with his good eye, Angel reached out and stroked my face. I slapped his hand away and told him impatiently to leave me alone.

"Luis will be angry with you," I said in Spanish. I realized how absurd the words sounded. Angel's grossest excesses of conduct had never displeased Luis. "Why don't you leave? I don't want you around. I hate you. I can't stand the sight of you. Go away."

I heard a new note in my voice: fear. Angel heard it, too, I was sure. Grabbing my shoulders, he pulled me toward him. His hands were like iron clamps, incredibly strong. He started to play cat-and-mouse. Loosening his grip, he allowed me to think that he was letting me go. When I started to run, he snatched at my arm or wrist and jerked me back. I heard a queer wheezing noise and forced myself to look at him. Angel was laughing at me.

Twisting my mouth into what I hoped was a smile, I said, "You're just being silly, Angel. Playing games with me. Well, it's been fun. But I have work to do. You'd better run along now. I don't want to play anymore."

He drew me toward him and nuzzled my face. His scarred cheek was surprisingly soft, hairless and silky, but I went stiff with terror. Something hard and vile-tasting lodged in my throat. A scream. I opened my mouth. No sound came out.

The old nightmare rose out of the dark waters of my memory like a familiar monster. Fear constricted my vocal cords, paralyzed my limbs. Once again I was helpless, a mute victim.

Angel was in no hurry. Lifting the skirt of my light summer dress, he kneaded my waist and hips. He had no reason to be gentle with me—we hated each other—yet he was gentle. He moved his lips lightly along my jaw and down the line of my throat to my breasts, covered only by sheer cotton that was soaked with sweat.

Then something strange and totally unexpected happened. A spark ignited the swirling ball of heat in my middle. That spark of desire blazed into a fierce longing to possess and be possessed by this strange savage. No, it was all wrong. I felt no raging passion for Luis, whom I admired above anyone I had ever met. But now, inexplicably, unbelievably, I found myself in a lather of desire for Angel, whom I feared and detested.

And he knew it. He had always known it. He had watched and waited and calculated his move. He knew that Luis was planning to be away this afternoon. He knew that I would be alone, and willing. He knew that I would respond to his caresses, even before I knew it myself.

Angel bent me back over the table. His hot breath was sour

with wine and cheap tobacco. I turned my face to the side. My eyes flickered open for a moment, just long enough for me to see the scissors that I had been using sitting not two feet from my hand. My arm slithered out, slowly and stealthily. Angel was an animal with highly developed instincts. If I weren't careful, he would sense danger.

My fingers touched the cold metal of the blades. As I drew them toward me, into my hand, they made a scraping noise against the surface of the table. Angel didn't hear. He was too absorbed in his pleasure. I gripped the scissors, holding them flat against my palm like a dagger. In a single, swift movement, I plunged the point downwards, into the hard muscle of his shoulder.

Sid Jenkins pushed up against me in the front room of the house in Monkey Gulch. Sid Jenkins breathed on me in the darkness. Sid Jenkins lay on his bed, his blood soaking through the mattress, through the floor and the floors below. Cascades of his own blood followed his soul all the way down to Hell. Good for him, I thought. Good for you, Mother. I'm glad you killed him. Glad.

Angel leaped away from me, his terrible face twisted by fury and pain. I shielded my eyes with my crossed arms. He was going to kill me. His fist struck the side of my head. I had never heard a louder sound, the crack of bone against bone. The floor rose to meet me. After Angel's fist, it felt soft, and welcome.

Throwing himself down on top of me, he forced my legs apart and drove himself into me even as his blood dripped onto my breast.

I heard noises from a long way away, a weak old man's voice whimpering in protest. Mr. Blumberger was trying to save me.

"Stop, stop, you must stop this!"

I heard a scuffle, a cry, the sound of a crash, a body hitting the wall, a chair tipping over. Pulling my skirt down, I rolled onto my side and drew my legs up. I sobbed until the muscles of my belly were sore.

Then I heard Diaz's voice, shouting in Spanish. He pulled

Angel away from the old man, whose head was bleeding. Mr. Blumberger offered a panting explanation of what had happened. I lay still, in a pool of blood and tears.

Diaz dressed Mr. Blumberger's bruises and escorted him down to his own apartment. Angel, his fury spent, sank into a chair and stared at me dully. I glanced up once and met his gaze, then closed my eyes. I knew what he thought: that I was mad and vicious and vile. I knew because I was thinking all those things about myself.

Diaz returned. He berated Angel in Spanish. "Crazy, you must be crazy. What if the old man calls the police? You'd better get out of here. The wound's not too bad. Here's money for a doctor. Take my jacket. You don't want the world to know you've been in a knife fight."

I was the last casualty to receive attention. After Angel left, Diaz helped me into a chair and wiped my face with a damp cloth.

"You are not badly hurt. Forget it. This will not happen again. He was excited by you, jealous. He did not understand that you are my woman, not his. We have often shared women in the past." Diaz frowned and sat back on his heels. "It is too bad about the old man. I hope he does not call the police. Angel would go crazy in jail."

I stared at him with dulled eyes. His inappropriate response stunned and angered me, and rage gave me back my voice. No words, only a shrill, keening screech that shook the windows in their sashes and caused the upstairs neighbors to pound the floor. Pure sound poured out of my wounded soul, like blood spurting out of a ruptured artery.

Diaz shook me. "Stop it, Theodora! Stop it at once."

Sound, blessed sound blotted out everything else: pain and memory and, most of all, the sickening realization that I had plunged a knife into human flesh. Given a chance, I would have struck Angel again, and again and again until he lay bleeding and dying, and then I would have cut into his flesh with the sharpest knife I could find. I was my mother's daughter. Poor

Mary, to have such a child. Poor child, to have inherited such a legacy of blood and violence.

"You must stop this," Diaz pleaded. "Someone will hear you. They will call the police." He slapped me once, and then three more times until I was half-conscious and weeping. He gathered me into his arms and held me. "Theodora, forgive me. I did not mean—I only wanted to silence you. Theodora, Theodora."

After a minute, I pulled away from him and staggered to my feet, ignoring the hand he offered me. Even though the temperature inside the apartment was suffocatingly hot, I went into the bathroom and filled the tub with steaming water, as hot as I could stand. I scrubbed my skin until it was raw, as my mother must have scrubbed after she murdered Sid Jenkins.

When Diaz came into the bedroom a short time later, he found me sitting at the window that overlooked Bedford Street. He spoke to me. I didn't answer. He told me that he was hungry, that it was time for me to fix dinner. I didn't move. After a while, I dragged myself to the bed and lay down. I didn't sleep. The next morning, I didn't go to work. My cameras sat idle in their cases.

"This is crazy, ridiculous," Diaz said. "How long are you going to keep this up? How long are you going to be silent? Do you think I want another mute around? Mother of God, I have enough trouble communicating with Angel as it is. Ah, I suppose that is what is troubling you. Angel tried to rape you. Well, so what? You weren't hurt. He was worse off than you. You think I don't care about you, is that it? You are wrong. I care deeply about you. But what good is it to weep about things that have passed? I have spoken to Angel. I have expressed my displeasure. He will not come here again, I promise you. What more do you want from me?"

Displeasure. Luis had expressed his displeasure.

"You are angry because I struck you. I had no choice. You were not behaving sanely."

No, because I wasn't sane. I had come face to face with my savage self. I knew now that I was capable of great passion and great violence, and that my soul encompassed the limits of the human potential for evil as well as good. Yes, I could love, deeply and loyally, or wildly and with joy and abandon. But I could also kill. Angel, knowing all about me, had mocked me silently because I had yet to discover the most basic truths about my own humanity.

Three days passed. I did not break my silence. I sat staring at nothing, doing no work, not leaving the apartment. I drank some tea when Diaz brought it to me, but I touched no food. I quickly became pale and drawn. Diaz pleaded with me to eat. He shouted at me, hoping to provoke some reaction, speech or tears or another fit of screaming, but I remained totally passive, like the deaf-mute idiot Evan Bradford had taken into his care.

On Wednesday morning, Gabe Rosati sent Eddie Powell down to the Village to find out why I hadn't appeared for work. Without admitting him into the apartment, Diaz informed Eddie that I was ill.

17

I watched Diaz prepare for his trip to Chicago. He wore his same old black trousers and a black vest over a wilted white shirt. His suit jacket, thrown over the open lid of his battered suitcase, was missing a button. I felt a pang. I hadn't been keeping up with the mending. At the last minute, Diaz found some notes and a dusty old book that he had forgotten to pack, and tossed them in on top of his underwear and clean shirts.

Stooping, he kissed my cheek. "I wish I did not have to leave you. But you will be better when I get back."

I didn't remind him that I had once maintained a stony silence for nearly a year. Mere words could not express what I felt. Silence spoke most eloquently of my pain and misery.

After he had gone, I shuffled to the door and turned the key in the lock. Diaz had promised me that Angel wouldn't return, but I didn't trust him, didn't trust either of them. I would never again feel safe in this apartment.

I sat in my accustomed chair by the window. The heat on this mid-afternoon in June had driven all the residents of Bedford Street out of their tenements and onto the sidewalks. Across the street, Mr. Blumberger and another old gentleman were seated on the stoop, exchanging stories and cigars. I could see clearly a purplish bruise on Mr. Blumberger's cheek. The old man had done battle for my honor. He wasn't a Spaniard, he wasn't the son of a noble family, yet his actions had proclaimed him to be more chivalrous than Diaz.

I lifted my hand to my forehead. My own bruises had faded considerably. Soon they would be gone, vanished as though they had never existed. Flesh was more forgiving than spirit, I thought. I would not soon forget that I had very nearly killed a man.

Childish laughter drifted up from the street. The mist of despair that had enveloped me for a week was beginning to lift. I was starting to notice little things again: the new lace curtains at the window opposite mine; a ginger cat dozing on a table behind a potted geranium; a little girl wearing a blue bow in her hair. The pattern of movement below my window altered slightly. People who had been strolling down the middle of the narrow street moved to the sidewalks to make way for a car, a black sedan.

The car stopped under my window and two men got out, both wearing hats and gray suits, even in this hot weather. One of them addressed a question to Mr. Blumberger.

"I don't know anybody by that name," the old man said with uncharacteristic brusqueness. "You guys are in the wrong place."

A fat woman projected her bulk into the discussion. "Diaz? That's the Spic lives across the street. Second floor. Lives with a high-class floozie, tall girl with brown hair."

"Shut up, you old bag," Mr. Blumberger said. "There ain't nobody—"

"She's up there," the woman went on. "She ain't been out of the house in days."

"Nobody's there, I tell you!"

I wondered who these men were, and why Mr. Blumberger was trying so hard to keep them away. The entry door opened and closed. Footsteps bumped on the stairs. They were on their way up. I looked down at my dress, a sheer summer thing, limp with perspiration, wrinkled from careless sitting. I wasn't even wearing a slip or a brassiere. But unexpected visitors had to be prepared to find women in states of deshabille, especially on a blistering hot day in June.

The thumping on the door seemed unnecessarily forceful. I pictured the two men looking around while they pounded with their fists, taking in the discolored linoleum in the hallway, breathing the hot stink of poverty, the stale cooking, the babies, the unwashed humanity. I would have to let them in, just to stop their infernal knocking. I dragged myself over to the door and turned the key.

The larger of the two men displayed a shield on his wallet identifying him as Agent Krumm of the U.S. Treasury Department.

"We're looking for Luis Diaz. Is he here?"

"No," I croaked, my voice rusty from disuse. "He's gone out of town." Pushing open the door, the two men surged past me.

Krumm jerked his head at the bedroom. "Go take a look, Matt," he said to his partner.

"Just a minute," I said. "Do you have a warrant? You can't come barging in here. Stop that!" I had followed the second man into the other room, where he was dumping the contents of my drawers onto the bed. After sifting through my things, he started to root around in my closet. "What do you think you're doing? Stop it at once!"

"When do you expect Diaz to get back?" Krumm ignored my protestations. "We'd like to ask him a couple of questions about some friends of his who have been engaging in a little counterfeiting." He mentioned the names of two prominent Communist Party officials who had been frequent visitors to our apartment.

"Why don't you ask them the questions?" I glared at the man who was emerging from the bedroom. "I don't know anything about them."

"We can get your fancy man out of this country pretty quick if we revoke his visa," Krumm said threateningly.

"My 'fancy man' has as much right to be in this country as you have," I informed him. "Go look for your counterfeiters somewhere else." I opened the door to the hallway and stood there, waiting for them to leave.

"Look, lady, if you won't cooperate here, you can cooperate at police headquarters. Take your choice. Matt, take a look through that stuff." Krumm indicated the mounds of paper on Diaz's desk, which included the enlargements I had been working on when Angel interrupted me. "Take a good look." The other man started to toss around photos and snatches of poetry. Picking up one of my Lowell photographs, he growled, "Damned subversive crap," and ripped it in half.

"Leave those things alone!" I grabbed his arm and tried to pull him away from the table. "You have no right to force your way in here."

He shook me off. I threw myself at him again and dragged at his sleeve. Krumm came up behind me and slung his arm across my chest, restraining me. Lowering my head, I sank my teeth into his hand. I bore down, hard, until my jaws hurt. With a roar, Krumm picked me up and threw me against the wall. I didn't release my grip on the other man's jacket. I heard a tearing sound, and another vocal expression of masculine ire.

For the second time in as many weeks, I found myself lying on the floor with a red-faced man standing over me. He was Angel. He was Sid Jenkins. He was a faceless stockholder of the company. He was a soldier of Spain's Guardia Civil. He was a man who liked to wield power over weak people who had none.

"You damned bullies," I panted, hauling myself into a sitting position. "Persecuting innocent people who don't have money or influence—"

"Take it easy," Krumm snapped. "We're not persecuting anybody."

"Oh, no? What do you call it? Get out of my house, do you hear me? Get out of here!" Scrambling to my feet, I hurled myself at them again. Krumm caught my arms and pulled them behind my back while his partner snapped handcuffs around my wrists. They dragged me down the stairs and out to the car.

When Mr. Blumberger saw me, he started to shout in a voice that was suddenly young and full of hatred and vigor: "Scabs! Filthy scabs! Why don't you leave her alone, you lousy scabs!"

I spent the night in the company of a listless group of prostitutes and a woman who had been accused of beating her lover to death with a hammer. She wailed all night, insisting loudly that she had no choice, it was either kill or be killed. When one of the prostitutes managed to impress upon her the very real possibility that she might not live to see the dawn if she didn't shut up, she finally subsided.

In the morning I was charged with sedition, interfering with a Federal officer in performance of his duty, obstructing justice, resisting arrest, and disturbing the peace. I refused to avail myself of the single telephone call that might have secured for me the services of a lawyer. I was too angry. That afternoon I was taken to the Tombs to await a hearing. My cell was small, but at least I had it all to myself. Solitary. Clearly I represented a very real threat to the Government of the United States.

After I had paced off the fifty-four square feet of my cell, examined the sink and the latrine bucket, and tested my mattress, I lowered myself onto the edge of my cot. I had always considered myself a loyal American, a good citizen. Yet here I sat, in a dank cubicle that reeked of carbolic and mildew and urine. Why? Because two suspected counterfeiters had visited my home? I knew for a fact that two of the city's more enlightened socialites had entertained those same Communist Party mem-

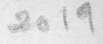

bers in their drawing rooms. Surely neither of those gracious ladies had been subjected to arrest and imprisonment, or a body
search that I had found almost as humiliating and degrading as
Angel's rape of me?

From the moment I renounced Evan Bradford's money and
left the protective shelter of his influence, I had become just another faceless, powerless member of the masses. No U.S. Treasury agent would have dared to barge into Evan's house on
Gramercy Park without proper authorization. But the occupants of a squalid apartment in Greenwich Village deserved no
such consideration. I was glad Diaz hadn't been there to witness
those indignities. They would only have confirmed his opinion
of the dualism in American justice.

Oddly, I felt no fear, no despair at my plight. I felt deeply
ashamed of my country, and deeply outraged at the way it had
betrayed me.

Anger sustained me during the four long days of my deten-
tion. On the morning of my hearing, a matron opened the door
of my cell. "Okay, sister, you're out."

I expected to be handcuffed and transported by police car or
paddy wagon to the Federal Courthouse in Brooklyn. Instead,
the woman escorted me to a room not much bigger than a telephone booth and instructed me to take off my prison smock and
to put on the dress I had worn on the day of my arrest. When I
had done that, she pressed a buzzer, summoning a uniformed
man who handed me a manila envelope containing my wristwatch, the only object I had had with me at the time of my arrest. I refused to sign a paper stating that everything I had in my
possession when I was admitted to the prison had been returned
to me. Taking note of my refusal, the matron and the uniformed
man signed the paper themselves.

Another door opened. The matron led me into a larger room
whose bare walls and high ceiling were scabby with flakes of
green paint. The room was furnished with a few scuffed wood-
en chairs and a small table, at which a guard was seated. The
windows had no bars.

Evan Bradford and Gabe Rosati stood together in the center of the room, carefully touching nothing that might sully their immaculate splendor. The two of them seemed to have dressed as if for a competition to see which could outdo the other in the race for sartorial elegance. Evan had chosen a tan suit with a yellow cambric shirt. He carried a yellow straw hat and a gold-headed walking stick. Gabe gleamed like cool marble in a white linen suit, striped shirt, and powder blue necktie. I decided that I would have to award Evan the prize: his cane added a worldly touch that Gabe's costume lacked.

A third highly polished man had decided to take a chance on one of the chairs. He sat with his briefcase displayed prominently in front of his chest like an identity badge: I am a lawyer. He got to his feet when I entered the room.

Ignoring Evan, I fixed my gaze on my employer, who came forward smiling. "Well, you're free, Theo," he said. "The charges have been dropped. The judge agreed that Krumm and Matthews had been a little overeager. Sorry this took so long, but I only found out about it two days ago. Some little guy who lives on your block came to the office yelling about scabs and strikebreakers. I had a hard time getting him to tell me what had really happened."

"What about Luis?" I asked. "Is he home yet? Is he all right?" Out of the corner of my eye, I saw Evan shift his weight onto his cane.

"I tracked him down in some flea—in a little hotel in Chicago," Gabe said. "I told him what happened. He'll be back tomorrow night."

The lawyer cleared his throat. "I am afraid Mr. Diaz may have a little trouble with the State Department when he gets back. They are reviewing his visa with an eye toward rescinding it. They don't like the articles he's written lately for certain organs of the leftist press, and they are disturbed by his potentially seditious influence on his students."

I said, "They'd better review the case very carefully if they don't want to be sued for a violation of his civil rights. Señor Diaz is an American citizen now."

The lawyer didn't like anyone telling him his business. "I'm afraid I don't understand, Miss Lowery."

"Then I'll explain it to you." Glancing at Evan, I said in a clear voice, "Señor Diaz and I were married last April. You can check the records at City Hall if you like."

I didn't tell them how sudden it had been, how ordinary—like applying for a license to drive or registering to vote. Because of Diaz's political sympathies, the United States Department of Immigration and Naturalization had advised him of its intention to refuse to renew his visa, due to expire on the fifteenth of June. At that time, he would be ejected from the country. One of Diaz's colleagues at the university suggested a simple solution: marry an American woman. Citizenship would be automatic, and he could stay in this country for as long as he liked.

"We might as well marry," Luis said to me. "It will show them that I have no intention of being bullied and coerced by their stupid bureaucracy." And that was that. We applied for our license, waited the required three days, then sought out a judge to perform the wedding. A couple of clerks served as witnesses. There was no party, no celebration of any kind. When we left City Hall, Diaz walked up Sixth Avenue to our apartment on Bedford Street, and I took the subway uptown to the *Mode* offices. I didn't tell anyone at work that I had just become a new bride. Diaz and I didn't exchange wedding rings. Ours wasn't a real marriage, after all; merely a protest at the way the government was treating him. I worked in the developing lab until nine or ten that night. Diaz was out when I got home, and I went to bed alone. I didn't bother to inform Mr. Blumberger that our union was legal now. He had been calling me Mrs. Diaz ever since I moved to Bedford Street.

"Well," said Gabe Rosati after a surprised silence, "that certainly puts a new light on things. Congratulations, Theo. You might have told us, you know."

He is a city

I felt suddenly sick and dizzy. "I think I'd like to get out of here."

Evan didn't move. Gabe Rosati sprang to my side and took my elbow. "Of course you would, Theo. We've been inconsiderate. How shall we celebrate your freedom? Lunch at the Algonquin? Champagne and lobster in my apartment? Or perhaps Evan has a better idea?"

We had reached the door. The guard moved to open it, but I held back. "I think I'd rather just go home alone, if you don't mind."

Evan spoke for the first time. "Don't be a fool, Theodora," he growled. "I have the Rolls. We'll drop you."

"Oh, I'm a fool all right." I shook off Gabe's hand and faced both of them. "I wasn't aware that you and Evan knew each other, Mr. Rosati. But here you are, sharing the same car, calling each other by your first names, springing the same girl from jail. It's quite a coincidence. Or maybe it's more than that."

Evan and Rosati exchanged quick glances. Evan said, "Gabe's a good friend of Hugo de Graaf's. You knew that. Hugo and I see a lot of each other out in Hollywood."

"But that doesn't mean he's your friend, too," I said. "You're certainly right up to date on what's been happening to me, aren't you, Evan? Thanks to Mr. Rosati of *Mode* magazine. He's been sending you regular reports on my progress, hasn't he?"

"You have no cause to act this way, Theodora," Evan said sharply. "We've been acting in your best interests."

"My best interests! That sounds like one of your fine evasive phrases, Evan. Why don't you just admit that Mr. Rosati has been spying on me for you? Well, hasn't he?"

"My dear girl," Gabe Rosati sighed, "you do have an unfortunate way of phrasing things. Evan and I have known each other for ages."

"Ages? You consider the nine months that I've worked for *Mode* ages?"

"Nothing of the sort," Evan put in. "Last fall, after you started the job, I asked Gabe to keep me informed of your whereabouts, your welfare, that sort of thing. You may have put me out of your life, but I couldn't just wash my hands of you, could I? I was concerned about you, Dory. I wanted you to be happy."

At this point the lawyer, murmuring something about a pressing appointment, slithered out. The guard continued to stand woodenly at the outside door. Hear no evil, I thought.

I said, "When Mr. Rosati found out that I was in trouble, he raised the alarm and you came rushing back east to rescue me, didn't you, Evan? You were probably on your way when you heard about my arrest. Eddie Powell came to the apartment while I was ill. I suppose he's one of your spies, too."

"I do wish you'd stop using that word," Gabe Rosati said.

" 'Look after the girl. Let me know if she needs anything, and I'll take care of it.' That's what you told him, isn't it, Evan? I've had two raises since I started at the magazine. I thought it was strange, times being what they are." I wheeled around to face my editor. "No wonder you were so nice to me. You could offer me the moon, knowing that Evan Bradford would reimburse you."

"You're jumping to all sorts of erroneous conclusions, Theo," Rosati began. "Your talent—"

I didn't give him a chance. "The spread you've scheduled for the fall, the gallery showing, all that talk about finding a book publisher—I have no doubt you would have found one. Who wouldn't publish a book of photographs, knowing that they'd make a profit even if it didn't sell one copy?"

The editor drew himself up. "My dear, no one could pay me enough to keep an employee that I didn't want. You're being unfair. You're a fine photographer, one of the best I've ever worked with."

"I don't believe you," I said. "Evan was paying for me all along, subsidizing my raises and bonuses and my project, and I didn't know it." I raked my fingers through my limp hair. In spite of the ablutions I'd performed at the sink of my cell, I felt like I hadn't had a bath in years. "*Mode* wasn't going to publish my pictures because they were good or important, but because

Evan Bradford wanted them to, and Evan Bradford has influence in this town, doesn't he? After all, he's a rich man. He could buy *Mode* if he wanted to, as easily as he bought the judge this morning. My position at the magazine wasn't something I'd earned, but something Evan bought for me. And I was too stupid to realize what was going on. It was so obvious, but I never dreamed—"

"It's a false and foolish kind of pride that makes a person think he can achieve success in this world without anyone's help." An odd note in Rosati's voice made me wonder whom he could thank for boosts up the ladder.

"You didn't have the guts to tell me what you were doing, either of you, so that I could decide for myself whether I wanted your help or not. Don't you see what this means? Everything I've accomplished so far is false. I'll never know if my work was any good or not."

The guard opened the door for me, and I walked out of the Tombs. Under an overcast sky, with a light rain falling, the place loomed up behind me, black and formidable, like Dickens' Bastille. My protective cloak of shock and pride and righteous anger was slipping away. I realized that I had actually been a prisoner, surrounded by high walls, guarded by men in watchtowers whose guns were trained on my freedom. I stood there trembling, feeling a deepening chill of horror in my soul even as the rain soaked through the thin fabric of my dress and chilled my flesh.

Evan came up behind me and draped his suit jacket over my shoulders. "I'll take you home, Dory."

"I don't want—"

He gripped my elbow and steered me toward the waiting Rolls. "Get in."

Too tired to argue further, I obeyed. I supposed that Gabe Rosati had gone the way of the lawyer, uptown in a taxi.

Evan settled himself beside me. "Would you like something to eat?"

"No, thank you. I just want to go home." I gave Evan's chauf-

feur the address on Bedford. The Rolls glided into motion, nego-
tiating the cramped and crooked streets of southern Manhattan
as effortlessly as if they had been Connecticut country lanes.

Bedford Street looked eerily empty, thanks to the menacing
and uncertain weather, which had discouraged stoop-sitting and
sidewalk games for the day. Throwing off Evan's jacket, I
climbed out of the car and entered the apartment building without a backward glance. My door was unlocked. I wasn't worried:
the neighbors would respect our belongings—not that we had
anything worth stealing. As I walked into the front room, I remembered that I had left the windows wide open. What Krumm
and his partner had failed to do, wind and rain had accomplished: Diaz's books and notes and my photographs were
ruined, soaked, stuck together, hurled to every corner of the
room.

Stooping, I gathered up a double fistful of papers. One of
Luis's notebooks lay open to a page somewhere in the middle.
Whole lines and phrases had been washed away, as if by a torrent of tears. I could still decipher a few words in Spanish: "The
old woman is a mother, a weeping girl, a laughing child—" Perhaps Diaz could remember enough of what he had written to re-
construct the words that had been lost. Words, responsible for
so much agony, so much joy. Words as fragile as spiderwebs, as
strong as steel girders.

Even as I heard the Rolls pull away, Evan spoke behind me.
"You don't love him."

Rising slowly, I let the papers I'd been holding drop to the
floor. The room was a shambles, worse than any scene from
Diaz's carefree slovenly bachelor days.

Evan said again, "You don't love him."

"No." Weariness began to press down on me. "I don't love
him. He doesn't love me. But we help each other."

"Dory, about this Rosati business: I promise you, I had nothing to do with his decision to publish those special pictures you
were working on."

"It doesn't matter." I moved to the windows and lowered the

sashes. Another storm was blowing up. "I should have quit that job long ago, but I didn't have the courage. Too interested in the regular paycheck, I guess."

"What will you do now?"

I gazed down at the street. Pieces of paper whirled past, sucked along like bits of ocean flotsam by an invisible undertow. "If we stay in New York, we'll be harassed and annoyed. Luis isn't a Communist. Neither am I. We're interested in freedom and justice. But in America that makes us dangerous radicals. Luis has talked about going back to Paris. I suppose I can find work there." I turned. "You don't have any influence in French publishing circles, do you?"

"Not that I know of," Evan smiled. "Dory—"

"I'm very tired, Evan. I think I'd like to take a bath and lie down before I start cleaning this place up. It would upset Luis to see it like this."

"Luis!" Evan's eyebrows converged over his aristocratic nose. "I can't believe it. After all you've been through, you're still eager to play housemaid to that second-rate Latin doggerel writer."

"I didn't realize you were a connoisseur of modern poetry, Evan." I moved past him. "But I suppose if anyone can judge if something is second-rate—"

Snatching at my wrist, he spun me around. "Damn you," he said through clenched teeth, "you have no right to talk to me that way."

"You have no right to interfere in my life. That makes us even."

He jerked me closer. His skin looked bad, sallow and unhealthy; his eyes were tired, etched with red. I could smell coffee and pipe tobacco on his breath, but, surprisingly, no whiff of bourbon.

"I'm impressed," I said. "You've managed to remain sober on the occasion of my release from jail."

He twisted my wrist sharply, hurting me, letting me feel his power. Every muscle and sinew in my body tightened and tensed, but I resolved not to cry out, not to struggle.

The room darkened, as though a veil had descended over the world, dark veiling but sheer, like widow's weeds. Thunder rumbled in the distance as sullen drops of rain smacked against the windowpanes. The air between us became stifling. Beads of perspiration trickled down between my breasts.

Suddenly the storm broke over the city with a deafening roar. I felt the anger between us flowing away. And something else rushed in to take its place.

Keeping my eyes on Evan's face, I began to twist the buttons on my dress with my free hand, opening them slowly, one by one.

18

"*Bon soir, Madame Diaz.*"
"*Bon soir, Monsieur Victor.*"

The concierge and I chatted for a few minutes about his rheumatism, the weather, the intriguing new tenants on the third floor. His wife called to him. Grimacing, he ducked behind a little door just inside the entrance. I shifted my load of cameras and groceries and prepared to assault the six flights of stairs to the summit. By early evening, most of the other occupants of the building were at home, preparing their meals for the table and their children for bed. I couldn't help eavesdropping on their lives as I passed their doors: "Look what you've done to my knitting, you bad cat!" "If you don't wash your face at once, I'll box your ears." "What do you mean, you're still in love with her? She hasn't given you a thought since she ran away with that fire-eater."

Up in our flat, Diaz and a young pianist argued the comparative uses of harmony and dissonance in music and poetry. Diaz flashed me a welcome with his eyes without breaking the rhythm of his rapid French.

The pianist's girlfriend followed me into the kitchen and asked if she could help with preparations for dinner. Since it looked like she and her companion would be staying, I gave her potatoes to peel and carrots to scrape and slice. I would make a simple chicken stew, American-style, without saffron or rice or hot peppers. Whenever Luis wanted Spanish food, he went to Angel's studio in Montmartre. Angel had a reputation among his artist friends for being able to make a fabulous paella out of nothing. Why not? I thought. He stole only the finest ingredients. He probably even stole his pots and pans.

I had caught only infrequent glimpses of Angel in the three years that Diaz and I had lived in Paris. The first time, Diaz and I had been enjoying an evening stroll after one of our rare evenings out together. We followed the Seine along the Right Bank until we came to the Pont Royal, one of the bridges that spanned the river near the Tuileries. I saw Angel standing against the wall of the embankment.

Stopping abruptly, I slipped my hand out of the curve of Diaz's arm.

"You talk to him, Luis. I'll go home alone."

"Nonsense. I just saw him the other day." We walked back the way we had come. Glancing back over my shoulder, I saw Angel grinning at us.

I prepared to light the gas under the stew pot. As usual, all the kitchen matches had found their way into the other room, for the convenience of the smokers.

As I entered the sitting room, Diaz said, "Theodora, you were very late tonight."

"The paper sent me out to Versailles to photograph a minor Rumanian prince being shown the sights. Diplomats and journalists stumbling all over each other. On the way home, some frustrated lover hurled himself in front of my train. We sat for hours until they located his legs, back under one of the second-

class carriages. I got out to take a picture, but it was too horrible. Paris will have to do without a glimpse of that particular
human tragedy."

"A pity," Diaz murmured vaguely. He resumed his discussion
with the musician. "The gods have not proclaimed any hard and
fast rules decreeing that melody must be an essential ingredient
of music, any more than rhyme need be a component of poetry."

Helping myself to a match, I returned to the kitchen.

My life hadn't changed much from those days on Bedford
Street. I worked part time for the liberal daily newspaper *Paris-
Matin*, and did some free-lancing for the glossier magazines. I
would have undertaken more portrait work, which I found en-
joyable and lucrative, but I couldn't seem to save enough money
to set up a private studio. In between photographic assignments,
I managed the household, paid the bills, cooked the meals and
swept the floors, and made sure my husband took an umbrella
with him when he ventured out into the rain. In three years, I
had spent a small fortune on umbrellas.

Diaz continued to devote the hours between midnight and
dawn to poetry. The critics praised his new poems, most of
them songs in the Andalusian gypsy tradition. They were beautiful, those poems: strong and sensual, earthy and violent, with a
strange vein of mysticism. I had been surprised, and moved,
when I read the dedication to his latest book: "For Theodora,
shining light."

After sleeping most of the day, Diaz rose after noon to receive
visitors or to meet his friends in their favorite cafes. Although
he and I usually spent our evenings together, we were seldom
alone. The students and intellectuals who used to visit the little
apartment on Bedford Street seemed to have followed us across
the Atlantic, to be joined on the Rue Ave Maria in the ancient
Marais district of Paris by a host of Spaniards eager to pay their
respects to a fellow countryman-in-exile.

I told myself that I had no regrets. I was older now. The gap
between expectation and reality had narrowed. Luis and I
would never share the searing, soaring bliss that I had known

briefly with Evan, but we had reached a plateau of understanding. These days I weathered his moods as calmly as if they were changes in atmospheric pressure. Together we were building a solid, enduring relationship, laying stone upon stone, making sure the joints were tight and the mortar strong before proceeding to the next layer. At times Luis's determined self-absorption infuriated and exasperated me, and I wanted to dynamite the whole structure. But I kept my temper under tight control. Since the incident with Angel, I knew what violence lay in my heart. I wanted never to unleash it again, no matter how Diaz or anyone else provoked me.

After dinner was over and the plates and glasses cleared away, the young pianist and his companion excused themselves.

"Did you see the way he was looking at her?" Diaz asked. "He couldn't wait to get her into bed. As a good host, I should have offered them ours, but as it will be occupied—" He slid up behind me as I stood at the kitchen sink.

Fists hammered at the door. I said, "Occupied with coats and babies, you mean. The evening contingent of visitors has arrived."

"Don't answer it," Diaz whispered, holding me tightly around the middle. "Pretend we're not home. We will go to bed and I will give you a baby of your own."

I was startled. Never before had Luis mentioned having a child. I had assumed he wasn't interested in fatherhood. Not that I had taken any precautions: I would have loved to have a baby. But so far, nothing had happened. I worried that my difficult teenage pregnancy had left me barren.

More pounding, and shouts in Spanish. I detached his arms from my waist. "You'd better let them in before they break down your door."

The arrivals were three Spanish Communist labor leaders who had fled their country after a revolution in the province of Asturias late in 1934, a year and a half earlier. At the order of the conservative government then in power, General Francisco

Franco had crushed the uprising. He brought in a contingent of
Foreign Legionnaires and Moorish soldiers, ruthless fighters
with no spiritual ties to the Spanish soil. For the first time, a
Spanish government had called in mercenaries to make war on
Spaniards. Hatred and bitterness at Franco and the leaders of
the conservatives still burned in the hearts of Diaz's countrymen.

"Such things will not happen under the new Republic," one
of the men said as they settled down to talk. "The Popular Front
won the last election handily. The people really support the
new government. President Azaña may be a pious old fart, but
he would never permit the army to abuse the people like that."

"Permit?" another yelped. "You cannot keep the army from
acting when they want to act. The army is the army."

The third man reminded them, "Election or no election, the
Catholic-Conservative element is still the most unified force in
Spanish politics. Those are the people with money, and money
is the equivalent of power."

I brewed some strong coffee for Diaz and his friends, then retired to the kitchen, where I began to dismantle my trusty Leica.
The sprockets had been tearing the film lately, which meant I
probably had a particle of film caught in the works somewhere.
Since I needed to take the camera apart anyway, I would give it
a thorough cleaning. I assembled clean rags and brushes and set
to work.

More guests arrived, but I stayed out of sight. Diaz's friends
weren't interested in me.

One of the new visitors was a woman, an American, who
started braying in that high-pitched voice adopted by some En-
glish-speakers when they try to communicate with foreigners.
Diaz welcomed her in English. Her companion boomed, "Jesus,
Luis, you're looking great. I see you've put on a little weight.
Better watch it. Pretty soon you'll look like me. I brought some
good Scotch whiskey for you and the boys. What say we drink
to old times?"

The voice sounded familiar, but I couldn't place it right away.

Coffee cups rattled as the men drained the last drops to make way for the whiskey. To my surprise, none of the Asturians seemed inclined to leave after the two Americans invaded. The man began to bellow in fair Spanish, and soon they were all talking not about politics but about the bulls, and the prospects for the upcoming corridas in Madrid, Barcelona, Sevilla. The American sounded knowledgeable, and even provoked some good-humored argument with his pronouncements about the strengths and weaknesses of this or that matador. Their names were all strange to me. I had never seen a bullfight, and I didn't want to. Bloodletting, however ritualized or ceremonial, held no glory for me.

Luis amused himself by translating the goriest tales of the bullring for the American's female companion, who squealed at each grim new revelation. "Oh, I've simply got to see one. Hugo, can we go to Madrid? Please, honey?"

Hugo? Of course, Hugo de Graaf, the film director, Fiona's mentor in Hollywood, the man whose conversation on that long-ago evening at Elf Hill had resulted in my banishment to the realms of outer darkness. My single encounter with Hugo de Graaf had changed my life.

At that moment Hugo's large figure filled the curtained doorframe. "Oh, hello there. Looking for a clean glass. One of the boys just dropped a cigarette butt into mine."

I glanced up from my dismembered camera. "On that shelf up there, Mr. de Graaf."

Hugo drew his brows together. "I know you. Never forget a face. Names, sure, but not faces. Something to do with Fiona Randall."

"I'm her niece," I said. "We met at her estate in Connecticut several years ago. My name is Theodora Lowery. Luis is my husband."

"No kidding? Luis didn't tell me he was an old married man. Hell, Luis and I go back about twenty years. I spent some time in Spain after the war. We did a lot of drinking together, and he took me to my first bullfight. Quite an experience. Like your first orgasm."

"I doubt that," I smiled. "I'm surprised. I wouldn't have thought that sort of thing would attract Luis. He's not sports-minded."

"Honey, bullfighting has about as much to do with sports as fucking. It's more like religion. Without the hypocrisy." Hugo looked over my shoulder. His bulk usurped most of the small space in the kitchen. "Nice old Leica," he remarked. "Sure, I know you now: kid who takes pictures. Still at it?"

"Oh, yes. Mostly magazine work, with an occasional portrait commission. We manage." I picked up the leaf shutter apparatus and dusted it carefully with a sable-haired brush. "Are you still making movies?"

"Sure am. I've got to pay my four ex-bitches their alimony somehow. Christ, I made three goddamn films last year and I'm still broke. Managed to talk the big bosses in Culver City into letting me shoot some backgrounds here in Paris. Strictly bull-shit. They can get the same streets on a sound stage, and cheap-er, but I won them three Academy Awards last year and right now I'm their fair-haired boy. 'Give de Graaf what he wants,' they said. I told them I wanted Paris. I got Paris."

"Congratulations."

"Fiona snagged herself an Oscar last year, too," Hugo said. "I didn't direct her. These days she's directing herself. What Fiona wants, Fiona gets. I haven't worked with her for a couple of years. We stopped seeing eye to eye long ago."

"Fiona always had very strong ideas about how she wanted her scenes to go." Using a bulb duster, I blew invisible particles of dust out of the inside of my lens.

"Strong, hell. The woman's a reincarnation of Lucretia Bor-gia. Poison rings and all."

I tried to keep my voice steady. "How is her husband? Evan Bradford?"

"For one thing, he isn't her husband anymore. She finally got tired of him. She's got a new one now, one of those ever-so-charming British lads. So goddamned refined that he makes Evan Bradford look like a caveman. You'd never know he was the bastard son of a Limehouse whore. But that's show biz."

"I guess Evan's gone back to New York?"

Hugo shrugged. "From what I hear, Evan's gone to the dogs, but I can't tell you where he's chosen to do it. Last time I saw him, after the divorce, he was drinking pretty heavily. Nasty drunk, too. Obnoxious. Bartender had to ask him to leave. I drove him home. Poor bastard was sick all over my damned car. Spent some time in the hospital after that, with pneumonia and God knows what else. They dried him out, but the minute they turned him loose, he fell right off the wagon. I know his doc. Says it's a race between Bradford's liver and his brain to see which will give out first."

I stood motionless. A tear rolled off the tip of my nose and fell onto the leaf shutter pieces.

"Better wipe that up." Hugo handed me a cloth. "You don't want that shutter to rust."

"Leave me alone. Please. Just go away."

Hugo picked up the shutter and wiped it carefully.

"Isn't a thing you or anybody else can do for a man like Evan," he said. He tested the shutter, the winding mechanism, the focus adjustment. "Just thank God that you're six thousand miles away. You can tear yourself apart watching something like that happen to somebody you love. Blaming yourself. Feeling guilty. Bad, all the way around." He worked steadily, capably. I watched his hands while I listened to the talk and the laughter in the other room. Hugo's female companion seemed to be trying to learn rudimentary Spanish from the Asturians. "Jesus, she's a stupid bitch," Hugo sighed. "Can't even speak English, and now she's trying out Spanish."

"Your wife?" I asked.

Hugo's solid presence had shored me up. He was right, I told myself. I couldn't help Evan. No one could. Even so, I wished that I could believe in a deity who took an active interest in people's lives. All I could do for Evan now was pray.

"No, thank God." Hugo started to reassemble the camera.
"Thinks she's going to be, but I haven't told her the bad news.
I'd have to be crazy to marry another actress. But hell, that's all
I meet in my work, and they're so damned sexy and willing.
Seem to think that if they lay the director, he'll be able to get a
better performance out of them. Who am I to disillusion them?
But this one couldn't act if she went to bed with Christ himself.
Don't tell her I said so. All finished." He snapped the lens cover
on and put the camera in its case. "You can out-Stieglitz Stieglitz tomorrow with this baby. Come on, you need a drink of that
whiskey worse than I do. If that bitch hasn't poured it all down
her beautiful throat, that is."

Hugo propelled me into the other room and thrust a generous
whiskey into my hand. I found myself seated next to a Spanish
miner, a man with gnarled hands and a ravaged face that would
forever bear the stains of the coal he had wrested from the earth.
He was articulate, soft-spoken. He had been educated by the village priest, he told me, in exchange for doing odd jobs around
the priest's residence. But no amount of education could keep
him out of the mines. In Asturias, one of the poorest of Spanish
provinces, the mines provided the only means of livelihood.

He talked about the strike, which had begun as a revolt of the
workers against their overseers and landlords. Yes, some of the
men had lost their senses, committed foolish acts, drawn blood,
killed. But surely not even those random acts of violence called
for the use of the Moors. Savages! A few years ago, the Spanish
army had been battling those demons in Morocco, trying to
keep them out of Spain. Then Franco invited the animals in and
turned them loose on his own people. The Moors weren't like
civilized men. Some of them were shrouded in burnooses; some
even carried curved scimitars. Jesus, Mary, Joseph, that was a
bloody time. They didn't just kill, they hacked honest men into
pieces. Children, too. And women. What didn't they do to wom-
en? And the Spanish generals who were commanding them let
them have their fill of blood. Workers' blood. Innocent blood.
On General Franco's hands.

The miner had seen his own son cut down like an animal in a slaughterhouse. His wife was raped by a half-dozen Moorish soldiers. Her insides were completely torn up. She died without regaining consciousness.

In my mind, the rough hills of Asturias looked like Monkey Gulch, Colorado. The miners were the men I had known as a child. Their children—I had gone to school with their children, Pilar and Joaquin.

As he talked, I sat composed and outwardly calm, my hands folded in my lap, while tears began to stream down my cheeks. The man noticed my distress and spoke softly to Diaz, who was engaged in lively conversation with Hugo. The room fell silent. Everyone stared at me.

Diaz said, "Theodora, are you all right? What is the matter?"

"I was just telling her about the strike," the miner said. "All of a sudden she started to cry. I am very sorry, Señora. I didn't mean—"

"No, no, it's all right." I stood quickly. "Luis, excuse me, I have to go out. Please don't worry about me. I forgot to do something at the laboratory this afternoon, very important. Don't let me disturb you."

Diaz looked puzzled, but he could hardly forbid me to leave. I snatched my trenchcoat off the rack near the door and tied the sash with shaking fingers. Conversation started up again.

"Gee, what's the matter with her?" Hugo's actress wondered.

"Shut up, baby," Hugo said wearily. "For once, just shut up."

I took the Métro to the Bureau de Postes et Téléphones on the Rue de Vaugirard, where the cable office stayed open all night. There I drafted a wire to Evan's mother in Southampton, Long Island, New York, U.S.A.: "Please send news Evan's welfare and whereabouts. Most urgent. Theodora." I gave my address as the cable office.

"I'll wait for an answer," I told the clerk as I handed over the form. Why was I doing this? To confirm what I already knew in my heart, that Evan was dead, or mad? Did I really want to torture myself with reproaches and regrets?

The clerk looked skeptical. "It could take some time, Madame. It is the afternoon in that country. This person may be out. Why don't you come back tomorrow?"

I insisted. He shrugged his shoulders, suggesting that if I wanted to make a fool of myself, it was no concern of his. Choosing a chair in a remote corner, I sat down to wait. It was nearly midnight, and all the postal services had shut down for the night. Only the telephone and telegraph desks were still operating, attracting a few customers. Their footsteps echoed in the vast, hollow chamber.

"Yes," I should have said to Evan, "yes, I'll be your friend, your lover, your mistress, your slave. Anything, I'll do anything if only I can be close to you." But instead I had put pride before love. Why hadn't someone told me that you shouldn't put anything before love?

Three years, and I still remembered every detail of our last meeting: the heat, the sweat, the drum of raindrops on glass, the frantic beating of our hearts. We hardly uttered a word after that first hurtful exchange. In the past, words had always obscured what we really wanted to say to each other. This time we had spoken with our hands, our lips, our bodies. We battled, we reconciled, we knew blessed peace, and all without saying a word. That day was our hail and farewell, the beginning and the end of the love affair we had once talked about. Three years after the affair ended, I still grieved for what I had lost.

I never told Luis what had happened, but he knew. He was too perceptive to attribute the changes he saw in me to the experience of four days in prison. With Evan, I had existed briefly as a whole person, a woman whose mind and body and passions and desires unified in a single overwhelming purpose: to love. Love had shown me myself as I most wanted to be. Without love, I disintegrated into fragments again. I became more dissatisfied with my life, uneasy. Luis knew that I hadn't acquired my new edge of bitterness in the Tombs.

Every time I heard the rattle of the telegraph, I looked up, hoping to see the clerk beckoning to me. Like some self-assured

demimondaine, the clock on the wall above the counter seemed to sneer at my slavish attention even while relishing it. Two o'clock. Four-fifteen. Five-forty. I drooped in my chair. I was wasting my time. Mrs. Bradford could be anywhere, Biarritz or Palm Beach or Boston. Why should she be at home to receive my wire, or receiving it, take the trouble to respond? She and I hadn't communicated in years.

Then I heard my name. The clerk handed me a cable:

"Evan missing past two months. Very worried. Last illness extremely serious. You have some word? Fondly, Edith."

Walking home through a cold misting rain, I felt cut adrift, rootless, like a person whose house has burned down.

Luis was alone when I got back to the flat. He looked up from his desk. "You have finished your work?"

"Yes. Yes, it's all finished." I hung up my coat and set my purse down on the chair near the door.

"Hugo told me about your Mr. Bradford," Luis said. "I have been wondering if the day will ever come when you will weep like that for me?"

The question sounded rhetorical, but it wasn't. He waited for an answer.

"I don't know, Luis," I said. "I'm sorry."

"So am I, Theodora." He bent his head over his notebook. "So am I."

1920

The political discussions in our apartment that winter and spring became more heated. Visiting Spaniards confirmed the newspaper accounts we'd read of increasing incidences of unrest and violence in various parts of Spain. The new leftist government, an uneasy coalition of nearly thirty special-interest groups, seemed incapable of controlling outbreaks of savagery in towns and in the countryside. Strikes paralyzed the cities, disrupting essential services. In the Basque country and the province of Catalonia, with their special customs and special languages, separatist groups worked to foment revolution in their regions.

Where would it end? The army could not act independently of the government to restore order, unless certain generals took it into their heads to stage a coup. Priests had forfeited their power to soothe and heal. Long allied with the wealthy landowners and the repressive monarchy, the Church had lost her influence with the working people. Communists, Anarchists, Socialists, and trade unionists vied with each other for the hearts and minds of the workers. Their leaders promised land reform, redistribution of wealth, a new utopia, while the Church offered more of the same: pain and suffering in this world, and happiness in the hereafter.

"God help the poor illiterate who tries to make sense of Spanish politics." Diaz and I were the guests of Fernando Casado, a famous playwright and dialect poet from Barcelona. Señor Casado had insisted on taking us to dinner at one of his favorite Parisian restaurants, the Café Procope, which such luminaries as Diderot, Voltaire, and Benjamin Franklin had reputedly favored. "JONS, PCE, PSOE, FNTT," Diaz named just a few of Spain's major political parties and organizations: *Juntas de Ofensiva Nacional Sindicalista, Partido Comunista de España, Partido Socialista Obrero Español, Federación Nacional de Trabajadores de la Tierra.* "These groups are like vultures circling over the dying body of Spain."

Our host replenished the wine in our glasses. "Then again, a pack of hyenas may devour the vultures. Either way, the bones of Spain will be picked clean."

I said, "It sounds like the country is ripe for the emergence of a fascist dictator, like Hitler or Mussolini."

"You are astute, Señora." Casado smiled. "Many Spaniards already have a candidate for such a position: José Antonio Primo de Rivera, son of the late dictator. He is an interesting figure.

Young, articulate, compelling, with an impeccable character and the looks of a film star. His party, the Falange, has a policy that demands the reestablishment of the old order, with the Church restored to her rightful prominence. In his speeches and his writings, he harks back continually to the noble history of Spain, when she led the world in art and culture, and when all of western civilization bowed to her superior military might. José Antonio has attracted the attention of Spain's wealthier citizens. They see him as their savior, and perhaps their last hope. The army might rally behind him, and so would that portion of the population with whom the Church still holds some sway."

"Money, military might, and numbers," Diaz grunted. "So the new savior of my country is a fascist."

"José Antonio disclaims any links with fascism."

"Blue-shirted facist uniforms, fascist salutes. What else are we to think?"

The old poet from Barcelona refolded his napkin and placed it alongside his plate. "I think it is time for you to return to your home, Luis."

Diaz looked up sharply. "To Granada? Impossible. My father and I haven't communicated in years."

"Not to Granada. Home to Spain. You are greatly loved there, my boy. Your works are popular with young people. You are a hero, a man who turned his back on his own family because he could not accept the way they discharged their duties to society. Everyone knows you have a high sense of morality, a conscience. Yours is a voice that commands attention. Speak to your people, Luis. Tell them, in your poet's words, about their foolishness and the price of folly. They must desist from violence. They must not move too quickly, or they will lose everything they have gained."

"How can I talk to them?" Diaz asked. "I am a poet, not a politician."

"Thank God for that!" Señor Casado said. "Spain needs no more politicians. Politicians lie, they dissemble, they embroider facts. But poets speak the truth. Truth is a rare commodity in Spain these days. Your voice has not been heard in Spain for a long time, Luis. You have been away for nearly fifteen years, but in everything you write, Spain is there, a presence. You love her. What kind of chivalrous knight are you, observing the trials of your beloved from a distance? Flee to her side. Defend her against those who threaten her."

"You expect too much of me," Diaz protested. "I am not a good speaker. I am not a lawyer, who can argue a case. I can only write what I think and what I feel. I cannot exhort, I cannot challenge, I cannot condemn. I can only observe, and respond."

"Then do that," Señor Casado urged. "Go to Spain. Look at what they are doing. Express your feelings. The people will listen, I promise you."

Diaz's smile was bitter. "When I tell the people that they are like starving dogs fighting over a rotting corpse, they will not welcome me. You remember what happens to messengers who bring bad news? They give their lives for the truth."

"What else can one give his life for?" Casado asked reasonably. He summoned the waiter and asked for the bill. "Your self-imposed exile was a fine gesture that attracted a lot of attention. But the Spain of 1936 is not the Spain of 1921. The old order is crumbling, as you hoped. But what is there to replace it? Madness? Anarchy, in the most destructive sense of the word? The danger is clear, my son. The threat is real. If Spain were attacked by a foreign power, would you not rush to defend her?"

"I would do what I could to help my people." Diaz chose his words with care. "I would not fight. I would work for peace."

"Then do your noble work now, before the battle begins. Use your gifts as a poet to communicate sanity, caution, love of country. We have seen what can happen. The revolt in Asturias was a shameful blot on our history. My greatest fear is that it will be overshadowed by worse horrors."

"Surely not." Diaz frowned. "In spite of everything, Spain is a civilized country. This is the twentieth century, after all. The days of the Inquisition are long past."

Señor Casado shook his head. "You are a Spaniard. You know that death holds no fear for the Spaniard, so long as it is death with honor. Remember the slogan of the Foreign Legion: 'Long Live Death!' The same slogan is engraved on the heart of everyone in Spain. Death reigns. Death is the only constant in life. The people on the left, the Communists, the socialists, all are willing to die for their beliefs. Those on the right, the landowners, the army, the monarchists, are equally willing to die for theirs. We can only hope that neither side will strike the fatal spark. All that will remain of our country after the conflagration will be cinders. Do you want to be known as the 'Poet of Ashes'?"

"A good line," Diaz said. "I congratulate you."

The elder poet acknowledged the praise with a nod. "I am fortunate, Luis. I am an old man, nearly eighty. My heart is weak, and my lungs are shrinking. I will not live to see Spain's fate. For that I am almost grateful. But who will speak for sanity after I am gone? A poet must sing the truth, even if no one listens. A poet who sits in Paris while flames engulf his country is like a man who dreams of beautiful women while he spills his seed into a jar. Forgive me, Señora." He smiled at me before returning his attention to Diaz. "This man does not have to worry about catching an unpleasant disease; he need never fear that a woman will reject him; and he will never be saddled with unwanted bastards. He experiences none of the hazards of lovemaking, and none of its incomparable joys."

Diaz's cheeks had flushed above his beard. "You need have no fears about my manhood, my old friend," he said. "I promise you, I will consider carefully everything you have said, and then I will make my decision."

"Go home, Luis. Go home to Spain." Our host stood up, signaling the end of the meal. "Good night, Señora Diaz. Luis is fortunate in his choice of a wife. At least I know that he is still

capable of making some sound decisions." Señor Casado raised
my hand to his lips.

Diaz and I began walking back to our flat through the cool
spring air. "Don't be angry with him, Luis," I said after a while.
"He meant no offense. He's truly worried."

"I am not angry," Diaz said. "But what can one man do at this
stage, and a poet at that? Poets have their uses as court jesters
and as obituary writers, but when their countries erupt into
chaos, they are swept aside with everyone else. I can do nothing
to change the course my people have embarked on. Could
Homer have stopped the fall of Troy? It's ridiculous to think
that I could be any more effective in Madrid than I am here."

"Do you really hate Spain so much?" I asked softly.

We stopped on the Pont Marie, which connected the Île St.
Louis with the Right Bank. Diaz gazed down at the dark waters
of the Seine, as if he were searching for his reflection.

"When I left Spain in 1922, I wanted never to go back," he
said after a long silence. "I felt as one does when a love affair
ends. You have been rejected. Your heart is broken. You hope
never to see this person again, and you want to put all thought
of her out of your mind. You are bitter, and angry, but mostly
your anger conceals the pain you feel whenever you think of the
happiness that might have been yours. But then you hear that
your old love is in trouble. Ill, or dying. You have a new life, a
new love, perhaps. What do you do? Do you abandon everything
and rush to the side of the person who has caused you so much
distress?"

I listened, head bowed, my heart constricting at his words.
Diaz didn't love me, but he couldn't forgive me for loving someone else.

He covered my hand with his. "It was a bad metaphor, Theodora. Forgive me. A country has no feelings. A country is a geo-
graphical location, whose mountains and shores endure the
passage of years and the troubles of humanity with no more
emotion than this bridge responds to our standing upon it. The
place we call Spain will survive, whatever happens, whether I

return or not. But the heart of a man is different." He breathed deeply, and straightened his spine.

"I have tried to serve truth all my life. I cannot betray her now. I must go to Spain."

"I thought this was supposed to be an express train." For the past hour, we had been standing in a station in the middle of arid, parchment-colored hills.

"You will soon find that Spain has no such thing as express anything." Diaz flipped his cigarette out the open window. "If the engineer is passing through a province where his aunt's cousin used to live, he'll spend an hour catching up on the local gossip, even though his aunt's cousin has been dead for five years." He stood up abruptly and left the compartment, taking yet another exploration of the corridor.

Diaz loved Spain, and he loathed Spain. For me, it had been love at first sight. The rugged evergreen mountains near the border, the brown hills shaded blue-gray in patches with olive orchards, the blazing sun, the cloudless sky, the wind-wrought buttes and arroyos, the dried-up rivers all reminded me of Colorado. Coming to Spain was like coming home.

A boy carried a basket of oranges up and down the platform. I hailed him, and, leaning out the window, completed the purchase of six pieces of fruit just as the train whistle shrilled and the engine started to inch forward. I pulled my head back in before it became enveloped in cinderous smoke. In spite of the rising heat of mid-April, I closed the window.

Diaz and I had had no real difficulty crossing the border between France and Spain at Hendaye. Upon noting that we were both American citizens, Spanish customs agents passed us through with only the most casual of inspections. They expressed some mild interest in my cameras, which evaporated as soon as I showed them a press identification card and a letter from the editor of *Paris-Matin* telling anyone who cared to know it that T. Lowery was a professional photographer in their employ.

Once we left the foothills of the Pyrenees, the terrain grew more rugged. The plains were vast, sand-colored, scored deeply with erosion. Diaz told me that the land had been stripped bare centuries ago by huge flocks of Merino sheep, at that time found nowhere else in the world. Spain's dependence on the profits from Merino wool had prompted the royal government to forbid any landowner or peasant to deny access to the roving herds. And so the sheep moved through the countryside like dingy poisonous clouds, consuming every root and blade in sight. Farmers locked themselves in their houses when they saw the herds approaching. Hours later, they emerged to find their crops decimated. They were forbidden to fence even the smallest plots to raise food for their families. Where the sheep roamed, famine followed.

"What can you say about a country that values sheep wool over human life?" Diaz had asked, not trying to conceal his scorn. "Anyone caught transporting these sheep out of the country forfeited his life. That's how Spain retained her monopoly on Merino wool, and cultivated her talent for oppressive savagery."

I dug my fingernails into the peel of an orange. What a contrast our voyage to France had been. Three years ago, as our ship had drawn closer to the port at Le Havre, Diaz had become more excited by the hour. His expectations of Paris had been unblemished by memories of disappointment, strife, or bitterness. He had looked forward to returning to the city that had welcomed him as a young poet.

But when we boarded the southbound train at the Gare de Lyon two days ago, his mood had gone into a decline. His depression deepened as we approached Madrid, where, fifteen years earlier, he had made his decision to leave his country forever.

The door to the compartment slid open and more people

struggled in, balancing their numerous pieces of luggage as they fought to remain upright while the train pitched and jerked. They were a family of four, a man about forty years old, his wife, and their two sons. They smiled apologetically as they boosted their baggage up on the luggage racks. I drew my legs out of their way. Diaz was still wandering the corridors, but he had left a book of verse on his seat, and they respected the book as if it were a human occupant.

The woman settled her children in their seats and began to forage in a huge straw basket. I made an innocuous remark on the heat. The family had assumed from my fair skin and the volume of English poetry on my lap that I was a Britisher or American who spoke no Spanish. They responded eagerly to the overture I made in their own language. They were going to Madrid, the father told me, where the mother's grandmother lay dying. Perhaps she was already dead. Well, he shrugged, so be it. God never intended for them to say farewell to her.

And while they were in Madrid, the younger son piped up, they would see the palace where the king lived.

"Shut up, stupid," his brother said. "We haven't had a king for thirteen years."

The little boy looked crushed.

"Surely we can see the royal palace, even though the king no longer lives there," I said. The little one perked up again.

The man told me that he was a baker. He owned one of the few cars in his village, but the blasted thing had broken down two days ago and it would have taken weeks to get it fixed, and with the old woman dying, they decided to leave it and come by train.

"I don't know where you would have gotten fuel for that car between here and Madrid." His wife spoke for the first time. "And what if you had had a flat tire?"

"Oh, be quiet, woman," the man grunted. "This isn't the middle of Africa, you know. Spain has roads, petrol pumps, and even garages that can fix tires."

"What about magnetos?" the little boy wondered. "It was the magneto that was broken. Could they fix the magneto?"

His parents shushed him. I offered to share my oranges, but the family had brought its own—half a bushel. They insisted that I take a glass of wine with them, and some ham and bread, and some olives, and a couple of the baker's little sweet cakes.

Just as I was wishing that Diaz would return to share the feast, he opened the compartment door and collapsed into the seat beside me.

The family fell silent. The baker stared at Diaz. "I think I know your face, but I do not know your name. Forgive me, Señor—"

"Diaz Albareda," his older son supplied readily. "The famous poet! I've read all your poems. I didn't know you were in Spain."

"Hush, Diego," his father said. "Diaz Albareda! I—we are honored, Señor. I too, have read your poems. *Songs of Spain. Gypsy Ballads.* I am not an Andalusian, like yourself, but I respect any man who can put his thoughts down on paper the way you do. When I read your poems, I think, 'Yes, that is the way I feel, too.' But I would never be able to think of the words myself. Yours is a great talent, a wonderful gift. May we—may I shake your hand?"

Diaz half-stood, and shook the baker's hand. The man introduced the rest of the family. The older boy was beside himself with excitement.

"Wait until I tell my friends that I saw you. They say you will never come back to Spain, and here you are! But how will I get them to believe me? Will you write me an autograph, Señor? The way the film stars do?"

Diaz turned to me. "Do you have any copies of that photograph you took of me, the one that was on my last book jacket?"

I selected one out of the dozen or so I had brought. My years of magazine work had taught me how important it is to have a face to go with a name. If Diaz wanted to be more than just a disembodied voice crying in the journalistic wilderness, he needed a face, a visible presence.

Diaz signed the photograph and handed it to the boy. His black eyes gleamed with pleasure and he expressed his thanks effusively. Instead of putting the portrait safely away, he attached it to the compartment wall with a tiny piece of chewing gum.

"You won't be able to get it off without ripping it," his mother scolded.

"Yes, I will. I only used a little."

Diaz accepted wine and bread and offered cigarettes in exchange. He talked about his years of exile, haltingly at first, as he tried to describe his complex feelings in simple terms that these people could understand. In turn, they told us stories of the general election, the troubles in the cities, the plight of the poor farmers in their area. We conversed until dark, when the boys began to nod off. Finally, exhausted by all the excitement, the occupants of our little compartment settled down to sleep.

I leaned against Diaz's shoulder.

"Now I know why I had to come back," he whispered to me. "I have missed them."

"They're wonderful," I agreed.

"They are typical," Diaz told me. "A man like that isn't going to let some Communist or anarchist or Jesuit tell him what to do. He will look at the problem, think it over, and then do what is right for himself and his family. It would take an army to change his mind."

The night in that mountainous country had turned cold. I shivered and pressed closer to my husband as the train crawled toward Madrid.

20

Madrid. Another walk-up apartment in another working-class neighborhood. Another bedroom furnished with odds and ends from secondhand stores. Another kitchen that I could convert into a darkroom at night, this time by tacking heavy Spanish shawls over the windows.

"Most efficient," Diaz remarked one evening as he watched me putting them up. "When I die, you can just take one down and wear it as mourning. Spanish widows remain faithful to their dead spouses forever, you know. You won't be able to marry again. You will roam over the face of the earth with this hideous rag draped over your head like a huge black wing, still taking your little black and gray photographs."

"Please stop, Luis." I spoke through a mouthful of nails. "I hate it when you talk that way."

"You will have to get used to it," Diaz shrugged. "You heard Señor Casado: In Spain, death is every man's mistress and the companion of every woman's old age."

As soon as we arrived in Madrid, we looked for a place to live. Diaz had many friends in the city who would have been delighted to shelter us, but he needed his solitude, and he decided that we would steal in quietly so as not to diminish the impact of his return. We would establish ourselves in an apartment, and then he would notify the press and the public that Luis Diaz Albareda had ended his long exile.

We moved into three rooms above a hatter's shop in Old Madrid, just off the beautiful Plaza Major. I learned that the king and his nobles had gathered there in the seventeenth century to watch *autos da fe*, the process by which heretics were tried and sentenced to death, and usually incinerated on the spot. In a neighborhood of crooked streets, small squares, crumbling churches, and quaint shops, we were half a world away from the throbbing center of the city, with its broad boulevards and massive nineteenth-century buildings.

Two days after we arrived in Madrid, Diaz presented himself at the offices of the Republican newspaper *El Globo*, whose editor was a boyhood friend from Granada. When the man heard Diaz's reasons for returning to Spain at this critical time, he offered the poet as much space in the newspaper as he could fill: "Not just on the editorial page, but page one!" The fact that Diaz had come back was news in itself; the fact that the poet wanted a forum from which to speak for sanity and peace was dramatic and exciting. And, the editor reasoned pragmatically, it would sell newspapers.

And so Luis abandoned poetry and took up a new pen, this time as a columnist and essayist. At least the literary requirements of prose were less stringent than poetry; he expressed his ideas in sentences that didn't have to be so beautiful or rhythmic or fraught with symbolism or layers of meaning. But he found the practical demands of a journalistic career more loathsome. His editor insisted on having his columns by six o'clock in the evening at the very latest, in order to make the morning edition. No more the luxury of writing until dawn and sleeping until noon. Diaz complained that he had to live like every other middle-class clerk in Spain, working from eight until one and from four until seven—even the most compulsive writers observed the siesta hours in Madrid. But actually he devoted much more time to his cause.

He spent many evenings with the leaders of the various factions of the left: the Communists, the Socialists, the Anarchists, and the labor unionists. Diaz knew that his readers would soon tire of his harangues in the press. He needed to use his influence while his popularity still ran high in order to persuade these people that the safety and security of Spain was at stake. Unless they ended their bickering and threw their support fully behind President Azaña and the fledgling Republican government, unless they discouraged strikes and threats and outbreaks of violence in their districts, then Spain would shatter, like a crystal goblet dropped on a paving stone.

" 'Diaz loves Spain and order so much, he must be a Falangist.' That's what one of them said to me tonight, can you imagine? Imbecile."

He tore savagely at a loaf of bread as he recalled his frustrating session with the Spanish Communists. We were dining in a small restaurant near the Puerta del Sol, not far from our apartment. Even at eleven o'clock, the streets were busy and the restaurant crowded. Late dining was the rule everywhere in Spain, and nowhere did people dine later than in Madrid.

"I said, 'No, I am a poet.' They didn't like that. 'What do you mean, a poet? You must be something else. A Jesuit, a monarchist, a militarist?' 'I am a poet,' I said, 'which means that I am an empty cup. When the cup is full of ideas and experiences, I write. When the cup is empty, I am nothing.' 'You are Andalusian,' they said, as if that were something to be ashamed of. 'No,' I said, 'I am Catalan, I am Galician, I am Castilian. I touch the Mediterranean, I touch the Atlantic. The bones in my body are the Guadarrama, the Sierra Nevada, the Pyrenees. My blood flows through the Ebro, the Manzanares, the Guadalquivir. I am Spain.' "

"And what did they say to that?" I wondered how anyone could resist such a beautiful and poetic declaration.

"They said, 'Your body has a tumor, Diaz. If we don't administer treatment immediately, you will die. Only one cure exists; only one: Stalinism.' 'Keep your Russian cures for Russian corpses,' I said. 'Treat me with Spanish medicine, or let me die.' And then I left."

"You didn't think it was going to be easy," I ventured, sipping my wine.

"No matter." Diaz lifted his shoulders and let them fall. "I can use these same arguments in my column tomorrow. One good thing about being a poet: you never run out of metaphors."

Our food arrived, plates of pork in a rich tomato and garlic sauce. Diaz took two bites and set down his fork. When I urged him to eat, he snapped at me, and then pressed his hand over his eyes, shutting out the world. I had never seen him like this, defeated and despondent, as weary as if the burden of Spain's safety rested entirely on his shoulders.

He slept poorly these days, often leaping out of bed to jot down a thought or an idea, remaining awake until he had exhausted his line of reasoning. His meals consisted mostly of tobacco and wine, with occasional nibbles of bread and cheese. He lost the few pounds he had gained in Paris. His skin took on a bluish pallor, so that he resembled one of El Greco's translucent saints.

When Luis and I did manage to spend some time alone together, he was so tense and preoccupied that he hardly spoke. He rarely confided in me as a wife; in fact, he seemed to have forgotten that I was a woman. His desire for me dried up. The demonstrations of affection and tenderness that he had shown me in Paris evaporated in the heat of the Spanish sun.

More and more, Diaz spoke of death. According to him, Death was as familiar to him as a member of his own family. Death was his friend, his lover; all-knowing, all-seeing, Death was as omnipotent and universal as God. Death did not discriminate between rich and poor. Death had no ideology, no philosophy. Catholic, Moor, Jew, atheist; Death treated all equally, without compassion, without mercy.

"Catalan, Galician, Castilian, it won't matter in the end," he said one day in early June, a month and a half after we had arrived in Madrid. "Death speaks all the dialects of Spain."

The afternoon was hot, the apartment seemed shabby and unbearable, and my patience had finally worn thin. I threw down the shirt I was mending.

"Why do you talk this way?" I demanded. "As if you expected the worst for yourself and your country. You act as though you already know your fate and have accepted it. But you're being foolish, Luis. You're not going to die. You are no one's enemy.

You are a beloved poet, a heroic figure. No one will harm you. They wouldn't dare."

"You do not understand, Theodora."

"No, I don't understand. Ever since we came to Spain, you've been so morbid. I feel like I'm already married to a corpse. I know you're concerned about the situation here, that you feel helpless and discouraged and that you're desperate for answers. But you solve nothing by going on and on about dying."

"In Spain, the central metaphor for life is death," Diaz informed me. "You cannot understand. You are not Spanish."

"No, thank God, I am not Spanish. I have no wish to be Spanish. I hate Spain! I loathe Spain! I loathe you!" Storming into the other room, I threw myself down on the bed.

When I emerged fifteen minutes later, Diaz was still sitting at his desk, his forehead resting on the heel of his right hand. The cigarette he was holding had burned down so low that it singed his fingers. Snatching the butt away, I sponged the burn with cold water.

"Speak to me, Luis," I begged. "I am your wife. I can help you. I can take on half your burden, if you'll let me. Just talk to me."

His black eyes were transfixed, as if he were gazing into the future. He didn't answer me.

After our arrival in Madrid in April, 1936, the situation had deteriorated rapidly. Rumor vied with fact in conversations in taverns and on streetcorners. The Anarchists were planning a strike. Fact. An attempt had been made on the President's life. Rumor. The generals were planning a *pronunciamento*, a coup. But who could say whether that was fact or rumor until it actually transpired?

I sent *Paris-Matin* some candid portraits of the people who figured most prominently in the ongoing conflict: President Azaña, politically moderate, fleshy and aging; chunky Francisco

Largo Caballero, a Socialist known as the "Spanish Lenin"; José Calvo Sotelo, the gentlemanly chief spokesman for the conservative Right; Dolores Ibarruri, known as "La Pasionaria," the shrill speaker for the Communists. Except for President Azaña, who graciously permitted the American lady to come to the National Palace for a photographic session, the others posed in the chambers of the Cortes, the Spanish parliament.

Knowing that I was Diaz's wife, Dolores Ibarruri took advantage of our half hour together to try to persuade me that the Communists' solution was the only possible one for Spain.

Her dark eyes boring into the lens of my camera, La Pasionaria spoke of her wretched childhood as the daughter of a Basque miner. She evoked vivid pictures of starvation, filth, overcrowding in company bunkhouses, pictures that struck familiar and chilling chords in my memory. Her marriage to a miner had offered no respite from suffering. Four of their six children had died, small sacrifices to the greed of the mine-owners, who lived grandly while keeping their workers in absolute poverty. Anger gave The Passion Flower a voice. Her outspoken condemnation of conditions in her region quickly earned her her first jail sentence.

"But not even the jailers wanted me around," she said with a scornful toss of her dark head. She was a handsome woman, squarely built, whose strong features seemed to have been carved by the wind and darkened by the sun. "I tried to organize the prostitutes. Ha! Can you imagine where this country would be without its whores? Where would Spanish men spend their Sunday evenings? What would they do after the bullfights?"

For the first time, I understood the challenge that confronted Diaz and the forces of rationality. Like the leaders of every other political party and faction, La Pasionaria was firmly convinced of the rightness of her own particular cause. She knew what was best for Spain.

Before we parted, she begged me to persuade Diaz to listen to reason. The poet couldn't go on condemning all sides. He had to choose a course.

"He has chosen," I said. "Peace."

"The only peace the Basque miners were destined to know was the peace of death," The Passion Flower snapped. "The time for words is long gone. If my babies had been able to eat words, they would be alive today."

I felt some of Diaz's despair. His task was hopeless. Too many voices wanted to speak for Spain. No one listened to anyone else. The few voices that called for reason and moderation were lost in the general clamor.

Madrid was a lonely place for me. I formed few friendships. In New York and Paris, I had worked with the same group of people on a regular basis: the writers and photographers at *Mode*, the editors at *Paris-Matin*. Here in Spain, I was on my own, a professional observer without a specific assignment, without a deadline. I met a few fellow photographers and journalists at the Cortes, but I remained aloof from them. Most were men living far from their homes. When they weren't occupied with their jobs or their mistresses, they gathered in the bars of Madrid's better hotels and exchanged cynical observations on the prospects of peace for Spain. I couldn't stomach their fatalism. From the moment the train had crossed the border into Spain, I had felt a special bond with the land and a strong sense of kinship with her people, which I retained in spite of my loneliness.

It was easy for the younger members of the foreign press to adopt a jaded tone when they discussed the likely casualties on either side should full-scale fighting break out. But I couldn't be casual about war. I knew without seeing one what a civil conflict would be like. I had been on intimate terms with violent death since I was a child, and I knew how terrifying and ugly it could be. Not peaceful and serene, like the drawing of a curtain across a darkened stage, not the dignified withdrawal of a man from this earth after a long and fulfilling life. War, when it came to Madrid and the rest of Spain, would be bloody, noisy, and supremely vicious.

One afternoon in early July, I happened to pass an air-conditioned cinema that was showing Fiona's latest film. Telling myself that I needed to escape from the heat and the tensions that beset everyone in Spain these days, I bought a ticket and followed the usher to my seat. The opening credits were already rolling, to the accompaniment of lighthearted music. Then Fiona appeared on the screen. She was driving an open sports car while she chattered brightly to her male companion. Her golden hair streamed back from her head, and the familiar crooked smile never left her lips. The people in the audience applauded her.

Although I knew very well that Hollywood artifice was responsible, at least in part, for Fiona's sleek figure, her flawless complexion, her glorious hair, I couldn't help but feel a twinge of shame at my own appearance. Most of my clothes dated from my last year at Radcliffe. Evan had always insisted on buying the highest quality, but he certainly didn't intend his purchases to last half a lifetime. Harsh developing chemicals had stained my hands. I still wore my hair short, in an easy boyish style that I could trim myself. As for makeup, I hadn't owned any for years, not even a lipstick.

I recognized the character Fiona was playing: the spoiled rich girl, pouty, saucy, and rebellious. Fiona had acted that role plenty of times with Evan, and it had never failed to get her what she wanted. A new fur, a trip to Europe, a play, written especially for her. Even when she stopped making demands, Evan didn't stop giving. When she no longer needed his money and his social and theatrical connections, he gave her his sanity, his health, his life.

The people in the theater laughed at the dialogue, which had been dubbed into Spanish. A couple of teenage girls near me had adopted Fiona Randall hair styles, bleached and swept back from the face in a series of never-breaking waves. The men and boys all looked smitten. They couldn't take their eyes off that two-dimensional giant of a woman. They would entertain her in their dreams and fantasies that night, never suspecting for a moment that in real life this goddess was a fiend, a demon who could kill merely by withholding her love.

I ran up the aisle and out of the theater. As I stumbled into the mellow twilight of the June evening, I pictured myself standing up in the auditorium and denouncing Fiona to the rest of the crowd. They would have shouted me down, and then ejected me bodily from the place. People don't like to hear the truth about their idols.

The sidewalks of Madrid were beginning to fill up. I had told Luis that I firmly believed that at seven o'clock in the evening, every single house and apartment in the city disgorged its inhabitants into the streets and shops and cafes, where they were required to stay until midnight, at the very earliest, when they could return to their homes.

Ahead of me, a group of men came out of a bar and turned in my direction. I recognized one of them: Angel. He saw me at once, and twisted his horrid face into a wide, mocking grin. The men pressed forward, surging past me like waves around a jetty stone. Passing close to me, Angel stroked my breast brazenly. I caught my breath.

"*Cabrón!*" I hissed. Bastard. Angel threw back his head and laughed silently.

Later I said to Luis, "You didn't tell me that Angel was in Madrid."

"You know he accompanies me wherever I go," Diaz said. "I respect your wishes; I never entertain him here." He began to rant: "What is your objection? Can't a man return to the land of his birth without provoking storms of feminine hysteria?"

Lately the public had started to object to Diaz's refusal to commit himself to one course or another. The newspaper *El Globo* had been bombarded with letters from all parts of Spain, demanding that the poet cease his eternal excoriation of their politicians and offer a real solution to Spain's problems. Diaz, who hated criticism of any kind, had become short-tempered and irritated by these negative reactions to his good intentions.

"No hysteria," I said quickly, hoping to soothe him before his annoyance erupted into full-blown fury. "It was an interesting coincidence, that's all. I watched part of Fiona's latest success at the cinema this afternoon, and I didn't expect to see my two *bêtes noires* on the same day."

The next morning, I bought myself a lipstick and a new pair of stylish sandals. I had my hair shaped, my nails manicured, my summer dresses starched and pressed. Luis would have no reason to be ashamed of his wife in front of his countrymen.

The heat in July made the memory of May and June seem like mid-winter. But even though many citizens of Madrid fled to the mountains and the seacoasts to escape the heat, the political passions didn't cool off. Groups of young Falangists, encouraged by their recently imprisoned leader, José Antonio Primo de Rivera, roamed through Madrid, conspicuous in their blue shirts, engaging in street fighting with toughs from the Left.

Then suddenly the spark that Casado the poet had warned about was struck. The Falangists assassinated a Republican army lieutenant in a Madrid street. The following day, José Calvo Sotelo, the well-known leader of the conservative Right, was taken from his home by unknown Leftists and shot.

"We will have more reprisals, more cries for revenge," Diaz said. "Who can stop it now? I have been speaking to Calvo Sotelo's constituency all day. These solid citizens, these Catholic bankers and farmers and professors at the University, are as angry as any mob I have ever seen. Violence begets violence. This is only the beginning."

On July 17, 1936, our afternoon siesta was disrupted by frantic knocking. Diaz and I had been lying naked on the bed, talking in listless murmurs as we tried to persuade each other that the breeze that floated in through the slats on the shuttered window was, in fact, cool. Diaz pulled on his trousers and hurried out of the room. I stood listening in the bedroom doorway, but I couldn't follow the hushed and breathless conversation.

The caller departed. "What it is, Luis? What's going on?"

"What we feared." Diaz finished dressing. "A *pronunciamento*. The army officers garrisoned in Morocco have rebelled against the government. This may be a signal for the forces on the mainland to rise up as well, to seize power." He moved to the door. "Stay here, Theodora. The streets are not safe."

"But what about you? Where are you going?"

"The radio station. I must talk to them, ask them to refrain from bloodshed and reprisals. This is the chance the hotheads have been waiting for. They've been longing to shoot down every Falangist and monarchist in sight. Someone must urge calm."

From my open windows, I could hear random pops of pistol fire. What was happening? Had the officers at the garrison in Madrid turned their guns against the civilians? Had the Republican government fallen to the rebels already? Had the generals claimed instant victory? To the south and to the east, fires sent up billows of black smoke. Madrid's churches were burning.

My heart began to pound. I couldn't remain safely indoors when history was unfolding only a few blocks away. I had a job to do in Spain. *Paris-Matin* and the wire services would want all the pictures I could send them. I pulled on a short-sleeved blouse and loose-fitting slacks with capacious pockets that could hold plenty of film. Snatching up my Leica, I scribbled a short note to Luis, and ran out of the apartment.

Down in the street, a burly worker almost knocked me down. "Wait, tell me, where are you going?" I shouted.

"The Montaña Barracks," he called back. "The army has guns. If we don't take them, the rebels will turn them against us. We must have guns if we are to defend Madrid!"

I hurried after him. The army in Madrid was headquartered in a collection of buildings massed at the summit of a hill on the western edge of the city, not far from the North Station and the

National Palace. Wrapped around with a high granite wall that bristled with turrets and watchtowers, the Montaña Barracks resembled a small feudal city.

The city began to awaken from its siesta. Traffic was still light on the smaller streets, but the Plaza Major was filling up with cars and people, most of them shouting questions and darting about in a bewildered fashion as they waited for someone to tell them what to do. I saw a small crowd armed with rifles and pistols and a variety of more homely weapons moving purposefully across the square, in the direction of the Barracks. I thought of the storming of the Bastille during the French Revolution. Here in Madrid, the Montaña Barracks had become the necessary symbol of the old order's intransigence, Spain's stubborn refusal to yield to the will of the people.

I fell in with a couple of boys at the rear of the group. They told me that the commander of the Barracks, General Fanjul, had refused to surrender.

"He expects his friend General Mola to come riding out of the mountains to save him," one laughed.

"He'll never get out of that place alive," said the other, brandishing an ancient dueling pistol.

We arrived at the Plaza de España, a park dominated by a great white monument to Cervantes, who was depicted sitting in a thoughtful pose in a vast marble chair. At his feet, life-sized bronze statues of Don Quixote and Sancho Panza seemed ready to charge westward, into the fray.

I heard a loud crack and a grunt at the same instant. Clutching his throat, one of my companions dropped to his knees. His mouth twisted, as though he were trying to speak, but no words came out, only horrible gargling noises. I reached out to him, but he fell, sprawling on his back, blood frothing on his lips.

"He's dead." I looked up at his companion, whose eyes had gone dull with shock. Another bullet buried itself in the ground just a few feet away from us. "Come on, we've got to get under cover!" I shouted, tugging at his arm. The boy grabbed the pistol that had fallen out of his friend's grasp. We started running together toward a grove of trees. I threw myself down, panting, and looked around for him. But he had disappeared.

Bodies littered the wooded area at the foot of the Barracks. No one made any attempt to remove them or to help the wounded. As cannons stationed in the park nearby hurtled shells into the Barracks compound, the earth trembled. Clouds of smoke and dust billowed high above the battlements. The wooden portions of the garrison buildings had caught fire.

"The gun bolts to all the army rifles in Madrid are in there." A man joined me behind a gnarled cypress tree. Wearing glasses and a crisp linen suit, he looked like a bank teller or a floor walker in a department store. A bullet smacked into the trunk just above our heads, showering us with dried twigs and bits of bark. "Azaña doesn't want to arm us. Can you believe that? He wants us to capitulate, to give in to these fat-bellied generals. They think they can maintain absolute control even though we have confiscated the rifles from outposts all over the city. So we'll arm ourselves. More simply." He displayed the fruits of his armory: a meat cleaver and a hammer. "We'll go in there and take the gun bolts for our rifles."

A young woman ran toward us from across the park. A bullet struck her and she fell. Ducking out from behind the sheltering cypress, I dragged the girl to safety. A bloody flower opened its petals on her white blouse, just above her left breast.

"No, no, forget about me. Fight them," she urged me in a feverish whisper. "Fight them."

I tried to staunch her wound with my handkerchief. "Don't worry, I'll get you to a hospital."

"I am not hurt," the girl insisted. "I wanted to see the victory, the people's victory. We will win, I am sure of it."

A plane passed overhead, dumping a load of small bombs on the Barracks. I heard muffled cheers. The girl in my arms moaned. "It is nearly nightfall. They must hurry and storm the Barracks before the sun goes down."

But it was still early afternoon, and the sun burned hot and high in the sky. I looked around frantically. The girl's life was ebbing away in my arms. What was the matter with the people of Madrid? Why didn't they do something? The angry voices that had advocated violence as the only solution to Spain's problems hadn't prepared to deal with the bloody reality of it. Killing fascists and Falangists and soldiers was all very well, but what about their own wounded? Where were the stretcher bearers, the ambulances, the doctors?

I became aware of men and women surging past me, rushing toward the main entrance of the Barracks. The ground shook as they blasted the gates open. I recognized the sound; my father's grave had been dug with dynamite.

The girl in my arms shuddered slightly. She seemed to be sleeping, but her eyes were half open and her pulse was gone. I laid her gently on the ground and folded her hands over her bloodied blouse. I wished I had asked her name and address; I wished I could take her back to her family.

All around me, hoarse shouts of "*Viva la Republica!*" and "*Viva España!*" supplanted cries of rage and terror and the crack of bullets. With the enemy breaching their walls, the defenders of the Barracks stopped firing on the Plaza and the surrounding parkland. Behind those high walls, soldiers and civilians were fighting hand to hand.

As I stood up, my camera bumped against my chest. In my shock at the events of the last few minutes, two strangers dead in my arms, I had forgotten all about taking pictures. The scene in front of me was beautiful and terrifying. Clouds of black smoke loomed over the Barracks like swollen thunderheads. Flames funneled up through the jagged ruins of the turrets, turning them into gigantic torches.

Uncapping the lens of my camera, I ran up the hill toward the battle.

Passing through the shattered gates, I entered Hell. The broad courtyard was strewn with bodies. Corpses blocked the

stone staircases, hung out of windows, draped over railings. I
stood in the entrance, not wishing to penetrate farther. I didn't
care about losing my life, but I feared losing my humanity.

A machine gun rattled. A woman coming in behind me
screamed and pitched forward, on top of another twitching casualty.

"Look, there he is! Up there!" someone shouted.

One of the last defenders of the Montaña Barracks stood on a
battlement, framed against a sheet of crimson flame, a tommy
gun tucked under his arm. Shots rang out. The soldier staggered
and dropped to his knees. He managed one more lethal spray of
bullets into the mob before he crumpled and pitched over the
edge of the roof. My finger moved on the shutter release.

"Come and look at the Last Supper!" someone shouted. "Look
at the brave officers of the Spanish Army!" I followed the voice.
In the officers' dining room, a group of men sat around a table
in a grim approximation of a feast. All were dead, bullets imbed-
ded in their heads or their hearts.

Outside, I heard shouts of victory. The people of Madrid had
taken the fortress, crushed the incipient rebellion in their midst,
taken the gun bolts they needed to defend their city.

Hearing cries of "Death to the traitors! Kill them! Kill them!"
I returned to the courtyard. The fighting had stopped, but the
killing had not. The Falangists and regular army officers who
had survived the battle for the Montaña Barracks were being
herded into corners of the courtyard and shot. As soon as their
corpses were removed, a new contingent was thrust up against
the wall and slaughtered. Bodies fell like wheat under the blades
of a thresher. Like gleaners, old women and looters descended
on the fallen to search their bloody clothes for wallets and coins
and to pluck their rings and wristwatches from their still-warm
hands.

My camera hung from the strap around my neck. I had been
taking pictures frantically for an hour or more, pausing only to
reload when my film ran out. I had captured images of bravery

and agony and madness and now atrocity. The victors, drunk with success, wanted still more blood.

I pushed my way close to the man who seemed to be in charge of the firing squad. "Stop them," I begged. "You've got to stop them!"

He shook his head. A wound in his arm had drenched his sleeve with blood, but he seemed not to notice. "No one can stop them."

"But you must! You've got your gun bolts. Why do you want more senseless violence!"

"Violence?" He whirled on me. "Violence in the hands of the people is justice," he snarled. Then he pointed his pistol at my heart. "Get out of here, you stupid bitch. How do we know you're not a spy for the army? Get away from here if you don't want to be next."

Stepping over corpses, shouldering my way through groups of rejoicing people who until that day had been simple workers instead of bloodstained assassins, I made my way out of the Barracks. The mood in the Plaza de España, in spite of the presence of the dead and the dying, was one of fierce jubilation and pride. The people had won. The Republic was saved.

As if in a dream, I saw a familiar figure coming toward me through the trees: Diaz. He looked defeated and weary. On this day of victory, he had lost the greatest battle of his life. He gazed at me with haunted, pain-filled eyes. I was exhausted, filthy. My shoes were caked with mud composed of blood and vomit and dust. On the front of my blouse, where the dying girl had rested, the crimson flower she had passed to me had dried to brown.

"The deathwatch is over," he said. I thought I detected relief in his tone. "Come."

Stumbling, shivering, supporting each other, we made our way home.

21 2019

Later, in the darkness of my shrouded kitchen, I removed the rolls of exposed film from their capsules and placed them in developing fluid. After I finished bathing them in a series of chemicals and rinsing them in the sink, I pinned them up on a line. When the negatives were dry, I grouped them on the plate under my enlarger and exposed them to light just long enough to transmit the images to the photosensitive paper underneath. More chemical baths fixed the images on the paper.

I showed the results to Diaz. The horrors of the day, reduced to black and white shadows on my proof sheets, still had the power to evoke the smells and sounds of the battle for the Montaña Barracks.

"I don't like what happened to me today, Luis," I said. "I became a robot, a picture-taking machine. You know what went on there. At first I was sick with horror. It was terrible. But all the while I was taking those pictures, I didn't feel a thing. Not shock or disgust. Nothing. It was as though the camera had the ability to block out fear and pain and horror. I've always known that I had a tendency to lose myself in what I was doing, but never like this. I wasn't a human being today."

"And so you don't want to take any more pictures," Diaz said.

"I can't. Not here. I won't be a paid witness to this war. I won't let it turn me into a machine."

Diaz gazed at the proof sheets on his lap. "Every artist lives for the moment when his hard work and training become so much a part of him that he is able to forget them. When the dancer steps out onto the stage, he becomes a dancer, not a person who watches himself in the mirror, who thinks about the position of his feet, who calculates the best way to cross the floor. He is able to forget the mechanics and to perform. The well-trained singer can sing an aria without concentrating on

297

how he must breathe in order to reach the end of the phrase. Today you became a photographer instead of a woman who takes pretty pictures. If you had stopped to analyze what was happening to you, you would have been paralyzed, unable to act. And these photographs would be lost."

"I want them to be lost. I hate them. I'll never forget what happened to me today. I was part of the madness, Luis. Now it's part of me."

"Don't be ashamed of what you do, Theodora. Somebody has to speak the truth about human triumph and human folly. People have stopped listening to my words; perhaps they will respond to your pictures. Your photographs speak. They speak for you; they speak of your concern for your fellow man. And from now on, they must speak for me."

"What do you mean?"

"I have written my last piece for the newspaper, made my last speech. Words are empty air now. The fate of our country will be determined by guns and bombs."

"But what about your poetry?"

He shook his head. "I will write no more poetry. In the past I worked to weave images and words and ideas; I was an artisan. But in times of war, artisans turn their skills to the forging of bullets rather than to the modeling of silver goblets. And I will not join this fight. I will not lift my hand against a fellow Spaniard. I would be killing part of myself. Whoever wins this conflict, Spain will lose."

Kneeling in front of him, I held both his hands. "Let's go back to Paris, Luis. We can leave Madrid now, tonight, before the battle comes here. Please, Luis. You don't want to witness Spain's suicide, and neither do I. Yes, I want to take pictures that speak the truth, but the only truth about war is that it's vile and terrible." I gripped his hands tightly. "We'll go back to our little apartment in the Marais, to the Rue Ave Maria. I'll cook for you, I'll make you healthy again. We'll go for walks along the Seine, as we used to. Remember, Luis? Remember how

beautiful it was, how peaceful? It's not too late. The borders are
still open—"

Diaz shook his head. "I cannot. If I leave Spain, everyone will
say that Diaz is a coward. I will never leave again. I must stay,
until the end." He looked into my eyes. "But you may go. You
must. I was wrong to bring you here. I knew what would happen." He touched my cheek. "You have been a good wife, Theodora. You deserve more happiness than I can give you. Go back
to Paris."

"I won't." I bent my head over his lap. "This is my country
now and you are my husband. I won't leave you, Luis. Wherever you go, that's where I shall be, too."

"How brave. How foolish." He stroked my hair. "But I thank
you. I cannot imagine life without you, Theodora. I would surely die of loneliness and despair."

I closed my eyes. Death again. Death was all around us, in the
streets and in the air. Death was a guest in our home, a stranger
in our bed. Sometimes I felt that I had married Death.

Within the next few days, the full scale of the rebellion became clear. General Francisco Franco, who had been stationed
on the Canary Islands, flew secretly to Morocco to take control
of the armies. At the signal of the initial uprising, army outposts
all over Spain joined in the rebellion. Foreign Legionnaires and
Moorish soldiers were transported to the southern part of the
Iberian peninsula. They began to press north, toward Madrid,
where they planned to join the forces of General Mola, which
were heading south.

Franco sent requests to Europe's two Fascist dictators for
men and arms. Both Hitler and Mussolini agreed to aid in the
fight against Communism. England and France, those two great
democracies, balked at offering similar assistance to the belea-
guered Spanish Republic. The United States also refused to intervene in a civil conflict.

As the rebellious Nationalist Army approached the city, panic seized Madrid. Violence broke out everywhere. Suspected traitors to the Republic were arrested, taken from their homes, imprisoned without legal redress, summarily executed. The specters of suspicion and terror stalked the streets. The prime minister resigned, the government collapsed. Another was hastily organized.

The enemy surged northwards, toward the capitol. Towns and villages fell to the Legionnaires and the Moorish soldiers who fought for Franco. The Legionnaires, who had no homes, and the Moors, age-old enemies of Spain, gladly sold their services to the generals who sought to reconquer their own people. Strength for hire, Diaz said.

The forces of the Republican Left, the Loyalists, marshalled themselves into a weak parody of an army. But the sons of the new socialistic state were unaccustomed to obeying orders. Because they regarded officers as comrades, they ignored their commands. They shambled into combat, certain that moral right guaranteed might. Overwhelmed by the power of the bloodthirsty Moors and the well-disciplined Legionnaires, they either fled or gave themselves up to slaughter.

The lines strung across my kitchen sagged under the weight of the images of a nation at war with itself: a mother searching through the endless rows of corpses in the morgue; requisitioned automobiles loaded with gun-toting boys; a lone corpse sprawled in an empty street, the victim of an assassin's bullet.

On the western edge of the city, La Pasionaria erected a banner bearing the slogan that would come to symbolize Madrid's resistance to the rebellious generals: *"No Pasarán."* They shall not pass. Knowing Dolores Ibarruri, I suspected that so long as she drew breath, the rebels would not pass, even if she had to hold them off with the strength of her invective and the blazing fire in her eyes.

Diaz acted like a man bereaved. He rarely left the apartment, but sat for hours poring over my photographs, a cigarette dangling from his lips. I knew that he despised himself for failing in his mission. The fact that no one could have stopped the rebellion or halted the madness in Spain did not console him.

One evening early in August, someone knocked at the door. My heart always gave a sickening lurch when that happened these days. One never knew what news a visitor would bring: the death of a good friend, the bombing of a town, the arrest of a respected citizen as a traitor or an enemy of the Republic. The caller was a young man, about twenty-five, dressed in a worker's baggy blue jacket and soiled cap.

"Good evening, Señora. I would like to see Luis Diaz Albareda, if you please." His Spanish was cultured, correct, polite.

I showed him into the front room, where Diaz sat in his favorite chair overlooking the street.

My husband had aged since coming to Spain. Ceaseless worry and long sleepless nights had taken their toll. Even though his part in the madness had ended, his suffering had not. Each photograph, each report of an assassination or an atrocity or an arrest pierced him like an invisible spike.

The young man stared at him. When he spoke, there was a note of disbelief in his voice. "Luis?"

Diaz looked up, frowning. His brow cleared slowly. He rose from his chair.

"Carlos? Carlos! Can it be?" His lean face broke into a smile, the first I had seen in weeks. "No, I don't believe it. You were just a boy when I left, a child. And now—" He opened his arms to his younger brother. The two men embraced.

The family resemblance was strong, although Carlos looked more like Diaz's son than his sibling. Fit and lean but not gaunt, the young man had the Diaz nose and the piercing Diaz gaze. His sleek black hair was untouched with gray. As he pumped his brother's hand and nodded politely to me, his eyes shone with excitement and delight. In contrast, Diaz's eyes were dull with weariness and despair.

"How is everyone at home?" Luis asked. "Mother? Elvira?"

"Father is very ill." Carlos' smile faded abruptly. "That is why I'm here. We thought you should know."

"I am sorry to hear it." Diaz's mouth hardened. "I don't suppose he has sent for me."

"No, not exactly." Carlos looked embarrassed. "But Mother decided—"

"As I thought. Father doesn't even know I'm back in Spain."

"Oh, but he does," Carlos assured him. "He has seen your columns in *El Globo*. I cut out a whole series of them for him. He refused to look at them at first, but I left the clippings within reach, and when I came in later, I caught him reading them. I asked him what he thought. He said, 'At least Luis is writing so that people can understand what he's saying.' I think he is pleased that you have come back, Luis, even though he didn't come right out and say so. Mother thinks that if you came home now, Father would be pleased. She says it's important that the two of you become reconciled."

"Impossible." Diaz dismissed the idea. "Our last meeting was so bitter. We both said harsh things that neither of us will ever forget. He ordered me out of his house, and I vowed never to return. I will not go back there unless he asks for me himself."

"But he is so stubborn," Carlos said. "You know he'll never relent. He wouldn't send for you, but if you came, it would make him so happy. Please, Luis. Come home. For Mother's sake. She misses you so much. And so does Elvira. She says she prays for you constantly. And besides, if you don't come at once, it will be too late. Father is—" He swallowed. "Father is very weak. The doctors say the end could come at any time." He gazed down at his well-scrubbed nails. He looked so clean, so patrician in spite of his rough garb. Anyone could tell that he wasn't really a laborer.

"As bad as that," Diaz murmured. "I am sorry to hear it."

"The priest came last week to give him the last rites," Carlos said. "We really thought the end had come. But Father rallied again. Just to prove the priest had made a mistake by coming too soon, I think. Father says he's glad he is dying. He says he

doesn't want to see what will happen to Spain in the next few months. But we don't believe him. You know how he is."

"Yes, I know." Diaz toyed with his cigarette pack. He offered it to Carlos, who refused, and he lit one for himself. "How did you get here? Granada has been part of the rebellion from the beginning. I'm sure the rebels in the city are suspicious of anyone who tries to leave."

"It was easy," Carlos said. "I left the city late at night, in my car. I drove to Frailes— you know where that is, the little village in the mountains?—and hid the car in the woods, near the home of a friend. Then I walked to Jaén, which is in the Republican zone. The trains are still running to Madrid from there. If anyone challenges me, I have a card saying I am a member of the Communist Party from Ciudad Real. I told the people I met that I was a student, on my way to Madrid to help defend it against the rebels. They believed me. Why not? Until last year, I really was a student, in the College of Medicine here in Madrid. I didn't finish."

"Why not?" Luis asked him.

Carlos said in a level voice, "I joined the Falange."

Coming in from the kitchen with a bottle of wine and three glasses, I stopped short and gave Luis an anxious look.

Diaz said, "You realize that if anyone around here finds out, they will shoot you? They will shoot me, too, for harboring you."

"I know. I'm sorry. I didn't mean to place you and the Señora in any danger." Carlos stood up. "I just wanted to tell you about Father. I won't stay any longer."

"Don't be stupid," Diaz growled. "Sit down, boy. You are in no danger here. The Falange, eh? So my baby brother is a fascist."

"We are not fascists," Carlos said with conviction. "We just want to save Spain from the forces that threaten her."

"Spain is on fire, and everyone wants to save her," Diaz grunted. "But the members of the bucket brigade are too busy squabbling with each other to throw their water on the flames."

He sighed. "Very well, I will go to Granada. But I will not intrude on my father's deathbed unless he agrees to see me first. I don't want to make his last hours unhappy."

Carlos' face broke into a boyish grin. "I thank you, Luis. Mother will be so pleased."

"Luis," I said urgently, "it's not safe. Everyone knows that your sympathies are with the Republic."

Diaz said, "The Diaz family is well known in Granada. No one will harm me while I am living in my father's house. Besides, my brother has influence with the rebels." He placed his hand on the boy's shoulder. "Carlos will protect me, eh? You will stay here, Theodora. I won't be gone long."

"No. I'm going with you," I said. "I must."

"The journey may be difficult."

"I don't care. It's better than staying here alone, wondering what's happening."

Diaz nodded. "Very well. Carlos, you can sleep here tonight. We shall leave tomorrow, on the early train."

That night, Luis slipped out of the apartment. He was gone for nearly two hours. The next morning, Carlos left at dawn for the Atocha Station. Diaz and I followed an hour later. We would ride in separate parts of the train from Carlos, not meeting or speaking to him until we reached the road outside Jaén. Diaz was an easily recognizable figure, thanks to the newspaper and magazine coverage that had followed his return to Spain. Everyone knew that his family was wealthy, landed. He didn't want to compromise Carlos by appearing in public with him. The mood in the countryside was too uncertain and dangerous.

The train was packed with people trying to leave the city before the rebels came. The corridors and even the toilets were jammed. Somehow, with the help of a friend, Diaz had managed to secure tickets. He and I shared a second-class compartment with two old women, an ancient priest, and a young widow and her two small sons. The priest said his rosary in a loud mutter, boldly defying current anti-clerical sentiment. The baggage racks and the floor space overflowed with suitcases, baskets, sacks of food. I held my camera case on my lap, the safest place I could find.

As the train crept through the suburbs of Madrid and headed south, the compartment became increasingly warm. Diaz, sunk as usual into thoughtful melancholy, didn't seem to notice. We stopped at every small village and town to take on more passengers, so that we reached Aranjuez, only fifty miles south of the city, about two hours after our departure from Madrid. I was feeling ill and claustrophobic, and since the train seemed likely to be stopped at the station for some time, I left the compartment, worked my way through the crowd in the corridor, and climbed down to the platform outside.

Glancing up at the open window of the carriage next to ours, I saw a young man in profile. Under crisp, curling black hair, his face was strikingly handsome, hard-edged and classical in its proportions. As he turned and grinned at me, his beauty dissolved into a hideous mask. Angel.

Fighting down rage, I resumed my seat beside Diaz.

"You couldn't bear to leave him behind for even a few days, could you?" I hissed in English. Even so, my anger must have been evident in my tone, for the other occupants of the compartment looked at me curiously.

Diaz said, "This doesn't concern you, Theodora. We don't need to discuss it now."

"Yes, we do, Luis. Why do I have to have that monster dogging my footsteps, following me wherever I go? You went to see him last night, didn't you, to tell him we were leaving? I suppose you moved heaven and earth to get a ticket for him, too. I just don't understand it, Luis. Or maybe I do understand. You love him, don't you? Or should I say you're in love with him? I know very well that you've never loved me. Our marriage was just a charade, a smokescreen, so that the world wouldn't know that the Poet of the People was a—"

"You are wrong." Diaz faced me squarely. His voice held no trace of anger, nor did his eyes. "I had my own reasons for bringing him on this journey. I can't explain now. We will talk about this, I promise you. But later." He pressed my hand. "Later."

The train chuffed along through barren sun-baked hills, past sleeping villages and pitifully impoverished towns, over parched fields and dry, cracked riverbeds. Neither Diaz nor I spoke much. Our companions dug into their baskets of provisons for lunch, and after the meal, they dozed. The old priest snored loudly, with his mouth open. The two little boys nudged each other and giggled at the old man's slack jaw and sonorous buzz. A few minutes later, their dark heads were nodding, and soon they were sound asleep on their mother's lap.

The interminable afternoon wore on. As we neared the province of Andalusia, the landscape lost its softness, becoming more ruggedly Spanish. Rocks shone warmly like burnished gold nuggets in the dying sun, their undersides cool and dark with deep green shadows. We passed gray-green olive groves and fields striped with neatly ranked vineyards. In the distant south, the horizon rippled with lavender-colored mountains.

Diaz murmured, "I had forgotten how beautiful this country of mine is. An odd sensation, to return home after so many years." He looked out at a village clinging to a hillside. "Angel came from a village such as that. He is probably a gypsy, a bastard whose mother abandoned him. He was always a thief. He never had a home. He was like an animal when I found him: brutish, self-centered, with an animal's sharp cunning and keen instinct for self-preservation. He was twelve years old, already mute and maimed for life. Like you, I was repelled by his appearance at first. And yet, for all his grotesqueness and savagery, I felt strangely drawn to him."

I remembered another mute twelve-year-old, another over-educated rich man's son, and the friendship that had blossomed between them. To Evan Bradford, I must have seemed every bit as crude and savage as Angel had seemed to Diaz.

Diaz said softly, "I felt that I was meeting my alter ego, my other self—the dark side of my personality. I can't expect you to

understand, and I know I am explaining it badly. Everything
Angel possessed, I lacked. For all my refinement and learning, I
didn't know how to live like a man. Like an intellectual, yes.
Like an effete and ineffectual pampered poet. But Angel gave
me color. And I gave him a voice. In trying to understand him
and to speak for him, I found a part of myself that I never knew
existed. I began to see the world through his eyes. I saw Spain,
its beauty and horror." He turned his head to face me. "We
were lovers for a short time. Angel wanted me to know that he
was grateful for my patronage and protection. No doubt he
thought I would enjoy it. But I had no wish to make him my
slave. I imagine he had frequently been abused in that way as a
child. As a man, he obviously preferred women. By that time,
the bond between us was so strong that it hardly seemed necessary to extend it physically."

"Yes," I said. "Yes, I can see that."

"We learned, as many lovers do, that we could not live together. He had his art, and I had mine. But we both knew that we
could never live far apart. It is folly to separate two halves of the
same person. We would slowly perish. His voice would grow silent, and I would lose my color, my passion."

He was right. For years, I had felt myself slowly dying inside,
shriveling like a plant without water or sunlight. And Evan-
—perhaps he was dead already. I closed my eyes. For the rest of
my life, I would feel incomplete, as though I had lost something.
And so I had: I had lost my other self.

It was nearly midnight when the train pulled into the mountainous city of Jaén, about two hundred miles from Madrid.
Even so, we could not look for a place to sleep. The three of us
would walk to Failes under cover of darkness, spend the day
resting at the home of Carlos' friend, and then drive to Granada,
arriving in that city after dark. I supposed that Angel would
find his own way.

As I climbed down from the railway carriage, I saw Angel
standing in a pool of light at the end of the platform.

As I passed in front of him, our eyes met. The scarred half of his face was in shadow. For the first time, he didn't mock or leer at me. Instead, he seemed thoughtful and a little sad.

22

"It is too hot to sit outdoors at this time of day, even here."

Diaz joined me on a bench in the shadiest corner of the tiled patio. A fountain bubbled in the center, lending a false impression of coolness.

"How is your father today?" I asked him.

He dipped into his shirt pocket for his cigarettes. "He is taking a long time to die. I think he wants to save my soul. He keeps trying to make me say that I was wrong, that thinking like mine led to the current crisis."

"He is proud of you, Luis. Remember what he said about your poems: 'Imagine people all over the world reading this stuff. Trees that talk, the moon making speeches. Now I know I have lived too long!' He's delighted with how famous you've become."

"It would never occur to him to tell me so." Diaz's smile was bitter. "Strange, that my father still has the power to hurt me after all these years. With the things he says, and the things he doesn't say."

"Are you sorry you came back?"

"Sorry? One cannot be sorry about fate. But I am sorry for you, Theodora. Except for Carlos, my family has not been exactly warm in its welcome to you. I apologize for them."

"I'm the last sort of person they would want their son to marry: American, not a Catholic. Childless," I added softly.

"They can blame me for that," Diaz grunted. "I haven't been

a very attentive husband lately." He gazed at the figure in the center of the fountain, a chubby cherub holding a fish that spilled water out of its mouth into a basin. "If we hadn't married, you might have felt free to leave me. You have wanted to, many times. I know that."

"No, Luis—"

"Please let me speak. I have waited too long as it is. I am a bad poet, Theodora, because I cannot express the feelings that lie most deeply in my heart. I have always known that you didn't love me. I could have set you free at any time, with a word, but I never spoke. Perhaps I feared that you would go back to your old life and your old love. My reasons for marrying you were more devious than you think: I cared nothing about an American passport. But I knew that once we were married, you would be reluctant to leave me. Your pride wouldn't allow you to admit failure. I used you. I exploited you as surely as landlords like my father have exploited the peasants who work their fields. I took the money you earned and shared it with Angel, whom you feared and despised. I enslaved you in my kitchen and in my bed. And in all these years, I have never once told you how dear you are to me."

Taking my left hand, he slipped a small gold band onto my fourth finger. "My mother gave this to me this morning. It was my grandmother's. She intended that I should have it when I married."

I touched the ring, the first, the only gift he had ever given me. "Luis, you don't need—"

"I am almost finished. Theodora, I ask you to forgive the hurt I have inflicted on you. I only acted as I did because I love you. Something happened inside me when our eyes first met, and I have loved you more every day we have spent together. I have never said that before. Diaz Albareda cannot speak with such simplicity and honesty. He has to embroider his feelings with images, metaphors, symbolism. But I am speaking the truth now, Theodora. I love you."

In the fountain, the water brimmed over the top of the stone basin and rained gently into the broader pool beneath, in which goldfish swam under coppery-colored lily pads.

"You act as though you were the dying man, instead of your father," I said after a while.

"We are all closer to death than we were yesterday." Diaz gave a little shrug. "My father may stand at the head of the queue, but I will follow him. Quite soon, perhaps. I could not let the opportunity to speak pass once more."

Doña Elvira Diaz came out of the house. Luis's older sister was a spinster, a deeply religious woman whose strong sense of duty to her family had kept her from joining a convent. She lived like a nun in the splendor of her father's house, dressing in severest black, sleeping on a hard cot in a sparely furnished room, attending mass twice daily, ministering to the poor.

Elvira stared disapprovingly at our joined hands. "Theodora, you agreed to come for a walk with me after siesta. You have not yet seen the Alhambra."

Diaz said, "Are you sure it's safe to go out? Didn't you hear the shooting throughout the night?"

"That has nothing to do with us," Elvira said. "I will tell Mother that we are leaving. I wish you would speak to her, Luis. She is upset that you refused to accompany us to mass this morning. It is Sunday, after all."

"My dear Elvira," Diaz sighed, "I have not attended mass for nearly twenty years. I hardly think it would be appropriate for me to do so now. My beliefs—or lack of them—have not changed."

Elvira sniffed. "Of course it would never occur to you to do something that might make someone else happy. But do as you please, by all means. This isn't my house, after all. I wouldn't presume to give you orders." She turned to me. "I would suggest you wear a hat. It's rather hot today." She went inside.

Diaz shook his head. "She's incredible. My parents are the same way. They act as though nothing at all had happened outside these walls. The rebellion, the civil war are as irrelevant as

my poems—merely an annoying disturbance, a squabble between two gypsy families. Meanwhile, in the Leftist zones, the
workers are shooting people who wear neckties. Here in rebel
country, a man can get himself killed for having a laborer's cal-
louses on his hands. The whole country is writhing in agony,
but as usual, my esteemed family prefers to remain blind and
deaf." His hand trembled as he lifted his cigarette to his lips.

"You're tired, Luis. Why don't you go in and lie down? I'll
come with you. Elvira will understand."

"No, you go to the Alhambra." He pressed my hand. "I'm
glad you'll have an opportunity to savor its beauties before we
leave. Don't let Elvira hurry you. She is incapable of appreciat-
ing anything more artistic than one of those bloody pietas in her
church." He stood up, stretching. Bearded and emaciated, he
looked like a crucified Christ. "I remember now why I never
wanted to come back to Granada: it's the most beautiful, most
boring city on earth. But even Mozart had his Salzburg." He
smiled down at me. "I'll speak to Mother. Like Father and Elvira, she needs to be reminded occasionally that a man's conscience is the one thing he cannot change to please his family."

I watched my husband disappear into the cool interior of the
Villa Diaz. A slight breeze arose, bringing with it the scent of
jasmine and dust and stale blood from the streets beyond the
walls. Diaz was right: Granada was a beautiful prison. Particularly these days. Heeding Carlos' cautions, neither of us had left
the house since our arrival a week earlier. Even so, we could not
forget the struggle going on in the world outside. Although
Franco's rebels held the city, the surrounding countryside was
still loyal to the leftist Republic. From time to time, Loyalist
planes scattered bombs over the center of town, causing heavy
damage and starting fires.

On our way up the wooded hillside to the Moorish palace that
dominated the city, Elvira and I were stopped by two tricorn-
hatted soldiers of the Guardia Civil who asked us for identification. Elvira told them in regally icy tones that her father was
Don Miguel Antonio Juan Diaz y Lasado. Would they kindly

permit her to show her guest their lovely city? The men bowed respectfully and let us pass. I wondered what they would have done if they had known that I was the wife of the poet who had made such cruel fun of them in his writing.

From the wall of the fantastic pleasure dome built by the Moorish kings of Granada early in the fourteenth century, I could see the city itself, dazzlingly white, nestling in a valley between two rivers, the Darro and the Genil, both nearly vanished now at the height of summer. Thick patches of greenery broke up the masses of buildings. Cypress, citrus, and olive trees cast shade over numerous private patios and public squares. I was astonished by such lushness, after the desolation I had seen in the rest of the country. Elvira told me that hundreds of springs flowed under the mountain on which the Alhambra had been built. The Arabs had regarded such an abundance of water as a sign of special favor from Allah. They had reveled in His goodness, creating water gardens, fountains, baths, fish ponds, and reflecting pools.

To the southeast loomed the chain of the Sierra Nevadas, their summits glinting with snow even in mid-August. Their foothills, rising out of the fertile plain, were yellow, the color of saffron rice. The Nationalists had adopted that Andalusian gold as one of the two colors on their flag; the other was red, the color of blood.

Gunfire rattled in the streets below us. Doña Elvira paid no attention. "Granada was the last Moorish possession in Spain," she informed me. "The capture of the city in 1492 by Catholic Spain was considered a triumph for all Christianity. I believe the celebration reached as far as St. Paul's Cathedral in London. And Cristobal Colón, your Christopher Columbus, was here in Granada for the glorious entry of King Ferdinand and Queen Isabella on January 2, 1492. Only a few months later, on April 17, here in Granada, they agreed to supply him with the money and ships he used to discover your country."

I tried to look enthusiastic, but I couldn't shake the feelings of foreboding and dread that had plagued me since Diaz and I came to Granada. Down in the streets of the town, men were dying because the rebels suspected them of being Communists or labor unionists. At my side, Elvira displayed a blithe disregard for the tide of blood that was engulfing her city, and her country. Somewhat listlessly, I followed my hostess into the Court of the Lions, where I posed Elvira against the famous fountain and took her picture.

We proceeded into the next section of the palace. Elvira pointed out some magnificent examples of carved Moorish lace. "My brother tells me you are an excellent photographer. You must take many pictures in Granada. Our home is the most beautiful of the Andalusian cities, the most beautiful city in Spain. Only a fool or a blind man would want to leave this place."

Her implication was clear: Luis was a fool. I defended my husband. "The beauty of one's physical surroundings isn't always enough for some people." I tried to keep my tone impersonal and vague. "Some minds require the stimulation of big cities; others prefer the quiet serenity of the country. A person's spiritual home doesn't necessarily have to be the place of his birth."

"Cities are capitals of sin," Elvira declared. "Why not? You are anonymous in a city, free to violate every stricture of morality and religion. A man who cares nothing about his immortal soul will leave the home of his parents and go to live among strangers, where he can escape shame." She turned her steely gaze, so like Luis's, upon me. "I suppose you are from the city?"

I should have told her that I had spent most of my life in New York, which I am sure Elvira regarded as the most depraved of all the world's sinful capitals. Instead I said, "As a matter of fact, I grew up in a small mining town in the western part of the United States. The countryside is a lot like Southern Spain: mountainous, with fertile valleys, and rivers that dry up in the summertime. The river near my home was called *El Rio de las Animas Perdidas en Purgatorio.*" Enjoying Elvira's startled expression, I told her the story of the murdering Conquistadores who had died at the hands of Indians, without absolution from a priest, so that their souls were doomed to wander forever in Purgatory. "Perhaps that's why I feel so at home in Spain," I concluded soberly, "because I grew up in a peasant's hovel in a land rife with legend and superstition."

Elvira gave me a blank stare. "This way is the Chamber of the Two Sisters. You will notice the two slabs of white marble in the floor. They say this was part of the Sultan's harem. The Honeycomb Dome is above us. It has five thousand cells, the most of any such ceiling still in existence."

We completed our tour of the buildings, some of them badly damaged by the French during the Peninsular Wars of 1812. I took a few photographs, not because I really wanted souvenirs of my visit, but because Elvira seemed to expect it, and she kept pointing out sights that she thought would make good pictures. The Alhambra was extraordinary, seductive, a fairy-tale palace that didn't seem to belong to the tortured Spain that I had come to know.

Gypsies and beggar children continually beseiged us, but we also saw a few other tourists: two or three local families with half-grown children, and an English couple, whom I greeted and later photographed with their own camera.

Elvira suggested that we go down into the city to visit the Cathedral next, which contained the tombs of those great Catholic monarchs Ferdinand and Isabella, but I pleaded fatigue, saying that I was unaccustomed to the heat in southern Spain. The two of us descended the steep road toward the town, through a forest reputedly planted by the Duke of Wellington after his victory over Napoleon's armies. Elvira, who believed in strengthening the soul by mortifying the flesh, charged briskly ahead, ignoring my feeble suggestions that we take a taxi or a bus back to the Diaz villa.

We reached the house at about seven, as the harsh shadows of the afternoon were beginning to lengthen and soften. The moment we passed through the gate from the street into the patio, I sensed that something unusual had happened. A servant scurried past. A door slammed. Elvira rushed immediately to her father's sickroom, thinking, as I did, that Señor Diaz had suffered another setback.

I waited outside, having no wish to intrude on the family's privacy at this sad moment. On the two or three occasions that we had spoken, the old man and I had discovered no instant rapport or natural fondness for one another. I felt somewhat relieved that the end had come at last. Soon Luis and I could return to Madrid.

Carlos came out of the house. He was wearing jodhpurs, high riding boots, and the dark blue shirt of the Falange, with its emblem of a yoke and five arrows embroidered in red over his left breast. He looked older, harder.

I stood, intending to express my sympathy for him and the rest of the family. He said, "It is Luis. They came for him this afternoon."

The strength left my legs, and I sank down on the bench again.

Carlos stood over me. "Try not to worry. They said they just wanted him for questioning. I'm sure it is only a formality."

"Who?" I found my voice. "Who took him? The army? The Falange?"

"I'm not sure," Carlos said vaguely. "They weren't wearing uniforms. I didn't recognize them."

"I don't believe you. You know and you won't tell me. Who was it, Carlos?"

My brother-in-law lifted his shoulders. I recognized the stubborn set of his mouth; I had seen it in Luis often enough.

"You must have noticed something. How did they come, by car or on foot? Did they walk like soldiers or like bureaucrats? Did they have guns? Could it have been the civil authorities, the mayor or somebody like that? Who, Carlos?"

Seeing that he couldn't or wouldn't answer me, I slung my camera case over my shoulder and strode toward the gate. "I'll have to find out for myself. The fascist military headquarters must be near the center of town. They'll know something. I'll find out where they've taken Luis, demand that they release him—"

Carlos ran after me. "No, Theodora, you can't. You must not go there. They don't know anything. It wasn't the military. I would have recognized them."

"Who?" I pressed him. "He's your brother, Carlos. Why won't you help him?"

When Carlos didn't reply, I answered the question myself. "Of course. You would have killed Luis long ago, but for the fact that he's your brother and you met under your father's roof instead of across a battle line. Carlos Diaz Albareda doesn't want to endanger his own safety and good standing in Granada, does he? He's a good Falangist, a friend of the rebels. How Luis must have embarrassed you by coming back to Spain! What did your friends think of you, having such an outspoken radical for a brother? You must have feared for your life! Don't worry, Carlos. If you don't draw undue attention to yourself by trying to save him, you can weather this crisis. You can easily restore your leaders' faith in you. Just tell them that when you had a chance to do something for your brother, you refused."

During this speech, Carlos had grown increasingly pale and tense. "The Guardia Civil," he said in a hoarse whisper. "I recognized one of them from meetings of the Falange. Lieutenant Sanchez. They have probably taken Luis to their *cuartel* on the Calle de los Reyes Católicos. But you mustn't go there! You'll only make it harder for him."

Ignoring this admonition, I flung open the gate and ran down the hill toward the center of the city. Having arrived in Granada in the dead of night, I had only the vaguest notion of how the town was laid out. I headed toward the highest church spire, assuming I would find the Cathedral. Surely the officers of the city and the Guardia and Franco's military government would not be far away.

"The Guardia Civil?" I asked passersby. "Where is their barracks, their *cuartel?* I am looking for the headquarters of the Guardia Civil. Calle de los Reyes Católicos?"

They met my questions with suspicious stares. Finally one old woman glared in the direction of a building draped with the red and yellow flag of Franco's Nationalists, and spat in the dust at my feet.

The Guardia Civil had been established especially to keep order in the provinces outside of Madrid and the other large cities. Its members were a familar sight in the small towns and on rural roads, where they traveled in pairs to insure against ambush and assassination. Soldiers of the Guardia were never assigned to their home provinces, lest their loyalty be corrupted by stronger loyalties to their families and neighbors. When the rebellion broke out in Morocco, most of the members joined with Franco's Nationalists in attempting to overthrow the leftist Republic. Those few who didn't want to join the rebellion deserted and headed for their homes.

Their belted gray-green uniforms and distinctive hats had been designed deliberately to intimidate and terrify the poor peasants. In foul weather, they wore dark, swirling cloaks. I remembered the line from one of Diaz's poems: "Patent-leather hats, patent-leather souls."

I told the officer at the desk that I wanted to see Lieutenant Sanchez. He gave me an uncomprehending smile. I repeated my request to no effect, and then demanded to see my husband, Luis Diaz Albareda. I thought I saw a flicker in the man's eyes, but he shrugged and shook his head.

"Who is your superior? I insist on speaking to him at once."

"They have all gone home, Señora," the man said blandly. "Why don't you come back tomorrow? Perhaps someone can answer your questions then."

I persisted. Ignoring me, he pretended to search for something in a file drawer.

The blades of the ceiling fan overhead swirled lazily. Flies buzzed over the contents of the wastebasket in the corner. The desk in the center of the room was battered, nicked and scarred as if by thousands of petitioners who, having failed to elicit a satisfactory response from the bulwark of integrity on duty, had vented their rage on the furniture.

"I mustn't get angry," I told myself. "I must be calm."

Momentarily thwarted, I left the office. The guard's studied nonchalance had convinced me that he knew very well what I was talking about, otherwise he would have looked confused and perturbed. He would never have turned his back on me. The Spaniards I had met were always gallant to women and polite to foreigners.

Foreigners. Like me, Luis had an American passport. The Guardia had no right to arrest a foreign national! I stopped a passing priest and asked if the American government had a consulate in Granada. Oh, no, the man told me. The city was much too small. In Málaga, probably. Certainly in Sevilla.

"A British Consulate, then?" I needed to talk to someone who could advise me on how to proceed.

Ah, there had been a British Consul once, fifty years ago, but not since then. The bigger cities, like Córdoba and Sevilla, now—

The priest was middle-aged, well-spoken, immaculate. Purple piping decorated the edges of his cassock, identifying him as a monsignor, a friend not of the workers and the peasants but of the rich men. Well, perhaps he would intercede on behalf of one of Granada's wealthiest citizens.

"My husband is the son of Don Miguel Antonio Juan Diaz y Lasado," I told him. "He was arrested this afternoon. I have reason to believe he was taken away by the Guardia Civil, but no one will tell me anything. Please, can't you help me?"

A veil descended over the man's eyes. Realizing that he wasn't dealing with an ordinary tourist, he suddenly became furtive and wary. "I am sorry, Señora. The name means nothing to me. I am sure this trouble of yours is a simple misunderstanding. Go back to your home. Ask no more questions of me. Of anyone."

He turned and walked briskly toward the Cathedral, the black skirts of his cassock flapping around his legs.

Heat radiated from the walls of the buildings that surrounded me. Heat rose up from the dusty paving stones under my feet, and pressed down on me from the darkening evening sky. For the first time, I felt the weight of despair. This was no ordinary case of a misplaced tourist, no simple misunderstanding that could be cleared up by a few minutes of conversation with an apologetic official.

Spain was at war with herself. The population of Granada was sympathetic to Franco's brand of fascism. They wanted to bring down the leftist Republican government, and they regarded liberal-thinking men like Luis as the enemy. Carlos had made some hazy remarks on the confusion that had followed the announcement of the rebellion and the taking of the town by the military. Luis and I had already heard that the good citizens of Granada had butchered several hundred of their own number, known members of the Communist Party or the Anarchist movement, men whose allegiance to the Republic was well known. What would they do to a man like Diaz, a writer who had made a career of parading his hatred of the Guardia and the royalists and the repressive forces of the Church and the landowners?

I walked around to a tree-shaded square, the Plaza de la Trinidad, a few short blocks from the Cathedral. My terror and desperation must have shown on my face, for the occupants of the other benches in the little park gave me curious looks and shifted away.

Should I go back to the Diaz house? I could picture the smug and censorious expression on Elvira's face. Luis's sister no doubt felt that her brother's misfortune had been brought on by his own sinfulness. Assuming that the forces of the state knew best, she would accept Luis's fate. Don Miguel might have fought to save his son if his health had permitted, but he was ill and weak, past caring about anything but his own immortal soul. Carlos had already shown his unwillingness to intervene.

No, the Diaz family would do nothing to help their oldest son, much less his godless American wife. Diaz had long ago forfeited his rights to their love and loyalty. Except for me, he had no friends in Granada.

No. One other person loved him. Angel. Angel was here in Granada. I had to find him.

Luis had told me that the most picturesque section of Granada was Albaicín, the old Arab town. Although some of the city's gypsies lived in caves on the high hill called Sacromonte, many more had settled in that congested quarter. If only we had been able to come at a different time, he had said somewhat wistfully, he would have taken me to his favorite haunts and shown me the real Granada, the throbbing heart of Andalusia. Yes, Angel would certainly make his home there, in Albaicín, among people like himself, artisans and gypsies.

I startled an old man out of his doze. "Where can I find *los gitanos*, the gypsies? Which way is Albaicín?"

North of the Rio Darro, the streets narrowed dramatically. The white houses had a Moorish cast, with tiled roofs, keyhole windows, low doorways. Gangs of grubby children congregated in the unpaved alleyways, ignoring the rough words from storekeepers and pedestrians. I rooted in my camera case for a coin, then approached the biggest boy in a group that was teasing a weary-looking burro.

"Do you know a man named Angel? He is a painter from Madrid, a stranger here. He cannot speak. His face is scarred on this side." I touched my hand to my cheek. "If you take me to him, you can have this coin."

The boy looked sullen and uninterested until he saw the coin. Flashing me a knowing if somewhat lewd glance, he darted off. I followed him through a maze of twisted streets. Through curtained doorways, I caught glimpses of sparsely furnished rooms, dark with rugs and draperies, whose whitewashed walls glinted with pots and vessels made of copper and brass. As we climbed the nearly vertical hill, the heat became less intense. I saw a hun-

dred intriguing corners that I wanted to photograph, but not
now. Later, when Luis was free, I would come back. We would
come back together.

Thrusting aside a curtain, the urchin motioned for me to pre-
cede him. While my eyes adjusted themselves from mellow sunlight to nearly total darkness, I felt his sticky hand brush mine.
When I opened my palm, the coin was gone, and so was the boy.

Below me, a lantern glimmered. Stumbling down a short
flight of stairs, I found myself in a dank, windowless room that
reeked of stale wine and garlic and perspiration. The floor was
marble, almost invisible under a coating of dust and grime.
Burning paraffin, tallow, and cigarette smoke had blackened the
walls, which had once been whitewashed. Copper pots hung
from the beams, along with strings of onions and dried red peppers, a few sausages, and joints of *jamón serrano*, ham cured in
the sun on snowy mountainsides. The stools and tables in the
place looked as old as the Alhambra itself, if not quite so ornate.

A short, big-bellied man came up to me. I said, "I am looking
for Angel, the gypsy painter, the one with the scars on his face."
The man shook his head. I seated myself on a stool near the entrance. The other patrons in the place satisfied their curiosity
quickly, then returned to their drinking. "Bring me a glass of
sherry. If you should happen to see Angel, tell him that the wife
of Diaz the Poet wants to speak to him."

I took only one sip of my sherry. It was the worst I had tasted
in my life, an astringent wine whose bouquet reminded me of
the stinking chemicals I used to develop my negatives.

Two old men shuffled in and sat on stools against one wall.
They both carried guitars, which they began to strum at the
same exact moment without looking at each other. Their music
sounded strange to my ears, throbbing and dissonant, more
Moorish than Spanish. Gypsy music.

A beaded curtain shimmered at the back of the room. Angel
sauntered into the tavern, followed by a swarthy gypsy girl
wearing vividly colored skirts and a low-cut blouse. She shook
the tangle of dark hair that lay on her shoulders, revealing glints

of gold at her ears and throat. Angel didn't glance at me, but something in his studied inattention told me that he knew I was there.

One of the musicians threw back his head and broke into song, wailing in a voice as cracked and rough and worn as the old stucco walls that surrounded him. The girl began to sway in time to the music. The heels of her shoes clacked on the hard floor. Some of the other patrons in the room clapped their hands in a broken rhythm, providing a jagged counterpoint to the music of the guitars. The girl dipped and whirled, tapping her heels, all the while fixing Angel with a smoldering gaze. Leaning against the wall with his arms crossed over his chest, Angel looked slightly bored.

The music swelled to a crescendo as the singer keened soulfully about the gypsy woman who had stolen his sanity and his peaceful dreams. With a final swirl of skirts and a wild drumming of heels, the girl finished her dance. The patrons applauded.

Unfolding his body with the languid grace of a cat awakening from a nap, Angel pulled himself away from the wall and moved to the center of the room. Holding his back straight, he tilted his head slightly forward. His arms bracketed his body in symmetrical S curves: elbows out, wrists touching the waist, fingers curled. The guitars were silent, waiting.

Angel stamped his feet and raised his arms sharply. Closing his eyes, he seemed to draw into himself, taking with him the rapt attention of everyone in the room. He snapped his fingers in a rippling motion that made them sound like rattling castanets. His heels punched out a rapid staccato burr. Unable to restrain their excitement, a few men cried out, "Óla! Óla!" One of the guitarists began to pluck out a quick, nervous tune, a strange melody punctuated with agonized chords and thumps on the instrument with the heel of his hand. The second guitarist joined him. The music gained urgency and intensity.

In that smoky cantina, Angel shed the role of the grimacing grotesque that I had seen him play so often. His scars seemed to vanish in a haze of dark hair and shadow. Although he never once glanced in my direction, I knew he was dancing for me. He moved slowly, with such exquisite control that even his smallest gesture seemed to suggest worlds of meaning beyond the movement. His concentration was absolute. Arms rising and falling, turning but never bending his torso, he reshaped the sculpture of his body into a succession of graceful postures that each had the hardness of smooth steel. Although he never made a single crude gesture, his dancing was suffused with a sensual awareness of his body as a powerful instrument over which he had total control.

The music and the clapping, the pounding of heels and the drumming throbbed like an excited pulse. The sound reverberated in my middle, spread to my limbs. I couldn't take my eyes off this man, this quintessential Spanish gypsy male: a creature so self-confident and arrogant that he could dance alone in front of strangers, rejoicing in the magnificence of his own body, sneering at old age and weakness and death. His boldness invited admiration. His beauty compelled desire.

I hated this man, this Angel. Every time I saw him, I learned something new and unpleasant about myself. I had come to this place hoping to help my husband, and instead I had lost myself in longing for this gypsy animal. As the dance drove to its fiery conclusion, my eyes began to burn. I knotted my hands so tightly that the ring Luis had given me that day cut into my flesh.

The pounding of heels stopped. The music ended. I sat dazed amid shouting and applause. Then I heard a step at my elbow and looked up.

Angel grinned down at me. His white shirt hung open to his waist, revealing a hairless chest slick with sweat. The gypsy girl, who couldn't have been older than fifteen, leaned against him, one hand clamped firmly and possessively on his smooth muscular forearm.

"They have arrested Luis," I said in English. "This afternoon, at his house."

Angel's grin vanished. He whirled and bared his teeth at the girl, who retreated to sulk against the wall. Jerking his head at me, Angel led the way through the beaded curtain.

I followed, aware of the studiously blank expressions on the faces of the other patrons of the tavern. We climbed three flights of stone steps, and entered a room at the rear of the house. The single bed in the corner was rumpled.

Angel turned and faced me, his eyes demanding more information. I told him what had happened, how my efforts to locate Diaz had failed. As I spoke, my fears dissolved into exhaustion and uncertainty.

"I'm not even sure the Guardia are still holding him. He could be at home right now, waiting for me. It's all a mistake. Of course, that's what happened. They questioned him and let him go. A mistake. I shouldn't have come here. Forgive me for bothering you. I—I'd better go."

But my trembling legs would carry me no farther. A strong hand pressed me down on the only chair in the room. When I looked up again, Angel was drawing a Basque beret down over the scarred portion of his face. He had already put on a dark suit jacket.

He thrust the palm of his hand toward me. I understood that I was to stay in the room until he returned. He set a bottle of sherry on the table in front of me, and then he slipped out of the room. I noticed the label on the bottle: Tio Pepe. In spite of my fatigue and worry, I smiled. Angel's taste in lodging and whores was simple, but he had a liking for fine sherry.

A dog-eared sketchbook lay on the floor near the bed. I flipped through it. To my surprise, I discovered that Angel could actually draw. He painted abstractly from choice, not because finer and more precise artistic skills eluded him. His sketches were strong, obviously done in haste, but with a deftness and confidence that denoted much practice and a keen eye. He had made several drawings of a gypsy whore lying naked on the bed. They weren't obscene or vulgar, but sensitive pictures of a woman grateful for a chance to rest from the rigors of her profession. Several studies of Diaz followed, in which the poet looked sombre and severe: his Madrid period, when he lived with the certainty of failure. Angel had captured him better than my photographs ever could.

Turning over another page, I was startled to see a fairly recent drawing of myself. At no time had Angel and I been together long enough for him to sketch me. He must have made the drawing from memory, on the train to Jaén, perhaps. He had given me a sad and pensive look. "Portrait of a woman married to a man she doesn't love," I thought, flinging the sketchbook away from me.

23

Darkness descended swiftly. A gentle wind from the east, carrying traces of rose scent and orange blossoms, softened the noxious odors that drifted up from the alley under Angel's window. I wanted to light the oil lamp on the table, but didn't dare. Franco's military commanders had ordered a blackout with which I couldn't comply, as there were no shutters at the window.

I hoped Angel would be cautious. He had good reason to hate the Guardia Civil, and to be wary of them. One of their soldiers had slashed his face and his vocal cords, transforming him from a handsome and voluble gypsy child into a maimed and hideous mute.

Another hour passed. The bells of a nearby church tolled eleven. A ten o'clock curfew had been imposed on the city. If Angel were discovered in the empty streets of Granada now, he would be arrested. He would not cooperate with the officials of the military government, being unwilling and unable to answer their questions. If the authorities discovered him to be a friend of the infamous Diaz, already their prisoner, they would throw him into jail as well.

The door opened and Angel slipped in, carrying a small candle in a saucer.

"Is it true, are they holding Luis?" I asked, going to him. He nodded. "Is there going to be a trial? Are they going to release him?" He shook his head. "Not tonight, or not at all?" A stronger shake of the head. "What will happen to him? Are they going to send him to another prison?"

Angel's good eye flickered and closed. Death.

"Oh, God."

Too numbed by shock and weariness to think further, I sat down on the edge of the bed. The sheets reeked of sex.

Moving silently around the room, Angel stashed his few possessions into a small canvas musette bag. When he had finished packing, he stood at the door and beckoned to me. I gave him a dazed look.

"What's happening?" I saw the bag. "You're leaving. Where are you going?"

Angel moved his hand in a gesture that encompassed both of us, then he whipped the tip of his finger across his scarred throat.

"If we don't get out, they'll arrest us, too," I interpreted. "But I'm in no danger from them. I'm an American citizen, like Luis. They won't do anything to me. But you go, Angel, before someone betrays you. I'll stay here until morning, when the curfew is lifted, and then I'll return to the Diaz house. Carlos will help me get back to Madrid."

The shake of Angel's head was vehement. His eye blazed. He wasn't going to leave me.

And then I understood. "Luis," I breathed. "Luis knew this was going to happen! He's known from the very beginning that he would never leave Granada, that he wouldn't survive the war. The way he talked—always death— And you." I gazed wonderingly at Angel. "He asked you to come to Granada because of me, didn't he?"

Angel represented the darker aspects of Luis's character. Angel, the animal, the brute. Angel. The sensitive artist, the loyal friend. In marrying Luis, I had married both of them. In Luis's absence, Angel would assume the role of friend and protector. He would not desert me.

We crept down the stairs and left the house by a back door. I carried my camera case, which contained my Leica and a few rolls of film, a comb, my passport and Luis's, a little money. Angel ducked into the tavern for a moment and returned carrying an immense black shawl, which he threw around my shoulders. I was grateful to him. Darkness in this desert country brought a deep chill that only the morning sun could banish, and I was still wearing the light cotton blouse and full skirt that I had put on that afternoon before going to the Alhambra with Elvira.

A three-quarter moon helped to light our passage as we descended through the darkened alleys and twisted streets of Albaicín toward the city. We had gone only a few hundred yards when Angel heard footsteps. He pulled me into a doorway and held me tightly as a pair of military guards approached. Shrouded in black, we blended with the shadows. The guards strolled past, noticing nothing.

I wondered where Angel was leading me, until I recognized the silhouette of the Cathedral spire and the boxy outlines of the Archbishop's Palace. As we crept along the alley between two buildings that faced the Calle de los Reyes Católicos, I heard gruff voices on the other side of the high wall to our right. We had reached the headquarters of the Guardia Civil.

Groping our way through the darkness, we came to a doorway in the wall opposite the *cuartel*. Angel must have fiddled the lock earlier, for now he simply lifted the latch and pushed the door open. Once inside, he lit a match and led me up a wooden staircase. We came out on the rooftop of the building across the street from the Guardia barracks. In the moonlight, I could see a couple of cars and trucks parked inside an enclosed compound. A few Guardia members lounged in front of the gate, exchanging idle gossip and cigarettes.

"Why don't the Republicans drop a bomb on this place?" I muttered. "Maybe we could get him out alive."

Crouching side by side, Angel and I watched the movement in the yard behind the barracks. Angel kept a grim vigil, neither moving nor dozing nor smoking, but gazing steadily at the scene below us. The blacked-out town was unnaturally dark, eerily silent. Somewhere a dog barked. The moon shimmered in the cloudless sky, casting hard-edged shadows in the clear night air.

Huddling inside the shawl, I struggled to stay awake. Angel draped his coat over my shoulders, giving me his tacit permission to sleep. Physical and emotional fatigue overwhelmed me. I folded my arms on my updrawn knees and lowered my head.

A touch on my arm awakened me. I looked up, immediately taut and alert. The eastern sky was brightening. Down in the courtyard of the *cuartel*, an engine sputtered into action and idled noisily. One of the trucks backed up to the rear door of the barracks. A small group of men shuffled out and climbed over the lowered tailgate of the truck while guards prodded them and urged them to hurry. Beside me, I felt Angel stiffen.

At that same moment, I caught a brief glimpse of Diaz's familiar profile. As he clambered into the truck, I saw that his hands were cuffed in front of him. I realized that I was gripping Angel's arm, digging my fingers into his flesh. He touched my hand briefly, and then he stood. The vigil was over.

At the foot of the stairs, we waited inside the alley door until we heard the rumble of the truck as it lurched out into the cobbled street behind the barracks. Keeping to darkened alleyways, darting occasionally into doorways, we pursued the truck and the Jeep that followed it. Angel seemed to be able to hear the roar of the motors long after I thought we had lost our quarry. We ran north, toward the Puerta Fajalauza and the Murcia road. Arriving at the top of the knoll just outside the ancient city walls, we halted for a moment. I could just make out the glimmer of red taillights disappearing over the next hill.

Panting, I stumbled after Angel, who moved swiftly but never carelessly. At the slightest unusual noise, he would motion me to take cover behind a rock or a tree. My heart swelled and

contracted with terror as well as with this unexpected exertion, but I managed to keep pace with him, all the while listening for the volley of shots that would signal that we were too late.

The truck and Jeep halted in open country, about two miles outside of Granada. The guards led their party of six prisoners to the edge of an arroyo about a thousand feet away from the road. With his unerring instinct, Angel seemed to know where they were going. We cut across a vineyard, keeping low between the fences of tethered grapevines as we ran up the hill on the other side of the gorge.

Angel half-dragged me up a steep face of wind-blasted yellow rock. Throwing himself onto his belly, he pulled me down beside him and motioned for me to be silent. Our prospect overlooked the arroyo; we were only a hundred feet away from the group of soldiers and prisoners, separated from them by a deep chasm. The rising sun at our backs cast a faint pale light on the scene.

The half-dozen members of the Guardia death squad were in no hurry. They shared cigarettes with the prisoners, checked their names against a list, removed handcuffs. A couple of the guards examined their pistols furtively, turning their backs to the men they were about to exterminate as if to spare them the anxiety of wondering whether or not the weapons would function.

Diaz paid no attention to the activity around him. He stood at the edge of the gorge, facing Angel and me. We could see his face plainly. I fought down an impulse to call out to him. The Guardia gunmen would shoot me, too, along with Angel. How could that help Luis?

The guards ordered the men to line up. One of the prisoners fell to his knees and began to weep loudly, his cries echoing off the rocks. Diaz went to him, and putting his arms around the man's shoulders, helped him to stand. The little group formed a ragged line about six feet from the edge of the abyss. I noticed that a couple of the men wore suit jackets and neckties. They had been arrested on Sunday afternoon, perhaps during dinner with their families, perhaps on their way to their favorite tavern.

I couldn't bring myself to watch what was about to happen, and yet I felt that I must witness it. My camera case pressed against my side. I took out my Leica and attached its telephoto lens. Bracing the camera against the rock so that it wouldn't wobble during prolonged exposure in dim light, I set the focus.

Luis stood at the end of the row, slightly apart from the rest. His head was bowed low, so that his chin rested on his chest. I recognized the attitude; I had seen it hundreds of times, when he was struggling with the line of a poem. Sitting at his desk, or standing at the window, he would lower his head and murmur the words to himself as he listened to their music. He called himself a singer, likening himself to the troubadors of ancient times, who never wrote their songs down, but who moved from province to province, teaching their stories and songs to people whose lives were starved for what Diaz called the unnatural beauty of the imagination, to distinguish it from the concrete beauty of flowers or landscapes or laughing children.

"A poet," Diaz once said, "is the most necessary and the most expendable of men."

The firing squad organized itself. Each prisoner had been assigned his own executioner, one to one. Standing erect but relaxed, utterly at ease with death, Luis Diaz Albareda faced the man who would kill him. He had come to the end of his long search for truth. I wished he could tell me what he had learned.

The leader of the squad barked a command, his words pounding on the rocks that surrounded Angel and me as we lay concealed on our promontory. I closed my eyes. This time my trusty Leica would have to take its pictures on its own, without my practiced eye guiding it from the view finder.

Six shots sounded like one shot, echoed like a thousand shots. My finger depressed the shutter release. I didn't need to see the men dropping to their knees or reeling backwards to sprawl over the edge of the arroyo. I advanced the film, clicked the shutter, advanced the film. My camera would record this event, but my own memories would stay with me always, more vivid and terrible than anything I had yet seen in that war.

A spell of silence followed, in which I could hear the agonized breathing of the man at my side. Angel was remembering, too. Remembering the lean aristocrat who had rescued him from the gutter, who had fed him and dressed him and loved him like a son. Never in his life had Angel experienced anything like that love; love that was demanding, uplifting, all-encompassing.

Then, one after another, six separate shots rang out. The guards were administering a *coup de grace*, insuring that no prisoner would crawl away alive, to speak the truth about what had happened on that Monday morning in August, 1936, outside the fairy-tale city of Granada.

I don't know which shot finished killing Diaz. My finger jerked on the Leica's shutter release at each hollow crack.

Its work complete, the members of the death squad dumped the bodies of its victims into the abyss. Then they trotted down the slope to the road, piled into their vehicles, and drove back to Granada as the sun was rising.

When they were out of sight and out of earshot, Angel slithered down to the base of the rock and ran around to the head of the arroyo, where he climbed down and made his way to the six corpses at the bottom.

I lay still, feeling as though the bullets had torn gaping holes in my own flesh and spirit. When the sun began to warm my back, I flung off my shawl. Diaz had joked about shawls like that, saying that I would wear one when he died. But I wouldn't wear black for him. I wasn't really his widow, because I had never been his wife.

Angel returned and crouched beside me.

"I never loved him," I said into the chamber of my folded arms. "I never loved him."

The morning sun rapidly heated our surroundings to an unbearable temperature. Gathering up our possessions, Angel urged me down from the rock. He led me to a shallow cave formed by an overhang of stone. Birds, frightened away by the pre-dawn cacophony, began to twitter again. A hawk circled overhead, inspecting the carcasses at the bottom of the arroyo. A car engine droned, coming nearer, halting. Footsteps scuffled on the graveled approach to the gorge.

"Luis! Luis!"

I stiffened. "It's Carlos," I whispered. "He'll help us." I started to rise. Angel pulled me back. As I drew a breath to call out to Carlos, Angel clapped his hand over my mouth. His arms pinned me like sturdy wooden stocks so that I couldn't move.

"Luis!"

Loose rocks spilled down the side of the arroyo. Carlos slithered down to search for his brother among the dead. After a moment, he clambered up again. The engine of his car roared. Tires squealed as he drove away.

When he was sure we were alone again, Angel relaxed his hold. Sobbing, choking, I unleashed my fury, slapping his scarred cheek so hard that the taut shiny tissue whitened under the imprint of my hand. Angel didn't move, but gazed at me with his one milky distorted eye and his one beautiful brown eye until I thought that Luis and Angel had actually merged into this single ugly-beautiful human, half god and half beast, who embodied every noble and disgusting trait known to mankind.

I lifted my hand to strike again. Angel waited. My hand wavered in mid-air, and then fell to my lap. I began to rock back and forth, weeping noiselessly.

Angel made me drink a little sherry, then he spread the shawl out on the rocky ground and forced me to lie down, bundling his coat under my head for a pillow.

Angel sat listening and watching for an hour or more. When he was sure we were safe from discovery, he lay down beside me at the front of the cave, shielding me from sight and from harm.

We slept until mid-afternoon. When we awoke, we drank the last of Angel's sherry. Angel left the cave and returned a few minutes later, having filled the bottle with some water from a well near the vineyard. We listened to the sounds of traffic on the road, the measured clop-clop of burros' hooves, the shuffle and subdued chatter of farmers on their way to their fields, the occasional churn and rush of a motored vehicle. Toward evening, Angel picked up his musette bag, indicating that it was time to leave the cave. Numb with shock and weariness, I obeyed him listlessly.

We avoided the main road, which was held by Franco's fascist troops, and confined our movements to the fields and vineyards where we could hide from their patrols. Angel pulled some oranges from a tree and shared them with me. I found that in spite of having gone nearly a whole day without food, I had no appetite.

We traveled eastward, over the foothills of the Sierra Nevada, toward the coastal plain, which was firmly in the hands of the Republicans. Once we reached Guadix, we could arrange for transit back to Madrid.

We had gone about ten miles when I sat down abruptly on a rock in the middle of a scrubby untilled field. I could go no farther. My feet, in rope-soled canvas espadrilles, were blistered and bleeding. My shoulders ached from the weight of my camera case. I thought longingly of the straw hat I had left behind at Villa Diaz in my rush to save Luis. My head throbbed from exposure to the hot afternoon sun.

"No more," I panted when Angel came back to see what was the matter. "Can't help it. So tired. Tired. You go ahead. Don't worry about me. I'll be all right. American citizen. Can't hurt me."

Angel slipped his hand under my upper arm and tried to drag me to my feet. I shook him off. "No, damn you! You don't have to help me any more. I don't want your help. We both detest each other—it's ridiculous for us to travel together, just because of Luis. Luis is dead. I'm only holding you back. For God's sake, Angel, leave me alone."

Seeing that I was on the verge of collapse and hysteria, Angel backed off. He glanced around, scowling. We were too exposed on this hillside, too far from any decent shelter. He may have wanted to travel farther before stopping for the night, but he could see that I had reached the limit of my endurance. I needed food and I needed rest. Looking northward, he spotted a small village huddled against the rising mountainside.

He set his musette bag down beside me, to show me that he meant to return. I stared sightlessly into middle distance, my shoulders sagging and my head bowed. I wasn't interested in Angel's movements.

I must have dozed off briefly, curled up on top of the shawl. A droning noise awakened me. Rousing myself, I looked up. A plane was approaching from the south. At first I thought it must be a Republican bomber, on its way back from a mission over Sevilla or Granada. Then I realized that the plane wasn't one of the Republic's old crates, but a sleek and modern machine of a wholly different design. It passed overhead, scouting the countryside, flying so low that I could see the Italian flag painted on the fuselage: one of Mussolini's contributions to Franco's Nationalist war effort.

One wing of the plane dipped as it flew toward me. Dressed in white, lying in the middle of my black shawl, I must have made a fine bull's-eye, a perfect target for sport.

Seeing the plane coming straight at me, I jumped up and started to run. Bullets chewed up a strip of earth only a few yards away from me, showering me with dirt.

Wheeling in the sky, the plane came back for another pass.

I saw Angel running down the hill toward me, but I was too terrified to pay any heed to his waving arms. He overtook me and tackled me, throwing me to the ground and rolling with me behind an outcropping of boulders just as the gunner sprayed the area around us with bullets.

The plane vanished over the western hills.

When Angel could no longer hear the engines, he moved away from me. Trembling, we sat up and looked at each other. Angel's scarred cheek was bleeding from a small cut inflicted by a piece of flying rock, and his left arm was bloody. But we were both alive. Angel permitted himself a twisted and triumphant grin.

My heart resumed a more reasonable pace. "You're hurt." I dabbed at his cheek with the hem of my skirt. His appearance no longer repulsed me. His scar was like a mask that concealed the man behind it, and that man didn't terrify me anymore. "Take off your jacket." His shirt was torn. The bullet had grazed his arm just above the elbow, inflicting a gash that was bloody but not deep. As I went to fetch our bags and the shawl, I saw that Angel had dropped some provender in his mad dash down the hill. On his foray to the village, he had managed to steal a loaf of fresh bread, a sausage, and a jug of wine from an untended kitchen. Some peasant's wife would blame a gypsy for the theft—and she wouldn't be wrong.

At my request, Angel removed his shirt. Moistening a corner of my skirt with some water from the sherry bottle, I bathed away the blood on his arm. As I bound the wound, I saw another old scar on the back of his left shoulder, a puckered crater where I had plunged my scissors into his flesh, on that long ago day on Bedford Street.

I touched the old wound, recoiling. I was never far from blood and violence. I carried it inside me, like a baby I could never deliver. My own soul must be puckered like this, I thought, from all the horrors I've witnessed in my life. So much blood, so much pain. I should be used to it by now.

Angel placed his two hands alongside my face, comforting me. Shivering, I leaned against him. I had lashed out at him again today. More than anyone else, Angel had a way of provoking me. Perhaps, like Luis, I recognized part of myself in him, my darker self. Angel aroused my most primitive passions: my ancient secret fears, my lust for blood, my deepest desires and cruelest hungers.

Darkness and its accompanying chill settled around us. Under my cheek, I could hear the strong vital pumping of Angel's heart. He felt solid and warm, as the earth still felt warm, radiating the heat that it had absorbed throughout the long hot day. A heavy fragrance of freshly dug soil rose up from the ditch the aerial gunner's bullets had ripped open in the turf, along with the delicate scent of the rosemary and wild thyme covering that poor land.

I touched my fingertips to Angel's blind eye, and lightly stroked his drawn cheek and silent throat. His skin felt taut and cool. I pressed my lips against the scar on his shoulder. It tasted of salt and blood.

"I am sorry for this, Angel," I whispered. "I didn't know. I didn't know then that I wanted you."

We sank down on the sweet musty earth. Angel shuddered with excitement, like a horse eager to start a race. I stirred impatiently, urging him to hurry, but he held himself back.

Theodora was Angel's woman now. He would master her, he would possess her, but in his own time and in his own way. He would show her what it felt like to be taken by a real man, a man who was as strong as a stallion and as tireless as a bull in the *corrida*. Diaz had been gentle, too gentle. He had made love with poetry, but they had never reached the summit. Angel would conquer her without words, without gentleness, as he had conquered Death that day.

The moon's light was kind to Angel's disfigured face. I kissed him again and again, and I called him beautiful. Later, I lay peacefully in his arms, under the blanket of the shawl he had stolen from the tavern-keeper's wife. The old woman wouldn't begrudge us her garment, not if she knew to what use we had put it. No one could deny us anything on this magical night.

For this night belonged to Angel and Theodora, two outcasts wedded to each other by the poet who on that same day had consummated his vows with Death.

24

Angel and I spent a week in a little inn in Guadix. We made love with inordinate frequency, if the looks given us by the proprietor's wife were any indication; we gorged on bread and fruit and sausages and drank so much wine that we were in a constant state of happy inebriation. Our strength restored, we decided to move on. Hearing that the roads to the north were blocked, we headed east toward the coast, to Valencia.

Valencia had suffered ghastly horrors and wholesale bloodshed immediately after the uprising, but now, far from the front lines, it offered warm sunshine, white beaches, and abundant food. But Angel seemed restless, eager to get back to Madrid.

"But I wasn't happy there," I told him. "I don't care if I never see my apartment again, or the Plaza de España, or any other part of that city. Why can't we stay here?"

Mute he may have been, but Angel had no trouble getting what he wanted. In less than a week, I found myself standing by his side on the platform of Valencia's gorgeously tiled railway station, awaiting the departure of the *talgo* for Madrid.

When Angel stepped inside his attic studio, he inhaled the stale odors of turpentine and linseed oil as if they were perfume. He looked around with satisfaction. Canvases in various states of completion were stacked against the walls. A vivid still life of oranges and red poppies stood on an easel in the center of the room. Light poured in through large windows that overlooked the classical Teatro Real and, farther on, the green and lovely Plaza de Oriente. We weren't far from the Palace, and the ruins of the Montaña Barracks.

Here, surrounded by the tools of his craft, Angel had no further need of me. Like Luis, his work was his life. I felt that I had become peripheral, unnecessary. The next moment, Angel dragged me to his bed and made fierce love to me.

The future fell into place. Here I would stay, until I tired of
him, or he tired of me, or we simply tired of each other.

That afternoon, Angel picked up a sketchbook and started to
plan a large canvas depicting the death of Diaz. He drew a horizontal line across the page, about two-thirds of the way from the
bottom. On top of the line he drew a pair of booted feet, and
above them, a hand holding a pistol: a soldier of the Guardia
Civil, standing at the edge of the arroyo. To the left he sketched
the head and shoulders of a man wearing a patent-leather tri-
corn: another Guardia member standing farther down the slope,
his face suffused with cruelty and cunning.

Below the line, all was darkness. A tumble of arms, legs, and
twisted torsos represented the dead. We were seeing the scene
from their point of view. I recognized Diaz, his body more tortured and distorted than any of the others, his face curiously
peaceful and alive.

The series of studies for the painting progressed from harshly
realistic to abstract, if no less chilling. Angel planned no use of
color, merely shades of black, white, and gray.

Seeing his watercolor studies, I thought of the photographs I
had taken that day. They were still in my camera case, still undeveloped. I wanted never to see them printed; but somehow, I
couldn't bring myself to destroy the film.

At eleven o'clock one morning in early October, Angel rolled
out of bed—we generally rose late—rummaged in his paintbox,
and brought me a couple of squeezed-out tubes of titanium
white and a bill from a dealer of artists' supplies.

"Oh, you need more paint. It's too early to go out now," I
mumbled. "I'll go later." He dragged me out of the bed, sheets
and all, and threw himself down on top of me. "You devil!" I
sputtered. "You're not going to get your own way this time."

Still protesting, somewhat less vigorously, I left the studio an
hour later. I carried my camera case. In addition to my passport
and photographic paraphernalia, it contained a little money and
one of Angel's sketchbooks, in which I had jotted down a list of

2019

what he needed. As I possessed no other purse, I usually took it with me when I went out.

The sun burned in a cloudless sky. As I strolled down the Grand Via, the broad boulevard that dissected the city, I reflected that Madrid wasn't such a terrible place after all. Living as I did, cut off from my past, with no dreams of the future, I could enjoy each small pleasure as a gift: a snatch of song, a child's laughter, a sip of good wine, a kiss.

The bombers of the Nazi Condor Legion flew over the city with their payloads of death while I was trying to persuade the art dealer that he couldn't really expect me to settle Angel's bill now, so soon after our return to the city.

"If not today, when?" the man demanded. "I can't eat these colors. I have bills to pay, too. Tell that mute that I want my money, war or no war. No money, no paint."

Just then the air-raid sirens began to shriek. Grumbling at this new annoyance, the man closed up shop and hurried me down into the subway, where we joined hundreds of others in waiting out the air raid. The all-clear finally sounded two hours later.

But when I got back to Angel's studio, the old building that had housed it was gone. Evaporated. Dust.

The facade of the building above me trembled. A few loose bricks rattled down, striking the pavement just a few feet from where I stood. Sparks snapped and hissed, adding light musical accents to the menacing roar of the flames. Timbers crashed, walls collapsed, and glass shattered with a sound like an icy avalanche sliding down a mountainside.

Women wept as they sifted through the wreckage of a nearby apartment house, half of which had been sheared off so that the remaining portion looked like the front of a dollhouse or a three-sided stage set. They called out the names of their loved ones who had disappeared, as if those persons could hear them from

inside their tombs of brick and plaster. A baby cried relentless-
ly, hardly pausing for breath. Air-raid sirens and fire sirens added their voices to the din.

Hell couldn't be any worse than this.

Angel had been like Diaz when he worked: self-absorbed,
oblivious to everything else. He would have paid no attention to
the sirens. When the bomb fell, he would have felt no pain.

After searching for him for a night and a day, I knew, without
really knowing, that he was dead.

Oh, NO

Days later, or perhaps only hours later, I was still standing
on the street where we had lived, staring at the madness and
straining to comprehend it. Vaguely, I became aware that
an open-topped Cadillac had screeched to a halt not far from
me. The driver cowered down behind the wheel and covered
his head with his arms. "Señor, it is not safe—the bombs—!"
he wailed.

"Damn it, man, when I tell you to stop, you stop!" A large
man stood up in the back seat. He wore dark glasses, a baseball
cap with the insignia of the New York Yankees over the visor,
and a short-sleeved safari suit with a belted jacket. He shouted to
me in clumsy Spanish, "Hey, you there, lady, look out!"

A few more bricks clattered down. One hit the sidewalk and
bounced up, striking my elbow. I tottered, but didn't move
away. The driver of the car began to beg the Virgin to deliver
him from fire and bombs and crazy Americans who insisted on
being taken to sections of the city that were under attack from
Nazis and Italian fascists and Franco's shells.

The big man picked his way toward me through the rubble. I
watched his progress with some interest. Didn't he know that
this building could collapse on top of him at any moment?

He yelled into my face, "Are you loco, lady? This place is going to come down on both of us if we don't get out of here. Wait
a minute—no, it can't be. Damn it, you are! You're that photographer, Fiona's niece—Diaz's woman! What in hell are you do-

ing here? Don't you recognize me? De Graaf. Hugo de Graaf."

Bombers, three of them, made a fresh pass over the western edge of the city. Through the smoke and the dust, I could see the bombs themselves, small and black, as innocuous as seeds floating on an autumn breeze. One struck a block of workers' flats two streets away. The ground trembled. Windows shattered above us, showering us with tiny shards of glass.

"Why are they bombing this part of the city?" I asked in a tone of mild irritation. "Madrid has no arsenals out here, no military targets."

"Who in hell cares why they're doing it?" Hugo tugged at my arm. "Let's get the hell out of here."

But I hung back. I had come to the end of a long road lined with corpses. Knowing what lay behind me, I had no wish to move ahead.

Cursing, Hugo picked me up and carried me over piles of brick and rubble to the other side of the street. At that moment, the burning apartment house in front of which I had been standing settled in on itself in a cloud of flame and dust. Throwing himself on top of me, Hugo sheltered me with his body and arms against the blast of heat and debris that spread out fanlike from the center of the implosion. Bits of plaster and stone sifted down around us. Screams rent the air, piercing the roar of settling rubble and the crackle of flames.

I peered up at my savior's face. "You're Hugo de Graaf, the man with all those wives."

"Damn right," Hugo said. "Come on, those flames are spreading. Whole damn block is going to go up in a minute." His arm around my waist, he propelled me toward the car. "Hit the gas, Manuel. This is no place to entertain a lady."

"Si, Señor Ugo!" The Cadillac jerked forward, throwing the two of us into a huddle in the back seat.

Righting myself, I sat in the corner of the car, my camera case clutched to my chest. "I've looked everywhere. No one's seen him. Some people asked me if I were his wife. I didn't know what to say."

"Who?" Hugo demanded. "What are you talking about? Diaz? Was Diaz in that building?"

"Twice. They killed him twice. I'm a widow. I don't feel like a widow. Not even once."

"You're not making any sense, kid," Hugo said. "What you need is a hot bath, a square meal, and a double shot of whiskey, not necessarily in that order. Manuel, head back to the hotel. The Señora needs some first aid. I could use a little tonic myself."

A few minutes later, Manuel pulled up in front of the Ritz Hotel on the Paseo del Prado. The big windows that faced the gardens in front were boarded up, giving the building the look of a place under seige. Nevertheless, the two bellboys who met Hugo in the lobby scurried away to do his bidding: tell room service to send up a plate of sandwiches and a couple of bottles of whiskey.

When I glanced into the mirror in the bathroom of Hugo's suite, I wondered how he had recognized me. I looked like a wild woman. Dressed in a stained white skirt and white blouse, my arms and face smudged with soot and mud, my hair disheveled and my eyes glazed, I hardly resembled the woman he had last seen in Luis Diaz Albareda's flat in Paris.

After I had bathed, I put on a vast black silk robe covered with rampant dragons embroidered in red.

Hugo was pacing the sitting room, a tumbler of whiskey in his hand. I glanced around. "This is very elegant."

Hugo shrugged. "It's okay. Service here's a little slow, but then it was even when Spain wasn't fighting a civil war."

I fingered the fabric on the robe. "These dragons look very fierce."

Hugo grimaced. "One of my wives," he said. "Bitch never did have taste." He proffered a plate of sandwiches. "Help yourself to some food and tell me what happened. You said Diaz was dead. When did it happen? Today? Yesterday?"

"A long time ago." I studied a ham sandwich. "I'd rather not talk about it."

"Look, kid, Diaz was no peasant, you know. He was no ordinary *campesino*. He was an important man, a symbol. You're going to have to talk about it sometime, whether you like it or not. Who did it, Franco's men? Were the Falangists in on it?"

"The Guardia Civil. In Granada."

"Granada, huh?" Hugo frowned. "I'm surprised we haven't heard about it up here."

"They killed him in secret, without a trial or any kind of publicity. They shot him and threw his body into a ravine." I spoke tonelessly, as if I were reporting stock quotations.

"But that's crazy. They know what kind of following Diaz has. Are you sure about this? Luis isn't just cooling his heels in a Granada jail?"

"No. I was there. I saw it all. Angel, too. Do you know him? The mute?"

"Sure I do. He has half his face all chopped up. Hell of an artist, though."

"Yes. Yes, he was." The touch of his hand, the crimp of his eyebrows, the flicker of his smile: I had learned to know Angel very well. I couldn't believe that I would never see him again.

Hugo demanded details of Diaz's death. I began with Carlos Diaz's visit to our flat near the Plaza Mayor at the end of August.

Hugo's scowl deepened as he listened. He said, "Wait a minute, I think I'd like some of the boys to hear this." He left the room and returned a few minutes later with a group of reporters in tow. I recognized some of the men from my days at the Cortes, before the rebellion. The bureau chief of *Paris-Matin* was there, along with representatives of the American and British press and a couple of photographers, one an old acquaintance from *Mode*. Hugo said, "They want to know what happened down there. I didn't think you'd mind."

"No, I don't mind." I felt exhausted but calm. Hugo offered me whiskey, which I declined in favor of some tepid coffee. "I'll tell you as much as I can remember."

As I talked, the reporters' pencils made scratching noises in their notebooks.

"Sounds like Carlos used the old man's illness as a way of luring Luis away from Madrid," Hugo growled. "I'm betting the Guardia and his fellow Falangists put pressure on him."

Carlos. Carlos, I thought: How had he found the arroyo so quickly? The other men looked at each other.

"You said Diaz was killed at the end of August," the reporter from *Paris-Matin* said. "That's over a month ago. Why didn't you tell anyone sooner?"

"Luis is dead," I said. "Getting this story into print isn't going to bring him back."

"What happened to Angel?" the correspondent from the *Times* asked. The *Mode* man snapped my picture. I winced at the flash. I'd always hated being photographed.

I told them about the bombing. "It's bad enough to kill a man, but to destroy his work—at least they couldn't do that to Luis." I glanced up at Hugo, who had assumed a protective stance behind the sofa where I was sitting. "When you found me, I didn't know what to do next. I didn't feel anything. I didn't feel frightened or angry or sad."

"That's normal." The man from *Paris-Matin* tucked his notepad away. "The cumulative effects of shock, one right after another."

"It's a remarkable story," Cecil Andrews of the *London Daily Mail* said. "They'll deny it, of course. Blame some other faction; blame the Left. Too bad we can't prove it."

"The photographs will make it very clear who was involved." I rubbed my eyes. "Those Guardia uniforms are unmistakable."

Everyone stared at me silently, their mouths gaping. Then Hugo said, "What are you talking about, kid? What photographs?"

"The ones I took of the execution."

"You what?" Hugo yelled. "Why the hell didn't you say so? Come on, let's see them."

"They're not developed. I didn't think I'd bother. They probably won't come out anyway. The light was bad, and I wasn't paying very good attention." I drew the edges of the dragon robe more tightly around me.

Hugo sat beside me on the brocaded upholstery. "Look, kid, I know you're upset. I don't blame you. Luis was a good guy, a friend of mine. All the boys knew him. We're on your side."

"What are you doing here?" I looked at him curiously. "Are you a reporter too?"

"Hell, no. I came over here to fight this war for the Republicans." Hugo made it sound as though the government elected by the Spanish people couldn't be trusted to fight its own war properly. "I know, I'm only a motion picture director, but believe me, nobody knows the value of publicity better than I do. This country is torn and bleeding, but half the world doesn't even know what's going on yet. I'm going to show them. I'm going to make the best damned war movie anybody has ever seen. People are going to walk out of their neighborhood theaters feeling like they've fought in Spain themselves. They're going to be so mad that they're going to get on the phone and call Roosevelt to ask him why in hell our country doesn't do something to help out."

I sighed. I felt tired, tired of watching the people I loved die, tired of war, tired of talk. Angel had communicated without using any words at all. Why didn't people like Hugo de Graaf realize how wasted words were?

"Diaz loved the Spanish people, and they loved him," Hugo said. "When they find out he was killed by the Civil Guard, arrested and shot in cold blood, without a trial, without a hearing, they're going to go after the sons of bitches who are responsible for his death. Every cause needs a martyr. The other side has Calvo Sotelo; so far all we have is an army lieutenant and a bunch of nameless trade unionists. But Diaz—Jesus, it's perfect!" His broad face glowed. "Champion of the common man, Poet of the People—"

"He hated this war," I murmured. "He said that it didn't matter who won. Spain would lose. He wouldn't have fought."

"These folks don't need to know that," Hugo said practically. "All they need to know is that he lived like a man and died like a hero. Give me the film. One of the boys will be happy to develop it."

For the first time that day, I felt something besides weariness and apathy. "I never let anyone else develop my negatives," I informed him.

Hugo grinned. "Then you'd better get to it, don't you think?"

The *Mode* photographer offered his darkroom, but I told him that I preferred to use my own equipment. After I changed back into my skirt and blouse, which the staff at the Ritz had cleaned and pressed, the entire party piled into Hugo's Cadillac and cruised over to the apartment near the Plaza Major.

Entering the flat wasn't the wrenching experience I had expected. Everything looked homely and familiar, not nightmarish or charged with vivid and painful memories. Diaz's favorite armchair near the window seemed ready to welcome him. His books stood in piles on his desk, as he had left them. In spite of his eagerness to divest himself of possessions, he couldn't help accumulating books. They had been more important to him than food or drink.

I dropped the black shawls down over the kitchen window and started to bring my developing equipment out from under the sink.

"I'm afraid this darkroom can't accommodate more than one," I told Hugo and the reporters.

"Okay, we'll get out of your way," Hugo said. "How long do you think this will take?"

"I'll make some contact sheets. No more than an hour. Please make yourselves comfortable."

Hugo turned around. "I brought the whiskey. Anybody have a poker deck?"

I lowered the curtain over the doorway and switched on my worklight. It would be so easy to pour too much developer into the tank, or to add the wrong chemical altogether. A mistake, I would tell them; I was upset; I wasn't thinking. I didn't want to see the pictures, any of them. Yes, Diaz had died like a hero that day, but so had five other men. Who would remember them?

One of the undeveloped rolls in my camera case had pictures of Angel, taken at a dusty bus stop in a wretched little town somewhere in southern Spain. He had insisted that I photograph him. I had refused, telling him that I felt like a ghoul for photographing Luis's execution, that I didn't want to take any more pictures, ever again. Angel had given me an amazed look, then he had laughed his silent laugh. He started to cavort in front of me, striking ridiculous and lewd poses. Finally, I took his picture just to appease him, and to explain his behavior to the other passengers, who were watching him with dismay and disapproval.

I poured out the developer, immersed the strips in the stop-bath solution, and finally in the fixative, before rinsing them in the sink. I reflected that my conduct since my husband's murder had been unseemly in every respect. Making love in the moon-light. Feasting on bread and wine and stolen sausages and oranges at dawn. Laughing like a lunatic in a public place. Dozing on a bone-rattling bus ride to yet another Republican town, my head bobbing against Angel's shoulder. We were a bizarre couple, the swarthy gypsy with the half-grotesque, half-beautiful face, and the tall fair-haired Anglo girl with the camera.

At first Angel had made a point of staying always on my left side, so that I could see only the unscarred portion of his face. But that aspect of him was strange to me; I preferred the scar, which had lost its power to terrify and sicken me.

I remembered standing naked in front of Angel and being filled with wonder that I experienced no sense of shame, no embarrassment or self-consciousness. We were staying in the ramshackle little inn in Guadix. Diaz had been dead only two days. For the first time since infancy, I felt truly naked, stripped of the layers of memory and guilt and regret that I had worn like heavy garments since childhood. Diaz was dead. I had nothing for which to reproach myself. I had done my best as companion and wife.

The past was done, the future lay in shadow. I had survived yet another trial by fire, and the experience had hardened rather than incinerated me. There, in that tiny shabby room, I had only the moment, and a man who desired me.

Shame and regret had not figured in the spectrum of Angel's emotions. In spite of his larcenous nature, he was the most honest of all the men I had ever known. Honest about himself, honest about his work. When he wanted to paint, he painted. He didn't agonize about how good or bad his art was, how worthwhile, how pleasing to this or that critic. He pleased no one but himself. Perhaps that was part of Angel's attraction for both Diaz and me: he showed us ourselves as we would have been without society, without family, without commitments to lovers or political causes or the inner demands of our own egos. Opportunistic, selfish, hedonistic: Angel knew what it meant to be truly free.

Each of the men I had loved had left me with something more than memories. Evan had taught me how to live with the pain of my early life, Diaz how to use it, Angel how to forget it. I was on my own now, for the first time since leaving Monkey Gulch. I wasn't afraid.

My timer rang. I removed the long strips of film from the water and hung them up to dry. One of the rolls had the shots of Elvira at the Alhambra. That day had been a prelude to terror. Even the smallest details of that visit had taken on a meaning and significance that they had lacked at the time. I took the strip down and threw it away. I wanted no souvenirs of Granada.

I don't want any paper images of Angel, either, I thought. Nothing of Angel that I wanted to remember could be captured in a photograph. I took the second strip down and discarded it as well.

I had purchased my enlarger in Paris, secondhand. It was a good one, the most expensive piece of equipment I owned besides my cameras. When the last strip of film was dry, I cut the negatives apart and arranged the pieces in a frame. After covering them with a sheet of emulsion-coated printing paper, I slipped the frame under the enlarger and exposed the film to the light for sixteen seconds. Then I slid the exposed paper into a tray of developing fluid and waited.

The pictures of the execution began to emerge. For the first time, I saw what had actually happened on that rocky hillside outside of Granada: pistol barrels belched fire and smoke; men dropped gracefully; the executioners advanced to administer to each victim a second and deadlier shot. When it was over, Luis lay on his back, his head tipped over the edge of the arroyo so that he faced the camera upside down. One half of his face was gone, like Angel's, the left side, vanished into bloody pulp.

My sweep-handed timer rang again, reminding me to remove the contact sheet from the developer and to put it into the stop bath. My hands shook. For a moment, I had felt the hardness of the rock against my belly, the heat of the rising sun on my back, the rush of blood in my ears. I was a child again, an unwilling witness to tragedy and violence. My own helplessness overwhelmed me.

I fumbled the contact sheet into the fixative solution and then dropped it into the kitchen sink and turned on the tap. Ordinarily, I would agitate the paper under running water periodically for the next hour, but I knew that the gentlemen of the press were becoming restless. Wiping the sweat off my forehead, I lifted the curtain and stepped into the living room.

The reporters studied the photographs carefully, almost reverently. Yes, they said, their excitement mounting, that was Diaz, all right. The evidence against the Guardia Civil was damning. The face of Diaz's assassin was clear, the details of his uniform and hat unmistakable.

Hugo was vehement. "Those bastards are going to be sorry for this," he said. "It's going to cost them friends all over the world, not to mention Spain itself. Jesus, these pictures are fantastic."

"It must have been hell out there on that rock," the *Times* man said. "I give you a lot of credit, Mrs. Diaz. I don't think I would have had the guts to do what you did."

"You know how it is," I said. "After a while, your reflexes just take over."

I promised to make copies of the photographs they requested. After murmuring words of condolence and congratulation, the reporters hurried away to file their stories.

Hugo lingered after the others had gone.

"Nice of you to put up with the boys' questions like that," he said. "Good sport."

I sank down on Luis's armchair. "At least they didn't ask the obvious sticky questions about me and Angel."

Hugo grinned. "From what I've heard, old Angel was quite a stud."

"I won't dispute that." I smiled wearily. "He certainly knew how to make a woman feel—like a woman."

"Tough for you, losing both of them."

"I'll be all right." I gave my wedding ring a turn. "The newspapers are going to give this big play, aren't they? I'm not sure Luis would have approved. But that hardly matters now, I suppose." I glanced at Hugo, straddling a hard chair near the window. "I think I'll have a drink of that whiskey now, if you don't mind."

"Sure thing." Hugo tipped the bottle over a glass, handed it to me, then dragged his chair closer to mine. "Listen, kid, I want to talk to you about something. I don't believe in fate, predestination, or Providence, but what happened today comes pretty damned close, and I'm not about to ask any questions." He sipped whiskey. I did the same. "I intend to shoot this movie myself. No crew, no assistants. Just me and a cameraman."

"That's sensible. You'll have an easier time getting around."

He nodded. "That's the idea. When I work, I hire the best. The best light men, sound men, cameramen. The best actors, the best set designers. I get Pulitzer winners to write my scripts, and if I need gowns and high fashion, I get Worth or Schiaparelli." He hitched his chair closer. "This film means a lot to me, kid. It's not just another slick de Graaf comedy with those serious overtones the critics like to talk about. This is the real thing. Real killing, real pain. War. Death. Brother against brother and all that other bullshit. This film may not earn me a fortune; in fact, I'll probably lose my shirt. But it will be something I can be proud of for the rest of my life."

"Of course, Mr. de Graaf." I wondered where all this was leading.

"Hugo," he corrected me. "I brought a cameraman with me when I came out here. Fred Somebody—worked with him for years. Wouldn't you know, the poor bastard went and got himself blown up in an air raid last week? I'm all ready to go on this thing, and all of a sudden, no photographer. I've wired Culver City, but they don't have too many guys willing to risk their necks after what happened to old Sam. I was wondering what in hell I was going to do next, and then I saw you standing under that burning building, looking like you'd just stepped out to check the weather and were trying to decide if you should take an umbrella or not. Something made me stop the car. Something made me want to get you out of there. Somebody's watching over ole Hugo today, kid. When I saw those shots of Diaz, I knew I'd found my cameraman."

I pulled myself up. "Oh, no, you haven't."

But Hugo was not to be deterred. "I'm producing this thing myself," he told me. "As a producer, I never stint on salaries. From the looks of things, Luis didn't leave you too well fixed. You'll get twice what I was going to pay Jim."

"Send it to Jim's widow. Or Fred's or Sam's. I don't need much to live on."

Hugo leaned forward, one of my teacups cradled in his big hands. "You don't understand, kid. My mind's made up. I'm going to get your okay on this if it takes all night. I need you. You know the country and the situation, you speak the language like a native, and you believe in the Republic. Well, don't you?"

I ran the tip of my finger lightly around the rim of my glass. "Before Luis died, I felt as he did, that any kind of armed conflict was hideous and shameful, something to be avoided at all costs. I still feel that way. But the civil war is here. We can't change that." I drained my whiskey. Hugo offered a refill, but I shook my head. "When Angel was dragging me over the Sierra Nevada, and I didn't care if I lived or died, I suddenly had a thought: what if this were happening in my own country, among the people I grew up with? What if those miners had finally managed to elect a government that really cared about them? What if that government, in trying to redistribute the wealth and weaken the hold of the Robber Barons and the big manufacturers, was suddenly threatened by an army made up of generals supported and encouraged by those same rich people? Which side would I be on then, I asked myself? Would I choose Monkey Gulch, Colorado, or would I choose Gramercy Park? Or would I sit it out? I decided that I wanted Monkey Gulch to win."

Hugo said heartily, "Good girl."

"I know what people are capable of doing when their dreams are threatened," I said. "The stories of atrocities you may have heard are not exaggerated. Government censors wouldn't let the worst pictures out, but the Republicans were every bit as vicious and insane as the rebels. They rampaged through this city after the rebellion, burning churches, killing priests, pulling innocent people out of their homes, taking them away to be executed. It's ironic, isn't it? Luis was killed in just that way, but by the other side. And now you're going to make him a martyr. But what about all the other innocent people who were killed? This war may have a right side and a wrong side, but it doesn't have any good guys. The good guys are all dead."

"I'm not going to tamper with the facts," Hugo promised. "This is strictly a documentary. Truth."

"Truth doesn't exist," I said softly. "Truth is like a kaleidoscope. You shake the cylinder, and the bits of facts fall into a picture. You shake them again, and the picture changes. But they're all true."

"You'll do it?" Hugo urged.

"I can't, Mr. de Graaf. I'm not able. I've never handled a movie camera in my life."

Hugo relaxed. He knew he had won.

"It's a cinch," he assured me. "No different from what you do now, except that you keep shooting as long as the action keeps moving. I'll get you the lightest, best-engineered cinema camera that exists—none of that old-fashioned hand-crank newsreel stuff. You don't have to worry about developing the film. Madrid has a lab only six blocks from here, and a big studio with some halfway decent editing equipment. We won't shoot with sound; we'll dub all that in afterwards. Means we won't be encumbered with any bulky equipment. We'll travel light and we'll travel fast, just you and me and Manuel in the Caddy. The government's given me an unlimited gas ration. That shows you how much they believe in this thing."

He stood up.

"Well, it's settled. We'll start on Monday, give you a couple of days to rest up. The Fascists look like they're ready to cross the Manzanares, and my bet is that our boys here aren't going to let them. *No pasarán.*" He waved his clenched fist. "We're going to get some damned fine footage."

I had to smile. He was like an overgrown boy looking forward to a new adventure, so excited that he could hardly sleep. "Monday," I said. "I hope I can measure up to your expectations, Mr. de Graaf."

"Hugo, remember?"

"If you insist. You're my boss now."

"You can call me God-knows-what, kid, as long as you keep taking pictures as good as the ones I saw today. Well, let's go. I've taken a room for you at the Ritz. Manuel will bring your stuff over tomorrow."

"I'd rather stay here tonight," I said. "I know it will be more convenient if I live at the Ritz when we start working. I don't mind. But just for tonight, I want to stay here."

I walked him to the door. "Wait a minute. You forgot your whiskey."

"Keep it," Hugo said. "This town is short on bread, short on meat, short on everything except whiskey. I suppose you could find worse ways of fighting a war."

When he had gone, I removed my gold band and put it away. I hadn't worn a ring as Diaz's wife; I wouldn't wear one as his widow.

I poured an inch of whiskey into my glass and walked over to the window. Through a haze of fog and smoke and cinders, the setting sun looked like a glass pitcher filled with blood. How long would it take before the pitcher emptied itself, so that the people of this country could return to the humdrum pattern of their daily lives free of fear, free of hatred, cleansed of the stain of crimson?

"Adiós, Luis." I raised my glass to the sun. "Adiós, Angel. Go with God."

25

The Moor slithered alongside the cliff that overlooked the Pindoque Bridge. He wore a khaki jacket and loose-fitting trousers, a bandolero loaded with ammunition, a belt weighted with hand grenades and a kit of rations. A black beret protected his head against the biting cold of early February. He held his rifle at the ready, his dark eyes twitching alertly for any sign of the enemy.

Hearing a clicking noise, he whirled, dropping to one knee to make himself a smaller target, and fired.

I ducked down behind the rock on which I had set up my tripod. The Moor's bullet ricocheted off the cliff above me, sending down a shower of gravel and sand. The camera motor continued to purr softly, undaunted by the noise and the danger. Another shot rang out, this one so close that a flying splinter of stone struck my hand. Grabbing the camera and tripod, I retreated to the shelter of a rocky overhang. I flexed my fingers to see if the stone had shattered the small bones in my hand. Nothing broken, only bruised. I wrapped my handkerchief around the bleeding wound and managed to tie it with my teeth.

Footsteps disturbed the pebbly sand on the other side of the ridge from where I sat. The Moor was coming up the slope to investigate. I looked around for a better hiding place. In spite of Hugo's continued insistence that I carry a pistol, I had refused. I would not fire a lead missile into living human flesh, not even to save my own life. Besides, I already had too much equipment to carry. Let the Moor come ahead. Folding up my tripod, I rested the camera on my knees and focused on the place where I expected him to appear. He would be silhouetted against the clear sky, facing directly into the sun. My angle couldn't be better, and the view was clear of obstructions.

My back pressed into the rock, I waited. I fancied that I could hear his panting breath as he picked his way up the sharply raked hillside. He would kill me at once, without waiting for me to explain that I was a member of the press. I decided that I would throw the camera at the last moment. With any luck, it wouldn't break open on the stony ground, and the footage inside would be saved.

The Moor's tanned face appeared over the top of the ridge. I started the camera. The soldier, his eyes momentarily dazzled by the glare of the sun, didn't see me at once. He stood at the crest of the ridge, moving his rifle from side to side in a fanning motion. Then he spotted me, huddled in a horizontal crevice, and took aim. A shot rang out. The Moor opened his arms wide, as if to receive an embrace. His rifle slipped out of his fingers as his knees crumpled slowly.

Astonished, I kept the camera running. A Republican soldier wearing canvas espadrilles and puttees ran over to the corpse and relieved it of rifle and ammunition. I heard another shot, which kicked up a cloud of dust near the fallen Moor. The soldier dashed for cover, throwing himself down beside me under the shelter of the overhang.

He grinned at me. "Looks like we're pinned down," he said in a crisp British voice. "I say, you don't happen to have any cigarettes, do you? *Cigarettes?*" he repeated with a Spanish accent, pantomiming smoking.

I said in English, "I don't smoke myself, but I usually carry some with me for occasions like this. Ah, here they are." I found a mashed packet under the cannisters of movie film in my knapsack. "Thank you for coming to my rescue. Your arrival was timely, to say the least."

The young man stared. He was about twenty-two, just a few years younger than I, lean and fair-haired. Then he grinned. "I do beg your pardon. I didn't realize you were a girl."

I gave a rueful glance at my rumpled trousers, sturdy brogues, and short leather jacket. "Silk frocks and high-heeled pumps aren't exactly appropriate attire for photographing a war. Are you with the Internationals?"

The boy nodded. "Fifteenth Brigade, British Batallion. I don't know what happened to my unit. We were engaged by the Moorish cavalry this morning. We didn't have any field artillery to back us up, and to top it off, we ran out of ammunition. Our commander ordered us to scatter and regroup north of the bridge. I'm afraid I lost my way, and when I finally found the place where we were to meet, I discovered it had been overrun by Moors. I had only the one bullet left, you know. If I had missed that shot, we'd both have been goners. I figured it was worth risking it, and it paid off. I got his gun, and his ammo besides. I'll have to tell my father that all those years of grouse-shooting weren't wasted." He sucked his cigarette down to the last half inch, and flipped away the butt with regret.

"Where are you from?" I asked.

"Devonshire. But we have land in Scotland. I never really cared for shooting. Hated it, actually. Odd, to find myself here, shooting men." He shrugged. "Not quite what Father envisioned for me. Or what I envisioned for myself, for that matter. Home seems awfully far away, so remote. Impossibly peaceful. Devonshire. Cambridge. It's hard to believe that England is enjoying such miraculous peace, while over here people are dying to protect the rights that we take for granted."

"Why did you join the Brigades?"

"I had to," he said simply. "All my life I've felt a kinship with people who are less fortunate then I've been. Some might call it guilt. But to my mind, it was only a trick of fate that saw me born in a manor house in Devonshire and not in some stinking back street in Liverpool or Manchester. I never joined the Communist Party, but I was a socialist of sorts. Wrote for a Fabian paper, went to all the right meetings. I'd be a hypocrite if I didn't fight for what I believed in, wouldn't I?" He gave me an earnest look. "That's why you're here, isn't it? Because you believe that it's the right thing to do, to support the Republic?"

I saw then that he was exhausted. His eyes were glazed with fatigue and the horrors he had witnessed, and his hands shook slightly as he lit another cigarette. He was just a boy, fighting a war in a faraway country whose language he didn't speak.

"Yes," I said, "that's why I'm here."

The battle for the valley of the Jarama river had been a terrible and costly one, with heavy casualties on both sides. The newly organized Fifteenth International Brigade had been thrust into the action with only a brief period of training, but the British and American volunteers had fought valiantly to keep Madrid from being encircled, and to keep the Valencia road open.

"Are you making a newsreel?" the boy asked me.

"Of sorts. A documentary film, with Hugo de Graaf."

"The American director? Oh, I say, how smashing." His eyes brightened. "I'm a great admirer of his. I especially like the films he's done with Fiona Randall. I wonder what she's really like."

"She's just what you'd expect," I said. "Fiona's my aunt." Or-

dinarily I would never have admitted that I shared a blood relationship with Fiona, but I wanted to give my companion the
additional pleasure of being able to say he'd shared a foxhole
with the niece of a film star he adored.

"Is she really? How extraordinary. I don't suppose you give
autographs?"

"Heavens, no," I said. "I'm nobody."

We laughed. A bullet whistled past, reminding us that we
were still under fire, unable to move from our shallow cave. The
British soldier hefted the Moor's rifle.

"I suppose I'd better figure out how to use this thing. If we're
surrounded, we might have to shoot our way out. Good line,
that. Right out of one of your American westerns."

I, too, had a task to perform. "I didn't think I'd live to change
the film in this camera, but thanks to you, I have." I took off my
jacket and wrapped it around the movie camera. Poking my
hands through the sleeves, I opened the camera, removed the
spent reel, inserted a new one. "Portable darkroom," I explained. "In the words of Mr. Hugo de Graaf, we travel fast and
we travel light, just the two of us, our driver, and the Caddy. Cadillac, that is."

"You're lucky to have a car," the young man said. "I feel as
though I've been marching for the last fifty years. We walked in
from France, you know, through the Pyrenees in a snowstorm.
The French have made it illegal to come into Spain to fight. The
non-interventionists don't understand that the more difficulties
they throw in our way, the more it makes them seem like they're
siding with Franco and the Nazis and the Fascists. Anyone
who hates those groups is going to want to fight for the Republic."

We settled down to await rescue or darkness.

Hugo and I had separated that morning, I to take some shots
of the fighting around the Pindoque Bridge from higher

ground, Hugo to discuss the military aspects of the situation with the leaders of the Popular Front Army. The notes he took for the script, while they didn't simplify events, made even the most complicated actions seem straightforward and easy to understand.

Sometimes Hugo's bombast and flights of ego made me forget that he was a master at communicating ideas on film. I had no regrets about agreeing to take part in his project. He had taught me a lot about cinematography. At one point early in his Hollywood career he had been one of D. W. Griffith's cameramen. And he had an unerring instinct about scenes that would add meaning and richness to the film, which he had decided to call *Spanish Blood*.

After the battle for Madrid had ended in a stalemate at the end of November, with the army of the Republic managing to halt the advance of Franco's troops at University City on the western edge, Hugo decided it was time for a change of pace. Manuel drove us to a remote village in the north central plain, a place that was as yet untouched by the war. We had filmed a peasant family living in conditions of unspeakable poverty. They told us that their land was owned by a nobleman who lived far away, in a place called Paris, on the other side of the mountains. Overseers came regularly to collect taxes and to take all the profits from the peasants' wheat crop. They had hardly heard of the Civil War. Their lives were as barren of information as they were of hope.

"That's why we're fighting this war," Hugo said as we drove away. "Scenes of street fighting and burning buildings aren't going to mean a damned thing unless we show the real reasons behind this conflict. If Franco wins, these people are finished. Back to the way it's been for hundreds of years. Church, army, landowners telling them what to do. No land, no food, no future." He shivered. "Christ, it's cold. Where's my flask?"

Hugo knew exactly what would appeal to an American audience. They had to have an underdog to root for, a villain to boo.

2019

2019

All that *Spanish Blood* lacked was a boy and a girl separated by
war. Somehow, I was sure, he would find a pair of lovers and
work them in, too.

"Do you like poetry?" the boy at my side asked. I said that I
did. Not wishing to overwhelm him with my collection of celebrities, I refrained from telling him that I was the widow of Luis
Diaz Albareda. He pulled a thin book out of his hip pocket:
Shakespeare's Sonnets. "A girl gave this to me before I left Cambridge. I hardly knew her; she was a friend of a fellow who lived
in the rooms next to mine. She said she'd heard I was going to
Spain, and she wanted to give me something of England to take
with me. She said this was the lightest and the densest book she
knew. I've been meaning to write to her, to thank her."
He opened the little book, and began to read softly:

When, in disgrace with Fortune and men's eyes,
I all alone beweep my outcast state,
And trouble deaf heaven with my bootless cries,
And look upon myself and curse my fate,
Wishing me like to one more rich in hope,
Featured like him, like him with friends possessed,
Desiring this man's art, and that man's scope,
With what I most enjoy contented least;

Yet in these thoughts myself almost despising,
Haply I think on thee, and then my state,
Like to the lark at break of day arising
From sullen earth, sings hymns at heaven's gate;
For thy sweet love rememb'red such wealth brings
That then I scorn to change my state with kings.

"That was beautiful," I said after a long silence. "Thank you."
"These sonnets have been wonderfully comforting," the boy
said. "All those verses about the march of time and the vanity of

human efforts." He looked around at the denuded windswept hills, the skeletons of shell-blasted trees, the body of the dead Moor lying only a few yards away. "They help to put all this in perspective."

We heard the rattle of gunfire. The soldier lifted his rifle, I my camera.

"Teddy! Teddy, where in hell are you?"

I relaxed. "Hugo to the rescue. I knew he'd be along. He won't admit it, but he hates to walk, which means the Cadillac can't be far behind. We'll drop you at headquarters. Maybe you can find out what happened to your unit."

"If any of them survived," my companion said.

But then we saw a group of Internationals moving in to secure the ridge. With a wave of his hand, the British soldier moved off with them.

Hugo came puffing up the slope. He stepped over the body of the Moor.

"What's all this?" he said. "Stopped in his tracks by your unassailable virtue?"

"The camera took his soul." I shouldered the heavy movie camera on its broad strap and tucked the tripod under my arm. "I got some fine footage of him shooting at me. And dying. And all close-up, too. Your fans will love it."

"I thought I told you that I didn't want you taking stupid chances," Hugo growled. "Looked around for you, couldn't find you anyplace. Damned inconsiderate. What if you'd gotten yourself killed?"

"Oh, you'd just go back to Madrid and find yourself another waif who looked like she could take pictures." I was unperturbed by his brusqueness. "What did you find out from the higher-ups?"

"Looks like another stalemate, but both sides will call it a victory. At least we've kept the Valencia road open. Good for morale. We need some good news for a change. Málaga fell last week. Nice swift victory for the Nationalists, thanks to Mussolini's 'volunteers.' They say the streets are running with blood."

We tramped down the hill. The Cadillac was waiting, its cloth top providing not the slightest protection from any stray bullets that might be flying around. As usual, Manuel was slunk down low in the front seat, praying feverishly. Lately he had taken to wearing a rosary around his neck, under his sweater.

Hugo and I spent a couple more days at Jarama, photographing the battle-weary survivors in camp. On the morning we were to leave for Madrid, a man from the British Battalion approached me.

"Excuse me, Miss, but I believe you know a fellow named Ken Champneys."

I thought. "No, I don't believe I do."

"Oh? Well, he asked me to give you this." He handed me the slender book of sonnets. "He was shot yesterday. Standing guard duty, he was, when a sniper got him. We were mates, sort of. He seemed very concerned that you should have the book."

"Yes, thank you." I patted my jacket pockets and pulled out a pack of cigarettes. "I'm not going to smoke these. I wish you'd take them."

"Luckys!" he said joyously. "Haven't had a decent smoke in weeks. Thanks, Miss. And good luck."

The little blood-stained book fell open in my hands. I read: "When, in disgrace with Fortune and men's eyes . . ."

My own eyes blurred, and I closed the book on yet another life.

Hugo burst into my room at the Ritz without knocking.

"We've got three days to edit ten thousand miles of footage into something that looks like a movie, or at least half a movie," he announced. He helped himself to whiskey from the bottle he kept on my dresser and flopped down on my bed. The springs sang under his considerable bulk.

I didn't look up from the desk, where I was filling in my log book. Since my very first day of work on *Spanish Blood*, I had kept scrupulous notes on our footage: how many minutes of each segment we had, a description, the date and circumstances under which it had been taken, even the weather.

"Some Hollywood money boys are going to be in Paris at the end of the week. They want to see what I'm working on," Hugo said. "If we can impress them, we're home free. They'll take care of distribution, in exchange for a share of the profits, naturally. They'll give us enough money to finish the project, and to enjoy ourselves besides. I always pad my budgets," he confessed with glee, "just enough to look convincing without being greedy. We'll give them twenty minutes. Even if I managed to come up with authentic footage of the parting of the Red Sea, their little minds can't take in much more than that. I'll write up a narrative that I can read while the film's running. Maybe we should concentrate on the human interest stuff. What do we have that will wring tears from their eyes and dollars from their pocketbooks?"

He bounced off the bed and leaned over my shoulder to examine the log.

"Here we go. Madrid bombings: 'Mother and dead child'—I remember those shots. I cry myself just thinking about them. 'Homeless old couple.' 'Soup kitchen.' Great stuff, all of it. We'll splice those shots together with some peasants at work and at play, throw in a few earnest young soldiers and some of that Moorish cavalry footage we shot last month, and top it all off with your charging Moor biting the dust."

"Underdogs and villains," I murmured. I shifted uncomfortably under the weight of Hugo's hands, which had moved to my shoulders. "You didn't give us much time."

"Plenty of time. I can write this stuff in my sleep, on the plane if I have to. Pierre Fouchard is going to give us a lift. He needs to talk to his publisher."

I knew Fouchard from Paris. He was an old friend of Diaz's, and he was a frequent visitor to Hugo's suite at the Ritz. The novelist and air ace was one of the first Frenchmen to volunteer for the Republican cause. He purchased aircraft with his own money, hired fliers, led them on bombing missions over enemy lines. He was always gallant to me when we met, pulling his long face into a dolorous yet slightly lecherous expression that suggested he would be all too happy to console the widow in her bereavement.

"But I don't need to go," I said.

"Like hell you don't. I'm not going to beard these morons without you. They'll love you: With your charm and my savvy, we can't lose." His beard tickled my cheek.

"That's silly, Hugo." I wriggled away from him and stood up. "I can't charm anybody."

"That's what you think." Hugo lay on the bed and locked his hands behind his head. "You've got what it takes, kid. Don't underestimate yourself. Put you in a Paris gown, slap on a little lipstick and powder, and you could be the next Garbo or Randall."

I shuddered. "God forbid. I don't want to be the next anybody. And I certainly don't want to go to Paris."

"Why not? Scared of flying?"

"Well, no, but—"

"But nothing. You're in my employ, and I need you in Paris. The break will be good for you. You've been looking a little tired lately, not to mention hungry. I, for one, am going to indulge in a feeding frenzy of unprecedented proportions when I hit Paris. You don't think I'm going to let you sit here chewing stewed garbanzos while I'm packing away filet mignon and escargots and washing them down with the best burgundy money can buy? I take my responsibilities to my employees very seriously."

"I'm sure you do, but—"

But Hugo had already reached the door. "Call Manuel. We'd better get over to the studio and start work. Bring that log of yours. I hope to hell their editing equipment hasn't been bombed."

Three days later, I found myself seated beside Pierre Fouchard in the cockpit of his little plane. Hugo crouched behind us, shouting words of caution over the engine noise. He was in no mood, he warned Pierre, to participate in a dogfight with the Germans of the Nazi Condor Legion. He'd paid too much for his breakfast of black market ham and moldy cheese to lose it.

The screening was scheduled for seven o'clock that evening, in the movie mogul's suite at his hotel. Our plane landed at Le Bourget at four. Hugo and I literally raced through customs. Fouchard had a taxi waiting. We checked into adjoining rooms at our hotel and headed straight for our bathtubs to wash off the dust of the journey.

While I was dressing, Hugo barged into my room and threw two large boxes down on the bed.

"The success of this act depends on costumes. I asked Pierre's wife to pick out something for you and send it over. 'Sexy Widow.' Let's see how she did." He flipped off the lid and lifted out a gown, black and sleeveless, sparkling with thousands of blue-black sequins. The neckline was fringed with black-dyed maribou feathers. "Not bad. Shoes and bag included. And I asked her to rent a sable." He opened the second box. "Nice set of skins, good for warding off the chill of Paris in April."

I pulled a robe on over my slip. "Are you out of your mind, Hugo? I can't wear this stuff."

"Why not? Looks like it should fit. I checked the sizes on the things in your closet and wired the statistics to Bebe. You'll get to meet her; she's a great gal." He held the dress up by a couple of feathers and turned it around. "Hey, no back. I like this."

"You're ridiculous," I fumed. "I brought a dress of my own that's perfectly suitable. This—this is in the worst possible taste. 'Sexy Widow,' indeed!"

"These people don't know anything about taste," Hugo informed me. "They're not going to spend money on a newcomer unless she can impress them that she has what it takes, namely, the ability to make money. If they ask about your experience, tell them the truth, that you've worked for *Mode* and *Paris-Matin*. They don't know what outfits like that cost. You might be better paid than Gable. All they have to go by is appearances. If you look like somebody, fine; you must be somebody.'

"Come on, kid, be a sport. It's just for tonight."

To my annoyance, Hugo introduced me to the men from Hollywood as Fiona Randall's niece. The fact seemed to impress the head of Hugo's studio, who patted my bottom and told me that I ought to consider a career on the other side of the camera. Later, when I expressed my irritation to Hugo, he shrugged it off. "In their world, everybody important is related to somebody else important. Wouldn't have done me any good to mention Diaz. Those bastards don't know anything about poetry."

Hugo's boss was tiny, hairless, immaculate, a miniature potentate surrounded by a half-dozen fawning courtiers, including a lawyer, an accountant, a tax expert, and a son-in-law.

When Hugo heard that their wives had remained in London for the weekend, he looked glum. "Should have knocked ten minutes off our running time. They'll be in a big hurry to get back to the girls at the Folies Bergère."

While one of the lesser courtiers threaded the film into the projector, Hugo drew me aside. "I forgot the script."

"Send somebody back to the hotel to get it," I said. "It will only take a few minutes."

"It will take longer than that to send somebody to Madrid."

"Hugo!"

"Look, why don't you do the narration, without a script? Just pretend you're talking about Spain to a room full of twelve-year-olds. That's about the level of their collective intelligence."

"But I can't," I protested. "I wouldn't know where to start. Oh, you're impossible! You wrote the damned script. Why don't you do the narration?"

Hugo smiled. He rarely heard me use even mild profanity.

"Look, the old man likes you. I've made a lot of money for him, but he hates my guts. Just talk about the scenes as they come on. Tell them about the people. The land. The war."

"All set, Mr. de Graaf."

"Okay, everybody, take your seats, please. Lights out." In the moment of darkness before the projector came on, Hugo kissed me lightly on the lips. "Go get 'em, Tiger," he whispered.

"I could kill you for this," I hissed. Then the first scene appeared on the screen, a shot of a Spanish peasant tilling a field with a wooden plow drawn by a scrawny burro.

I took a breath and began.

"I suppose to most people, the word 'Spain' conjures up images of romance, gypsy dancers with castanets, moonlit nights in the Alhambra, bullfights. But to the ordinary people of Spain, the reality is much different. They break their backs, toiling on land that doesn't belong to them. Their babies die in infancy. Their wives age rapidly, so that at thirty, they look sixty, or older. In the face of such grim reality, a farmer like this one has only a dream of a better life. With the election of the first Republican government in 1931, something else was added to that dream: hope."

Out of the corner of my eye, I saw the mogul inch forward slightly in his chair. One of his sycophants leaned over to whisper in his ear, but the old man waved him away.

When the lights came on twenty minutes later, the tiny mogul turned around in his chair and looked at Hugo. "How much do you need to finish it?"

Hugo lifted his shoulders. "The people at the studio back in Madrid have been working for love for the past two months. Theodora here hasn't been paid since November, when we started. We still have a lot to do—two more months of shooting, or more, depending on how the war goes. I'd say another ten thousand would do it."

I suppressed a gasp. So far, the filming had comprised the least of Hugo's expenses. Food and lodging, Manuel and the

Caddy cost far more than film or camera repairs. As for the people at the studio back in Madrid—they weren't on any kind of payroll at all. Hugo had persuaded them to donate their services to the Republic. True, I hadn't been paid yet, but Hugo was footing the bill for my room at the Ritz and for my meals and transportation. Even for the clothes on my back, I thought, with a rueful glance at my black sequins and maribou feathers.

The mogul nodded. "Albert, write the man a check. And you, Miss, ah, Randall." I started to correct him, but decided not to bother. "If I give you a personal check for those little kids I saw, do I have your word that it will go to help them?"

"I know at least five agencies in Madrid that work with homeless and displaced children," I said. "But I have another suggestion, if you don't mind."

"Speak up, speak up, don't be shy." He winked at me. "Fiona's never shy about asking for anything." The courtiers chuckled.

"The biggest problem in Madrid now is food," I told him. "The city is virtually sealed off, except for the Valencia road, and half the meat and produce that is destined for Madrid never gets there, because of bombing raids and strafing attacks by the Nationalists and the Nazi pilots of the Condor Legion. I happen to know that Pierre Fouchard, the aviator, is here in Paris. He'll be returning to Madrid in a few days. Flying over Spain is dangerous. As you know, the Nationalists have tried to impose an air blockade, too. But if anyone can fly in food and medical supplies to those children, Pierre can."

"Great publicity for the studio," a courtier whispered in the mogul's ear.

The little man frowned. "Perhaps. Albert, another check. Make it for two." He turned his gimlet eyes on me. "If you need more, you tell me, okay? And if you want to work in Hollywood, come and see me. A talented girlie like you can go places out there."

Out in the cool evening air, I waved the check. "Two dollars, or two thousand, it's still just a little piece of paper."

"That's the trouble with you socialists," Hugo said cheerfully, "you don't appreciate the true value of money."

"You robbed him."

"He'll take it out of my hide on the next picture I do for him. But who cares? Tonight we live!"

We feasted on duckling at the famous Tour d'Argent, drawing out the delights of our first real meal in months for over two hours. Afterwards, Hugo insisted that we go dancing. After sampling a number of better-known clubs, we found a little cabaret in Montparnasse that advertised American jazz.

"Don't you ever get tired?" I asked Hugo at two in the morning. We had been dancing for nearly four solid hours.

"Not when I'm celebrating. And we have a lot to celebrate. We're working on a great picture, we're in Paris, and we're rolling in dough. You're not mad at me for forgetting the script, and you can be proud of yourself for persuading that old son of a bitch to feed a thousand orphans. My God, but you're beautiful tonight, Teddy. I'm glad I'm not too drunk to see straight." He stroked my naked back lightly as he propelled me around the tiny dance floor.

"You remembered that my name was Theodora back there with the money boys," I said. "I was surprised."

The band played a Frenchified version of "Good Night, Ladies." The music ended to a spatter of applause from the few remaining patrons in the club.

"And so Cinderella and the Prince hail a taxi and ride back to their humble hotel," Hugo sighed as we stepped out into the crisp night air and climbed into a cab. "If I were writing this scene, it would be different. We'd stroll along the Seine in the moonlight, past the Eiffel Tower, stopping to smooch a little on a bridge. You'd tremble as I took you into my arms. I'd make reassuring noises. You'd say you never knew love could be like this. I'd say I didn't either, until I met you. The camera moves in for a close-up. Nice long kiss, your hands fluttering lightly on

my shoulders. I don't move my hands; that would look too sug-
gestive. We'd continue our stroll, closer together this time, you
resting your head on my brawny shoulder—"

"I wish this taxi would hurry up," I said. "My feet are killing
me."

"So much for Hollywood." Hugo sounded wistful. "Well, I
still have hope. Good line, that: 'With the election of the *et cetera
et cetera*, something else was added to that dream: hope.' I think
we can use it."

"Yes, when you get around to writing your script," I said. "I
wondered why you never let me see it. I suppose you never
wrote anything at all. Left it in Madrid, ha! You might have
warned me, you know. What if I had become tongue-tied?"

"You didn't have a chance to get stage fright," Hugo said.
"Listen, I know how to handle my actresses, and my producers.
If I had read that script to them, they would have fallen asleep
in their chairs. Another slick de Graaf special. But you—you're
so damned sincere, Teddy. Sincerity isn't something they know
much about. I knew they'd be crazy about you."

Hugo walked me to my room. As I opened the door, I saw a
big bouquet of red roses sitting on my dresser. Next to it stood a
bottle of champagne cooling in a bucket of ice. The card attached to the neck of the bottle read: "With love to the only cameraman I've ever bought a dress for."

"Why, thank you, Hugo," I said. "I see they've provided two
glasses. Care for a little nightcap?"

As I worked the wire off the cork, Hugo put his hands on my
naked shoulders and kissed the nape of my neck. A moment later he sneezed, expelling a noseful of feathers. I started to laugh.

"If you're trying to seduce me—"

"I am not." Hugo turned me around to face him. His expression was serious. "I'm courting you."

"Oh." I went limp with amazement. "I—I didn't expect that.
But I forgot, you're in the habit of marrying the women who
work with you."

"It's called auditioning. As of tonight, the part's been cast. Will you?"

"No." I detached his hands from my shoulders. "No, Hugo, I won't. I don't think I'll marry anyone, ever again."

"No problem," Hugo said, undismayed. "I get two more chances before I'm officially struck out. Now about this love scene." He scratched his beard. "The audience is wondering, will he or won't he? He seems like a decent guy, not too pushy. He's kept his hands to himself so far. But maybe he's had all he can take. Maybe it's time to show her who's boss." He pulled me into his arms and kissed me hard.

"I won't play it that way, Hugo." I slipped away from him.

Hugo yawned and stretched. "No harm in trying, I always say. Well, time to turn in. We've got a lot to do in the next couple of days."

"What?"

"Stock up on supplies for the Spanish kiddies and head back to Madrid on one of Pierre's planes. I'll wire the press boys and tell them to expect us. Whether or not the studio wants to take credit for this, I can sure use the publicity. And then it's back to work. We've got a film to finish, in case you've forgotten. 'Night, kid. Thanks for the help tonight."

"You're welcome, Hugo." I followed him to the door. "And thank you for the dress. It really is lovely."

"You look terrific in it." Hugo grinned at me. "You can't blame me for falling in love with you, kid. You're cute as hell in long pants and army boots, out there taking pictures, but right now you look—well, the old man knew it. We both know star quality when we see it."

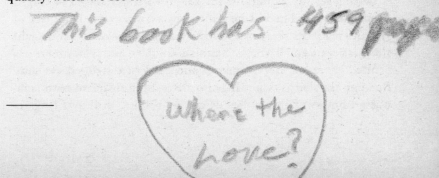

26

Hugo's second proposal came in July, following the Battle of Brunete. The campaign took place in an area about fifty miles southwest of Madrid. It was the first Republican offensive of the war, an attempt to break through the rebel cordon that was choking the capital. *Spanish Blood* was nearly finished, needing only some editing in the Madrid studio, but Hugo had promised the American Committee to Save Spain a short film showing American soldiers in action. They were volunteers, fighting with the Abraham Lincoln Battalion of the International Brigades.

"Strictly for propaganda purposes," he told me. "I know Stalin and the Communist Party are responsible for recruiting a lot of the Internationals, but I don't care about that. Our boys are damned good soldiers, and the folks back home should know it."

We visited the little village of Quijorna soon after the Republicans had taken possession. Fighting in the vicinity had been fierce, following the lines of a scorched earth policy, with Franco's retreating Moors and Legionnaires leaving very little of the town intact. The stink of death still hung over the ruins of the village. Bloated burros, long dead, lay rotting in the hot sun, their stiff legs pointing to the sky.

"Christ," Hugo choked as Manuel guided the Cadillac along a rubble-strewn alley, "you'd have to be brave just to stay in this place for more than five minutes."

Setting up my camera in the middle of the ravaged square, I silently agreed. The village really was a corner of hell, a place of horrors made all the worse by the way the men who had fought the battle accepted them. Spanish soldiers and volunteers recruited from all over Europe and America strolled casually through the debris, scanning the ground for cigarette butts, taking no notice of the bodies of enemy soldiers still awaiting removal.

I was sick of the war, sick of looking at it with coldly professional eyes that gauged not the depth of human suffering but the depth of field, not the quality of life but the quality of the daylight. After Brunete, I vowed, I would study war no more, not through the lens of my camera, and not on the battlefield.

After the success of Pierre Fouchard's foodlift to Madrid, paid for by the Hollywood studio, I had found myself turning more and more to the plight of Spain's orphaned and abandoned children. I could see the future of Spain in their sunken black eyes. Would anything remain for them when this was all over, beyond yawning blackened craters left by the bombs and shells?

Battered trucks arrived in Quijorna to collect some of the wounded and take them to Madrid's already overcrowded hospitals. A few of the wounded lay in the shade of an olive grove on the edge of town. A hot, searing breeze carried the echoes of their moans and wracking coughs to the nearby village.

Hugo bent over a makeshift stretcher and spoke to a wounded veteran of the battle who was waiting for his turn to be taken into town. As I started toward them, Hugo looked up and saw me. He patted the man on the shoulder, said some words that I couldn't hear, and left the stretcher. Taking my elbow, he led me away from the olive grove.

"Poor bastard," he said. "Bullet shattered his hip. It's going to take some fancy orthopedic work to get him back on his feet."

"Someone you know?" I twisted my neck to look around. His arm upraised, the soldier shielded his face from the glare of the sun. From the waist down, his body was covered with blood, already darkened and stiff.

"Not really. Fellow I ran into once or twice out on the Coast. Listen, take a couple of shots of those guys setting up headquarters in that church, and then we'll get out of here."

"Don't you want some pictures of your friend?"

"He's not my friend." Hugo's tone sounded unusually brusque. "Just some guy. Forget it. We have all the shots of the wounded that we need."

That evening, we sat down to our usual supper of boiled garbanzo beans in the dining room of the Ritz. The staff served the humble food apologetically, on fine china set on acres of sparkling white linen. The journalists who shared our table agreed that the Republicans' gains at Brunete had been offset by their horrendous losses, estimated to be almost a hundred planes and twenty thousand men.

I frowned down at my plate. Twenty thousand lives. Twenty thousand human beings. I couldn't even comprehend such numbers.

After dinner, the party adjourned to Hugo's sitting room for a typical evening of whiskey, poker, and war gossip. Hugo was generous with his liquor, which he imported at great expense. When Americans from the Lincoln Battalion came to call, accepting his invitations to drop in for hot baths and whiskey, he treated them to cigarettes and food from the private hoard of provisions he had brought back from Paris: tins of caviar and salmon, a few bottles of champagne, some cans of asparagus and endive.

As they settled down to play cards, the journalists recounted their various troubles with government censors that day, their difficulties in telephoning or wiring their stories to offices in Paris or London. They complained good-naturedly about the food, the fleas, the body lice they had picked up in the trenches. Their conversation was interrupted from time to time by the racket of a shelling attack. When the noise started, they made bets on how near or how far the strike was from the Ritz. Later, a bellboy would be dispatched to investigate. The bathroom window in Hugo's suite was boarded up, having been blown out by a shell that had hit the street outside. That time the bets had been placed in terms of inches and feet.

I made myself comfortable in the corner of the sofa with a whiskey and soda at my elbow and my log book on my lap. I liked the company of these writers, who accepted me as a fellow professional. At first I hadn't been able to get used to their cynicism. Then I realized that it was a buffer, a device they used to distance themselves from the horrors they had witnessed. My viewfinder reduced scenes of war and suffering to a comprehensible dimension, smaller than life. But those who reported the war had to try and distill the thoughts and impressions and facts they had gathered into a coherent and readable story. I didn't envy them their job. My pictures explained themselves; the correspondents had to explain the war in a few insufficient paragraphs.

Sometime after midnight, when the other men had left, Hugo unlocked the armoire in his bedroom and produced a bottle of champagne. "Bar the door," he said. "I hope to God they don't hear this cork when it goes off."

"Celebrating something?" I made a last jotting and closed my book.

"I hope so."

The cork exploded out of the bottle with a loud report like a gunshot. Champagne foamed over Hugo's hands and onto the sitting room carpet. Hugo poured two glasses, and then he lifted his to me.

"Okay, you've had plenty of time to think it over. What about it? Marry me?"

I had been expecting this. "No, Hugo. I can't."

"You're still in love with that poor bastard Evan Bradford, aren't you?" Hugo gulped champagne.

I felt myself turn pale under my sunburn. "What in the world made you say that?"

"A hunch. I keep remembering that little scene in Paris. You were scared silly, really worried about him."

"I couldn't help it." I watched the champagne bubbles rising from the bottom of my tumbler. "Even now, scarcely a day goes by that I don't think about him, wonder what he's doing, if he's all right, if he's still alive. It wouldn't have been any good between us, I know that. He could never stop loving Fiona. But that doesn't stop me from loving him."

"Forget him, kid," Hugo advised. "You can't do anything for

him. You need a fresh start. Diaz is dead. You're still young, and
God knows you've still got your looks. I'm not such a bad bar-
gain. Sure, I know my record is lousy, but I'm a reformed character now. My whole trouble was that I kept marrying stupid
women who spent so much time worrying about their faces and
their hairdos that they didn't have a thought to spare for anything else. But I can talk to you. We've been good pals, good co-
workers. By the way, I'm giving you credit as co-director. I
couldn't have made *Spanish Blood* without you."

"You don't have to do that."

"I want to. If this film goes over in a big way, we're going to
have enough money to finance another project. No more wars.
Africa this time, big game and jungles and natives in their villages. We'll make movies in places where no white man has ever
been before. We'll do important work. But better than that,
we'll have a lot of fun. What do you say?"

"What would I be, wife Number Four or Number Five?"

Hugo looked slightly embarrassed. "Four—but I married the
first one twice. Some of my friends hired an actor to play the
judge at the wedding, thinking I'd be too drunk to know the difference. They were right. When she found out, the bitch insisted that we make it legal. By that time I'd had enough of her, and
I wanted out, but I let her talk me into it. I've always been a
sucker for demanding women. I wish you were more demanding, Teddy. I'd give you anything you wanted. You know that."

"But I don't need anything," I said. "I have my work, and
that's enough for me right now. I don't want to get into the habit of marrying famous men—Diaz, you. If I ever marry again—
which I doubt—I'd want him to be an ordinary man with no
particular talents and no all-consuming ambition. I like you,
Hugo, but I'm exhausted just being with you. I felt the same
way with Luis. In a way, I was always competing, fighting for
my own identity, fighting for a sense of myself. I know now
what Evan must have gone through, being married to Fiona.
She was so brilliant, so beautiful, but she cast an enormous shad-

ow. Most of the time, Evan was floundering around in darkness."

"But we're not like that, you and me," Hugo insisted. "We're
partners."

"No, we're not. You're the driving force, the inspiration. I do
what I'm told, and I'm thankful that the responsibility for the
success or failure of this film doesn't rest on my shoulders. I
don't crave fame or recognition. You do. I don't want to live ostentatiously or lavishly, but that's important to you. This film
has satisfied my lust for travel and my capacity for hardship,
and I'm glad that it's over. But I have the feeling that if we were
married, if I made any kind of commitment to you at all, it
would never be over." I smiled. "Thank you for asking me to
marry you. I'm just sorry you've wasted another bottle of champagne on me."

"Still one more turn at bat," Hugo said. "But that was a pretty nice rejection. Let's kill this bottle and start another."

In the middle of September, 1937, Hugo flew to Paris to show
Spanish Blood to some French millionaires who wanted to finance his next project. According to Hugo, the meeting was
critical. He wanted to work independently of a large studio
from now on, and he needed new backers. I suspected that he
really wanted to replenish his larder.

Spanish Blood was finished. Hugo could boast truthfully that it
had been made entirely in Spain. He had scored a coup of sorts
when he secured the services of a famous British actor, who like
many other celebrities had come to Madrid to investigate the
war. The actor recorded the narration in tones so sonorous and
dignified that they brought tears even to Hugo's eyes.

"The guy's a twenty-four-karat son-of-a-bitch and queer as a
three-dollar bill, but he could make the Sioux Falls telephone di-
rectory sound like Shakespeare," Hugo told me privately.

"We were lucky to get him."

"This whole film has been lucky," Hugo said. "It's you, kid."

I resisted his suggestion that I accompany him to Paris. Now that my work on the film was over, I wanted to spend more time at the children's shelter on the Calle de Columela, not far from the hotel. In addition to helping out where I could, I was putting together a photo essay on the children of war. My experience with the diminutive Hollywood mogul had taught me that the plight of suffering children would stir even the hardest hearts. I planned to send copies of my pictures to the American Committee to Save Spain, as a way of spurring donations.

The girls at the shelter, so dark-eyed and sober, reminded me of Pilar, my childhood friend in Monkey Gulch. And the boys, unnaturally watchful and wary, reminded me of Joaquin, Pilar's brother. Their shattered lives reminded me of my own. In a way, the violence that had sundered the serenity of my childhood was not unlike a war.

When Hugo returned from Paris, he was downcast. The Frenchmen had had their own ideas about what they wanted him to do; a film promoting the wine industry. While he was in Paris, he had received an offer from the studio to direct an important film with an all-star cast.

"A Biblical epic," he told me over champagne that night. "The old man must be getting religion. But the money he offered me was so good that I couldn't turn him down."

"I'm sorry your plans for Africa didn't work out," I said.

Hugo was philosophical. "Africa will still be there when I'm ready. Oh, I forgot. I bought you a little something."

"Perfume," I guessed. "A wheel of camembert."

Hugo dug into his pocket, then opened his hand. A huge diamond in a gold setting winked up at me. "It occurs to me that I haven't gone about this courtship in the proper way. I've heard that most girls can't resist diamonds."

When I found my voice, I said, "I can't accept this. You shouldn't have done it, Hugo. You could have gone halfway to Africa on what this cost."

"What could I film halfway to Africa?" he asked. Taking my hand, he pressed the ring into my palm and closed my fingers around it. "I gather the answer is still no. Keep this anyway. I haven't paid you for your work on the film, and I'm not going to. I'm flat broke. It's a good thing the old man is paying my way back to Hollywood. Otherwise I'd never be able to get there."

"How were you able to afford the ring?" I wondered.

"He sent two steamship tickets, one for you. Thought you'd be great for the part of Mary Magdalene or something like that and wanted me to bring you along to take a screen test. I knew you wouldn't come, so I cashed in the ticket and bought the ring. Something to remember me by," he added softly, with a touch of Hollywood pathos.

"What if I had said yes to your proposal?"

"I would have told him to shove his epic, accepted the Frogs' offer to make a film about the wines of France, and you and I would have had the best damned honeymoon the Riviera could offer. How about it?" he coaxed. "No law says you can't change your mind. We could have a lot of fun together, kid."

I held the ring up to the light. "It's beautiful. I wish I could say yes. But I can't. You'd better keep this, Hugo. You'll find someone to wear it, I know. Your Mary Magdalene, maybe."

"No. No, it's yours, kid." His massive shoulders sagged. "Christ, I'm tired. You'd better shove off. I need to catch up on my sleep. I'll be leaving in a couple of days." He looked around his suite. "This place is paid for until the end of the year. It's bigger than that closet you're sleeping in. You might as well move in. Since they boarded up the window, the john should make a pretty good darkroom."

Pierre Fouchard had gone back to Paris to write his book about the war. Since Hugo didn't trust any of the other pilots he knew to get him safely out of Spain, he decided to have Manuel drive him to the French border, where he would catch a train to Le Havre. On the morning of his departure from Madrid, Hugo said his good-byes to his journalist friends. They would miss his whiskey, his humor, his unflagging enthusiasm for a war that most of them had come to loathe.

I went down to the lobby of the Ritz to see him off. A huge pile of luggage awaited Manuel and the Caddy.

"One thing I forgot," Hugo said as he supervised the loading of the car. "You're interested in kids. Take a look at the Children's Pavilion at the Provincial Hospital some afternoon around four. Nice human-interest story there. You might get some good pictures."

"Thanks, Hugo, I will."

I knew that if I announced that I was going with him, he'd give a roar of delight, sweep me into a crushing embrace, and then bear me off to Paris and the Riviera. And we would have fun, making films in out-of-the-way places, spending wildly when we had money, coming up with schemes to finance new projects. I liked and respected Hugo. He was generous, egotistical, stubborn, imaginative—and never boring.

At the same time, I knew that I had been right to keep my distance. We weren't right for each other. I didn't love him, and I would probably tire of his bluster and bombast. We had little in common beyond our belief in the value of film and photography. Over the years, Hugo had constructed a personality for himself that was larger than life, a Hollywood creation that obscured and concealed the man within. Where was the real Hugo? Who was he? He would be as difficult to find, and to know, as the real Fiona Randall.

The Cadillac was loaded, ready to go. Manuel, ensconced once again behind the wheel, prayed to the Virgin to see him and his passenger safely to the French border. A fervent Anarchist, Manuel had joined in sacking and burning several Madrid churches in the first days of the civil war. His acquaintance with Hugo had sent him secretly scurrying back to the faith of his fathers.

"Looks like this is it," Hugo said. "So long, kid. The stuff in the armoire is for you. Don't let those jackals of the press know you have it, or they'll clean you out."

"I won't. Thank you, Hugo." Impulsively, I threw my arms around his neck and kissed him. He held me for a moment, and then he released me.

"That's enough of that." His voice was gruff. Armed with government passes that he hoped would get them farther than Manuel's prayers, Hugo strode toward the exit shouting, "Let's get the hell out of here, Manuel. We've got a lot of miles to burn before sunset."

"Si, Señor Ugo!"

The engine roared, and they were gone.

I went up to Hugo's suite, where I opened one of his tins of sardines and a bottle of burgundy and had a silent and solitary lunch. Afterwards I lay down on his bed and tried to sleep, but sleep wouldn't come.

All through October, I continued to help out at the children's shelter while working on my photo essay. One day near the end of the month, I decided to follow up the lead Hugo had given me. I showered and changed into a beige woolen dress, combed my hair, dabbed on a little lipstick, and set off with my Leica for the Provincial Hospital.

I found the main building of the hospital just a few blocks away from the Atocha Station. I asked directions to the Children's Pavilion. A young nurse escorted me through the south wing.

"Most of our children are from Madrid," the nurse told me. "They have been hurt in the bombings and the fires. Many of them have no family."

"You send them to shelters when they are well?"

"So few get well," the nurse said. "Only the most serious cases are here. We have no room for the ones who can be cared for in private homes or shelters."

We passed through hallways jammed with small cots and pallets on the floors. The wards were overcrowded, the staff overworked, medicines in short supply.

I was struck by the silence in the wards and halls. Even more than the war orphans at Madrid's shelters, these children had lost their energy and joy. They bore their suffering mutely, with a dignity and forbearance that would shame adults.

I took a few pictures, promising my subjects that they should have copies. The nurse said, "Down there is the solarium. We call it the schoolroom now. The children who are well enough to leave their beds take instruction from the American. That is why you are here, no? To see him?"

I confessed that I didn't know precisely why I had been advised to come, only that I would find something newsworthy. "Who is the American?"

"A soldier who is recovering from a serious wound. As soon as he was able to sit up in a wheelchair, he asked to be taken to see the children. He reads stories to them, teaches them the alphabet and their numbers. The little ones have never been to school, and as for the older children, the war has interrupted their schooling so that they have forgotten most of what they have learned in the past. Go in," the girl said pleasantly. "He doesn't mind visitors."

The solarium was a small lounge at the end of a long corridor, whose windows overlooked the grimy railroad yards near the Atocha Station. At the center of a small group of children sat a man in a wheelchair. He was reading aloud to them in fluent but slightly accented Spanish. Sunlight poured through the window, glinting on his longish golden hair. The children were so absorbed in the tale that they hardly noticed me come in.

Turning the page, the man in the chair looked up and smiled at me.

"Hello, Dory," Evan said. "Won't you join us?"

27

Under the rough brown robe and faded striped pajamas, Evan's body looked frail and wasted. He had lost his excess flesh, and with it half his years, so that he seemed even younger than my memories of him, like a boy prematurely aged by harsh experience. The Spanish sun had bleached his hair to a new fairness and given his skin a falsely robust look. A cushioned footstool supported his left leg.

Years ago, I had convinced myself that I would never see Evan again. Since then, I had lived like a pauper, eking out a frugal and bitter existence on a watery diet of duty and pride. I subsisted on work, taking great bites of it in order to persuade myself that I wasn't really hungry. In all that time, I had been slowly starving to death, growing weaker and weaker, my capacity for enjoyment shrinking, so that when a banquet finally offered itself, I could only stand and stare, dizzy at the prospect of unlimited feasting, afraid to sample even the simplest delights. Proximity to such richness was enough to intoxicate me. It went right to my head, like wine on an empty stomach.

Gazing at Evan, I felt that I was basking in warm sunlight, engulfed in happiness greater than any I had ever known. He was alive. My love was alive.

After a few minutes, my wonder and delight were joined by curiosity. How did Evan come to be here, in Madrid, a soldier, recovering from his wounds in a Republican hospital? The situation seemed impossible, bizarre. How long had Evan been in Spain? Why was he here?

My fingers twitched on my Leica. I uncapped the lens. I would need nothing to remind me of this moment; memory alone would suffice. But the scene itself deserved to be recorded: the battered soldier, clearly American, reading aloud to a group of wounded Spanish children. Evan's listeners laughed at his story, which concerned a clever mouse named Pablo who had

383

persuaded a rich man that he was really a physician who could cure all ills. Some of the small members of the audience were ambulatory, with bandaged heads or arms. Most were badly scarred from burns. A few wore plaster casts. But their eyes gleamed, and their laughter sounded healthy and spontaneous.

Two nurses came in to tell the children that it was time for them to rest before dinner. Evan promised to finish the story at their next meeting, tomorrow afternoon. The children were led away, still protesting loudly that they weren't a bit tired. They wanted to hear more of Pablo's adventures.

"And you?" I asked Evan when we were alone. "Are you tired, Evan?"

"Lord, no!" He closed the storybook and shoved it down beside the seat of his wheelchair. "Your face is a better tonic than anything they've given me so far." Smiling, he held out his hand. I gave him my own. He grasped it warmly. "Let me look at you for a few minutes," he said. "You taught me long ago that sometimes words are unnecessary."

"Are you all right, Evan?" I couldn't restrain my anxiety. "Where are you hurt? How long have you been here?"

Laughing, Evan released me. "I can see you're not going to let me have any peace until you know everything. Very well. I have been here nearly three months. I was hit at Brunete, a dum-dum bullet in the hip, breaks in five places. The surgeons here did a fine job of putting me back together again. Everyone says it's a miracle that I'm still alive. They take special delight in reminding me that if the bullet had been just a few centimeters to the right, I'd be singing soprano right now. Nevertheless, my cast came off last week, and I've already taken my first steps, with a pretty nurse on each arm."

"Hugo." My jaw dropped as realization dawned. "He knew! You—*you* were the man on the stretcher at Quijorna. He spoke to you and he didn't tell me!" I felt my cheeks growing hot with anger. "I could shoot him. That, that monster! He knew!"

Evan nodded. "I was pretty far gone that day. I thought I recognized him, but I decided later that I must have been hallucinating. Hugo de Graaf, bending over my stretcher, telling me to keep my chin up?" He laughed easily, without rancor. "Then someone here told me he was in Spain making a film. I'm glad he's on our side. He's pretty good at his job."

"I know all about Hugo and his film," I said through my teeth. "I've been working on it with him, doing the photography. The selfish pig. I'll never forgive him for this."

"Perhaps he wanted to keep you all for himself." Evan spoke cautiously. "I don't blame him. Tell him for me that he's a lucky guy."

"He's lucky that he's left Madrid," I seethed, hardly noticing the look of relief that flashed over Evan's face. "Otherwise I'd wring his neck. Do you know, he was on his way out of town when he suggested that I come here? Even then he didn't tell me why. If he hadn't said anything—that was almost a month ago—if I hadn't decided to come—we'd never—I'd never—oh, Evan!" My lower lip started to tremble. Not wishing to upset the invalid, I turned aside and dashed away my tears before they could fall.

"I'm okay, Dory," Evan said softly. "Honestly. I should be back to normal in a month or more. With a slight limp, but I'm used to that. Funny, but since I've been wounded, I haven't had any trouble with that old back pain. Remember how it used to bother me?"

Gazing at him, I could read the story of his recent past in the new lines and shadows on his face. "You've been through hell, haven't you?"

Evan lifted his shoulders. "No more than any of the other people in this place. I'm nothing special. I'd be willing to bet that you've had your share of hell, too, Dory."

"But why, Evan? What are you doing here? You, of all people, fighting a war—"

"—against capitalism," he finished with a wink. "It's a long story. Why don't you push me out into the garden, and I'll tell you all about it."

I wheeled him out into the courtyard that lay between the

two newest wings of the building. The modernistic fountain in the center was idle, its concrete basin holding a few inches of stagnant rain water, scraps of litter, and a few leaves. A man on crutches limped past and grinned at us. "Howdy, Evan. Got yourself a new nurse, I see. She's even prettier than the last one."

"This is Mrs.—ah, Miss Lowery, Bob. She's a photographer."

"Ma'am," the soldier saluted me, two fingers touching an invisible cap. "When we saw the Captain had been hit, we thought his luck had finally run out. Guess we were wrong." He continued his slow progress across the courtyard.

I pushed Evan's chair close to the fountain and sat on the edge of the pool, facing him. "So you're a captain."

"Battlefield promotion," Evan said, dismissing his rank. "They're easy to come by if you happen to be one of the lucky few who survived a couple of encounters."

I knew that wasn't so. The leaders of battalions were chosen carefully by the International Brigade hierarchy.

"I'm astonished you passed ideological muster," I remarked. "Are you sure you're really Evan Bradford, glorious crown prince of the Four Hundred?"

"I've abdicated that throne, thank God." Evan grinned. "Otherwise I am still myself, glorious or inglorious as that may be. I told my superiors right off that I wasn't a Communist and that their jargon didn't impress me. Since each of the battalions has numerous political commissars who take care of propaganda and morale building, they let it pass."

The delirium of the first moments of our reunion had begun to dissipate. Now that we had moved outdoors, within full view of a hundred windows and several other patients who were enjoying the afternoon sun, I felt the atmosphere between us becoming slightly strained and awkward.

"So you haven't actually become a convert to Marxism since I saw you last," I said. "I'm not sure I understand why you're fighting with the Left rather than the Right."

Evan answered easily, "I guess I thought I had a better chance of dying if I picked the losing side."

My fingernails dug into the palms of my hands. "Oh, no, Evan."

"You haven't by any chance taken up smoking since we saw each other last?"

"No, but I usually carry some cigarettes with me these days. For purposes of bribery and barter." Thankful for the diversion, I rummaged in my camera case and handed Evan a pack of Luckys.

"Tobacco assumes an unnatural importance out in the trenches." Evan struck a match. "It helps pass the time, breaks the monotony of endless waiting, especially when you've nothing else to do, no letters to read, no one to write to." He exhaled the smoke gratefully. "No one knows I'm here. Not even Mother. Before I left New York, I telephoned her and told her I was going to Europe for a few months to think things over. I was in pretty rotten shape. I think she was glad to be rid of me for a while. I'd been staying with her off and on, and I'm afraid I behaved rather badly."

When his divorce from Fiona became final, Evan had hurled himself into what he called a downward spiral, drinking around the clock, not eating, spending his nights with prostitutes or in drunk tanks in Los Angeles, Chicago, New Orleans. He was victimized time and again by thieves, until he literally had nothing left but the clothes on his back. His mother dispatched private detectives to find him. When they brought him home, she committed him to a private hospital. After six months, the doctors pronounced his alcoholism cured. Evan celebrated his new freedom by running up an enormous bar bill at one of New York's posher clubs and then refusing to pay it. Another night in a cell. His mother decided to keep him at home for a while, in the care of a muscular male nurse, but he saw that his presence pained and embarrassed her. He had decided then to commit suicide.

"I had nothing to live for, you see. Fiona didn't want anything more to do with me. You were gone, married to someone else. My own mother was beginning to despise me. My behavior was obnoxious, even to myself. My old friends deserted me as if I had contracted leprosy." He winced as he remembered those pain-filled months. "I escaped from my keeper—I made a ladder of knotted sheets, if you can believe it—and hitchhiked into the city. I rented a room high up in a cheap midtown hotel, bought a half-dozen bottles of expensive bourbon, and promised myself that when the bourbon was gone, I'd perform a graceful swan dive out the window."

"Oh, Evan," I murmured.

Evan didn't acknowledge my heartfelt sigh. Having begun his painful narration, he didn't want to stop. "By some strange quirk of fate, the man checking into the room next to mine was a garrulous young fellow from the Midwest who'd come to New York to join the Lincolns. He was a Communist Party worker, a union organizer, utterly committed and sincere. He made Spain sound like a new crusade, a good fight, a noble cause. As I listened to him, I decided that just pitching myself out the window would be an empty gesture, a further cause of embarrassment and sorrow to my mother, and a scandal besides. How much better it would be if I could quietly disappear and perish on a Spanish battlefield, in the service of a good cause. I asked him where I could join. He was delighted to have made a convert, and the next day we hurried off arm in arm to a dank little cellar somewhere in Brooklyn, where a Party worker described life in Republican Spain in such glowing terms that it brought tears to my companion's eyes. Equality, fraternity, liberty—and the villainous Fascists were trying to take it all away. The recruiters promised that each man would receive a bonus when he returned from the fight, that we'd only have to spend six months on the front, and that we could leave at any time if we were dissatisfied. Peculiar way to run an army, I said to myself, but my new comrade ate it all up with a spoon. We signed up then and there. The Commissar smelled the bourbon on my breath and told me sternly that the Brigades would tolerate no drinking. I told him that I'd been celebrating my birthday, and I promised I'd lay off if only they took me. And I meant it, too. When my comrade and I got back to the hotel, I took one long last drink and poured the contents of the remaining bottles down the toilet. A few days later, we received fake passports and steamship tickets to France. Oh, and I'd given them a phony name: Evan Bradley. I suspected that if the Communists knew the truth about me they'd capitalize on it for publicity, and I wanted to spare Mother that agony. Three days after that, we set sail for Le Havre."

"So they don't know who you are," I said. "Didn't anyone guess?"

"How could they? I kept my most offensive Exeter-Yale mannerisms in check, and I didn't flash any gold cigarette cases or diamond-studded lighters. I tried hard to become one of the boys. They thought I was a minor bond salesman down on Wall Street, divorced, disgusted with the inequities of a capitalistic system that kept my bosses on vacation in Florida while I pounded the streets looking for a commission."

During the voyage, Evan had suffered from a combination of delirium tremens and seasickness, but when the ship finally docked at Le Havre, he was sober and reasonably free of his craving for alcohol, if somewhat weak and undernourished. When his leaders found out that he spoke fluent French—he invented a French grandmother—they put him in charge of a group of twenty men. He watched over them after they arrived in Paris, kept them out of jail and away from the whores and the tourist traps, and saw to it that they were properly clothed and shod for what promised to be a grueling hike through the Pyrenees. The French had closed the border three months earlier, in March, 1937, making the passage of International volunteers into Spain illegal. The new recruits followed smugglers' trails through the mountains.

"It was agony," Evan recalled. "I was horribly out of condition, of course, and I fully expected to collapse on the spot and perish at any moment. Joe Binnering, my recruiting buddy, kept me going. He half-carried me over the worst stretches, pushing me to go one more mile, one more step. I couldn't bring myself to tell him that the whole point of this adventure, so far as I was concerned, was suicide, and that he really didn't have to bother."

Evan's unit reached Barcelona in early June and shipped out immediately for training. They marched, drilled, and received instruction in the use of weapons. They weren't allowed to practice with real bullets, ammunition being in critically short supply. Evan, who had learned to shoot as a boy, gave his companions extra advice and training. They showed their appreciation by electing him squad leader. His body became harder, leaner, tougher. He realized that he hadn't felt so well in years. His resolve to offer his flesh as cannon fodder didn't weaken, but he began to consider the possibility of taking some of the enemy with him. Why not go out in a blaze of glory, a suicidal hero?

Just two weeks after their arrival in camp, the word went out that their unit was going to see action. The men began the long march to Brunete, west of Madrid. They were excited. At last they would have a chance to put their beliefs into action. As the oldest among them, Evan became the repository of their confidences, their questions, their stumbling search for truth. The members of his squad gave him the addresses of their mothers and their wives. Clearly, they trusted and respected him. This was a new sensation for a man who only a few months before had been a bum and a drunkard. Evan couldn't tell these boys his own shameful reasons for joining the International Brigades, so he listened in silence, envying their innocence, marveling at their willingness to die for what they believed was right.

"The youngest kid in the squad was only seventeen." Evan helped himself to another cigarette. "A Jewish boy from Brooklyn. His parents had been socialists for years. They were proud of him for joining the Internationals. The night before we saw action, he came to me and told me that he was scared. He was afraid that when the fighting started, he would turn and run.

He didn't want to be a coward. If I saw him running, he said, I was to shoot him. He'd rather die than live with the knowledge that he was a chicken. I told him that I was scared, too. So were all the rest of the guys. I promised that if I saw him running, I'd go after him and bring him back and get him pointed in the right direction again. He was so relieved that he started to cry. We moved out at dawn. We were supposed to take a hill about fifteen miles north of Brunete. Our esteemed leaders didn't tell us that the hill was occupied by Legionnaires with machine guns. The first of my men to fall under fire was that boy."

Evan didn't forget that his reason for coming to Spain was to get himself annihilated at the first opportunity. When their captain asked for a volunteer for a dangerous mission, Evan offered himself. While his men created a diversion by firing on the hill from the south, Evan loaded himself with grenades, crawled up a gully on the eastern side, and hurled them at the guns on top. At this signal, the members of his unit swarmed up the slope. Only six Legionnaires were waiting for them, but they might have been fifty. Hardened professionals, seasoned and experienced fighters who were well armed and well supplied, they defended their outpost with a ferocity and stubbornness that the green recruits from New York couldn't match.

After their captain fell in the earliest fire, Evan assumed command. Using the bodies of their own dead as shields, he and his men advanced on the cornered Legionnaires, firing and lobbing grenades until the thunder of return fire ceased. They had taken the hill. The cost had been high: twelve men out of thirty wounded, and six dead, including their commanding officer.

They waited for fresh troops to relieve them, but no relief came. No medics appeared to offer first aid, no ambulances arrived to remove the wounded. Hearing no word from headquarters, Evan dispatched a runner to tell them that the hill was theirs.

Exhausted and benumbed by their initiation rite, the men lay listlessly under a blazing sun and stared at the tattered remains of the enemy. To their astonishment, the Legionnaires were men like themselves, some handsome, some ugly, some carrying pictures in their wallets, or letters from girlfriends, mothers, sisters. Late that afternoon, planes swooped low overhead, their own Republican planes. At first the men cheered, and then dove for cover as the aerial gunners started to strafe them. Evan's message had failed to get through in time. Brigade Headquarters didn't know yet that the hill had been taken. Two more members of Evan's squad died, including Joe Binnering, with whom he had joined the Lincoln Battalion.

The unit spent a wretched night on the hill, fearing to light a fire for warmth in the chill that fell in the Guadarrama mountains after sunset, listening to the moans of their wounded comrades. In the morning, the runner returned with a message from headquarters: abandon the hill and regroup with the rest of the Battalion at a point two miles downriver. Because the enemy surrounded the entire area, the hill offered no decent point from which to press an attack. It wasn't worth defending.

Carrying their wounded on their backs, they retreated. Evan lost no more men that day. He received a battlefield commission with the rank of lieutenant. By the time the Popular Front Army occupied Brunete, he had earned the rank of captain, the dislike of the generals at headquarters, and the fierce loyalty of his men. He abandoned his original scheme for the time being. He had assumed responsibility for lives other than his own; someone had to protect his men from the deadly blunders, lethal errors, and gross miscalculations of their own military superiors.

"I saw right away that the quarreling and infighting between the Communists and everyone else in the Popular Front Army was going to cost a lot of innocent men their lives," Evan said. "I let my boys know that I would never force them to obey an order that I considered unnecessarily risky or suicidal. Nice irony, that. When you come right down to it, I guess I'm not really fighting for Spain at all. I'm fighting for the men who are fighting for Spain."

At that moment I recognized how much the war had changed

Evan. He had a purpose now, a mission. Spain had revealed to him an aspect of his character that he never knew existed. This pampered, overindulged scion of great wealth discovered that he was a natural leader. He had a rare combination of charisma and courage that inspired confidence and trust. Maybe he didn't believe in the Republican cause, but he believed in the men who were fighting for it, and in turn, they believed in him.

"Where did you get hit?" I asked.

"We were still at Brunete. At the end of July, Franco's armies moved in again, and recaptured the town. Some German planes from the Condor Legion bombed the church where we had a ton of ammunition stored. The explosion was tremendous. But by that time, I'd been shot by a sniper and I was past caring. I rode to Quijorna in a two-wheeled cart pulled by a mule. No Rolls Royce suspension on those things, I can tell you."

"If only I'd seen you," I said, remembering the blood-soaked soldier lying under the olive trees. My anger at Hugo renewed itself.

Evan shook his head. "I'm glad you didn't. It's bad enough seeing a stranger shot all to hell, but when it's someone you know—" He passed his hand over his eyes, trying to brush away the memories of the boys who had died—his boys. "All that time, I kept telling myself that I didn't mind dying. After all, that's why I had come to Spain, to die. But as I lay on the ground, watching my own blood seeping into the sand, I decided that I didn't want to die anymore. I even figured out what I wanted to do when I got out of here."

"What's that?"

"I'm going to start a school at Elf Hill. A school for poor children who can't function in public schools for one reason or another, but who can't afford a private school. I was a teacher once. My sole pupil hasn't fared too badly, I hear." He smiled at me. "Tell me about yourself, Dory. You look different. You're even more beautiful than I remembered."

The compliment gave me pleasure. Being close to him, basking in the warmth of his smile, I felt beautiful.

"Diaz is dead," I said.

"I know. The newspapers back home gave it a big play. I saw the pictures you took. I know what they must have cost you."

I told him briefly about Diaz's involvement in Spanish politics before the war, his death in Granada, my life since then.

"Hugo literally picked me up off the street and put me to work. He couldn't have found a better cure for shock and apathy." Aware that Evan was looking at me searchingly, I blushed slightly and glanced away. "I think your idea about a school is wonderful, Evan. If you ever need someone to teach photography, let me know."

"You're hired," Evan said with stunning promptness. "I can't promise a very large salary at first."

I said, "I'd work for nothing. You know that."

"I can offer long-term employment," he told me. "A lifetime if you like. And excellent benefits. How does it sound to you?" He extended his hand, once so smooth and perfectly manicured, now roughened and calloused, still stained by grease and gunpowder, even though three months had passed since he had last seen battle.

I slipped my fingers into his palm. The link between us, once so brittle, so easily shattered, had been mended, welded by time and hardship into a stronger and tougher bond. I felt whole again; complete.

"You always were extravagant," I said when I could speak. "I remember the first day I saw Elf Hill. You gave me Muffin. I couldn't believe that anyone could be so generous, and so crazy."

"Oh, I'm an old hand at trying to buy affection," Evan said with a rueful smile. "I'm learning that money isn't the best currency to use. You mean it, Dory? You'll help me?"

"Of course I will. I'll help you even if we have to build your schoolhouse out of pebbles, using spit for mortar."

"I thought I'd remodel the stables, turn them into dormitories." Evan's eyes shone with an excitement and enthusiasm I'd never seen in him before. "Keep a part of the house for us, and use the rest for classrooms. That way, the kids won't feel like we're breathing down their necks."

"The downstairs sitting room would make such a fine art studio," I suggested. "All those windows."

"Your darkroom's still there, down in the root cellar. Remember how hard you worked on me to get it?"

"You'll have to move the location of your wine racks," I said. We laughed.

Love could change the landscape of a life more quickly than a hurricane, more dramatically than a bomb blast. A few minutes ago, my future had been barren, empty of hope. But love, stronger than a tidal wave, swifter than a magic trick, had given me a home, a role as companion and teacher. Evan and I would work together, grow together, learn from each other. As a woman who had come quickly to experience and slowly to wisdom, I had much to give, much to gain, much to share.

Elf Hill. The only place on earth I had ever wanted to call home. I had despaired of ever going back. And now it was mine again. Ours. I started making plans of my own. As soon as Evan was strong enough to travel, we would leave Spain and sail westward, like Christopher Columbus, to a new life.

Love even transformed the bleak world of war-scarred Madrid. I thought I had never seen a more beautiful sight than the Atocha train yards and the debris-filled fountain behind the Provincial Hospital.

An aide came out to announce that it was the patients' dinner hour. Evan wrinkled his nose. "How they expect their patients to recover on a diet of tomatoes and garlic and olive oil is beyond me. But it won't last forever. My doctor says I should be out of here in another month. I'll buy you a real dinner before I go back to the front."

"Go back!"

I said the words incredulously, half-laughing. I thought he was joking. Then I saw his face, set in an expression of regretful determination. I remembered that look. It had accompanied words like, "I love Fiona"; and "I won't go with you."

"I have to, Dory," Evan said. "If the doctors will let me, that is. Spain gave me back my life. I owe her something. And I owe my men even more. They trust me, depend on me. I can't let them down now. I have to finish what I've started. You feel the same, or else you would have left with Hugo, wouldn't you?"

"I don't know." I stood up and brushed out my skirt. "I don't know why I stayed. Maybe I just didn't want to become another notch on Hugo's gun barrel." My mouth felt dry. I tasted ashes. "I'll send some more cigarettes, if you like. Hugo left plenty."

"Thank you, I'd like that very much. Will you visit me again?"

His words sounded faint. A deafening roar filled my ears: the thunder of dreams crashing down around me. Fool. Fool! So eager to hurl yourself into the flames, to throw yourself under the wheels of the first dream that comes along.

I couldn't bring myself to look at him. "Of course I'll visit you," I said automatically. "Although I'm rather busy these days at the children's shelter on Calle de Columela. I'm working on some pictures for the American Committee to Save Spain. Of the children."

"You're angry with me," he said. "Because I want to go back to the front."

"I thought you had abandoned the idea of suicide." I marveled at how cold my tone had become. But I felt frozen inside.

"I have."

With horrible swiftness, the love in my soul twisted, shriveled, and died. He had done it again. How could Evan hold out a promise of happiness, and then snatch it away so quickly? He was heartless, evil, the kind of man who would dangle a shining apple just out of the reach of a starving child. Nothing had changed. Love was a bitter joke, a whoopee cushion hidden under a brocaded chair seat, a champagne glass that falls apart in your hands, a pretty flower that squirts water in your eye. Love hadn't changed at all. It still meant betrayal. It still meant pain.

I looked around. Life was smoke and cinders and battered railroad ties. Life was dried leaves and cigarette butts floating on water the color of urine. I walked away from my dream without saying farewell.

When I entered the lobby of the Ritz, the lounge-sitters hailed me. "What's the matter, duck?" Cecil Andrews of the *London Daily Mail* called. "You look like you've lost your best friend."

My eyes blazed. "Oh, go to hell, Cecil." Ignoring the elevator, which failed to function half the time anyway, I strode toward the stairs.

Cecil trotted after me. "My dear child, please forgive me. Of course you miss Hugo. How thoughtless of me."

"Hugo can go to hell, too." Pulling my hands into fists, I whirled and faced him. "Damn Hugo. Damn you, Cecil. Damn all of you. If it weren't for men like you, we wouldn't have wars. We wouldn't have a thousand kinds of misery and suffering. Women didn't invent guns. Women didn't invent factories and coal mines that destroy more lives than they improve. Women didn't invent rape or brutality or—or love!"

Cecil and the others stood open-mouthed at the bottom of the stairs. I ran all the way up, gasping and sobbing until I reached the safety of my room, where I gave full vent to what they would consider a very feminine rampage of hysterical tears and fist-pounding fury.

28

I dropped a set of prints into a pan of fixative, nudged them with a pair of tongs, and set my timer. On the other side of the bathroom door, I could hear the creak of bed springs as one of my fellow journalists made himself comfortable. For some reason, the tub in my bathroom was the only one on our floor that still worked. Wartime etiquette demanded that I share it with my colleagues. But because my bathroom doubled as a darkroom, bathers often had to wait. The manager of the Ritz,

Don Faustino, had tried to charge me extra for the hot water. I refused. Since the weather had turned cold, my radiators provided barely enough heat to warm the inside of a shoe box.

To keep prospective customers from barging in and spoiling my work, I had printed a large sign and tacked it up on the other side of the door: "*No Pasarán!* STOP! Do Not Enter!" To discourage the truly rash or illiterate, I had appended an enlargement of a ferocious gun-toting Moor.

I heard Cecil Andrews of the *London Daily Mail* announce in his loud bray, "Not available, old man. Developing. Come for a bath? Have to wait your turn. Oh. Well, in any case, help yourself to some booze. We're still working on Hugo's stock. Thank Heaven Theodora's as generous as her late-departed mentor in passing it out to guests. Not that I mean to suggest that dear old Hugo has left this earth, merely gone to pastures where the greenbacks are greener and the cigarettes don't explode in your face."

Sighing, I transferred my prints to the sink and turned on the water. Cecil Andrews was the worst gossip in Madrid. The other person in the room murmured a question. Cecil responded with warm expansiveness.

"Oh, simply ages, old man. I've been in this bloody hole for six months, and she and Hugo were here when I arrived. Theodora was occupying a different room then. Not that any of us was ever invited in, more's the pity."

I opened the bathroom door. Cecil glanced up from the bed, where he was reading a ragged-looking *London Times*. Portly and moustached, Cecil wore his bathrobe and slippers, and he had rolled a towel around his neck. Between paragraphs, he sipped from a whiskey glass on my nightstand.

"Ah, there you are, dearest heart. It's about time."

"I'm afraid you'll have to go up to the fourth floor after all, Cecil. I've got too much stuff in the sink and on the line." I looked around, and saw Evan leaning against the dresser.

"Oh, I say, Teddy, that's dreadfully unsporting of you. Can't we move the bloody clothesline in here? I'll help you." The bed creaked as he raised his bulk upright and swung his legs around. "You did promise, after all. I won't take a long soak, just a little sponge bath. How's that? I beg you, don't make me go up there. Bloody prostitutes all over the place, never let a man have his bath in peace."

Evan was wearing the makeshift uniform of the Lincoln Battalion: baggy trousers tied at the ankle with string, a short khaki jacket, beret folded and tucked in his belt, stout but worn shoes. He spared his wounded leg by resting his weight on a hand-hewn cane.

"Sorry, Cecil," I murmured. "No bath today."

"Can't I at least retrieve my shampoo from your tub, then?" Cecil sniffed. "I promise I won't touch any of your precious photographs." He padded into the bathroom. Evan and I continued to gaze at each other. "I'll be going now," Cecil announced loudly. I blinked at him, surprised to see him still in my bedroom. I followed him through the sitting room to the door. "No need to show me out," Cecil protested. Nevertheless, I ushered him out into the hallway and closed the door firmly behind him.

"I didn't mean to disturb the routine of this happy little dormitory." Limping, Evan emerged from the bedroom. "I thought Cecil looked rather put out."

"He'll get over it. I guess you'd better sit down."

I knew I sounded ungracious. I couldn't help it. Four weeks had passed since our meeting at the Provincial Hospital. I hadn't visited. I hadn't sent cigarettes. I was still trying, without success, to forget that I had seen Evan there.

"Sitting down is easy," Evan said with a wry twist of his mouth. "Getting up again is the real challenge. I want to be sure of my welcome before I commit my body to the ordeal. I upset you badly that day at the hospital. I'm sorry."

I leaned against a small chest of drawers, a fake Louis XV commode. "I'm sorry, too. I shouldn't have gotten angry with you that day. What do your doctors say? Will you be well enough to go back to the front soon?"

"I'm supposed to take it easy for another month or so, and

then get myself checked out by a Brigade surgeon. But the doctors here think I should be able to fight again, if I want to."

"And you still want to?" I heard the coldness in my voice, but I couldn't stop it.

"Yes, Dory, I do."

"Then there isn't anything else that I can say." I untied the strings of my apron and tossed it onto a chair. Underneath I wore a tweed skirt and brown pullover sweater. "You shouldn't have come here, Evan."

Setting his cane aside, Evan braced his hands on the back of the sofa. "I didn't really think you'd come back to the hospital, although I kept hoping. Every time my door opened, I was sure it would be you."

I didn't tell him that at times during the past four weeks my longing to see him had been so strong that I could hardly keep myself from running over to the Provincial Hospital and throwing myself at his feet. I would have done it, if I hadn't been so sure of his resolve to return to the front.

"I've already been widowed once by this war." I tried to keep my voice even. "Another man who loved me died in a bombing raid. I've seen too much to be idealistic anymore, Evan. Too many lives lost." I picked up one of my wartime keepsakes. "A soldier I met at Jarama sent me this little book as he was dying. Shakespeare's sonnets, hymns to love and life. They didn't do him any good. 'When, in disgrace with Fortune and men's eyes—' "

I tossed the book aside.

" 'I all alone beweep my outcast state,' " Evan supplied. "That sonnet's always been one of my favorites, especially the last lines: 'For thy sweet love rememb'red such wealth brings that then I scorn to change my state with kings.' Your love has meant a lot to me, Dory. When I was at my lowest ebb, I remembered how much you had loved me once. If only I'd had the sense to take your love when you offered it. I'll never forget that day in your apartment—"

"It's no good, Evan." I couldn't listen to his reminiscenses. I had lived too long on those same memories, sucking them dry of nourishment. "I'm not going to put my heart on the chopping block again. I wouldn't have stayed in Spain at all, except I knew that this war couldn't take anyone else away from me. Then I saw you. And what did I find? That you couldn't wait to go back and get yourself killed."

"I had to tell you my plans. I couldn't spring it on you later. You needed time to get used to the idea."

"My God, Evan," I cried, "don't you know the box score? While you were sitting in the hospital, a thousand Americans fought at Teruel. Two hundred survived. You may have cheated death once, but you won't do it again. The odds are too high. The other side is too strong. It's only a matter of time before the Republic collapses completely. I respect anyone who believes in an ideal strongly enough to die for it. But only a fool would die for a dream."

My harsh words didn't seem to make Evan angry. He shrugged. "I've made a fool of myself before."

I walked to the door and put my hand on the knob. If Cecil was listening, he was certainly getting an earful. "I don't love you anymore."

"Ah, so it's that easy, is it?" Evan said. "You just say the words often enough, until you start to believe them. I wish I'd known. I could have used that technique a few years ago. Dory, don't you know that you're part of me? I'm part of you. As precious as life is to me now, you are infinitely more precious."

I glared at him over my shoulder. "What would happen, Evan, if you suddenly found out that Fiona was here in Madrid?" He jumped a little. "You don't have to tell me. I'd lose that contest. Again. You haven't stopped loving her. We may be part of each other, but Fiona's always had the lion's share of your love. If she crooked her little finger at you, you'd go running."

Evan raised an amused eyebrow. Dressed in the roguish uniform of the Lincoln Batallion, he had still managed to achieve his old style, his look of careless elegance. "You don't credit me with very much intelligence, Dory."

"Intelligence has nothing to do with the way men like you feel about women like Fiona. Why should I care? Whether you're killed by the Moors, or whether you let Fiona destroy you, you might as well be—" My hands flew to my face. "Oh, my God, what am I saying?" I whispered. "What's happening to me? Talking like I wished you were dead." Tears started to roll down my cheeks. With an angry swipe of my hand, I dashed them away.

"Why did you have to come here, Evan?" I cried. "I didn't need you. I was doing fine without you, just fine. Even after Diaz and Angel died, I was all right. I kept busy. I didn't think. I didn't feel. I just took my bloody pictures of this bloody war and forgot about everything else."

"Had you really forgotten me?" Evan asked.

"No, because I'm the biggest fool that ever walked this earth. Years ago, I even thought you were dead. I should have stopped caring then. But things are different now. If you want to get your head blown off by some Legionnaire, that's your affair. But I don't want to know about it."

Turning the key, I wrenched the door open. Cecil, still wearing bathrobe, towel, and slippers, stepped back, dumbfounded. Collecting his wits, he pretended he was about to knock.

"Theodora, I just wanted to ask you if I might borrow—"

"No, you may not."

I turned to Evan.

"And you, Mr. Bradford, can take your wound and your cane and your ideals back to Belchite or Brunete or Teruel or Jarama. I don't want anything to do with them. Or you."

I ran into the other room, slammed the door behind me, and hurled myself face down on the bed. I decided that I had finally lost my mind. My mother's daughter. But madness was the only logical response to this insane world, a world that offered happiness with one hand and snatched it away with the other.

The hall door closed. The sound had a grim finality about it. Not even Evan Bradford, in his new incarnation as idealist and war hero, could tolerate being humiliated in front of a stranger. He had gone out of my life again. So be it.

Evan's cane bumped in the doorway. "My doctors didn't want to release me yet," he confessed. "But I told them that my girl was here in Madrid. So they let me go." He stood at the foot of the bed. "I'm sorry, Dory. I don't want to hurt you. But I made a vow after I was hurt: If I lived, I would go back and finish the fight. I never dreamed then that I'd find you here. When I saw your face, I couldn't believe my eyes. I couldn't believe how much I loved you."

Within the corral of my arms, I squeezed my eyes closed. Once I would have risked anything for those words, committed any crime, made any sacrifice. Now they struck me like hammer blows.

"If I betrayed that vow, I'd always feel that I hadn't done all I could for the people who had done so much for me. Can you understand that? I had no right to speak as I did, of Elf Hill and the school and our future together. I can't promise you any of those things, not yet, anyway. But that doesn't mean that we have to stop loving each other. A hundred things could happen between now and the time I'm ready to go back. A bomb could fall on this hotel tonight and kill us both. The war could end."

I knew better. The war wouldn't end until it had claimed the last person in the world that I held dear.

Evan shifted his weight, grunting softly at a twinge in his wounded leg. "You know, Dory, in some ways you remind me of Fiona."

I bounced into a sitting position, ready for a fight.

"No, let me finish. I've taken a long time to accept it, but I finally realized that Fiona couldn't love me. She wasn't able to. She could play-act at love, make all the right gestures and all the right noises, but it wasn't real. I don't know why—maybe something had happened to her in childhood—but she was terrified of being hurt, and so she built up a lot of powerful defenses. She never let anyone get close enough to touch her, much less hurt her. Do you see what I'm talking about? You're doing the same thing right now. Building walls, constructing an iron-clad shelter. But the cost is too high, Dory. Let the walls crumble. Come out. Let yourself love me."

"You still love her," I charged.

Evan didn't deny it. "I spent too many years loving her to forget her. I gave her too much of myself. I've forgiven her for hurting me, because I understand her so well. I wish her every happiness, although I don't think she'll find it. But I can't say that I love her the way I did once."

He had been honest with me. His old feelings for Fiona still lingered. Perhaps they always would.

But he loved me, too.

And Fiona was far away.

Beyond the winter-blighted garden in front of the Ritz, the setting sun produced a half-hearted display of mauve and orange. Shadows like dirty mist gathered in the corners of the room.

I got up to close the shutters and draw the blackout curtains.

Grasping the bedpost for support, Evan lowered himself carefully onto the side of the bed. He was sure of his welcome now. I switched on the lights, hung up his jacket, parked his cane between the nightstand and the bed, where he could reach it if he needed it.

Standing in front of him, I began to apologize. "Evan, I didn't mean—"

He placed the tips of his fingers on my lips. He knew what I wanted to say. He knew that the time for words had passed.

The evening shelling began, muffled popping that sounded as innocuous as distant fireworks, reminding us that a war that brought lovers blissfully together could also wrench them cruelly apart. Evan folded his arms around my waist and pressed his face into my belly. I smoothed his hair.

I think we were both a little afraid of each other, and afraid of the changes that the years had wrought. Evan's wounds made him cautious; he still lacked strength. I could have reassured him, but I held myself back. I, too, feared that love would be the inevitable prelude to pain, the pain of loss that was my legacy as well as my destiny. My mother. Evan's loving friendship. Luis. Angel.

Our first kisses were tentative, even shy, but they awakened a passion that overwhelmed us with its strength and suddenness. Like a mighty storm, passion lived for itself alone. Powerful and magnificent, it spoke with words that existed in no other language; it healed breaks and hurts and sicknesses that would have defeated even skilled physicians; like the rising sun, it sent pain and fear scurrying like rats into the shadows. Passion was life, love triumphant. Without it, life was bland, gray, an approximation of death.

My life with Luis had been no life at all. Life had flared briefly with Angel, and died with him. Now, with Evan, I lived again, a pure flower bursting out of the muck and mud of Purgatory, that gray land without love. A bloodflower.

Evan wanted to return to the war, to fight the Fascists. Lying with him, I could hear the enemy's shells falling on the northern part of the city.

I would fight, too, I vowed. I would be as ruthless and vicious as any Fascist in my fight to keep him.

On Christmas Day, we went to the Provincial Hospital and spent the afternoon with Evan's wounded children, singing carols and playing games. But we took them no candy. I could no longer find decent food for ourselves in Madrid. Hugo's dwindling stock couldn't even provide proper nourishment for Evan, still convalescing. So when Manuel and his Cadillac turned up in Madrid after New Year's, I decided to hire him to take us to Valencia. Food from neighboring villages and collective farms was readily available there, but because of air attacks and enemy raids, little of it reached Madrid, even though the roads were still open. I expected the winter weather at the seaside to be more bearable than in Madrid, where the dry winds howled down out of the Guadarrama mountains.

Enemy bombs and shellfire continued to punctuate our dreams. Evan, who seemed so eager to return to the battlefield, was not unscarred by the suffering he had endured and witnessed. On several occasions I had to shake him awake to free him from his nightmares.

I never mentioned his plan to return to the front, but I never forgot it, and I never stopped hoping that his scheme would fail. Surely no doctor would permit a man who had sustained such a serious wound to return to action in less than a year, I reasoned. In that time, the fighting might well be ended.

"Our side can't possibly win," I told Evan on the night before our departure for Valencia. "Franco and his generals are fighting a Holy War, another crusade. Even without the help of Hitler and Mussolini, they'd be winning, because they're united and they're determined. They want to protect institutions that are centuries old." I retrieved one of Hugo's enormous socks from the depths of the armoire and added it to the pile of "items to be left behind," already as large as "items to take." "The Republicans have nothing to defend, except a government that never worked right in the first place, along with dreams of a fine and happy socialistic state. I've heard stories about Communists assassinating Anarchists on the battlefield. Does it make any sense, when all the members of the Popular Front want to defeat a common enemy, for them to turn their guns on each other? It's just a matter of time before the whole defense collapses and Franco's tanks roll across the peninsula to the Mediterranean."

On the bed, Evan looked up from the book of Diaz's poetry he had been reading. "When this thing started, some people said that the war would last only six months, with the Germans and the Italians throwing their weight behind Franco. Madrid was supposed to fall in a matter of weeks, remember? But it held. Two years later, the war is still going on, with no sign of a ceasefire any time soon. The people of Spain won't give in, so long as they have hope."

"Hope is dead." I tossed a pair of slacks into my suitcase and wondered if a second threadbare pair was worth packing. "It sickens me to think that men are bleeding their lives away on battlefields for a cause that's doomed. The fight may have been a good fight once, but it's hopeless now."

"Not if it shows the world that some things are still worth fighting for, and dying for." Evan set the book aside and reached for his cigarettes, the last of the Luckys. "At Brunete, back in July, our unit overlapped with a French battalion during an action to capture a hillside above Quijorna. The planning was messy, poorly organized as usual. I won't go into details. We were pulling back—in full retreat, actually—when I saw a young soldier fall about fifty feet in front of me. He'd been hit in the shoulder. I cut his shirt away so that I could staunch the bleeding enough to get him down to the medics." He smiled, recalling his amazement at the time. "I uncovered a breast. A small, shapely, perfectly delightful alabaster breast. The soldier was a woman, a French girl of about nineteen, from Normandy. She begged me not to tell anyone. She and her sister had joined the Brigades together, because they hated Fascism. I got her out of firing range, patched her up myself, and sent her back to her unit. I saw her again once or twice. Her name was Émilie, but she was calling herself Émile."

"You loved her," I said, feeling a twinge of jealousy.

Evan said thoughtfully, "I loved her spirit. She reminded me of you, Dory. You were always so passionate about things I could never understand. The experiences that shaped you were utterly foreign to me. But they made you strong, because you survived them. I understood Émilie very well, because I'd met her before."

"Is she—?" I could hardly bring myself to ask the question. I already knew the answer.

"A sniper got her. She's buried on some unnamed hill, with-

out a marker, without an epitaph. But I'll remember her." Evan
held out his arms to me. I went to him. "We don't need to talk
about this. We both know why we're here, why we have to stay.
Not so much for Spain as for ourselves, because if we left, we
would be leaving something beautiful and important behind."

Leaning against his shoulder, I prayed silently for a miracle.
Dear God, don't let him be well enough to fight again.

But every day since his release from the hospital, I saw Evan
growing stronger, moving about more freely, putting greater
stress on his shattered bones and severed muscles. I rejoiced
with him, and mourned for myself. I loved him for his courage,
and I despised myself for my selfishness.

Manuel had agreed to take us to Valencia, but only if he could
remove his family from Madrid at the same time. Accordingly,
five adults and three small children piled into the capacious
Cadillac, along with an assortment of photographic equipment,
household goods, clothing, and toys, and set off for the little city
on the Mediterranean Sea. We ran into some minor skirmishes
along the way, and once we had to delay our trip for half a day
while an officer of the Popular Front Army subjected our papers and our persons to intense scrutiny. But compared to what
we had experienced in the last year, our journey was unevent-
ful.

Manuel's cousins ran a hotel on the Paseo de Neptuno, not far
from the Port of Valencia. Every morning, Evan and I tramped
along the beach, always increasing the distance we covered, relishing our silences as much as our conversation. We hadn't
spent such long hours in each other's company since I went
away to Miss Frasier's school. The passing years and our disparate experiences hadn't spoiled our friendship. The old barriers
between age and youth and rich and poor and educated and ignorant had vanished. We were equals now, if lovers could be
equals.

"Which of us loves, and which permits himself to be loved?" I wondered one morning as we set out for our after-breakfast walk.

"Our love could never be so one-sided," Evan declared. "I feel sorry for the moronic Frenchman who made that one up."

The men in Manuel's family were away fighting the war. Some had died in the early days after the rebellion, when vicious street fighting raged in Valencia as it had everywhere else in Spain. Blood had run in every alley, and the Valencia bullring had been the scene of mass executions. But two old women ran the hotel with an ease and competence that suggested that menfolk, even in normal times, were superfluous. They took a natural interest in us, the wounded American soldier and his young bride. Manuel had conveyed a somewhat blurred impression of our situation.

"When I went down to the kitchen for our coffee this morning, they asked me why I wore no ring," I said as we tramped along the line of sea shells left by the receding tide. That morning we headed north, toward the smoking paper factory at Malvarossa. "I pulled out Hugo's diamond and told them that it was too big. Not true, but I had to have some excuse for not wearing it. They thought it was the most gorgeous thing they'd ever seen."

I handed Evan the ring. "Magnificent," he said. "Our oversized Cupid doesn't have such bad taste after all."

"He wanted to marry me, didn't he? Evan Bradford, I do believe you're still jealous of Hugo."

"Not at all. I thank him for sending you to me. And for providing me with an engagement ring. I'm out of pocket right now, and on a soldier's pay I could never afford something as sumptuous as this." Grasping my hand gently, he slipped the ring onto my finger. "Be careful how you swing it around. You could knock a man out with it."

I stared at him. "You want to get married!"

"Of course I do. As soon as possible. I thought it was all settled."

"But what we have is so perfect, Evan," I argued. "We don't

need to get married. Wouldn't it be better just to let things go on as they are?"

"Indulge me, Dory." He tucked my hand through the curve of his arm and tried to resume our stroll. I pulled away. "I have a special reason for asking."

"You want to make me a widow again." I couldn't conceal my bitterness.

"Not at all. I want you to have Elf Hill. A will would be sufficient, but marriage is simpler, and it would leave you in a much better position legally. As it happens, the American vice-consul at Barcelona is an old classmate of mine. He can marry us and take care of our legal business at the same time. He won't be terribly pleased to see me; the Department of State has ordered him to have nothing to do with the members of the Lincoln Battalion. But he'll play along. And so will you, I hope."

"But I don't want Elf Hill!" I cried. "I don't want anything of yours. Not without you. For God's sake, Evan." I huddled miserably inside my coat. When the sun ducked behind a cloud, even warm Valencia felt the taste of winter.

Evan put his hands on my shoulders. "We're going to come out of this, both of us. We are going back to Elf Hill, to start our school, and to teach our children that long, loving relationships provide the only islands of sanity in a crazy world. Please, Dory. A man needs to protect those he loves. I have no intention of dying, but I'll fight with a clearer conscience knowing I've taken care of you. Smile, won't you?" His fingers caressed my cheek. "We don't have much time left."

Stepping back, I glared at him. "I'm going with you," I announced. "I can take pictures; somebody always wants to buy more bloody pictures of this stupid war. I won't bother you. The other men don't even have to know about me. I won't ask you to slip away and visit me. You don't have to sleep with me. You don't even have to look at me when I come around with the other reporters. Jackals of journalism. Hugo called them that once. He was joking. But he and I were the biggest jackals of all. *Spanish Blood*! That film isn't going to help the people who have died here. Nothing can help them. It isn't going to do much for the ones who are left alive, either."

"Dory, I can't allow you to—"

"No, Evan." I was trembling all over. "I need to know that you're all right. That's all; just to know. I'm not going to wait behind the lines. If being your wife means I have to obey you blindly, then I won't marry you, not now, not ever. I won't obey any order that keeps me away from you. I'll put on a uniform myself, or ride an ambulance, or sleep with your generals."

"This is getting very dramatic," Evan sighed.

"I'm serious, Evan." I stamped my foot on the soft sand, which defeated the whole purpose of the gesture. "I will not sit in a hotel room in Barcelona or Madrid, wringing my hands and praying for some word about you. I'm not going to walk through some olive grove five years from now, wondering where they dumped your remains. You have your work to do and I have mine. If you want to go and get yourself killed, that's your business. But I want to be there to see it, to mark the spot, to take some pictures for the jackals."

"Dory, please." He took a step toward me.

"Like Luis." I retreated out of his reach, my voice rising in a crescendo of agony. "I saw what they did to Luis. I even made his death part of history, didn't I? Why should my second husband be any different from the first? Front-page news. You can't stop me. The whole Guardia Civil couldn't stop me. I'm not afraid of seeing you die. Why should I be? It's happened before, over and over, seeing the people I loved bleeding to death—"

"Theodora!" Gripping my elbows, Evan shook me. "No!" he shouted, and watched my wild face crumple. "No," he said in an anguished murmur. "No." He held me close.

"We'll go to Barcelona tomorrow," he said when I was quiet. "We'll see Tony Manchester at the embassy first thing, get that business taken care of, and then I'll report to camp. If the doctors declare me unfit for duty, I'll accept it, and we'll take the next ship home. Otherwise, I'll go where they send me. I won't hold back. I won't use the lives of my men to spare my own life.

Honor isn't something you grab once and wear like a badge. You have to keep earning it—like love. I'd like to think of you safe, out of harm's way, but if you want to take pictures of the action, I can't stop you. You have to do what suits you best. You have your art to serve, and your conscience. And I have mine."

The breeze from the sea dried the salt streaks on my cheeks. "If I had a gun, I'd shoot you through the foot," I said.

Evan laughed. Sitting awkwardly on the sand, he pulled me down beside him. His kisses had never tasted sweeter. I felt like the condemned man eating his last hearty meal. After Barcelona, we would have no more kisses. No more anything.

"We'll arrive for lunch looking suspiciously sandy and rumpled," Evan promised, "and really give those old ladies something to talk about."

29

Barcelona: like Madrid, a city under seige, torn from within by an ongoing dispute between the Communists and the Anarchists, and battered from above by Italian bombers. When the Republicans made it their official capital in November, 1937, Barcelona became a riper and even richer target.

Arriving at the end of February, 1938, Evan and I found an inexpensive hotel on the Calle Moncada in the Gothic Quarter, the most ancient and picturesque part of the city, whose tangle of narrow streets and sooty ochre buildings dated from the fourteenth century. With lines of clothes strung across alleys too narrow for cars, the neighborhood reminded me of the Spanish towns I had seen on the stage, in operas like *Don Giovanni* or *The Barber of Seville*. But no light-hearted music accompanied the furtive scurrying of persons moving through the shadows after curfew, only the occasional snap of a sniper's rifle, or the drone of an airplane engine.

"I'll go see Tony Manchester at the Consulate right away," Evan said after we checked into our room, which wasn't much bigger than Hugo's armoire at the Ritz. "Will you come with me?"

"Your friend can't perform a wedding without the bride." I arranged Evan's shaving kit and my toiletries on top of the dresser.

"No, he can't." Evan watched me from the doorway to the dank hallway. "Are you coming?"

"I don't think so." I directed my attention to the contents of my suitcase.

He nodded. "I'll just see about making a new will, then. You can still change your mind, you know. Be my wife, Dory?"

I held a pair of his socks in both hands. "I won't be your widow."

"I understand. It's all right. A wedding won't change anything. It's just a formality, a piece of paper." Coming up behind me, Evan wrapped his arms around my waist. "I couldn't love you any more if we were married." He kissed my earlobe. "I don't love you any less because we're not."

"Please leave me alone, Evan." I wriggled away from him. "I'll be all right. Just do what you have to do."

A few days later, Evan received a thorough examination by a Brigades surgeon, who gave him permission to return to action within the week. He was told to report to the headquarters of the Fifteenth International Brigade in the desolate war-ravaged town of Belchite, about a hundred and fifty miles from Barcelona. The Fifteenth Brigade included battalions of volunteers from English-speaking countries such as Great Britain and Canada, as well as the American Abraham Lincoln Battalion.

Evan and I spent three pleasureless days exploring Barcelona. In wartime, I noted, one city under seige looks much like another. Barricades of sandbags appeared everywhere. With their boarded-up windows, the facades of otherwise handsome buildings had curiously blank expressions, like aged beauties with cataract-blinded eyes. Everywhere, people walked past scenes of sickening ruin and devastation without a second glance. To my mind, the symbol of Barcelona was its fine old Gothic cathedral: stripped of its artwork, denied its function as a place of worship, it retained a certain bedraggled dignity, but it had lost its warmth and its sense of purpose.

One evening I sat with Evan in a cafe on the crowded promenade called the Ramblas. Our talk was stiff and superficial, as though we were two incompatible strangers suffering through a first date.

After a few minutes, I said, "I'm having a terrible time and so are you. You don't have to stay here any longer, Evan. We've already had our time together in Madrid and Valencia. I have plenty of memories."

And plenty of souvenirs, among them several rolls of exposed film containing photographs of Evan, Manuel and the Caddy, the old women at their seaside hotel, even a couple of shots of the two of us together on the beach, taken by an obliging old fisherman who had never held a camera before. I decided that I wouldn't develop those pictures. Not right away. Hugo de Graaf wasn't around to urge me on; no panting newspapermen demanded that I produce photographic proof of our love. The day might come when those pictures would haunt me, and I would print them, so that I could see what two people in love looked like.

"I'll come back," Evan promised. "Believe it, Dory. Keep saying it to yourself over and over, until you believe it."

I twisted Hugo's ring. "I can't. I won't lie to myself."

"Lies aren't the same as dreams," Evan said. "But you turned your back on dreams a long time ago, didn't you, Dory? You think that dreamers are fools and weaklings who can't face facts. But people need dreams. Not just creative people like Diaz and Hugo, but simple people like me. We all need to be able to make plans, to hope. We've got to tell ourselves that the future holds happiness instead of misery and pain. That's the only thing that keeps any of us from sinking into madness or suicide. You've always been so practical and realistic. You insist on seeing things as they are. Well, I think it's time you started seeing things as they ought to be. Relax your fierce grip on reality. Let yourself dream a little."

"Supply trucks are leaving for the front every day," I said. "You can hitch a ride on one of them." I swirled the wine around in my glass and tipped it into a nearby potted plant. "How about tomorrow morning?" Why had I ever thought I could drink red wine? Why had I ever consented to come to this city, where red flags fluttered like so many remnants of my bloody past, and reminders of my worst fears for the future?

"If you like." Evan sipped his mineral water. He touched no alcohol these days, not even wine. Long minutes passed before he spoke again. "You know, for the first time since I left New York, I have a real craving for whiskey," he said. "I don't want to get drunk, particularly. I just want to erase the picture of what I'm doing to you."

"Sorry I can't fake a smile to brighten your last hours with me." I tilted my chin, displaying no sign of sorrow. "But I've never been much of an actress. I guess I'm my father's daughter. I say what I think. I can't pretend to be happy when I'm not. You must wish you were back with Fiona."

I don't know what made me say that. Neither of us had mentioned Fiona for weeks. I took Evan's silence to mean that he still loved her. Of course he did. He had been ready to destroy himself once because she no longer wanted him; he seemed no less ready to do it now.

Evan paled slightly. "You can always get word to me through Headquarters in Belchite," he said, ignoring my last jibe. "I'll send my messages to you by way of Manchester at the consulate. You might want to change hotels. Don't worry about my finding you. If all else fails, our meeting place will be that monument to Columbus down near the waterfront, any day at noon."

I led the way out of the cafe. "You seem to have spent the last few nights making plans."

"Why not? I had nothing else to distract me."

Stung by the implication that I had failed him as a lover, I stopped in my tracks. People surged around us, jostling us as they hurried to get back to their homes before the evening blackout. "I'm sorry, Evan," I said. "I hate myself for acting this way, but I can't help it."

"I'd give anything to take you home to Elf Hill right now and never leave you again," Evan said. "But it's not possible." He put his arms around me and drew me close. "We still have tonight," he murmured.

I began to tremble, as much from desire as from terror. For the first time in all the weeks we had spent together, Evan had to lend me support, rather than the other way around. We stopped in the middle of the busy street and kissed. The wretched world slipped away, becoming as insignificant and unimportant as the odd scraps of newspaper that fluttered at our feet.

An old woman limping past us hissed, *"Puta."* Whore. Lowery's a who-ore. The world was the same, still filled with ignorant persons who resented the need of other people to be loved.

Evan and I didn't speak again until the following morning. As soon as we closed the door of our hotel room, we tore into each other with heated violence and breathless urgency. We were like illicit lovers bent on achieving new dimensions of delight and forgetfulness in a few forbidden hours. But sex brought no release, no relief from tension. The ecstasy we shared only heightened my despair. I knew in my heart, with full certainty and conviction, that I would never experience love this way again, love drenched with longing and anguish, yet softened by friendship and long familiarity.

The next morning, while Evan was shaving in the bathroom down the hall, I dressed in slacks, a shirt and jacket, and sturdy shoes. When he returned to our room, he found me packing extra rolls of film into my camera case.

"What are you doing?"

"I'm going with you." I threw a few personal items into a small canvas bag, and checked things off against a mental list:

salt tablets, bandages, lens cleaner.... I still possessed a large canteen of Hugo's, which I filled with bottled drinking water.

"I won't allow it."

"You can't stop me. I told you back in Valencia that I wouldn't sit here waiting for you. You go right ahead with your fighting and killing. I have my own work to do."

He grabbed my arm. "I don't believe you. You've told me time and again that you're sick of this war, that you don't want to take any more pictures of the fighting. You're just doing this to keep me here. I know how stubborn you can be."

I closed the flap on my canvas bag. "If you don't want me to ride out with you, I'll hitch a ride with someone else."

"You're still trying to make me change my mind. Well, I won't, Dory. I can't."

"Neither can I." I shrugged. "You'd better hurry up and get dressed. The trucks start pulling out at seven."

Who wants War?

And so Evan and I went off to war together, bumping along in the back of a Soviet-made truck filled with barrels of diesel oil and boxes of medical supplies. We joined six other soldiers also on their way to the front: three Spaniards, a Frenchman, and two Ukrainians.

As we neared the iron bridge that spanned the River Ebro at Mora de Ebro, the road became clogged with fleeing soldiers and refugees. The men called down to the passersby to ask for news. Spanish soldiers told us that the headquarters of the Fifteenth Brigade at Belchite had disbanded. They advised us to turn back. The Nationalists had redoubled their efforts to reach the Mediterranean, which would divide the Republic in half and isolate Barcelona. Outgunned and outmanned, the Popular Front Army was in full retreat.

"What about the Lincolns?" Evan shouted. "Where are the Americans?" No one knew for certain, although a couple of journalists who were on their way back to Barcelona remembered hearing that the Lincoln Battalion had withdrawn to Caspe, east of Belchite.

Our Spanish driver stopped the truck. "How can I go on if I don't know my destination?" he demanded. "I am supposed to deliver this stuff to the headquarters. But where are the headquarters?"

Climbing down from the truck, we huddled for a conference in the middle of the road. The driver and the other passengers voted to go back to Barcelona. What was the point of joining a battle that was already lost? I remained silent during the discussion, hoping that Evan would agree with them. But he said, "This isn't what I came for, to retreat before I've even seen a fight." He turned to me. "Go back with them, Theodora. I'll get word to you through Tony Manchester at the consulate, as soon as I catch up with the Battalion."

"This isn't what I came for, either," I said, "to be treated like a naughty little girl and sent home with no supper."

The other men boarded the truck again, which turned around and headed back toward Barcelona. Evan and I started walking toward Caspe.

We hardly spoke at all that day; we were still furious with each other. Late that afternoon, we encountered a squad of British soldiers bivouacked on the shore of the River Ebro, still about fifty miles east of Caspe. Evan introduced himself to the major in charge, who armed him and told him he could stay with them until they joined the Lincolns, two days' march from there.

Neither the major nor his men seemed surprised at seeing a woman photographer stroll casually into their camp. The International volunteers had been photographed, sketched, filmed, and interviewed on numerous occasions during their participation in the fight for liberty. As one of them remarked when I was working for Hugo, "Your snapshots won't win this war." I told him then that I had hoped my photographs would discourage future wars, but I had since abandoned that naive wish.

"We haven't a chance in a thousand of holding Franco's armies back at Caspe," the officer confided to us as he stared out at the barren ochre hills that surrounded us. "All we can do is slow them down a little. The town is nicely situated for defense. Now if we were in the Middle Ages, without threat of air strikes, we'd be in fine shape. If you ask me, Captain Bradley, you didn't know when you were well off. I was wounded myself at Teruel. I should have gotten out of here when I had the chance."

"Why didn't you?"

The major shrugged. "Crazy, I guess. I didn't want to give those Francoist bastards the satisfaction of seeing my backside."

"I hear Teruel was bad," I said.

"It finished us," the man said bluntly. "A hundred men deserted every day—and that's a conservative figure. I don't blame them. This isn't a war anymore, it's a travesty. Or perhaps I should say tragedy. The Republic's resources have run dry. Stalin hasn't come across with the men and materiel he promised. Why should he? He knows it's a lost cause. Besides, I hear he's got Spain's gold reserves in Moscow, where the Republic sent them for safekeeping. Good joke, that!" His laugh sounded more like a broken wheeze. "The Internationals aren't international anymore. Half of them are Spanish kids, recruits and draftees. They hardly know how to handle a gun. I'm afraid they'll have a chance to learn at Caspe. The hard way."

According to the major, Caspe was a vital railroad center, easily defensible—if you have the wherewithal, he added without much optimism. He told us that the Lincoln Battalion had been ordered to engage and hold the enemy there for as long as possible, while the Popular Front prepared further obstacles to the east that would impede the Nationalist march to the sea.

That night I slept on the ground like the others, with my canvas bag under my head and a rough blanket covering my body. Evan took his turn on guard for two hours after midnight.

As he was coming off duty, he stopped just a few feet away from where I lay. He stood watching me for a minute or two. I could see him clearly in the light of a half-moon, dressed in his rough uniform, a beret on his head, his rifle slung over his shoulder.

He crouched down beside me. "Let me go, Dory," he said softly.

"I can't, Evan. I'm afraid."

"I can't do my job if you're around. Can't you see that? Please, Dory. Go back to Barcelona where it's safe."

I could see the steam of his breath on the frosty air. "I'm not going to follow you around, Evan. Don't worry. But I won't go far away. I need to know where you are, what you're doing. That's all."

Nearby a sleeping soldier rolled over, muttering, "Can't you see it's a bleedin' fish, for Christ's sake?"

"So long as you love me," Evan whispered, "I'll be fine."

"Then you'll live forever."

So I returned to Barcelona, but just long enough to offer my services at the headquarters of the International Brigades and to receive an assignment. The members of the Propaganda Committee glowed as they reviewed my credentials: well-known photographer for liberal publications, political prisoner in New York, widow of the poet Diaz, and co-worker of that great humanitarian filmmaker, Hugo de Graaf. I made a valuable addition to their staff, if only for my propaganda value. They asked if I would make some newsreels for them. I agreed, provided I could travel freely and take plenty of footage of the International volunteers in action. The committee accepted my terms, and promised to provide passes that would permit me and my crew to commandeer rides on Brigades vehicles to any part of the front.

As an official Brigades newsreel photographer, I was able to follow the course of the battle through the spring of 1938. I filmed green recruits in training, veterans in trenches, soldiers of all ages engaged in earnest political discussion. From time to time, I filmed soldiers dying. The work wasn't much different from what I had done for Hugo, but I had had my fill of Spain's war. I longed to pitch my newsreel cameras into one of the deep arroyos that scored the bleak hillsides of eastern Spain. But I stuck with it, for Evan's sake, and my own. I would gladly have endured any hardship, just so I could place myself where I could receive regular news of him. Although I disliked seeing my work used to distort the truth—"This wounded soldier is happy that he was able to give an arm to the Cause"—I had to keep my objections to myself if I wanted to keep my job.

Soon after being given command of a transmission squad responsible for communications in the field, Evan and his men had come under fire. They were still south of Caspe, which the Lincoln Battalion had secured at great cost. The area was thick with Italian tank squadrons, Nationalist battalions, even cavalry. Moving at night over rough terrain, without maps, with only a compass to guide them, they passed through the enemy lines. Two men were wounded in an aerial strafing attack, but otherwise Evan managed to get his whole squad into Caspe without any serious casualties.

Evan and I managed to see each other only two or three times that spring, when his squad was camped within a few miles of where I was filming. In front of his men, we addressed each other as "Captain" and "Miss Lowery." We managed to snatch only a few minutes together when we could exchanged whispered "I love you's."

When I couldn't reach Evan by field telephone from Fifteenth Brigade headquarters, I sent him written messages with the drivers of ambulances or supply trucks. In return, he wrote me long letters describing his life as a soldier. In one sentence he told me how much he loved me, and in the next, how glad he was that he had returned to the fighting. Lacking decent weapons and proper support from the air and the ground, the men of the Lincoln Battalion needed strong leadership if they were to stay together and survive.

The Lincoln Battalion held Caspe for a few weeks against overwhelming odds, but the victory soured quickly. As had happened so often throughout that war, the Americans had staged a successful offense, only to find themselves stranded without tactical support and crushed by superior might. The Lincolns pulled back to the hill town of Corbera, hoping to regroup and stage another defense. Again the enemy routed them. By mid-March, intelligence reports suggested that the Nationalist push to the sea was many-pronged and that nothing could stop it.

While Evan was camped near Corbera, I received word from the Propaganda Committee in Barcelona that they required my presence at once. I had been filming the leaders of the Fifteenth Brigade at their headquarters in Corbera. Now that it looked like the Lincolns would need to defend themselves against an imminent and forceful assault by the Nationalists, I wanted to make sure that the hierarchy of the Fifteenth Brigade intended to arrange an organized retreat for the soldiers who had fought so bravely, with plenty of artillery support and protection from air attacks. Still, I couldn't refuse the urgent summons from Barcelona.

Arriving in the city, I learned that my employers wanted me to film nothing more important than a hand-holding session of officers of the International Brigades, the Popular Front Army, and the Prime Minister and cabinet ministers of the Republican government. Furious, I left the Ayuntamiento Palace as soon as the meeting ended. I wanted to get back to the front as quickly as possible, so that I could be closer to Evan. But I had promised the Propaganda Committee that I would help edit the footage I had just taken into a short film that they could show to the world as proof that the Left in Spain was still united, and that the Republic's determination to resist the rebels had not flagged.

As I hurried toward the film laboratory near the Plaza de Cataluña, I heard a familiar droning noise. Shading my eyes with my hand, I looked up at the sky. A group of three planes soared overhead, disgorging bombs onto an unsuspecting, unready city. For some reason, the air-raid sirens were silent. After a long, sickening moment, a series of muffled explosions came from the direction of the docks. As if to voice their shock and outrage at being so rudely aroused from slumber, the sirens began to scream. People raced past, heading for shelters in basements and subway tunnels. In the east, the sky grew dark with clouds of smoke and dust that obscured the planes.

An old man came up to me. "You'll get a terrible sunburn if you don't wear a hat," he scolded. "You girls with white skin should always wear long sleeves and hats."

Just then a bomb struck the building across the street from where I stood. As the shock wave hurled me against a wall, I saw the old man's mouth opening wide in a loud roar of anger.

It kept opening, wider and wider, engulfing me in a deafening swallow, until I could see right into the blackness of his belly.

I awoke in a white room to see a white-clad nurse bending over me. Raising my hand to my head, I encountered a helmet of tightly wrapped bandages.

"Evan," I rasped. "Evan."

The nurse said, "Do not try to talk. You have had a serious wound in your head, a bad concussion. But you will be all right. Rest. Rest, Señora."

My recovery was slow. I faded in and out of delirium for weeks. When I was finally able to move around on shaking legs, I suffered from raging headaches and dizzy spells. The hospital staff refused to release me. My nurses told me that in all the time I was semi-conscious I spoke only one word: "Evan."

Sitting in the solarium of the Gothic-looking Hospital de la Santa Cruz y San Pablo one afternoon, I heard my name.

Cecil Andrews of the *London Daily Mail,* my old comrade from Madrid, flopped into a wicker chair beside mine.

"I'm glad they've finally taken off the bandages, dear girl," he said cheerfully. "For a while you looked positively mummified. I must say, you've gotten marvelous care. But then you're a favorite at International Headquarters. They dote on you. The Prime Minister himself sent you flowers, I hear."

"Evan," I said. "Have you heard from Evan?"

Cecil skirted the question. "You know how impossible communications are during a war, even from a communications officer. I was lucky to get to Barcelona at all, once the Nationalists completed their push to the sea. The city's cut off from Valencia and the south now, you know. But we're used to that, aren't we, old girl? After all, we survived the seige of Madrid. We're veterans."

"What's happened to Evan?" I grabbed his sleeve. I would grip him like a terrier, I vowed, until he told me the truth. "The Lincolns? Tell me, Cecil!"

I had to drag the story out of him, but in the end, Cecil was unable to resist an opportunity to display his military knowledge and to parade his vocabulary. I listened with growing horror.

Fleeing from Corbera in disarray, the Lincolns had been forced right to the edge of the Ebro River, swollen in early April by spring rains and melting snow. Strafed from above, pressed by cavalry and artillery units on land, the Americans turned to the river as their only means of escape. The Republicans, however, had blown up the bridge at Mora de Ebro as a means of holding back the enemy. Since it was the only bridge within thirty miles, the American soldiers had to cross the river by any means at their disposal: crude rafts, leaking rowboats, swimming. Hundreds drowned in the swift torrent that rushed to the Mediterranean. All this had happened soon after I was wounded in the bomb blast, over a month ago.

"I've got to go to him." I struggled weakly to my feet. Cecil jumped up and supported my arm.

"Get me out of this place, Cecil," I begged. "I've got to find Evan."

The surviving members of the Lincoln Battalion were camped on a hillside near the village of Darmos, overlooking the Ebro. I scanned their faces, still drawn with fatigue and shock. They felt betrayed by their leaders, who had blown up the bridge without providing an escape route for their own men. They felt cynical about the chances for victory against an enemy so awesomely well equipped and supplied. They felt embittered, angered, and desperate. After the Ebro, many had deserted.

"No boats, no planes, no rafts. We had to swim for it. Lot of guys from the city didn't know how. They didn't make it."

"Evan Bradley?" I used the *nom de guerre* that Evan had adopted when he joined the Lincolns. "Has anyone seen Captain Bradley? Please, try to remember. I'm sure you know him. He was wounded at Brunete last summer. He fought with you at Caspe."

None of them remembered seeing Evan. Some knew him, but thought he had died at Brunete. I found only one boy who had served with Evan's transmission squad at Caspe. But the boy was in shock, and he hadn't spoken a word in weeks. No matter how hard I tried, I couldn't persuade him to tell me what had happened.

Exhausted, my head throbbing, I rested in the shade of an olive tree. Cecil Andrews lowered himself down beside me.

"Evan," I murmured. "Got to find Evan."

"It's no good staying here, old girl," Cecil told me. "He'll turn up sooner or later. When he does, you'll hear. Let's go back to Barcelona."

"He's not dead," I said. "I would know, Cecil. I would feel it. We're so close. I would have felt the bullet in my own heart."

I visited every Popular Front Army encampment and dugout on the eastern shore of the Ebro, searching for Evan. I located a few more men from his squad, who told me that during a strafing attack by German fighter planes, Evan had given the order to scatter. The hills around them had been crawling with Nationalists. Unable to regroup, each man had made his own way to the shore of the Ebro. But none of them had seen Evan.

Not without grumbling, Cecil loyally accompanied me on my search. After two fruitless weeks, he persuaded me to go back to Barcelona with him. We rode to the city on a truck full of wounded, a young boy from Alicante resting his bloody head in my lap for the whole journey.

As soon as we reached the city, I went to the American consulate on the Via Layetana and demanded to see Tony Manchester. Looking alarmed, the receptionist told me that Mr. Manchester was engaged. I became insistent. At her signal, a U.S. Marine standing guard near the entrance approached the desk. Speaking soothingly to me, addressing me as Ma'am, he asked me to leave.

"Evan Bradford," I said. "Tell him that I'm a friend of Evan's." My voice rose shrilly. "I won't go until I see Tony Manchester. I've got to see Tony Manchester!"

After a hushed exchange on the house telephone, the receptionist directed me to the office of the vice-consul. Tony Manchester, well tailored, fair-haired, and plump, seemed to regard my bad manners as an affront to the country he represented.

"Frankly, Evan Bradford was the last man I expected to see in Spain," he sniffed. "Since that Ebro nonsense, I've been swamped by telegrams and letters, asking for information about all sorts of people. I can't be expected to serve as a postbox for every American who chooses to come to Spain in violation of State Department orders. My government takes a dim view of—"

"He's your friend," I cried, "and the man I love!"

His attitude softened slightly. He promised, in the name of Exeter and Yale and an old friendship, to let me know as soon as he heard any word of Evan.

During our short interview, I noticed that Evan's friend seemed leery of me, even frightened. He was certainly eager to be rid of me. When I got back to my hotel room and peered into the mirror, I understood why. Still dusty from the road, with my filthy cheeks streaked with tears, an old scab on my forehead, blood smears on my clothes, and an expression of utter desperation in my eyes, I resembled a madwoman in the grip of an obsession.

I stayed in Barcelona, doing some photographic work for the Propaganda Committee, living in the little hotel on Calle Moncada that Evan and I had chosen when we first came to Barcelona. Every day at noon, I went down to the waterfront, to the monument to Christopher Columbus. I waited for Evan to find me.

He wasn't dead; of that I was quite certain. He was lost somewhere, temporarily misplaced. But he would make his way back to Barcelona as soon as he could, and he would meet me there, at the monument, one day at noon.

30

In July, 1938, the Republicans mounted their last big offensive of the war, recrossing the Ebro River and attacking the Nationalists from the north in an attempt to draw some of their power away from Valencia. The fighting dragged on for two months, taking a fearful toll, with the last of the Lincoln Battalion fighting bravely.

At the end of September, as part of an effort to negotiate a peace, the Prime Minister of the Republic of Spain announced that all international volunteers in Spain would be sent home. The Lincoln Battalion withdrew from the battle a few days later. After a period of rest, they traveled to Barcelona with the rest of the International Brigades for a farewell parade along the broadest boulevard in the city, the Diagonal, on November 15.

Early on the morning of the parade, I staked out a good vantage point along the route of march. Battalions from nearly twenty nations strode past a weeping, cheering crowd: Poles and Hungarians, Germans and Italians, Britons, Canadians, Frenchmen. None looked more ragged and more pathetically noble than the Americans of the Fifteenth Brigade, the Abraham Lincoln Battalion. Ignoring the cheers and shouts of the crowd pressing around me, I scanned each and every face. The people of Barcelona had come out to thank their brothers for their assistance and support. Girls tossed flowers at the marchers; red banners streamed in the sunlight. I counted sixty American soldiers. Only sixty, out of the hundreds who had come to Spain. Where were the others? Wounded or prisoners, deserters or dead. Where was Evan?

Day after day, ignoring the cold, the approach of the enemy, and the rising hysteria in the city, I kept my vigil at the statue of Columbus. Every morning, I went down to the waterfront, arriving at the monument a half hour before noon. The few people whom I saw there regularly, refugees or old women who lived nearby, started calling me *La Loca*, the Crazy Woman.

Food in Barcelona became scarce. Like everyone else, I was beginning to experience the first symptoms of starvation: listlessness, lightheadedness, but no immediate sensation of hunger. The dining room at my hotel had long since closed. Hoarders had stripped the nearby shops of goods. Enterprising citizens always managed to find the food they needed, but I couldn't afford to pay inflated black market prices. And besides, I no longer cared about food.

Although my funds were almost gone, the manager of my hotel declined to evict me. "I don't want any stinking refugees living in my hotel," he told me. "Country bumpkins, trash. They can't pay, either. I would rather have people of quality around, like yourself."

I offered to do photographic portraits of him and his family. His wife hung them on the wall behind the front desk. The manager would point to them proudly and say: "See? Who says picture-taking isn't art?"

Beating back a crumbling Republican defense, Franco's Nationalist army crossed the River Ebro and advanced on Barcelona. The Government talked of evacuating the city's children by ship, but ceaseless air raids on the port made that plan unfeasible. Now refugees streamed out of the city instead of into it: Communists, radical labor unionists, anarchists, loyal sons of the Republic who feared reprisal and execution after Franco's soldiers took the city. A few rode burros. Most walked. Those persons who owned cars piled them high with possessions, loaded family members inside, and headed north, toward France.

One cold morning in mid-January, 1939, nearly a year after my arrival in Barcelona, I received a message to come to the American consulate.

Tony Manchester welcomed me with stiff cordiality. "I have no word about Evan," he said at once. Clearly, he didn't want to let me nurse a false hope. "I don't wish to distress you, Miss Lowery, but for your own safety, I think you ought to leave Spain. A certain document has come to my attention. It may be spurious, but even so, it is always best to err on the side of caution. It's a list of one thousand names, people whom Franco's aides have marked for execution. Your name is on it."

For some reason I found this amusing. My laughter ended on a shrill note. "That's ridiculous! I'm no threat to them."

"The pictures you took of your—" he coughed delicately, "—your late husband's assassination were a cause of considerable embarrassment to General Franco and the Nationalists. I realize that you still retain your American citizenship, but to some rigidly Spanish minds, you are a Spaniard by marriage."

"They're just trying to scare me," I sniffed. "Well, I'm not leaving."

"I think you should consider the matter more carefully before making a decision, Miss Lowery," Manchester said. "Assuming that Evan is still alive—"

"What are you talking about?" I snapped. "He is alive! I know it!"

"Of course he is," Manchester said hastily. "But he would hardly be likely, as a former member of the International Brigades, to come here to Barcelona, where the threat of danger is so acute. He would contact me through diplomatic channels, from wherever he happened to be. I would inform him of your whereabouts, and the two of you could be reunited."

He paused a moment, letting this sink in.

"I am Evan's oldest friend," he went on in a less official-sounding voice. "He wouldn't thank me for allowing you to expose yourself to possible reprisals from the new government. Go to France, Miss Lowery. Go back to the States, if you'd rather. Just give me an address. Money is no problem. I have the numbers of Evan's bank accounts in Paris, Geneva, and New York. With the power of attorney he gave me when he was here, I have already drafted authorizations for you to draw out as much money as you wish when you reach Paris. I'll advance you some cash now—"

"No." I stood up, leaning heavily on the arms of my chair. These days, even simple exertions seemed to require tremendous expenditures of energy. "I can't leave. Evan is in Spain. I can't leave Evan."

"Then I can't be responsible for what happens to you, Miss Lowery," Manchester said in a sharp tone. He must have regretted his impatience, for he added more kindly, "Please, I urge you to reconsider. I know of a couple who are leaving the city this afternoon. They have room for you in their car; it's all arranged. You owe it to Evan to take precautions. Save yourself. This war is over. Even if the Nationalists spared your life, they could make things very difficult for you. They could imprison you or detain you under house arrest indefinitely. We don't know what kind of government we'll be dealing with, or what the American government's position will be regarding them. I can't even guarantee that I'll still be here to help you in a few months. If Evan knew how you were sacrificing yourself for him, he would be most unhappy. Can't you see that?"

I knew he was right. As Evan's friend, Tony Manchester had made himself responsible for my well-being. Evan would want me to do as Tony advised.

After a long silence, I said, "You'll let me know, the minute you hear from Evan? I'll go to the Hotel Lutetia in Paris. He knows it—we stayed there long ago, when I was a child. You swear?"

"You have my solemn word." The American vice-consul seemed relieved that his diplomacy had succeeded. "Don't worry about anything. The car will pick you up at your hotel in one hour. Good luck, Miss Lowery."

My luggage was scant, a single valise and my old, worn camera case. I gave Hugo's ring to the manager of the old hotel, in partial payment for my room. My wardrobe was in a shocking state, I reflected as I packed my suitcase. I promised myself that I would buy some new things when I got to Paris. Some really stylish dresses, a couple of silly hats, and some frothy lingerie, including the most diaphanous peignoir I could find. For Evan. For us. To celebrate.

My fellow travelers turned out to be a prominent official in the Spanish Communist Party and his wife. I don't know how they had become acquainted with Tony Manchester, but they must have owed him a favor, for they clearly suffered my presence unwillingly. The car had barely enough room for me, much less for my things. The two bickered constantly as the man drove through rubble and refugee-filled streets.

"My God, can't you go any faster than this?"

"What do you want me to do, woman, run right over these people?"

"We should have left long ago. Look at all this traffic. If you had listened to me—but no. You had to wait. Wait! Now see what's happened. The enemy will be here before we're even out of the city!"

"Shut up. I'm sick of your nagging."

Gazing out the rear window, I saw dispirited groups of humanity streaming north, toward the border. The winds were raw and cutting, carrying with them the cruel bite of the sea and the crueler sting of humiliation and defeat. The dream of a free and democratic Republic was dead, and with it the hope that had once made it seem possible.

"Stop the car." I leaned over the back of the seat. "Stop the car! I'm going to walk."

Turning their dark, well-groomed heads, the two stared at me as if I had gone mad. I couldn't explain to them that the widow of Luis Diaz Albareda would not leave Spain riding in the cushioned comfort of an expensive automobile. The dream wasn't dead until dignity and pride died, too. The man halted the car beside a particularly bedraggled-looking trio of refugees, a mother and her two small daughters. Holding the back door open, I called to them.

"These people will give you a ride to France. Hurry up!"

Sobbing gratefully, the woman and her weary children piled in. The car roared off, choking me on a plume of exhaust.

I buttoned my coat up around my throat, knotted a kerchief under my chin, and hefted my camera case higher on my shoulder. Straightening my spine, I joined the retreat.

After a few hours on the road, I decided to wear most of the clothes I had brought and leave the rest behind with my suitcase. In my camera case I carried everything I would need when I got to France: my passport, letters to Evan's banks in France and America, Evan's battlefield letters to me, the money Tony Manchester had given me. I still had my old Leica, a few canisters of exposed film, and some rolls of fresh film that Cecil had scrounged for me on the black market. I had an idea that I wanted to photograph Evan when I saw him, at the moment of our greatest happiness.

The road to France followed the coast for about thirty miles before veering sharply north, into the foothills of the Pyrenees. Winter had brought icy rain and near-freezing temperatures to Barcelona, but farther inland, away from the warming currents of the Mediterranean, the cold grew increasingly bitter and numbing. With my sturdy shoes and woolen sweaters and trousers, I was more warmly dressed than most of the women on the trek. Those from the temperate coastal areas didn't even possess overcoats. They wrapped themselves in blankets and shawls, and fashioned leggings out of rags and scarves.

The nights on the road offered little relief from the days of walking. Huddling together in burned-out churches, in taverns, on the streets of the villages that lined the tortuous route between the Catalonian capital and the French border, the refugees endured cold, hunger, disease, and despair. No one knew what fate awaited them once they reached France. They didn't care. They were fleeing a future more terrible than any of the horrors they had endured in three years of civil war.

The grueling march quickly depleted my small reserves of strength. In the mountains, we encountered snow and howling winds, as well as rumors of bandits, avalanches, and wolves. Food was nearly impossible to find, the towns along the way having been stripped bare by previous travelers. Hunger claimed the lives of old people, infants, the chronically ill. Their bodies lay stiff and snow-covered at the side of the road like grim milestones.

Toward the end of my journey, I traveled with the Solers, a socialist schoolteacher and his wife who knew Diaz's poetry and respected his work in Madrid before the war. Reaching Figueras, a moderate-sized town within one day's walk of the border, we took shelter for the night in an old stone church. I fell asleep before either of the others, and awoke in the middle of the night with a raging fever and the sure knowledge that Evan was dead.

What a fool I had been, believing his promises, swallowing his lies, standing at that monument every day, lying to myself, lying more desperately than my mother had ever lied, in those dark days back in Monkey Gulch. Someday. Someday. Someday. Evan and I would be together. Teaching school, making love, having babies, exploring the woods at Elf Hill, showing the children the first flowers of spring, the trillium and the violets and the bloodroot, *sanguinaria canadensis*. Be careful, children, don't touch the bloody bloodroot with a stain so penetrating that you can't erase it, not even if you try for half a lifetime.

I had been an idiot, a dupe. What right had I to dream, to hope? Did I really believe that Evan was alive somewhere, that he had escaped the fate of hundreds of other members of the Lincoln Battalion? I thought that bullets, shells, and grenades couldn't touch him because my love was like an armor plate that shielded him from harm.

By morning, I was delirious. The Solers exchanged helpless glances. What could they do? They had no medicines, not even aspirin.

"We cannot leave her behind," Señor Soler said. "She is the widow of Luis Diaz Albareda. We must do what we can for her."

We joined the last refugees straggling out of the church. A light snow was falling. In spite of their fatigue, everyone walked more quickly now. France lay just ahead, around the next curve, over the next hill, or perhaps the next. Even children caught the spirit. They skipped ahead, ignoring their mothers' warnings that they would tire themselves out. I trudged doggedly along, Señor Soler keeping a sharp eye on me. Whenever he saw me flag, he tugged at my hand and gave me a beseeching look that reminded me of Angel.

"Angel was the beast," I muttered aloud. "Luis was the brain. Articulate, but he had no feelings to articulate. Angel knew all the secrets of life and death, but he didn't talk about them. He used pictures instead. I used to make pictures. With a camera. Stupid machine."

Soler told me to shut up, to save my breath for the next mountain. I obeyed. I pretended I was an engine and that my legs were pistons, pumping up and down with admirable regularity, even though the hand on the controls was faltering with exhaustion. Left, right, Paris, France, don't, stop, Evan's, dead, left, right—

Once I collapsed in the snow. "I am so tired, Angel," I protested. "Let me sleep. Let me stay here."

"You can sleep in France." Soler hauled me to my feet. "Peaceful sleep is not possible for anyone in Spain these days, except for the dead."

How had Evan died? I wondered as I slogged through the deepening snow. Had he drowned in the Ebro, like so many of his men? Pulled downriver by the swiftly moving current, never to be seen again, like the souls of the Conquistadores who had given their name to the River of the Souls Lost in Purgatory.

But no, Evan knew how to swim. He had pulled me out of an icy pond one day long ago. More likely a bayonet had ripped him from gullet to groin, or a bullet had smashed into him, leaving him helpless and immobile while retreating Republican soldiers passed him by, until a Moor or a Legionnaire administered the *coup de grace*.

We knew we had reached the border when some young men started surging past us, racing toward their new dreams. The people around us wept, and laughed. Some jeered and hurled snowballs at the cars that overtook us, cars full of dignitaries who had left Barcelona that very morning. "Lazy good-for-nothings!" they shouted. "We made it on our own!"

Because we are strong, we are brave, we are Spaniards.

French gendarmes and military guards tried to impose some sort of order onto the crowds that milled around them. They asked for names, addresses in Spain, names of relatives in France. Relatives? We have no one. Anything to declare? What a joke. We were lucky to get out with our lives.

"Name?" A gendarme shouted into my face. Swaying unsteadily, I blinked into the glare of the lights that flooded the compound with an eerie unnatural brightness. "Name!"

I opened my camera case. My papers were gone. Money, vital documents, passport. All gone. Only my camera and rolls of film remained.

"She is the widow of Luis Diaz Albareda," Señora Soler volunteered.

"Address in Spain?"

"I don't know. She came from Barcelona. Look, she is too ill to speak. Why don't you leave her alone?"

"I didn't ask for your help. Is she a relative of yours?"

"No, of course not. She's an American."

"Can she prove it?"

"She has no identification. Her papers must have been stolen on the road from Barcelona."

"Section Four," the man declared, making a note. "Unidentifiable Persons Having No Familial Attachments."

Señora Soler protested, "Let her stay with us. We are her friends."

"Be quiet, woman," her husband hissed. "Don't make trouble. Do you want them to send us back?"

The gendarme gave me a little push, propelling me toward another group. Lifting my head once, I gave the Solers a last sorrowful glance, then I slumped against the wire fence and closed my eyes.

Our group of unidentifiable persons shuffled into a recently constructed shed to await processing. Processing: as if we were so many gallons of milk, or bits of paper on a bureaucrat's desk. Latrines overflowed, beds were nonexistent, the wind whistled through cardboard walls. Babies squalled, the sick moaned. Those who had recently held positions of power in the Communist Party or the Republican government looked affronted at being thrown in with the rabble. But the rabble had fought the battles, just as the rabble had mined the coal and tilled the rocky fields. In the dream, they were all brothers under the same flag, but war had nurtured new classes, new divisions. In defeat, the dream of equality lived again.

I lay shivering in a corner of the shed. From time to time I coughed, making such a racket that the sleepers near me muttered angrily and told me to be quiet. I slept poorly in spite of my exhaustion, pulling myself awake every time I started to dream. My fever made my dreams hideous, bloody, more terrible than any of the scenes I had witnessed in Spain. In all that time, my camera had absorbed the horrors and arranged them in interesting configurations of black and white. But now I could no longer use the camera, my third eye, my protective shield. Nightmares licked at the fringes of my sick and tired mind like a hyena sniffing at a carcass.

In the morning, the women of Section Four were loaded into trucks and taken to a hastily erected camp on the dunes near Port Vendres, overlooking the Mediterranean. Our new home was a building that resembled a packing shed. The women sized it up, muttering to themselves: bunk beds, three latrine buckets for over a hundred users, no facilities for bathing. The first day passed slowly, with no diversion other than the arrival of a truck bearing vats of weak soup and baskets of stale bread.

I was too weak to stand in line for food. A week passed before a doctor visiting the camp ordered me removed to a hospital. Impossible, he was told. We can't provide hospital care for everyone who wants it. A lot of these women would fake illness just to get out of the cold.

The young girl who slept in the bunk above mine had overheard Señor Soler telling the border guard that I was Diaz's widow. She knew Diaz's poetry. She had even heard him speak once, in Paris.

"He was so handsome," she sighed. "I think I became a Communist because of him. Oh, I know he always said he wasn't a Communist, but I think he was, in his heart."

Diaz had no heart, I thought. Only a mind.

"I saw those pictures of the Guardia shooting him." She shivered. "Whoever took them must have been very brave, or very sick in the head. I felt as though I was there. I could almost hear the bullets. It was horrible."

No, I hadn't been brave. Angel was the brave one. I was sick in the head. I coughed, a ragged ugly sound.

"Why don't you speak, Señora Diaz?" the girl asked. "Are you a mute?"

Yes, I was mute. Mute with anger, mute with despair. What good were words to me now? Words could not revive the dead. Words could not bring Luis or Angel or Evan back to life.

As I had done after my mother's death, I withdrew into a sanctuary of silence. In the past I had used silence to shut out feeling, to block out pain. I could do it again. Having opened that old familiar door, I could follow the path that I had abandoned long ago, when Evan dragged me out of the icy water of the pond at Elf Hill. That path would lead me away from sanity, away from consciousness, straight to the ultimate silence of death.

As the weeks passed, the women grew mutinous, but not noisily or destructively so. They knew that the French were searching for any excuse to send miscreants and troublemakers back to Spain. According to unverifiable rumor, Catalonia had fallen. General Francisco Franco had declared himself *el caudillo*, the leader of Spain. Let him try it, the women said bitterly. Let him try to rule that troublesome collection of Catholics and Falangists and Monarchists, Catalonians and Andalusians and Basques. He won't have any better luck than poor old President Azaña, with his labor unionists, Communists, and Anarchists. No one can rule Spain.

My cough worsened, although by March the coldest weather had passed. Muttering fearfully about tuberculosis, my neighbors in the bunkhouse complained to the military guards in charge of the camp. The women thought they would all die because the French refused to remove the sickest person among them. The officials paid no attention. Most of the women in the camp had a variety of complaints: bronchitis, migraine headaches, ulcers, anemia, palpitations of the heart, liver, and other organs. A few, succumbing to despair, stood for hours and days weeping at the fence that separated them from freedom.

I never wept, as I never spoke. I felt no interest in my own fate. Because they thought I was mute, the other women talked freely in front of me. Here, as in Barcelona, I was *La Loca*, the Crazy Woman. But they were the crazy ones, I thought to myself as I listened to their conversations. As impossible and hopeless as their lives seemed now, they were still able to invent futures for themselves, to describe reunions with lost husbands and lovers and children. In hard times, I thought scornfully, dreams are as useful a currency as any other.

The Communist student who had befriended me early in our captivity continued to watch over me. When we were together, she chattered brightly to lighten the heavy pall of my silence.

"Look, there's Señora Montalba."

The girl had urged me to leave my bunk that morning. I balked, but she persisted, literally dragging me to my feet. Supporting me, she led me out of the shed, into sunlight so bright that it made me stagger. We sat on the sand near the fence, watching the other occupants of the camp.

"Do you know, she's gained even more weight since coming here? She buys food from whoever will sell it. She's asked me a couple of times, but I told her to get lost. She has a lot of money stashed away in that bosom of hers. Some of the girls think she was a secretary to the Prime Minister or something, and got her fat hands on the wealth of the people. I think she must have been a madame in a whorehouse. She came here by car—was she surprised when they slapped her in this place!" The girl sighed. "If only we could see the ocean. It wouldn't seem so bad, being here, if we could look out at the sea. This part of the Mediterranean near Port Vendres is called the Gulf of Lions. Did you know that?"

The sea lay on the other side of a barbed wire fence, just beyond a fringe of dunes, unseen but always making its presence heard. The rumble and crash of the surf punctuated the hours of waiting. Waiting for liberation, waiting for transport to Paris or Marseilles or Lyon. Waiting for someone to claim them. Waiting for the warmth of the spring sunshine.

I gazed at the other women in the yard. I knew most of them by now, although they didn't know me: Pepita, who had been the mistress of a Russian commissar; Señora Montalba, who had grown fat during the seige of Madrid, while the rest of the city starved; Monserrat, who had clubbed an old priest to death while the other women in her village cheered her on. I didn't despise them. In ordinary times, they would have lived ordinary lives, going to church, marrying young, raising families, honoring their husbands and thinking very little about the state and politics. But war had turned their world upside down, set it on its ear. Everything became scrambled, hard to understand. The violence of war forced people to confront different aspects of their personalities. To despise the women who had explored the extremes of lust and hatred would be to despise myself.

Violent upheavals had changed my life, too. When the roof of a mine shaft caved in on top of my father, our family's little

2019

world caved in with it. Without a husband to temper her wilder flights of fancy, my mother discovered the power of her beauty, and the dark consequences of her foolishness. Without my father to shelter and protect me, I discovered the meaning of fear.

If my father had lived, I might have come to womanhood gradually, my heart open and trusting, my head filled with a girl's bright dreams and hopes. I would have known better than to attach myself to a man like Diaz, whom I could not love. I would not have needed an Angel to reveal my capacity for passion, for life. And when I found a good and gentle man like Evan Bradford, nothing would keep me from loving him.

Like my father, my mother had died quickly, but her dreams for me lingered, like a bad odor from her coffin. I felt relieved that I could relinquish those wretched dreams at last. Here in Port Vendres, a refugee, a prisoner behind barbed wire, I had become reconciled to an essential fact about myself: happiness would always elude me. The world was no place for me. The poem Diaz had written for me long ago was false. My life may have been rooted in blood and pain, but I drew no sustenance from that source. I was a blighted, withered creature, a flower destined never to see the sun.

Learn to dream, Evan had said. When life is hardest, that's when people need dreams most. Without dreams there would be no poetry, no music, no storybooks filled with tales of adventure and yearning. Evan, sitting in a Madrid hospital, had dreamed of starting a school. Every man and woman on the long march from Catalonia had once dreamed of a new Spain, a modern nation freed of the domination of class and clergy. Many of them had killed for that dream. They had left behind all those who had died for it.

I turned my face toward the sea, to the universe beyond the fence. A clump of gray-green grass that grew on top of a dune reached toward me, yearning. Rustling in the wind, it spoke softly of beauty and hope. I could smell its salty, musky fragrance; I could almost feel the touch of its feathery fronds on my cheek.

2019

441 ◆

NATASHA PETERS

Overhead, a gull wheeled and dipped on strong wings, floating on the wind, not resisting, but using the wind's force to lift itself high above the dull earth. Behind me, a woman sang a gypsy song about love's pain. To the accompanying throb of the surf, she sang in a fine, strong, human voice about the agonies of living. She sounded unafraid, almost joyful.

Sinking down on the sand, I wound my hands around the strands of wire, between the barbs, and closed my eyes. The earth was offering its small joys to me, Theodora, one of her daughters, who had had her fill of horrors. But I wanted no part of the world and its gifts! Yet I couldn't shut out the soft murmur of the sea, and the strange, sad melody of the gypsy love song.

I saw myself as I had been in the happy days before my father's death. That little girl lived inside me yet, wide-eyed and expectant, still waiting for life to reveal its beauties. In spite of all my attempts to stifle her with my silence, to kill her hope by denying her a chance to dream, that little girl refused to give up. I wanted to die, but she wanted to live.

A commotion was taking place in the yard. Voices were raised in French and Spanish. Feet raced toward me across the sand.

"Dory!" Arms closed around me and held me for a long moment. "Dory. Thank God. Thank God."

"The water—so cold." Clinging to him, I began to sob. "Black, and cold. Help me, Evan. Help me."

31

Evan looked up from the note the French messenger boy had just delivered. "Miss Penelope Poindexter has consented to interview me between the hours of four and five this afternoon. Listen to this part: 'I do hope this new school of yours won't be one of those haphazard affairs in which the chil-

2 0 7 9

dren are permitted to indulge any fancy that comes to their minds. Learning, Mr. Bradford, requires discipline.' "

I set aside the novel I had been reading. "Miss Poindexter sounds formidable. Are you sure you want to hire someone who's going to tell you what to do?"

"Why not?" Holding the arm of the sofa, Evan eased himself down beside me. He couldn't walk more than a few feet without his cane or some other support. "I've never run a school before. I'll need all the help I can get. When Miss Frasier wrote to tell me that Poindexter had retired down here, she said it would be a lucky coup if I could persuade Penny, as she calls her, to come out of retirement. As a math teacher, Penny is one of the best, and she's a sound administrator, too. I'm driving up to Grasse to see her. Want to come along?"

"I don't think so." I wriggled deeper into the sofa cushions. "I'm feeling particularly lazy today. I need to go to the market, and I promised Madame Laurent that I'd do a portrait of her as a gift for her husband's birthday next week. Today we're going to select just the right dress."

"Are you sure this is wise? Her face will break your new camera."

"Please don't say anything to Monsieur Laurent. It's supposed to be a surprise."

"Poor man. He spends sixteen hours a day at the café on the corner, trying to get away from her, and now she's going to give him something to remember her by."

"I think it's very romantic," I said, defending my sex. True, Madame Laurent was shrill and somewhat severe-looking, but some spark must have burned within her iron bosom to make her want to present her husband with a glamorous image of herself.

"Your opinion is highly colored and biased." Evan tried to look stern. "You think everything's romantic these days. Are you by any chance in love?"

"How clever of you to guess. Are you?"

"Most definitely."

"But aren't you afraid I'll turn into Madame Laurent when I get old?"

"You couldn't. Your nose is too small, your teeth don't have gaps, and your figure, while far from being what one might call ample, has taken on some rather pleasing contours lately." Evan accompanied this catalog of my physical attributes with appropriate kisses and caresses. "If Madame Laurent looked like you," Evan concluded, "Monsieur would gladly tolerate a little nagging now and then, and the café would lose its best customer."

Evan had taken me to a private clinic in Paris, where I was treated for pneumonia, bronchitis, and malnutrition. Evan, too, had needed to regain strength and vigor after a prolonged internment in a Nationalist prison camp. We decided to spend the period of our convalescence in the south of France. Since the playgrounds for the rich, like Cannes and Monte Carlo, no longer suited Evan's taste, he rented a small apartment on the outskirts of Nice, high on the hill overlooking the town. We planned to stay there through the end of June. Evan wanted to open the school at Elf Hill in the fall. We needed to do a lot of work before we could welcome our first students.

Making his way to the shores of the River Ebro after the German air attack, Evan had been captured by three Italian infantrymen, who had taken him to their field headquarters. During an interview, Evan and their commanding officer discovered a common love of opera and nineteenth-century Italian poetry. Over glasses of Spanish sherry, they agreed that the war was a tragedy, a scandalous waste of valuable lives. Then the officer received an order to execute all captives immediately. Shaking Evan's hand, he expressed elaborate regrets and condolences. Evan joined a scraggly band of other prisoners of war, mostly British and American.

As he faced the firing squad with them, he thought of me with love and regret, smoked a last cigarette, and prepared himself to die. This, after all, was why he had come to Spain in the first place.

The guns were cocked and ready when a messenger arrived with a reprieve.

In the weeks that followed, the prisoners were moved from one miserable jail to another, until they finally reached a camp in Málaga at the southern tip of Spain, hundreds of miles away from Barcelona. An infection developed in Evan's wounded hip. Without medicines and decent food, he grew steadily weaker as the infection spread and an abcess formed. After the fighting ended in February, 1939, he and the other Internationals in the camp were exchanged for some Italian prisoners of war. An ambulance took him to a military hospital in France, where the doctors confirmed what he already suspected, that the abcess had affected the joint. He would recover from the infection, but he would live with pain and walk with difficulty for the rest of his life.

The exchange of prisoners took place one month after I had left Barcelona. As soon as he was able, Evan wired Tony Manchester for information about me. When he couldn't find me at the Hotel Lutetia in Paris, he began to search the various concentration camps in which the French were holding Spanish refugees. He visited Section Four at Port Vendres in mid-April. The guards in charge informed him that they had no Americans in the camp, and that the only Diaz on their list was a woman of about fifty, with yellowed teeth and a blind eye. Just as Evan was leaving, a girl rushed up to tell him that Luis Diaz Albareda's widow was indeed an inmate of the camp.

"Albareda?" The guards consulted their records. "Why didn't you say so? Stupid Spaniards, with two names. One surname ought to be enough for anyone."

Extricating himself from my embrace, Evan smoothed his hair and tucked in his rumpled shirt. "Siren. You won't get

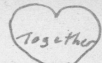

away with that sort of behavior when I'm headmaster of a prestigious New England private school."

"Then I'd better take advantage of you now."

"Absolutely not." He stood up. "Miss Poindexter will rap my knuckles if I'm late."

"Don't let her intimidate you."

"I am prepared to give her whatever she wants in the way of salary and working conditions," Evan said cheerfully. "I never could resist a woman who knew her own mind."

"I'll try to remember that." I must have sounded distracted, for Evan asked me what was the matter. "I feel nervous, Evan. We've been so lucky. I keep waiting for the ax to fall, or something terrible to happen. I imagine the most awful things—car crashes and sinking ships. It's horrible. Tell me I'm being foolish."

"You're being foolish." Grasping my hands, Evan drew me to my feet. "You're right, we are lucky, Theodora. We're lucky because we can appreciate the value of what we have. I don't care if the roof caves in on me. Hitler can declare war on Europe if he wants to; Mussolini's Brown Shirts can march into Nice tomorrow. I'll worry about those things when they happen. But for now, I want to enjoy what I have, and I want you to do the same. No more dark forebodings and intimations of doom and disaster." He kissed me. "Don't invent problems, Dory. You have enough to worry about, just making Madame Laurent's portrait look beautiful."

"That was a very nice scolding," I said meekly.

"Just getting into practice for my students." Picking up his cane, Evan saluted me from the door. " 'Learning requires discipline, Miss Lowery.' "

When he had gone, I took my new Leica apart and tinkered with the shutter. I enjoyed the work, and didn't hurry. After an hour or so, I reassembled the camera and returned it to its case. Stretching to ease the cramped muscles in my back, I went out onto the small balcony that overlooked the street. I loved the late afternoon in this part of the world. The colors were richer, the air warmer, the fragrances riper. In the distance, over the rooftops of Nice, the Mediterranean glinted under a cloudless blue sky. I had told Evan that I wanted an apartment from which I could see the ocean without hearing it. I could never again listen to the murmur of the surf without thinking of the fenced compound at Port Vendres.

I pictured Elf Hill, landlocked and peaceful. We would be there soon, in just three more weeks. Evan had already booked our passage. Home. I smiled to myself. I hadn't permitted myself to think of Elf Hill as home for a long time.

A silvery limousine turned onto the road and purred up the hill. A few pedestrians, startled by the appearance of such a magnificent vehicle in this working-class section of town, turned and stared. Some children raced shouting after the car.

To my surprise, the limousine pulled up in front of Madame Laurent's house, right under our balcony. A uniformed chauffeur stepped out, hopped around to the back of the car, and opened the door. After two suspenseful minutes, a woman emerged in a flurry of pale blue silk, one gloved hand holding the wide brim of her straw hat to keep it from blowing away. The small crowd that had gathered laughed and pointed.

"What's going on?" A woman in the house across the way leaned out of her window.

"Mademoiselle Randall is here," a boy shouted back. "The American movie star. Fiona Randall!"

Fiona glanced up at the balcony. Our eyes met.

Just then, Madame Laurent burst out of the house, her apron flapping. She greeted the visitor shrilly and volubly, tossing around words like "pleasure" and "honor."

I stepped back into the sitting room, my heart pounding. Of all the terrible things I had imagined, this hadn't been one of them. But of course, this was the biggest threat of all. Fiona, here. Fiona. She had come to see Evan, who still loved her with that portion of his heart that he had given her long ago. Evan, who couldn't resist a woman who knew her own mind.

Glancing around the room, I felt as if I were seeing it for the

Dec
2019

first and last time. The furnishings were shabby but serviceable, typical of rented lodgings at the seaside, where people are accustomed to treating their surroundings with less care than in their own homes. Evan and I had made fun of the garish floral wallpaper and the prim lace curtains that billowed gently in front of the long windows. On the credenza near the door, a bouquet of enormous peonies had started to drop its petals onto the floor, each one as large as a page in a notebook. We had bought the bouquet together at Nice's Marché aux Fleurs, the big flower market down near the Quai des Etats-Unis. Evan and I had been happy here.

Knuckles rapped on the door. "Madame Bradford! Madame Bradford, you have a visitor!" Ordinarily, Madame Laurent never escorted guests up the stairs. That she did so now only confirmed my suspicion that under that homely exterior beat a heart that thrived on romantic fantasy: Madame was one of Fiona's fans.

As I crossed the floor, I felt weightless, made of gauze. I was vaguely aware of the excited chatter of the people in the street, the fragrance of the dying peonies, the slight stickiness under my arms and across my back.

Taking a deep breath, I opened the door.

Looking past the chattering landlady to the woman who stood in the cool darkness of the hallway, I said, "Hello, Fiona. Please come in." Madame Laurent offered to bring up coffee, tea, brandy—"No, thank you, Madame." I closed the door firmly and turned to face my visitor.

Doffing her hat, Fiona shook out her red-gold hair. She wore it in loose curls that somehow managed not to look tumbled or messy.

"I need a minute to catch my breath," she said. "Those stairs are murder."

Tossing her hat onto the credenza, where it dislodged another shower of flower petals, she strolled around the room. "I'm surprised. The Evan Bradford I knew in the old days didn't stay in cheap rooming houses. He must be drinking again."

"No," I said. "No, he isn't." 2019

Fiona grunted, a sound that bespoke disbelief. "Where is Evan, by the way?"

"He's out. He had an errand."

"How sweet. Did you run out of butter and eggs?"

Fiona sat on the sofa. She fished in her handbag, an oversized wicker briefcase with white leather handles that matched her sandals. She wore no stockings. Her toenails were painted a pale apricot color. She studied me over the top of her gold cigarette lighter.

"You haven't changed much, I see. Still sullen and skinny. My spies tell me you and Evan are honeymooning. Forgive me, Dory, but you don't really look like a blushing bride."

"We're not married yet. We plan a small ceremony at Elf Hill, as soon as we get back." I took a breath. "What do you want, Fiona? Why did you come here?"

"Just curious," Fiona shrugged. "I heard from a mutual chum in Monte that the two of you were here, and I thought I'd pop in to say hello." She looked around for a place to deposit her ash, spotted a saucer on a table within reach, and extended a slender arm loaded with sparkling bracelets. "Please don't glower. You always did it as a child. I don't like it any better now than I did then."

"Then you'd better leave," I said. "You're not welcome here."

"Such a frosty greeting," Fiona clucked. "I thought you'd be pleased to see me. Evan will be, though. He's always been glad to see me in the past, even when we were feuding about something. He used to say that my looks made up for my multitude of sins. What do you think? Have I changed much?"

"No," I admitted. "You're still beautiful."

"That's right," Fiona nodded. "Not bad for an old bag of thirty-nine. This is the dangerous age, you know, when the producers start looking around for younger women. The fans are loyal, though. They don't care if I'm playing a sixteen-year-old or a thirty-year-old, as long as I give them the performance they've

2019

come to expect. I figure I've got five good years left, and then it's out to pasture somewhere. I'll be damned if I'll play character parts. Aging movie stars ought to slink quietly into retirement, without attracting any attention. No one should be able to say, 'My God, Randall looks old.' I suppose I could go back to the theater. The stage is more forgiving of age than the camera. But somehow I don't think I will."

I waited. Surely Fiona wasn't looking for sympathy.

Fiona glanced at the Leica lying on the table beside her. "Still taking pictures, I see."

"I haven't done much photography since I left Spain. I didn't want to. Evan persuaded me to start again."

"That sounds like Evan. He used to be good at bucking me up when I felt low."

"That's more than you ever did for him," I charged.

"Ah." Fiona's smile broadened. "I was wondering when we'd get around to the tears and recriminations. So you think I treated Evan badly?"

"You saw him destroying himself, and you didn't try to stop him."

"What was I supposed to do?" Crossing her silky tanned legs, Fiona leaned back against the cushions. "Drop my career and play the happy housewife at Elf Hill? Sorry, my dear, but that's not my style. That's not why I married Evan. He wouldn't have wanted it. It bothered me to see him making such a fool of himself, but I couldn't save him. He didn't want to be saved. Drowning his sorrows in liquor was easier than facing the hard facts about himself."

"The hardest fact was that he loved a woman who was incapable of loving him, or anyone else," I said. "He gave you everything he had. What did you ever give him?"

"He knew what I was when he married me. I never pretended that I was interested in anything else but my career. Whatever you may think of me, I am not a hypocrite. Any other woman would have pressed her dead sister's kid to her bosom and made all the right motherly noises, but not me. I never liked you and I never wanted you." She lifted her chin. Diamonds glittered on her earlobes. "At least you knew where you stood with me."

"I knew what you were like even before I met you." I shoved my fists deeper into the pockets of my full skirt. I was conscious of the contrast I presented to Fiona's perfumed and perfect elegance, with my short, boyish haircut, cheap cotton skirt and blouse, rope-soled espadrilles that laced around the ankle, no makeup. "I knew that you let my mother die of heartbreak and despair, when you had it in your power to save her. She was so proud of you. She talked about you constantly. She almost believed she was you, I think. Beautiful, talented, wonderful Fiona! And when she needed you, you turned your back on her. She wasn't just a stranger trying to touch you for a loan. She was your sister! Even if you hadn't sent money, if you'd just written a few kind words after Papa died, it might have made all the difference. You killed her hope. And when you did that, you tied the rope around her neck."

A flush had mounted to Fiona's cheeks. "She brought it on herself. I won't accept any of the blame for what happened to her."

"No, of course you won't. Love carries responsibility, and you've never wanted to be bothered with that. If you had loved Evan, you would have done something to help him, just to reassure him that he wasn't a failure in your eyes. That's all he needed. A word, a touch, a smile that wasn't Hollywood-bright or stage perfect. But you couldn't spare a thought for anyone but yourself. You knew how desperate my mother's situation was: widowed, with a child, no home, no money, no place to go. If she had come crawling up to you on the sidewalk, you would have stepped right over her, or kicked her in the teeth. You were lucky you could do it by mail. So much easier and tidier."

"How dare you talk to me that way." Fiona rose with less than queenly dignity. We faced each other. "You don't know—"

"I know that when you had a chance to do something for someone other than yourself, you refused. You can justify your actions all you like. We both know there's no excuse for what you did." I was breathing hard. "You're afraid of getting old, aren't you, Fiona? You're beginning to find out that the only cure for loneliness is love, but you don't know how to love, and it's too late for you to learn. When your career is over, you can sit on top of your bags of money and talk about how marvelous and beautiful you used to be, and as long as the money holds out, you'll find people to listen—young boys looking for a leg up in Hollywood, girls hoping to learn some tricks. Well, you can teach them how it's done, Fiona: 'Set your sights on what you want, think only of yourself, don't give a thought to the ones you've hurt.' "

Swirling away from me, Fiona stood at the open doors of the balcony. A little crowd in the street below applauded and shouted greetings to her. She retreated a pace or two into the room again.

"I want Evan back," Fiona said without looking at me. "He's never been able to refuse me anything, ever."

I felt myself falling into an abyss. Fiona had found the flaw in her dream with the rude intrusion of real life: old age and loneliness. She wasn't the kind of woman who paid idle calls on ex-husbands just to stir up mischief. She had come to Nice looking for Evan, looking for love.

I said, "You could have anyone you wanted, anyone in the world. Why don't you just go away and leave us alone?"

Fiona glared at me over crossed arms. "I'm not leaving here without him."

"No."

I rubbed the scar on my forehead, the memento of the Barcelona bombing. From time to time, I still suffered from bad headaches. I felt one starting now.

"It's not just that you want Evan back. You want to hurt me, don't you? Why, Fiona? I never gave you any reason to hate me. It's my mother you hate. She's been dead for nearly seventeen years, and you still hate her." I picked up my new Leica. My cameras had always provided comfort and security in uncertain situations. As long as I held a camera, I knew what I could do, I knew who I was. "I'm going out. Evan should be home in another hour, if you care to wait."

I had just reached the door when I heard Fiona's voice behind me.

"I loved your mother."

I paused, my hand on the latch.

"Mary could have had anything she wanted," Fiona said. "A career, a name. When you said she used to think she was me, you didn't understand. She really was Fiona Randall. We used to sit around and dream about what it would be like to have money and carriages and servants. Even then she knew she wanted to be an actress. 'I shall call myself Fiona Randall,' she said. She thought Fiona was a beautiful name, and she always liked that poem about Lord Randall, that handsome young man who feels sick because his girlfriend has poisoned him. It was certainly a better name than plain Mary Murphy, and better than Rose Murphy. That was my name in those days: Rose. I hated it, of course. All little girls hate their names. When I got to New York, I used Mary's stage name. It was my revenge."

I turned slowly. "Revenge?"

Fiona lit a cigarette. The flame from her lighter wavered. "When things were rotten at home, the old man drinking and beating Ma, the other kids carrying on and fighting, the two of us would go upstairs to the attic. Mary would tell me what it would be like when we grew up. We'd go to the theater in New York and see Sarah Bernhardt in *Camille*. And on the way back to our hotel, we'd ride in a beautiful carriage drawn by a pair of matching black horses. She even described what we'd wear. She loved pink. Her gown would have big sleeves puffed at the shoulder and tight at the wrist, and it would have a high neck and a pleated peplum at the waist. Mine would be the same, only blue. My coloring was right for blue, she used to say." Fiona looked down at her dress. "I guess she was right. I still wear a lot of blue."

"But I don't understand," I said slowly. "You went to see

Bernhardt. She told me all about it, exactly as you've described."

"It was one of her dreams." Fiona exhaled a billow of smoke. "She believed in them so hard that in her mind they came true. She invented a whole different world for us to live in. Instead of East Chicago, Indiana—"

"No, you lived in Chicago, on—"

"—on West Lansing Avenue, in a big stone house with a circular driveway. Our mother had died, and Father worked for the railroad. He was away a lot, and we were brought up by—"

"—by two old aunts," I finished.

"You see, you got the same dreams as I did." Fiona gave me a bitter smile. "They saved me, those stories of hers. I was the weakest kid of the bunch, sick with asthma, always crying over something. Mary was the only one who could calm me down. She'd hold me in her arms and talk about our other home, our real home. It was so real, so believable. That's why I became such a good actress, because I already knew how to put myself into another world, inside my own head."

I felt my head start to reel. "Then there were other children, besides you and Mother?"

"Nine, when I left home, and another on the way. East Chicago, Indiana, is probably crawling with Murphys. You ought to look them up some day, all your aunts and uncles, and at least a hundred cousins. Pop worked in a steel mill. Ma used to meet him at the plant door on payday, to get a little money before he spent it all on drink. Mary was the oldest, our second mother. I was five years younger. Her favorite."

I lowered myself onto the straight-backed chair near the door. I knew that Fiona's story was true. Somehow, Mother's tales of her childhood had always seemed too highly polished, too well rehearsed. Even when I was young, I had suspected that my mother had edited her reminiscences, rearranging some details, omitting others. But I never imagined that the stories were complete fabrications. I thought of the family Bible. She had probably found it in a pawn shop, and filled in the geneology with her own fictitious family tree.

Fiona perched on the edge of a frayed sofa cushion. "I was only twelve when she ran off with Frank Lowery. I couldn't understand it. I asked her how she could give up everything we'd talked about and hoped for. 'It was only a dream, honey,' she told me. 'It didn't mean anything.' I wanted to die. I very nearly did. I cried for weeks after she left. Didn't eat. Pop had to shell out money for a doctor. He was furious. 'Damned kid always has something the matter with her. Should have drowned her when she was born.' That's what my own father said about me. A lot of men have felt that way about me since then. I pretended that Mary was dead. She might as well have been. She never wrote to me. I didn't hear from her for twelve years, and then the letters started coming. I never read any of them. I threw them away as soon as I saw who they were from. When Frank Lowery died, she sent a telegram. She wanted money."

I said nothing. Fiona looked at me, her eyes bright.

"I got out of East Chicago when I was fourteen, and I didn't look back. I didn't want anything to do with the Murphys. Mary threw away her dream, but I took it and made it work. I would have done it without Evan, without anybody. I didn't need him. He just made it a little easier. You're right: if I had seen Mary begging in the street, I would have stepped right over her. Why not? She abandoned me for the first good-looking man that came along. Her love for me didn't mean anything. It was all a lie, like those stories she told me. I was furious with her for dumping her kid with me. Why didn't she send you to East Chicago? In the Murphy household, one more wouldn't even matter. But no, she wanted you to have a piece of the dream. My dream. Damn her! Damn you." Fiona mashed out her cigarette. Her hand shook. "I don't know why I'm telling you all this."

"Does anyone else in your family know who you are?" I asked after a long silence.

Fiona shook her head. "I'm nothing like the skinny little kid who ran away from home twenty-five years ago. They probably think I'm dead. They'd never connect plain Rose Murphy with the blonde they've seen on the movie screens in their neighbor-

hood. In those days I had an accent, a flat nasal voice. Horrible."
She shivered. "My hair was darker then. This famous Fiona red-
gold comes out of an assortment of bottles, in case you hadn't
guessed. Evan toned it down a little, and he worked on my
voice. Underneath all this makeup, I have unremarkable eyes
and practically no eyebrows. But the business of theater is illusion, isn't it? Evan gave me beauty and culture. Hollywood gave
me a fortune. My press agents gave me a past."

"And Mother gave you a name," I said.

"Yes, Mary gave me a name. Some people would say that she
gave me a career, too. If it hadn't been for those fairy tales of
hers, I never would have suspected that there was anything better out there than East Chicago. But I don't owe her anything."
Fiona's voice sounded hard, but the venom in her tone was
weak.

I stood up. "If she'd had an outlet for all those dreams, she
might have been all right. If she could have acted, or sung, or
written poetry. But mining towns like Monkey Gulch don't
have much to offer people like her. Life was too hard. Everybody had too much work to do. No money. No time. My father
was able to pull her back to earth when her dreams and talk got
too wild, but after he died, she went spinning off, like a kite
with a broken string. She couldn't cope with real life. Her
dreams would never have come true. She didn't have your
strength, Fiona. Dreaming was easier than doing." I picked up
my camera, thought better of it, and set it down again on the
chair near the door. "Evan should be back in an hour or so. If he
wants to go with you, I won't stop him."

Fiona had covered her face with her hands. She might have
been weeping. If so, she was doing it with none of the theatrical
flair I had witnessed in the past.

I started down the stairs. Madame Laurent darted out of her
sitting room, expecting to see Fiona again. I explained that Mademoiselle Randall wanted to see Monsieur Bradford, and that
she preferred to wait upstairs. I thought Fiona would appreciate
some coffee or a little brandy, if Madame could spare it.

The little mob in the road outside had swelled. The neighbors continued to drift over to see Fiona's limousine and to catch a glimpse of the American movie star in person, when she emerged from *chez Laurent*. Whatever could she want in such a place, they wondered? I found it amusing that Mary Murphy's dreams had reached even this sleepy little town on the Mediterranean.

I walked down the long road to the sea. I had balled up my string shopping bag in my pocket, but neglected to bring my purse. The merchants who knew me would give me credit, but how could I go shopping if I didn't know whether I'd be cooking for one or for two? I supposed I was a fool for leaving Fiona to see Evan alone. But I didn't want any man to stay with me out of guilt. Only Evan knew best how to balance his love for the two women in his life.

"I don't want to see them together," I said half-aloud.

That was it, of course. Evan still loved Fiona. He loved me, too, but with a different sort of love—more paternal, less complex. In many ways he was still teaching me. Evan had changed, gained confidence, new respect for himself. He was Fiona's equal now, no longer her mentor, her secretly frustrated competitor. He was a man who knew his limitations, a man with a dream of his own.

The breeze over the water dispersed the warmth of the late afternoon sun. I picked my way carefully along the uneven surface of the beach. The foamy surf licked at the gray pebbles, rubbing them smooth, tumbling off the corners, rounding the sharp edges. Ultimately, I thought, we all conform to life's pattern. Life has a way of wearing you down, of forcing you to accept things as they are. Some people, like Angel, know instinctively how to deal with life on its own terms. Others, like Diaz and Evan, learn only after years of struggle. A few, like Mary Lowery, go mad, because no matter how real their dreams may seem, they are merely seaspray, misty fragments that any strong wind can blow away.

A freighter moved eastward across the horizon, on its way to

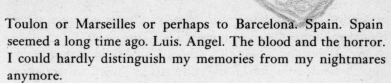

Toulon or Marseilles or perhaps to Barcelona. Spain. Spain
seemed a long time ago. Luis. Angel. The blood and the horror.
I could hardly distinguish my memories from my nightmares
anymore.

Sitting on a jetty stone, I forced myself to consider the possibility of a future without Evan. According to the most recent
news reports, appeasement hadn't satisfied Hitler's lust for new
territory. War in Europe was imminent. I knew very well that
when wars start, journalists and photographers are in high demand. I decided that I would get myself a job with one of the big
newspapers or international wire services. Or I might offer my
skills to the British government, which seemed certain to become involved when conflict erupted.

A plane flew overhead, sparking thoughts about the problem
of taking detailed pictures while flying high out of the range of
anti-aircraft fire. It would be hard to get good shots of installa-
tions on the ground from that altitude, because the cold would
make the cameras freeze up. One would have to construct a
heated chamber, perhaps in the belly of the plane.

Yes, I could make myself useful, in one way or another. A
woman on her own, unattached, experienced, with no family except a hundred Murphys in East Chicago, Indiana.

My spirits raised by this practical communion with myself, I
walked back through the town, stopping to buy a long loaf of
bread and two lamb chops, a bottle of wine, a good-sized piece of
camembert, and, as a treat, two appallingly rich cream-filled
cakes. As I turned onto the road on which we lived, I remembered that I should have bought flowers. Those peonies in the
sitting room really were pathetic.

I stopped abruptly. The limousine was gone. So was Evan's
car. I was going to have a solitary meal after all, with memories
for appetizer, main course, and dessert. I would skip the hopes
and dreams for tonight. They might leave a bad taste in my
mouth.

Just then, Evan hailed me from a side street.

"I've been looking everywhere for you," he said. "I'm in need of comfort. My interview with Miss Poindexter was very sober-ing." Evan limped over to me and kissed my cheek. "According to her, I'm going about this school business in a thoroughly muddle-headed fashion. But Penny has promised to straighten me out." He took my string bag in his left hand.

"Where's your car?"

I slipped my hand under his elbow, taking care not to bump his cane. Arm in arm, we walked up the hill toward Madame Laurent's house.

Evan made a face. "It broke down about three miles outside of Grasse. It must have heard Miss Poindexter telling me that she doesn't approve of automobiles."

I stood still, dragging on his arm.

"Fiona was here."

"I know, I saw her. After the car gave up the ghost, I hitched a ride home on a vegetable wagon. Her car passed us going to-ward Cannes. We chatted for a few minutes. I didn't dismount from my vehicle, and she didn't get out of hers. Finally, when some of the flies that were buzzing around our donkey sought more civilized company, she decided she'd had enough. She rolled up her window and off she went."

"She still looked beautiful," I said.

"Did you think so?" Evan frowned. "I thought she looked a little bored with it all. But she can't turn her back on it now. She's worked too hard to get where she is." He gave me a pene-trating look. "Theodora Lowery, you thought—"

"I did not," I said quickly. "If you look in that bag, you will see two chops and two cream cakes."

"You did! You thought that if she so much as wiggled her lit-tle finger at me, I'd go rushing off after her like a dog after a juicy steak. Admit it, Theodora, the thought crossed your mind."

Laughing, I declined to incriminate myself.

We climbed the steep flight of stairs to our apartment. Evan had insisted that the only way he could regain the strength in his leg was to exercise at every opportunity. Our ascent was slow and giddy. Evan described his visit to Miss Poindexter in such a way that I didn't think I could possibly meet the woman without disgracing myself.

When I opened the door at the top of the stairs, my laughter became an astonished gasp. Flowers bloomed everywhere. Fresh peonies bobbed in the vase on the credenza. Snowy roses spilled out of urns that sat on the floor near the balcony doors. Wisteria trailed over the kitchen table, winding itself around a bucket of ice and a bottle of champagne. Iris, anemones, tuberoses, lavender—the wares of the Marché aux Fleurs had somehow made their way to our little home, transforming it from a shabby suite of rented rooms into a bridal bower.

Dumbfounded, I looked to Evan for an explanation. He appeared as astonished as I.

I moved slowly around the room, touching the flowers, trying to persuade myself that they were real. Their fragrance was intoxicating, as overwhelming as their beauty. When I completed my circuit, I sank down on the sofa and continued to stare around me with wonder and amazement.

Evan picked up a card tucked under the ice bucket. "I don't have to tell you that this sort of gesture is most unlike Fiona," he said. "What did you say to her?"

"I didn't say anything." I gazed at the urns of white roses. Flowers from Purgatory. "She did most of the talking."

He read aloud, " ' Best Wishes. Mary and Rose Murphy.' "

Looking even more baffled than before, Evan joined me on the sofa and put his arm around my shoulders. I leaned into the curve of his body.

Evan felt solid and warm. Real. Love was real.

The evening shadows deepened around us, bringing soft unmenacing darkness, in which the roses gleamed like ghosts. My tears began to fall.

"Oh, Evan, I wish my mother could have seen this," I said after a long while. "It would have made her so happy."

THE END

ABOUT THE AUTHOR

Natasha Peters is the author of *Savage Surrender, Dangerous Obsession, The Masquers, The Enticers,* and *The Immortals.* Under her real name, Anastasia Cleaver, she lives with her husband in a drafty old Victorian house on a hill near Philadelphia. The ideas for her books have taken her to many foreign lands in the East and the West, and through volumes of history and biography. She is also an actress, an artist, a singer, and a grower of old-fashioned roses.